Malevolent

VJ Nash

The characters and events portrayed in this book are fictitious. Any similarity to real persons, living or dead, is coincidental and not intended by the author.

ISBN-13: 978-1-7395539-3-7 (digital)

ISBN-13: 978-1-7395539-4-4 (print)

10 9 8 7 6 5 4 3 2 1

Book cover design by ebooklaunch.com

Also by

I'm very much looking forward to populating this page considerably over the next few years. Right now, all I can offer you is...

The Bermuda Covenant

Jack Kidd and Annie Ingels' happy life in New York is shattered by the sudden death of his estranged father in England. Now they are dragged into the brutal darkness of Jack's past – a past he'd so carefully buried. The reading of the will sets Jack and Annie in direct conflict with his sisters - Rosalind and Veronica. They're rich, devastatingly attractive and have an other-worldly power over men... except their brother. And they hate him for it.

As Jack and Annie are plunged into a murderous nightmare, they uncover the disturbing truth that a mythical evil is at work and will stop at nothing to destroy them and those they love. From England to the Italian alps, to the rich playground of the Hamptons, Jack and Annie must fight for survival as they are drawn inexorably to a final confrontation in the place it all began... Bermuda - the Isle of Devils.

About the author

As someone who is Canadian by birth, Hungarian/Yorkshire by blood and brought up in the south of England, it's fair to say I've never quite fitted in. I didn't help my already slim chances of fitting in by becoming a DeadHead in 1983. Nobody knew who the Grateful Dead were in rural Surrey in the 1980s, so I had to follow that obsession all alone. I have always had a love of horror and spent much of my childhood terrifying myself by reading books and watching films that I really shouldn't have. It probably didn't help that my grandparents' ancient house (it pre-dates the founding of the United States by 200 years) was undoubtedly haunted. Neither did the fact that all the sensible adults in my life had stories to tell of bizarre, unexplained happenings they'd experienced. One of my Hungarian aunts – a reasonable and intelligent person – was even convinced that werewolves and vampires actually existed back in 'the old country'. So, it's hardly surprising I'm writing horror. Also, maybe like you, I often wonder what's out there in the dark, just beyond the bounds of human knowledge.

THANK YOU

To my family for their support and love.

To everyone who read my first book The Bermuda Covenant, thank you so much for taking a chance with an unknown author. Thanks also for your reviews on Amazon etc and for feedback via Facebook. You've been very encouraging and it means a lot to me.

Finally, thank you for getting this book. I hope you enjoy it!

Contents

Chapter One

Hide And Seek

"You bring me to the most romantic places," said the hulking bruiser caustically, as he trudged along the unmade road.

"It's because I love you," winked the smaller man walking alongside him.

The two men made an incongruous pair as they picked their way quietly through the puddles and potholes of the neglected urban back lane. The smaller man looked around thirty, with deep brown skin and a perfectly shaved head. He wore a faun-coloured leather jacket and black jeans with a style the other man could never hope to achieve. The lumbering lummox beside him looked over forty, was pasty, and his ill-fitting grey suit and badly tied blue tie gave the impression that he'd dressed in the dark. They didn't even look like they were together, let alone highly rated detectives in the Metropolitan Police.

"Great... it's a dead end," the big man said with an East London growl. If there was one thing Detective Sergeant Andy Harper had learned in twenty years, it was that if things went sideways, it was handy to have escape options.

Walking next to him, Detective Inspector Ray Ennis didn't like it either. To their right there was a set of dilapidated garages, some with broken doors, others with collapsed roofs. To their left, ancient, looming railway arches had been converted into lock-ups. The crumbling brickwork left spaces for buddleia and other plants to grow, but their presence, far from cheering the place up, made it seem all the more desolate. At the end of the lane a ten-foot wall buttressed an overgrown slope that rose another twenty feet to the railway tracks above the arches. Ray's lean jawline tightened briefly, but then a wicked gleam came into his dark brown eyes,

"And guess what?" Ray said playfully in a voice that wasn't as deep as Andy's and with a less abrasive South London accent.

"What?"

"The lock-up we want's the one at the end."

"Bollocks!" said Andy with feeling.

They fell into silence as they approached the last of the bricked-up arches. It had stopped raining, but the clouds above them weren't helping to make the dismal scene any more inviting. Just another beautiful English summer's day. Now they slowed their pace and sharpened their senses, exchanging a knowing glance when they saw the last lock-up in the row. It wasn't like the others. Of course it wasn't. While every other one had large double-doors held firm with big padlocks, this last one was completely bricked up apart from a single steel door, unpainted and bloomed with rust.

"Doesn't scream 'potential serial killer' at all," said Ray quietly.

Andy smiled briefly, then asked,

"Shall I?"

"Please do," said Ray, ushering Andy towards the door.

Andy banged on the cold metal with the side of one of his enormous fists,

"Mister Titheridge, this is the police," Andy bellowed, "We'd like to talk to you please."

Silence.

"I liked the 'please'. Nice touch," Ray smiled.

"Politeness costs nothing," Andy replied, then set to on the door again,

"Mister Titheridge, this is Detective Sergeant Harper. We met last week..."

Thickening silence.

Andy looked over questioningly at Ray, who gave him the nod for one last try. The sound of Andy's big fist beating on the thick metal filled the dead-end once more.

"Mister Titheridge, this is the police. If you're in there, we need you to open up and come out to talk to us."

Now the silence was heavy with possibilities.

Ray looked at Andy. His doughy face with its heavy cheeks had taken a few too many knocks on the rugby pitch, but his blue eyes were quick and piercing and flicked down to the two locks in the steel door, then back to Ray. The question was posed and Ray answered it with the briefest of nods. Andy immediately felt in his jacket pocket and produced a well-used set of lock picking tools. He went down on his haunches and looked at the locks – there was an old rim lock by Chubb and, below it, a mortice lock. With his tools, he could spring the Chubb, but if the mortice was locked, that could give him some problems. He smiled and gave Ray a thumbs up. The mortice hadn't been engaged. There would be no signs of forced entry and they could say the door had been left open. Ray hadn't seen a single security camera on their walk down the lane, so they should be fine – their word against that of a man who might be a killer. Normally, there'd be at least one camera somewhere, but this wasn't a 'normal' place. The people that owned the garages and lock-ups in that part of Loughborough Junction were the sort of people who preferred not to be caught on camera.

It didn't take Andy long to pick the lock and soon he was up and pushing the door open. As it swung inward, the piercing sound of metal dragging across metal made both men wince as it reverberated into the darkness beyond the door.

"Fuck me!" Andy muttered as he produced a small torch from an inside pocket. He clicked it on and its powerful beam revealed the extent of their problem.

"It's bloody huge!" Andy said with annoyance.

"Because there's six railway tracks above it. For all we know, this could go all the way through to the other side," said Ray, taking out his own torch and clicking it on,

"What the hell?"

The beam of his torch was illuminating a pile of old dining chairs that rose up in a higgledy-piggledy tower eight feet high, as if the chairs were climbing towards the arched ceiling above. Ray ran his beam across the pitch-black vault – it seemed to be crammed to the roof with piles of bric-a-brac. Furniture, crockery, toys, sports equipment, military memorabilia and general oddments including a hatstand - every possible variation of mouldy old tat seemed to be there.

"On the plus side, he's a hoarder, so if he's our man, he's bound to have kept things," said Ray.

"And on the minus side, we're going to have to sift through all this crap to get to it," Andy reflected.

"Yeah," Ray sighed, "Ok, let's get on with it."

"Mister Titheridge!" Andy shouted, "This is the police. The door is open and we are concerned that you might be in some sort of difficulty..."

Ray liked that and smiled at Andy's ability to make things up on the fly,

"...We are entering now. If you are there, please show yourself..."

They stood, coiling themselves by the door for ten seconds,

"Mister Titheridge?"

Another five seconds,

"Right, we're coming in!" Andy called and the two men stepped out of the light and into the darkness.

It was colder inside, with a musty smell of damp, mould and rats. Ray shivered slightly at the temperature change, then picked out a carver dining chair that was upside down on top of a rotting sofa and used it to wedge the door open. The two men shone their torches into the gloom. Incredibly, the first ten or fifteen feet were the least cluttered. The decades of detritus gathered from God-knows-where were pushed to the sides of the space, but ahead of them it was a different story. A huge pile of junk rose about seven feet high in the middle of the vault, leaving only narrow paths either side between it and the crap piled six feet deep against the sloping side walls.

Ray looked at it and sucked his teeth. Now they had a choice – both go down the same side so they could watch each other's backs, but risk Titheridge slipping away down the other side, or split up and risk Titheridge jumping one of them. What to do?

"I reckon we should split up," said Andy, who had gone through the same thought process, "We're both big boys... well, I am, anyway," he added, looking down at Ray, who rolled his eyes at the well-worn jibe.

"Okay, but we keep talking to each other, right?" said Ray.

"Yes, boss," Andy replied and he slowly started to work his way down the right hand side.

"Love what he's done with the place," said Ray loudly as he picked his way forward, shining the torch carefully over the looming piles of tat either side of him.

"Sort of 'American Pickers' meets 'The Hoarder Next Door'," Andy replied as he strained his eyes to see if there was anything suspicious behind a rack of old army surplus coats.

"Great smell of rat," Ray observed, "They must love it in here. All these crevices to hide in."

"Probably hundreds of 'em," said Andy. The thought unsettled him. As if it wasn't bad enough already that Titheridge might leap out at him, now there was the possibility of a rat going for his throat. Ah! There was a solution! Andy reached out and took an old wooden tennis racquet from a jumble of sports gear. It was cold and unpleasantly damp, but as he hefted it in his hand, it gave him the consolation that if a rat did go for him, he'd have an even chance of thwacking it into next week.

In the other aisle, Ray was carefully scrutinizing every nook and cranny with the beam of his torch, horribly aware that the darkness outside that beam might be concealing a killer. Then he suddenly stiffened at the unmistakeable shape of a head and shoulders,

"Hey!" said Ray, loudly.

"What?" Andy called.

Ray sighed as he realised there was no danger,

"I've got a mannequin," he said, running his torch over the shop dummy dressed in out-of-date military clothes.

"Is it creepy?" Andy asked.

Ray regarded the bland features,

"Nah!" and he moved on slowly.

"So long as it's not a ventriloquist's dummy - they scare the bejesus out of me," Andy said as he advanced slowly down his aisle, gripping the tennis racquet that little bit harder. Now he was about thirty feet down the looming canyon of clutter and he didn't like it. An ambush would be all too easy. And even if someone came straight at him, what could he do? Turning to run would leave his back exposed, so he'd have to stand and fight. But what if they had a knife, or a sword, or a gun? Christ, they could probably find a spear or a battle-axe in all this tat and then what would he do? Suddenly, a pair of eyes glinted at him from the darkness. Sharp teeth bared in a snarl. Andy cried out and slashed instinctively with the tennis racquet. The move dislodged a badly stacked collection of garden furniture and now he was deluged in plastic chairs and tables as he tried to strike at the thing coming at him from the gloom. As he stumbled backwards into the central pile of rubbish, bringing even more bric-a-brac down on his head, he could vaguely hear Ray shouting and running round to him, but it was too late – whatever was in there was on him. There was a stale, animal stench and he could feel sharp teeth on his hand as he dropped his torch and fell to the ground. He struck again and again at the thing, but it didn't make any difference.

Ray was off as soon as he'd heard Andy's cry. In a couple of seconds, he was back near the entrance and then he was sprinting down towards Andy. Ray's torchlight flashed haphazardly as he ran, but as he got up close, he steadied himself to see Andy on the ground beating the assailant on top of him with a tennis racquet. Ray stood transfixed for a moment and then burst out laughing as he watched Andy trying to kill the large stuffed badger that had fallen on him.

"Andy! Andy! It's all right! It's just a badger!"

"What?" Andy shouted, while still hitting his assailant.

"It's a stuffed badger, you twat! Look!"

Andy stopped hitting and looked at the thing on top of him, illuminated by Ray's torch. Yes, it was a stuffed badger.

"Fuck!"

Andy scrabbled clear of the badger and the jumble of garden tat and picked up his torch as Ray joined him. Andy dusted himself off and looked sheepishly at Ray,

"Sorry. I overreacted. All I saw was the eyes and the teeth, so I lashed out and brought the whole bloody lot down."

"No harm done," Ray replied and, as he shone his torch on the badger, he could see why Andy had reacted. With its open mouth and snarling teeth, it was fairly unsettling.

"Ho-ly shit!" Ray breathed as he pointed his torch at the rubbish piled against the wall. There, stretching off into the gloom, was a chaotic jumble of stuffed animals – foxes, birds, dogs, cats, more badgers...

"Is that a fucking Shetland pony?" Andy asked in amazement.

"Yeah, that is a fucking Shetland pony," Ray replied as their torches picked out the unmistakeable shaggy head and body of the pony standing amidst the mess.

"Who stuffs a pony?" Andy was struggling to compute what he was seeing, "I mean, museums used to do it, obviously, but... what's it doing here?"

"God knows. But it tells us something about Mister Titheridge."

"That he's a psycho?"

"Yeah," said Ray, lingering on the word as he thought ahead. Should they get out, call for back-up and sit on the place until it arrived, or continue the search? What actual evidence did they have that Brian Titheridge was their man? They were there playing a hunch. That was all. He and Andy both had a feeling about Titheridge, but was that really enough to call out the uniforms? The man had a creepy storage facility, hoarded crap and collected taxidermy. None of those were crimes. And all that had happened was Andy had got spooked by a stuffed badger. No, it wasn't enough to start up a hue and cry.

"Right, I've got an idea," he said, "Let's pull a load of this stuff out to block this aisle, then we go down the other one together, see what's down there and if we flush Titheridge out, we catch him right here."

"Works for me," said Andy, "But I'm keeping the tennis racquet just in case."

"Tit!" said Ray, shaking his head pityingly.

It didn't take them long to block off the narrow passageway with a heavy sideboard piled with bits of furniture, stuffed animals and black bin bags filled with some sort of heavy material. Then they went back down Ray's side. They took it slow and easy, shining their torches into every dark corner to make absolutely sure no one was hiding in the clutter. The further they went, the colder it got and the more their sharpened senses could pick out the occasional skittering of tiny, clawed feet running somewhere out of sight. Ray noticed that there was a new note to the smell of must and rats, something sour but indefinable. Like one of those stars that can't be seen by directly looking at them, but only by looking at a point of sky nearby. Ray shone his torch straight down the aisle and tapped Andy on the arm,

"It opens out,"

Andy nodded in reply and, as they made their way towards the end of the aisle, they could gradually see the back wall of the lock-up looming out of the darkness. When they'd finally picked their way to the end of the aisle, they looked at an open area about twenty feet across with a large Persian rug laid in the middle of it. In the centre of the rug was a small, square table with a single chair lying on the floor next to it as if someone had got up in a hurry.

Ray and Andy looked at each other. How to play it? Was someone in there with them? If it was Titheridge, and if their instincts were right, he was a man who had killed and dismembered three people. Ray indicated for Andy to announce their presence again.

"Mister Titheridge, this is the Police and we'd like to talk to you," Andy said firmly as Ray stepped out into the space and scanned the clutter around the edges with his torch. More of the same mouldering crap, but there were some interesting military-style storage boxes on the far wall that would need closer investigation. Andy joined him and ran his torch across the clutter in the middle of the two aisles.

"Bloody hell!" Andy cried.

"Wha...?" but the word stopped in Ray's throat as he saw the nine-foot grizzly bear towering over them with its glinting fangs and razor claws outstretched.

"I don't like it in 'ere," Andy said bluntly as he regarded the vicious-looking stuffed bear wedged between a large wardrobe and a big coat stand with a long, black coat hung on it.

"Not much more to check, then we can get out of here," Ray said, training his torch on an area of the back wall that looked like a good place to hide.

After searching through the rest of the clutter around the edges of the open space, Ray stopped and looked up the aisle to where they'd made their makeshift barricade.

"I'll check this out. You stay down here and watch out for Titheridge," he said and he started off down the dark, narrow alleyway of junk, leaving Andy to guard the back end of the room.

As he moved away from the open space, Ray noticed that the air was getting more breathable.

"Is it just me, or is there a funny smell back there?" he called back over his shoulder, before taking a broom handle and poking it into a pile of curtain material under a desk.

"Smells like something's gone off," Andy called back, "And it's a funny place for a rug, too."

"Yeah..." Ray was glad they were singing from the same hymn sheet. Now, as he worked his way up the aisle, looking into every dark recess and throwing the occasional glance back from where he'd come, Ray wondered what might be under that rug. None of his ideas were pleasant. So, when he finally got to the barricade and found precisely nothing, he turned back towards the open space with the grim foreboding that whatever they were looking for was waiting for them somewhere under that rug.

"There's that smell again," said Ray when he was halfway back to the open space. Now that he was expecting it, he noticed it more strongly than before. There was definitely something stomach-churning in the air.

"Nothing," Ray said as he re-entered the open space, where Andy was stood, eyeing the angry-looking bear with suspicion.

"Shall we?" Andy asked, indicating the Persian rug.

Ray nodded in reply, then walked across to the fallen chair, picked it up and took it to the side of the rug. Andy used his large wingspan and strength to pick up the table unaided and carry it over to the side. At last, they were able to roll back the rug.

"Trap door," said Andy as they revealed a heavy wooden square in the concrete floor and, with the carpet fully rolled up, the unmistakable stench of spoiled meat rose up from the floor.

"I'll lift, you take this and be ready to hit anyone who comes out," said Andy, handing the tennis racquet to Ray.

They stood for a moment looking at each other. Both knew that something nasty was down there. Both knew that things might happen very quickly. But both knew that there was no one else they trusted more in that moment than each other. Andy grasped the inset brass handle of the trapdoor,

"Mister Titheridge, this is the Police. We're opening the trapdoor now."

He gave Ray a nod and pulled the door up as Ray shone his torch into the chamber below. Ray was instantly enveloped in a wave of stinking air that made him gag, but that seemed to be the worst of it. No one charged out at him and the room below was still and silent. Andy opened the door fully and gently rested it on the floor, then got down on his haunches and pointed his torch into the room,

"Jesus shitting Christ!" he gasped.

"Fuck me with a hammer!" Ray said in shock at what their torches were revealing.

About ten feet below them and accessed by a metal ladder, was a large room in the middle of which was a blood-soaked operating table. Strapped to the table was the mangled body of a middle-aged man, whose eyes had been ripped from their sockets and whose teeth grinned up at them from a mouth without lips. From the smell of him, he'd been there a few days. Wherever Ray shone his torch there was dried blood – the walls, the floor, the trolley with a selection of medical instruments, the desk strewn with papers and a mug – even the area to the back of the room with the sink and what looked like a tea-making setup.

Andy gave an inarticulate moan and then asked,

"Are those hands?"

Ray looked to where Andy's torch was shining and there on the floor next to the operating table was a plastic bucket. Christ!

"Yeah," Ray said, fighting his rising gorge.

The bucket contained a selection of hands in various states of decay.

"So, we were right," said Andy through the handkerchief that he'd got out to cover his nose and mouth.

"Yeah," Ray said through gritted teeth – that smell was intolerable! Then Ray had a realisation that made his flesh crawl,

"Look at the mug on the desk."

Andy did so and within a second experienced the same sensation as Ray.

The mug was steaming.

Chapter Two

"I've Seen Him!"

The thought process: steaming mug + empty kill room = vicious killer somewhere in the darkness, took about a third of a second in the minds of both men. They instantly stiffened and shot each other a look that registered they both fully understood the danger they were in. An unpleasant silence filled the vault of the railway arch. Ray's mouth had suddenly dried, but he had to break the silence,

"What a nightmare," he said, trying to sound natural, while signalling to Andy that they needed to get out and call for backup. Maybe it was the preceding silence, or the note of insincerity in Ray's voice – whatever the reason, Titheridge made his move before Andy could reply.

The roar was an animal sound of strain and fury which startled both men, who turned to see the unthinkable.

"Bear!" Ray shouted as the grizzly lunged down at them, its teeth flashing in their torchlights. Ray rolled sideways, but Andy couldn't move in time and was pinned by the great beast. Ray scrambled to his feet, but before he could orientate himself, he felt the blade of a large knife press against his throat,

"Don't move, Detective Ennis, or you'll end up like the others."

Ray immediately recognised the well-spoken voice of Brian Titheridge talking into his left ear.

"Alright," Ray choked, allowing Titheridge to move him as he pleased.

"Good lad," said Titheridge.

They could hear more than see Andy fighting to get out from under the grizzly, but then he was up and shining his torch at them.

"Stay back, or I cut his head off!" Titheridge shouted.

In Andy's torchlight, Titheridge looked wild-eyed and unhinged, his thinning hair was all askew, but the way he held the carving knife showed expertise.

"I mean it! One move and he's dead!"

Andy made a great play of stopping in his tracks and staying very still.

"It's all right, Andy..." Ray began,

"Shut up! And you, stay back. Stay back!" Titheridge shouted over Ray, before running his free hand through hair that was soaked with a cold sweat,

"Right... right... right..." he gabbled, "All right... this is... this is... this is what we're going to do..."

As Titheridge marshalled his thoughts, Ray's left hand moved slowly towards the back of his belt.

"I'm going to take your car and this one's coming with me... no, no that won't work... bugger! Why'd you have to ruin everything? I had it all perfect... perfect!" Titheridge accused with a rising voice.

"Mister Titheridge, please try to calm down," said Andy with surprising softness, "I'm sure we can sort this out without any unpleasantness."

"But you don't understand what you've done!" Titheridge snapped, "I can't go to prison! Who will stop *him* if I'm gone? No one! Only I can stop him! I need time... Time! I'm too busy to go to prison. Without me, he'll have a free hand..."

As Titheridge raved, Ray's hand reached back to the small pair of push daggers that were clipped to the back of his belt. With infinite care, he slipped the left one out of its sheath and manoeuvred it so that the elongated triangle of its blade jutted out from between his second and third fingers, while the T-shaped handle nestled reassuringly into his palm. He was set. All he needed was a moment when the carving knife was not pressed firmly into his throat.

"Without me, the streets will run with blood," Titheridge babbled to himself, "They'll all get away with feeding *him* new victims and *he'll* get stronger every day... do you know what you've done?" He screamed and Ray winced as the knife dug into his skin.

"Right..." Titheridge said with unsettling finality as he started to back towards the unblocked aisle leading to the entrance,

"I'm taking your car. Yes, that's it! Get a head start. I can disappear so that neither you nor *he* can find me... then I can slip back and start my work over again."

Andy could see that Titheridge was in his own little world, talking to himself and seeing nothing, with his bulging eyes staring into a darkness deeper than anything on this earth.

"Who's got the car keys?"

"He has," Andy replied calmly.

"Is this true?" Titheridge increased the pressure of the knife against Ray's throat so that Ray didn't dare move. All he could muster was an

"Mmmm," which he tried to make sound as positive as he could.

"If you're lying," Titheridge said quietly into Ray's ear, "If this is a trick, I will give you a deliberately clumsy tracheotomy," his breath smelled of the coffee he'd recently abandoned in the kill room.

"Ngggn," Ray tried to make the sound seem sincere.

"Okay, you!" Titheridge shouted at Andy, "Throw your phone at my feet. Come on! Throw your phone!"

Andy held the hand with the torch in a calming, supplicatory way as his other hand reached...

"Slowly!" Titheridge shrieked,

...slowly into his jacket pocket, taking his phone between the tips of his fingers and thumb to bring it back out carefully so Titheridge could see it was just a phone.

"Toss it over here!"

Andy complied and the phone clattered onto the concrete and skittered towards Titheridge, who dragged Ray with him to it before stamping hard on it three times. Andy tried not to look pissed off, but it was a nearly new iPhone and he inwardly groaned at the thought of having to go through the rigamarole of setting up a new one.

"Now yours – where is it?"

The pressure of the knife eased enough for Ray to choke out,

"Inside jacket pocket. Right side."

"Okay, hold still. You've seen the playroom. You know what I can do with this..."

Titheridge was holding the knife to Ray's throat with his right hand, so had to reach his left hand all the way across Ray to get to the pocket. The problem was, Titheridge wasn't a big man – maybe five-six in his shoes – so reaching around Ray proved to be difficult. After a failed attempt, he repositioned Ray and tried again. This time, his hand found the pocket and started fumbling around for the phone. Ray measured the pressure of the knife on his throat with infinite concentration as he felt Titheridge's fingers finding the phone and struggling to get a grip. He had to strain to reach it, it was right there at his finger-tips, just a bit more... the extra stretch to grasp the phone caused the knife to come away from Ray's throat and in that moment, Ray drove the push dagger into Titheridge's left thigh. A high scream filled the vault and Ray slapped the hand with the carving knife aside as he leaped away. Titheridge wasn't a tough man and he dropped the knife as he looked down with horror at the thing sticking out of his leg. Out of his peripheral vision, Ray saw a huge shape leap from the darkness at Titheridge, who was flattened under Andy's bulk. The sound of the smaller man's breath being knocked out of his body was unpleasant and reassuring at the same time. And now Titheridge's world was nothing but pain. He was vainly trying to breathe, but it wouldn't come, then there was a sunburst of pain as something crashed into the right side of his face, then a crack as another blow exploded on his left cheek. That was all he knew.

"Stitch that, cunt!" Andy shouted, before getting up to roughly turn Titheridge over and handcuff him.

"Is he alive?" Ray asked.

"Unfortunately, yes," Andy replied.

"I'm all right, thanks for asking," Ray said, rubbing his throat.

"You're a big boy. Nothing that a few pints of liquid counselling can't fix. You'd better call it in. My phone's buggered," said Andy with venom, barely restraining himself from giving Titheridge a sharp kick in the ribs.

Ray took out his phone and made a couple of calls, then came over to look at Titheridge's leg. The push dagger was still sticking out of it and blood was soaking the fabric of the blue overalls the man was wearing.

"You're gonna get in trouble for that," Andy chided, pointing at the embedded dagger, "A Detective Inspector with an illegal blade. Shame on you."

"Who says it's my blade? This place is full of dangerous stuff. I picked it up during our investigation. Lucky I did, or I'd be dead."

"Nice story. Very believable," Andy smiled, "Well, it looks like you didn't hit anything vital, so no need to do anything before the ambulance gets here..." then he looked at Titheridge's blood-stained overalls more closely, "Nice that some of the blood on there is finally his."

"I think I'll close that trapdoor – keep some of the smell down there," Ray said, moving across and putting the trap door back in place, "Besides, the last thing we need is someone falling down the hole in the dark."

"Would be quite funny, though," Andy liked that thought - it appealed to his sense of the macabre.

"Keep an eye on him, I'm going to look for a light switch," said Ray, heading back up the unblocked aisle towards the entrance.

"Don't worry, I'll keep both eyes on him, boss."

"And don't call me 'boss'," said Ray, "I know you're only taking the piss."

"All right, cap'n," Andy said with a salute.

"Muppet!" Ray muttered as he headed for the door.

It took Ray a few minutes to find the switch hidden behind a pile of clutter by the door and when he turned it on, an ironic cheer came from Andy in the depths. The lights, strung at intervals across the top of the arched ceiling of rough bricks, gave only a dismal light and made the place seem even more weird and unpleasant than when it was dark. The jumble of stuff was a window into a very disturbed mind. Now, Ray could see that in amongst the everyday household tat, there were weapons. Some were on their own – near the door was what looked like a First World War Lee-Enfield rifle with bayonet – others were in caches: a selection of fencing swords, bundled in sack cloth; a battle axe, a mace and a war hammer in an umbrella stand; half a dozen nail-studded cricket bats in a pile by the back wall. Ray smiled – he'd easily be able to make his story of finding the push dagger stick. His thoughts were broken by the distant sound of a siren and he went outside to direct the paramedics to where they were needed.

Ten minutes later, Ray and Andy were standing outside the lock-up, in the painfully bright sunshine of what had become a sparkling July day. They watched as two paramedics tended to Titheridge, who was now strapped to a gurney next to the ambulance and annoyingly wide awake.

"You must understand, I don't have time for this!" Titheridge declared as one of the paramedics – a sturdy woman with a blonde ponytail – gave him an injection of morphine.

"I'm at war! At-war!" he repeated, giving extra emphasis to each word, "*His* acolytes are everywhere and I have to kill them!"

"Why?" asked Ray.

"Why? What sort of a question is that? Because they're evil, of course!" Titheridge said sharply.

"Please stay calm, sir. Until we get you to the hospital and get that knife out of your leg, you really need to stay calm," the blonde paramedic said in a firm, but sympathetic voice.

"All right, yes, sorry," said Titheridge, visibly calming, "And sorry for holding that knife to your throat, Inspector. You're just doing your job. No reason to take it out on you. No, no reason."

"Thanks," said Ray, "But what about the people in your 'playroom' as you call it?"

"Oh, don't worry about them. They were all evil," said Titheridge in a matter-of-fact way, "They were all *his* acolytes. They deserved everything they got. You see... you see... it's quite simple – I hunt and kill *his* servants.

I hunt them, I kill them. Simple. And you know what the best thing is?" he continued conspiratorially,

"What is the best thing?" Ray asked, leaning closer.

"I can see them for what they are... but they can't see me!" Titheridge tittered like a child giving away an embarrassing secret.

Ray and Andy flashed each other a look.

"So, you're invisible?" Ray asked.

"No, don't be ridiculous! That would be silly. No, I can see their auras, but they can't see that I can see their auras."

Of course, yes, that made much more sense!

Andy and Ray's blank looks made Titheridge explain things further,

"You see, people with the gift of second sight can see the auras around other people. They can see if they're good, if they're bad, or whatever else. And *his* followers have a very particular aura – black, would you believe it!"

Ray and Andy didn't, but they continued to listen attentively while Ray recorded it all on his phone.

"But, because they have been imbued with some of *his* power, they can spot people with second sight. And if they spot you, they feed you to *him*. He loves to feed on psychic power. And blood, of course."

Titheridge said, giving them one of those 'Ah!' expressions that engaged all the muscles of his face and throat so that his shoulders shrugged upwards slightly.

"So, who is..." Ray began, but Titheridge cut him off,

"But I'm too clever for them! I have an amulet that means they can't see that I see their auras."

"A magic amulet?" Andy snorted with derision.

"Yes!" Titheridge was delighted that Andy seemed to understand, "And it cost me a pretty penny. Took me over a year just to track down a druid to make it. Then it cost me ten thousand for the amulet and another five to have it implanted in my body. Clever, eh?" Titheridge searched their faces for approval, but found only idiotic confusion. He'd have to spell it out for them,

"That way I can't lose it. See?" and he laughed at his genius.

Andy and Ray smiled politely and Titheridge continued,

"That's why I've been able to hunt down sixty-eight of them!"

At this, Andy, Ray and the two paramedics stopped and stared.

"Hang on, Mr. Titheridge, have you just admitted to killing sixty-eight people?" Ray asked, his eyes widening.

"Yes, yes... oh yes!" Titheridge seemed to be remembering something particularly satisfying, "And I didn't just kill them, I tortured them, too! I tortured and defiled every last one of them."

The paramedics and the detectives looked at Titheridge with open-mouthed disbelief.

"Oh, I know it sounds terrible, but they were all very, very evil."

"All of 'em?" Andy asked.

"Yes!" said Titheridge with a hint at wounded pride that his word wasn't being accepted as truth, "They were *his* servants."

"And *he* is...?"

"Can't say. Won't say!" Titheridge shook his head firmly and his gaze went from the world around him to some memory, "I saw *him*... I *saw* him... I *saw him*!"

Titheridge broke down into uncontrollable tears.

"We've got to take him now," said the male paramedic who was in his late forties and more overweight than was healthy.

"No, it's all right," said Titheridge, regaining his composure, "I'm fine... mustn't think of *him*! Don't look inside – shut him out... all good."

"But if you killed all them people, where are the bodies?" Andy asked.

"Here and there," Titheridge replied lightly, "I've got places all over. I had to. *His* servants are everywhere. Everywhere! And the police are no help – poking their noses in where they're not wanted. Although I must say, I'm appalled that you found any of them... blasted Dry January."

"Dry January?" Ray said as he and Andy looked at Titheridge, confused.

"The bits of the three people you found... I killed them in January last year. I was trying to be healthy, you know, cutting out drinking – Dry January and all that rot – but the lack of sleep must have made me sloppy. I need the best part of a bottle of Macallan to get to sleep. Otherwise, I see *him* when I close my eyes. Yes, January last year was very difficult – hardly slept at all. Was it worth it? My liver might be thanking me, but look where it's got me!" Titheridge exclaimed, struggling vainly against his restraints.

"But all the others... are you going to tell us where they are?" Ray asked.

"No need. No need. I logged it all. The book's got everything in it."

"And where's the book?"

"Listen, I know you two are good men. You're good, but you can't trust anyone. You've got to promise me, promise me you won't let it fall into *his* servants' hands."

"We promise," said Ray.

"Say it like you mean it!" Titheridge snapped.

"Are you taking the piss?" Andy started angrily.

"It's all right, Andy!" Ray said quickly, "Come on Andy, let's promise properly," and he gave Andy a thunderous look, then turned back to Titheridge,

"Mister Titheridge, we solemnly promise to protect the book," said Ray.

"Yes," said Andy, with his hand on his heart.

Titheridge gave them both a long, hard stare.

"All right. Twenty-five B, Hillside Terrace, Peckham Rye. Master bedroom, bedside table, top drawer. It's all there."

Ray looked at Titheridge sceptically. They had been to his house and it wasn't in Peckham Rye. Titheridge picked up on the look and sighed,

"I rent half a dozen houses around London. All under different names. These are the lengths I've had to go to in order to avoid being caught by the police. And it's been very wearing, I can tell you!"

"Well, I'm sorry for your inconvenience," Ray replied, "But can you give us the other addresses?"

"Yes, yes, all in good time. Christ, you've caught me now – all I've bloody got is time. Oh, and the keys to the Peckham house are in my right pocket."

Andy reached in and produced a large set of keys.

"And you do realise you've admitted to sixty-eight murders?" he said, placing the keys in a clear plastic bag.

"Yes, I just wish I'd had time for more," and he sighed heavily, "I can't tell you how inconvenient this is – I had another two scheduled this month and a very busy August planned," and he relaxed back into the pillow as the morphine started to take hold.

"May we take him now?" said the paramedic.

"Yes," Ray replied.

Ray and Andy stood back to allow the paramedics to load the gurney with Titheridge on it into the back of the ambulance.

"Constable!" Ray beckoned a uniformed officer who had arrived not long after the ambulance. He looked young, new and shiny in the white light of the day,

"Go with him to the hospital and take down as much of what he says as you can. Once they've patched him up, stay with him until he's back at headquarters."

"Yes, sir," said the young man, relishing the idea of playing a part in nailing a serial killer.

"Ta-ta!" Titheridge called as he gave them a merry little wave before the doors closed and the ambulance drove away. As it did, two nondescript vans came down the lane.

"The crime scene investigators have got here bloody fast," Ray said.

"Must be having a slow day. I hope one of 'em's got a flask of tea – I'm gasping!" said Andy.

Chapter Three

Complications

Within half an hour, the railway arch was full of busy people doing their specialist jobs. The crime scene investigators, along with the medical examiner, were down in the kill room, while Ray and Andy (now happily united with a mug of tea) were going over the clutter surrounding the space around the trapdoor. They were joined by Detective Constable Emma White, who had been with their team for about a year. She was small – around five-foot-two – with short, dark hair and a wiry physique, which she kept in shape with kickboxing. Andy and Ray had always found her calm, steady and capable, and they liked her instincts. She had a nose for 'wrong 'uns', as she called them. Now she was trawling through the clutter at the back of the railway arch, looking for any evidence that might put Titheridge away for good.

"So, Andy landed right on top of him?" she asked, unzipping an ancient Pan Am carry-on bag and shining her torch inside.

"Yup," said Ray, sifting through the contents of the wardrobe that was next to the gap left by the fallen bear.

"And he wasn't crushed to death? It's a miracle."

"Ha bloody ha!" Andy said dryly.

"I hope he doesn't sue for police brutality," Emma added.

"It was Captain Fantastic who stabbed him, not me," Andy protested.

"Inspector Ennis, could you come down here, please?" the enquiry came from the open trap door.

"Coming!" Ray called, going over and looking down into the hell hole below, which was now well lit. Right below him stood Belinda Warburton, the medical examiner. She was a large woman of about fifty, standing with her hands on her hips and her feet firmly planted. She and the other crime scene investigators were in full white coveralls with their hoods up.

"We need to talk. Pop on some shoe protectors and come on down," she said in a well-spoken, no-nonsense tone.

"Sure thing," said Ray, putting on some blue polythene shoe protectors from a container by the top of the ladder.

"You wearing gloves?" Belinda called up.

"Yes," said Ray before positioning himself at the top of the steel ladder.

"Careful! That's slippery as hell," Belinda warned.

Once he got down, Ray turned and saw for the first time the full extent Titheridge's 'playroom'. It was more oblong than square and the rough concrete walls and floor were caked in blood. The area nearest the ladder was clearly where most of the 'action' took place and it was dominated by the bloody operating table with two trolleys on the far side of it. One had a set of dirty surgical equipment on it, while the other had a collection of tools, all of which looked designed to inflict maximum pain. One of the crime scene techs was carefully looking through them and taking notes. Beyond these, there was the messy desk with the tell-tale coffee mug over by the left wall, which was being photographed by another tech. An old, rusty fridge stood against the wall opposite the desk. Next to the fridge was a dirty counter-top, above which there were mould-encrusted cupboards, one of which had a hinge missing on its door. As the third tech carefully opened one of the cupboards, Ray could just make out a mass of something rotting in it. Whatever was oozing from it had stained the underside of the cupboard and the wall below. The area under the counter hadn't been boxed in and it was a jumble of rusting electrical equipment and opaque plastic storage boxes. Ray didn't want to think about what they might contain. Down at the end was a Belfast sink that would normally have been white, but which was spattered with dried blood. Above the sink, hanging on hooks nailed into the concrete walls, were what looked like the intestines of some of the victims. The floor was strewn with bits of the insides of the people who'd presumably once owned the intestines on the wall.

Ray was trying not to breathe, because even breathing through his mouth gave him a taste of the stench.

"Here, have some Vick's," said Belinda, offering an open jar to Ray in a gloved hand.

"Thanks," he gasped and gratefully smeared the vapo-rub under his nose. Better!

"You've got a right one here," said Belinda.

"I guessed that from the bucket of severed hands," Ray smiled, but Belinda Warburton wasn't smiling.

"No, the hands – and they're from nine different people, by the way – the hands are probably the least disturbing thing down here," Belinda said, pursing her narrow lips.

"Oh," said Ray.

"Yes, 'Oh'. This unfortunate gentleman was raped a number of times while he was alive..." she said, moving towards the body on the operating table, "And none of them in the orifices God gave him," she added, arching her left eyebrow.

"Jesus!" Ray exclaimed, glancing across at the nightmarish grinning corpse. Close up, he could see that the lips had been removed with a sharp knife.

"Indeed. Looks like Mister Titheridge used this home-made device to create his own 'tunnels of love'," and Belinda indicated a large metal device on the far trolley that had a passing resemblance to an apple corer.

"Judging from the symbols he's carved into the victim around each newly cut orifice, it seems to be ritualistic. Look..." and she indicated a rough design around a blackened, oozing hole in the man's right side just below his ribs.

"Any idea why?" Ray asked.

"God knows!" Belinda exclaimed, "Not my line of country. Probably some sort of satanist nonsense. It usually is... all I can say with surety is that his main aim was to inflict as much pain as possible. He had all this surgical equipment and yet this man's eyes were torn out of his head by hand."

Ray didn't know what to say, but unfortunately his mouth decided to have a go before his brain could engage,

"Any idea where the eyes are?" he asked and then inwardly kicked himself for it a second later.

Belinda paused for a moment and looked hard at Ray, then replied,

"Not yet, but they'll probably turn up – unless he's fed them to something. Sometimes they do that. Now, if we go over here..." she continued, leading Ray past the corpse on the operating table, "You can see a lot more of those symbols on the walls."

Ray looked and it was like looking at one of those magic-eye pictures – once he tuned his gaze to see the designs, they stood out clearly. He was no expert on the occult, but it all had the look of some sort of demonic iconography.

"Je-sus," he said quietly.

"Literally," Belinda replied, pointing to a word that was repeated over and over again amidst the designs, "My ancient Greek is a bit rusty, but that word is Jesus in ancient Greek. And this symbol is the Arabic word 'Allah'," and she pointed to another symbol that was also repeated across the wall,

"And this stuff is over all the walls and floor and ceiling," said Belinda pointing her torch upwards.

Ray stood there amazed as he looked. The entire ceiling was covered in designs and words. Then he looked down and, through the blood and gore, he could just make out more of the bizarre scrawls across the floor.

"I'd say he carved all these into the concrete before he started killing people in here. Like some sort of consecration," Belinda said.

"That's a lot of work," Ray mused. He didn't like it. It opened the door wide open to a 'diminished responsibility' judgement,

"Fuck. So, either he's a religious nutcase who's on some insane crusade to kill everyone with black auras, or he's a meticulous, forward thinking, cold-blooded sadist... and he's cooked up all this to ensure he ends up in a secure hospital instead of prison," Ray thought out loud.

"Sorry, what black auras?" Belinda asked, looking at Ray as if *he* was the nutcase.

"Sorry, it was something Titheridge was burbling about as they put him into the ambulance. He says he can see people's auras and he's been killing anyone whose aura is black."

"Right..." Belinda replied slowly, "I don't know why that should seem surprising, given what we've got in the fridge."

Ray's heart sank as they moved over to the rusty fridge. Whatever was in there wasn't likely to be yesterday's moussaka neatly stored in a Tupperware box.

"Not sure who they are," said Belinda, wrenching the door open, "But at least the thing's working, otherwise this would be even more revolting."

And it was about as dreadful as it could get. The fridge had two items in it. On the glass divider above where the veg' would go into the 'crisper', sat the head of a man. Above it on the upper shelf was the head of a woman.

"Probably been in there about six weeks," said Belinda as Ray stared, "But I'll be able to work timings out when I get them back to the lab."

"In her mouth..." Ray began, looking at the woman's head. The mouth had been wrenched open and inside were,

"A man's genitals," Belinda replied, "Possibly his," she indicated the man's head, "And yes, his mouth is stuffed with the surgically removed outer parts of a woman's genitals."

"Ffff..." was the only sound Ray could muster as he fought to keep his breakfast down.

Belinda closed the fridge.

"Sorry, but I thought you ought to see it 'in situ'. The photographs never quite capture the feeling of what's happened."

And this was all about feeling, Ray thought as he focussed his gaze on the rusty door and mastered his urge to vomit. The energy of it was very strange. On the one hand, it all seemed utterly insane, but on the other, there was meticulous planning and frighteningly clear execution. This was a man in total control of his organisational faculties, but who had absolutely lost control of his mind.

"Anything else?" Ray asked, looking at Belinda.

"Probably, but we haven't found it yet. Plenty to be going on with, though," she replied, glancing over to the plastic boxes under the countertop.

"Belinda, can I have your opinion on this, please?" asked the tech who was looking into the cupboards.

"Sorry, do you mind?" Belinda said, looking to Ray.

"Of course," he replied and she hurried away to look at something nightmarish.

Ray stood and slowly turned around on the spot, trying to fix everything into his memory. It was worse than a slaughterhouse - at least slaughterhouses had to meet public health standards. But this... this was something else. In a way, it was journey's end. He and Andy had been working on the case for more than six months and now it looked to have finished right there in that pit of horrors. They would undoubtedly get a conviction. Titheridge was caught armed at the scene, in a lock-up that he owned, wearing overalls most likely covered in the blood of the man on the operating table, and his DNA would be all over the rim of the mug on the desk. And presumably in every orifice he'd cut into his victim. There was no barrister alive who could talk his way out of that. Plus, Titheridge had confessed. But why had he done all this? Until three years ago, he'd been a senior partner in a big accountancy firm in the City. Then suddenly, he'd cashed in all his equity, taken his huge retirement settlement, divorced his wife, left her and his kids half his wealth and disappeared. And this – he looked around in disbelief at the grisly 'playroom' – was what he had been doing since. How could anyone go from solid, middle-aged family man to depraved monster so completely in so short a time? Or at all? How could that happen? It was bewildering. Unless... what? Something was nagging at the back of his mind, which he wanted to ignore, but couldn't. Unless... there was something else going on here. As Ray looked at the eyeless corpse, the entrails nailed to the walls and the religious symbols scrawled everywhere, he had the feeling that this wasn't all about Titheridge. Ray felt an energy in the place that hinted at something greater than any single man. This was an ending to a case... so why did it feel like a beginning?

"I'm afraid it'll be a while before I can give you my preliminary report," Belinda apologised coming back from the other end of the room, "You all right?" she asked, looking at Ray keenly.

He shook himself and said,

"I'm fine and no worries about the report. We've got plenty of time. We've nicked him. He's off the streets and he's not going anywhere. Take the time you need to make this stick."

"Will do. Are you going to be here a while?" Belinda asked.

"Oh shit!" Andy's cry came from above before Ray could reply.

"What?" Ray shouted up.

"Got to get everyone out!" Andy called.

"Coming!" Ray started up the ladder, shouting "Get your team out, Belinda!" and, as she began to give orders behind him, he emerged from the kill room to see Andy holding open the lid of one of the military style boxes. Ray stepped forward and then stopped. The box was full of heavy stick-grenades.

"Fuck!" Ray swore. Could today get any more complicated?

Chapter Four

Born Cross-Eyed

Vicky Ennis usually loved the start of the school holidays. As an English teacher in a secondary school, she was invariably wrung out by mid-June and was only holding on by the skin of her teeth by the time the holidays finally arrived around the twentieth of July. Normally, the final bell of the last day of term was like a great exhalation where the stress of exams could be released and batteries could start to recharge. This year it was different. The first full day of the holidays found her and her seven-year-old daughter Chloe getting up and out of the house as if it was a school day. To make matters worse, they were heading into central London with the commuter crowds. And it was raining. They hurried from their house under a big, red and black striped golfing umbrella and headed up to the top of their road, which ended in a T-junction with Streatham High Road. As one might expect for one of the arteries into central London, all four lanes of the High Road were busy with traffic and the wheels of the passing cars, trucks and buses were loud with a wash of white noise from the water on the road. Vicky and Chloe turned left and, dodging the puddles, they jogged towards the nearest bus stop past the rows of four storey buildings that had been overlooking Streatham's bustle since the end of the nineteenth century. Across the street, six storey apartment blocks from the nineteen thirties with ground floor shopfronts had largely replaced the older buildings, which Vicky felt gave that part of the High Road a split personality. It had the solidity of the late Victorian and Edwardian eras to the west and the forward-looking style of the 'thirties to the east.

A few lucky people were standing under the shelter by the bus stop, but when Vicky and Chloe arrived, they had to join the large group standing in the heavy summer rain. Vicky's long, dark, gently waved hair was already getting damp in spite of the umbrella, but she couldn't bring herself to put the hood up on her blue anorak. Vicky was very aware that she was still carrying some of the extra weight she'd put on during pregnancy seven years earlier, and she thought the anorak with the hood up made her look like a big, blue potato. Even though Ray and Chloe disagreed with this assessment, she never put the hood up. Meanwhile, Chloe was sporting red wellies and a white raincoat with strawberries printed on it. Her hood was very firmly up, and she was enjoying the sound the rain made on the stiff material.

Their wait wasn't long and soon they were on a crowded, steamy bus, lurching down Brixton hill. As it was impossible to see through the steamed-up windows, Chloe looked around the bus at the people. Most of them were sitting or standing with their heads bowed over their phones, so Chloe was able to stare at them with impunity. Why would they look around them when they could look at anything in the world on their phones? The passengers were a typical south London mix of races, but Chloe wasn't interested in the colour of their skins – it was the colour of their auras that fascinated her. Ever since she could remember, she could see vaporous colours surrounding people. They were like layers of energy, always in motion. Most were a mix of colours, but some were very clearly a single colour. Her dad's was red, while her mum's was green. Chloe felt these reflected their personalities, because Ray was intense and competitive, while Vicky really connected with people and understood how to encourage their potential. Looking around the bus, she could see lots of different auras – energetic orange, peaceful blue, spiritual silver and many more. There were also one or two brown auras. Chloe could feel that these people were struggling in some way or were in pain. A middle-aged woman sitting nearby had a brown aura and Chloe could feel that she had recently lost someone close to her. She was finding life difficult, so Chloe concentrated all her positive energy in her direction. Maybe it would help.

After about twenty minutes, they bundled off the bus and were swept down into Brixton underground station with the crowd of commuters. Although they were able to get a seat on the tube at Brixton, when they changed from the Victoria line to the Piccadilly line at Green Park, they were wedged into the standing space among the soggy commuters. Chloe didn't like crowds at the best of times, so now, crammed in amongst the big people with nothing to see but the vast back of the man in front of her and the smell of damp coats in her nostrils, Chloe squeezed her mum's hand and sucked her thumb for comfort. Vicky looked down at her and felt a bloom in her chest of maternal protection and love. Poor little mite! She returned the squeeze of Chloe's hand and smiled at her when she looked up with her large, blue eyes that shone all the brighter from the contrast with the light-brown skin of her face.

Chloe's eyes had always been a talking point, given that both Vicky and Ray had brown eyes.

"It's 'cos my grandmother had a dalliance with a white man up in Sav' la Mar, an' the result was my dad," Ray's grandmother had announced at some family get-together when Chloe was two,

"Those baby blues've been hidin' in our genes since the eighteen seventies. An' don't they look lovely!" she'd exclaimed in a Jamaican accent that nearly sixty years of living in Britain had hardly changed,

"An' they get it from you, too," she'd added, pointing at Vicky's dad. Even though he'd passed neither his blonde hair nor his blue eyes to Vicky, the blue eyes had come to Chloe. And Chloe's eyes were the reason they were packed into the tube train, screaming through the tunnels under London towards Knightsbridge. It wasn't the colour that was the issue, but how they worked. Chloe had always struggled with writing and she was a reluctant reader. She loved stories, loved being read to and had lots to say about them, but Vicky had always thought there was a disconnect between her daughter's verbal abilities and her reading and writing. Since her school assessments were slap-dab in the middle of the range, her teachers insisted that there was nothing out of the ordinary. Vicky wanted to disagree but hadn't made a fuss out of professional courtesy – although she'd still felt there was something not quite right. Even Ray had eventually noticed it. Of course, it had been in the confessional of the car that the truth had come out. Vicky had been talking about Pride and Prejudice, and how funny it was, when Chloe had said,

"The problem with books is the words keep falling off the page."

That statement had been enough for Vicky to take matters into her own hands. Through sheer luck two years earlier, she and Ray had seen a documentary about Meares-Irlen syndrome in which the symptoms of visual stress such as moving words could be alleviated with simple coloured lenses. After Chloe's revelation, they both agreed that her symptoms fitted the bill and took her to the optician for testing. Vicky thought that it was freakish good luck that their local optician offered services for that exact problem. Within a week, they'd confirmed that Chloe's visual stress could be managed with light blue tinted specs. The excitement they'd all felt when the specs arrived was only matched by how damned cool they made her look. Her love of reading exploded from that day.

But Vicky wasn't finished. She knew that visual stress could be prevalent in people with dyslexia, and that the earlier dyslexia could be identified, the better. She fiercely wanted the best for her daughter and knew that until she had an official diagnosis, there was no way she could level the playing field when it came to exams that were all designed for 'normal' children. The result of months of research was this trip into central London. Chloe was going to see an educational psychologist for a full evaluation. It wasn't cheap, but they could just about afford it. And now here they were, emerging from Knightsbridge tube station into the sort of cold rain that only Britain can serve up in the summer.

"Come on, it's just down here," Vicky said encouragingly as she noticed Chloe's look of unease. They stood at the entrance of the station and Vicky wondered how they were going to get into the mass of people passing by. After a few moments' hesitation, they took their chance and darted out into the heavy traffic of the crowd (mainly composed of tourists) that was flowing like a human river towards Harrods a few hundred yards away.

Chloe didn't mind the dull day. She found bright light very tiring, but the rain brought its own problems. The constant shushing of car tyres on the wet road seemed loud to her – like waves on a pebbly beach on a stormy day. The crowds and the sheer amount of sensory stimulation all around her weren't helping her anxiety levels. Although her parents had said that this wasn't too important and that she should relax and be herself, Chloe knew that this *was* something important. Exactly why, she wasn't sure, but she could sense her mother's tension as they hurried along. Thankfully, they soon took a left turn away from the crowds and made their way down various side streets until they reached a big, white building with a big black door in the middle. Vicky announced them through the intercom system and then there was on over-loud buzz and click as the door was unlocked and they went inside.

It smelt just like school and had the same sort of hard floor, but the ceiling was much higher and here they were looked down upon by statues and busts of important people. They walked across the big entrance hall to a desk on the far side and the sound of their feet on the floor made Chloe feel self-conscious. As Vicky introduced them to the receptionist and explained why they were there, Chloe looked around. Like an animal at the vet's, she could sense something was 'off' here. They seemed to be trying too hard to make the place 'friendly' for children. There were lots of pictures drawn by children blue-tacked to the walls, in between murals of cuddly animals. The waiting area had magazines for the adults on a low table, as well as various kinetic puzzles, picture books, drawing equipment and paper to keep children with short attention spans occupied. But Chloe felt it was all fake. This was a place where children like her came to be tested and labelled. Even if it was supposed to help her it wasn't a place *for* her, but for grown-ups to do grown-up things. It made her tummy feel fluttery and she wished she could go home and pull the duvet over her head.

"Do you want to play with one of the toys or do some drawing?" Vicky asked once they'd sat down.

"No thanks, I'm fine" Chloe said quietly.

"I don't blame you," Vicky said equally quietly, "Some of this stuff looks rather grubby!"

Chloe smiled and relaxed just a little.

Vicky wanted to reassure her that everything was all right, that there weren't any 'wrong' answers, that only good things were going to come from seeing the psychologist, but she kept her counsel. She knew what Chloe was like. Someone fussing over her and talking at her would only overload her systems, make her flustered and cause her to withdraw into her shell. So, she sat and tried to be as relaxed as she could.

"We could go to Five Guys afterwards. Get a shake," Vicky suggested lightly. She knew Chloe adored the Five Guys chocolate shakes.

"Yes, please," Chloe replied happily. Yes, it was an obvious bribe, but she'd take it.

"Chloe?"

Chloe and Vicky looked up to see a kindly-faced woman of about forty with her blonde hair in a ponytail standing at the double-doors which opened into a long corridor on their left.

"Yes, that's us... well, her," Vicky spluttered as she stood.

The woman paid her little attention, but directed her welcoming gaze on Chloe,

"Hello Chloe, I'm Thalia. I believe we're going to be having a chat today," she said in an amiable voice with a hint of an Australian accent.

"Hello," said Chloe, getting up and going towards her.

"So, how long will it take?" Vicky asked.

Once Thalia was sure that she had made a connection with Chloe, she replied,

"About two hours."

"Wow!" Vicky was slightly taken aback. She'd been expecting maybe an hour, but two...

"Sometimes it can be two and a half or three, but don't worry, Chloe, the time will fly by. Shall we go in?" and she smiled such a reassuring smile that Chloe couldn't help but smile back.

"Ok, well... have fun, little one – oh, have you got your glasses?" Vicky couldn't help a moment of maternal fussing as they started moving away from her.

"Here," Chloe said, producing the case from her coat, "See you later, Vicky," she waved as they walked towards the doors.

"I'll text you when we're done," Thalia smiled and then the double-doors closed behind them and Vicky was left alone. God, this was worse than dropping her off for her first day at school! She watched them through the small, reinforced windows of the doors until they finally went into one of the rooms. Vicky stood for a moment wondering what to do, then realised that she was being watched by the receptionist, who probably saw this every day – worried parents handing their children over to total strangers for evaluations that might determine the course of their educations or even their lives.

"Right," said Vicky as brightly as she could, "I'll be back later."

The receptionist smiled in an unconvincing fashion and watched as yet another discombobulated parent left.

Vicky walked out of the door and into the steady rain. She needed coffee and hurried off to the nearest non-chain Italian coffee place she could find. Fortunately, it being Knightsbridge, that didn't take her very long. As she sat soggily in a corner at the back of the rather warm, rather narrow café, she wondered if Thalia's first question might be,

"Why did you call your mother 'Vicky'?"

She thought about the first time Chloe had done it and smiled. The reason was so... logical. As a baby, Chloe had always been a late developer. When other people's kids were crawling like crazy, Chloe had stayed firmly in one spot. Occasionally, she'd butt scooch from one place to another, but that was all. When other kids were toddling like drunken sailors, Chloe was still firmly on her arse. Then one day, she'd heaved herself up onto her feet, sidled along the edge of the sofa and walked six steps to the Garfield book in the middle of sitting room floor. She'd flumped down and started turning the pages. After that, she'd walked whenever it had suited her needs. She was months behind the other kids, but she'd gone from sitting to walking, bypassing crawling altogether. Talking was the same. They had always talked to Chloe and reinforced this communication with basic sign language. Unlike other kids, who seemed to babble incessantly, Chloe had been quiet. It was unsurprising that she was months behind other kids before she first said 'mama' or 'dada'. And she'd almost seemed reluctant to say 'dada' at all. It wasn't long before she'd ditched 'dada' for 'Ray'. Vicky had found Ray's frustration at losing his paternal title amusing until Chloe ditched 'mama' too. And, even though they'd tried to dissuade her, they were 'Ray' and 'Vicky' from then on (however much grandparents tut-tutted or sucked their teeth). When Chloe was a little older, Vicky had asked her directly,

"Why do you call me Vicky?"

Chloe had looked at her with a curious gaze and replied,

"That is your name, isn't it?"

Vicky couldn't argue with her daughter's logic.

Now she sat and stared into space and drank her mocha, wondering what questions and tests the psychologist was trying on her daughter. She herself wasn't sure what she hoped they'd find out. She felt that Chloe might be somewhere on the dyslexic spectrum, but did that matter? Only insofar as making sure her school days weren't miserable. She didn't need Chloe to be academic, or a high achiever. All she wanted was for Chloe to be Chloe and not to have her potential crushed by a system that loved to mangle square pegs by trying to hammer them into round holes. Today was all about that and she needed to keep that in mind. Whatever they discovered was already there. This was just going to make it official and help them chart an easier course through the next ten years.

For Vicky, the next three hours passed in a distracted daze. She thought it might be fun to go into Harrods... it wasn't. The sheer number of people in the store made it like an expensive rush-hour tube train. When she finally fought her way out, the rain had abated, so she decided to go for a wander. Now it was painfully bright outside with the July sun reflecting off everything. Even the road sparkled. Vicky kicked herself for leaving her shades on the hall table and worried about how Chloe would cope with the intense light. Eventually, she found herself in South Kensington and decided to recce the Five Guys restaurant. She knew that if Chloe was tired from the tests, she'd get upset if the promised milkshake wasn't forthcoming. No worries. The place was open 'til late...

***

"... a very gifted girl. You are truly lucky," Thalia Moncrief said, smiling at Vicky.

They were in the small, functional room where she'd spent the last three hours putting Chloe through her paces.

"Yes, we are," Vicky smiled back, then cast a glance at Chloe, who was squirming with embarrassment.

"Now, I will be emailing you my full report at the end of the week and I'd like you to come in a week today to discuss our detailed findings,"

"Yes, I think that was the schedule we agreed," Vicky replied.

"But I can confirm what you probably already know... in spite of the visual stress, Chloe's understanding of what she reads is very advanced – about double her age."

"Wow," Vicky couldn't help smiling. She was proud, goddammit!

"Whereas her ability to write is far behind what we'd expect."

"Yes," Vicky agreed, reigning in her pride and focussing on the job in hand.

"There are various aspects of cognition where I guarantee she is going to score very highly. I think our challenge is taking what she understands and putting it on the page. You need to start thinking about typing... now, I realise this seems like I'm jumping the gun, given that we haven't got the full report yet, but my experience is that typing will be the way forward for her and the sooner you start her learning, the better. You've got a long holiday ahead, so by the beginning of next term, you can hit the ground running."

"What a good idea," Vicky said, "Will you be okay learning to type this summer?"

"If it means I don't have to write," Chloe replied.

"Great," Thalia smiled, handing a sheet of paper to Vicky, "This is a list of good websites for teaching children to type. I'd experiment to see which one suits her learning style best."

"Thanks," said Vicky.

"But overall, she is a wonderful person to spend time with and is very perceptive. Thank you, Chloe."

Chloe smiled back with a mixture of embarrassment and happiness.

"And it was interesting to discover that I am green," Thalia added.

Vicky exhaled with a slight chuckle,

"You told her that?"

Chloe nodded without meeting her mother's gaze. If she'd done something wrong, she didn't want to know. And besides, she was tired.

"I hope you don't mind," Vicky apologised to Thalia.

"Not at all."

"It's just something that she's always done. Different people have different colours around them. I'm green, too. That makes us nurturing, creative and loving, doesn't it?" Vicky looked to Chloe, who twisted slightly in her chair,

"Yes," she said quietly.

"Well, that can't be bad," Thalia smiled.

"My husband is red – passionate, intense, competitive and a leader... which just about sums him up. Although he's also a sceptic."

"Mmmm," Thalia smiled politely and Vicky immediately wished she hadn't said anything. She didn't want her husband or her relationship with him analysed by a stranger.

"Okay, so we'll book you in for the same time next week?" Thalia said, standing up. Vicky mirrored her and encouraged Chloe to stand up too. It was time to go. Vicky and Thalia had a short, functional exchange about next steps and within a couple of minutes, Vicky and Chloe were out of the building and heading towards Five Guys for a well-deserved chocolate shake.

"So, how was it?" Vicky asked as they walked hand in hand past the white stucco townhouses of Walton Place.

Chloe took some time to reply – the bright sun shining off the houses was hurting.

"Ok," she said, shielding her eyes.

"What sort of questions did she ask?"

"I don't remember," Chloe said honestly. The last three hours were already a strange blur to her, like a fast-fading dream.

"Did you have to do some writing?"

"Yes."

"Was it hard?"

"Yes," Chloe said with a sigh. Vicky knew how hard she found writing, so why ask?

"And was there lots of reading?" Vicky had picked up on her daughter's prickly response, but she knew that if she left the questions to later, all the information would be gone.

"Some."

"Anything interesting?"

"Not really."

"And what did you do the rest of the time?"

"Talked."

"What about?"

"I can't remember," Chloe couldn't. All she could remember was Thalia's warmth and friendliness.

"You really can't remember anything?" Vicky was having to work to keep the exasperation out of her voice, but this was frustrating. Forget herding cats, this was like trying to teach a disinterested cat how to talk.

"No. Honest. I remember her and that it was nice, but tiring," and Vicky could tell from Chloe's tone that that was all she was going to get out of her. She sounded exhausted. Not surprising after three hours.

"Want to get a burger, too?" Vicky asked, deliberately bringing the conversation to something Chloe could manage.

"No."

"You're not hungry?"

"No, I don't want a burger. Can we have noodles?"

"Of course!" Vicky smiled, "You can get anything in South Ken. We can even look at some dinosaurs after lunch if you want," the teacher in Vicky couldn't help but try to make the trip an educational one.

"Yes, please," Chloe loved dinosaurs, "But the milkshake first."

"Of course, a milkshake should always come first!"

Chapter Five

"I Don't Believe In Evil."

The crowd of people with nothing better to do than gawk and wait for a disaster to happen seemed to have magically appeared from nowhere. As Belinda Warburton and her team drove their vans back up the lane and away from Titheridge's lock-up, about thirty people were already craning to look at them from the far side of the police cordon. Belinda directed her assistant to park at the side to give easy access for the bomb squad vans to get through, then she got out. As she drew back her hood and slipped under the tape slung across the lane, a twenty-something woman in a pink onesie with fluffy pink slippers, a fag in one hand and a toddler in the other shouted,

"Wos 'appenin? They won't tell us nuffink."

"It's nothing to worry about," Belinda called back.

"Oh yeah? Then aa' come you look like someone off of Resident Evil?" shouted her fat boyfriend, who was wearing nothing but a pair of baggy shorts and flip-flops with socks.

"Haven't you ever seen CSI? This is how we roll," Belinda replied and decided that she'd had more than enough of the general public, ducked back under the tape and got into her van to do The Times crossword in peace. Meanwhile, the crowd passed around her comment and speculated further on what was happening.

Ray and Andy were the last two out of the lock-up and they trudged back up the lane grumbling,

"I 'ate the bomb squad," said Andy, "So fucking superior. Treat us all like children."

Ray nodded in agreement,

"And they take so long!" he said, looking at his watch irritably. Almost two already. That was it for the rest of the day – all they had to look forward to was the tedium of waiting for the show-offs to do their stuff. Of course, this time it was complicated by the fact that it was happening directly under six railway tracks. That would make the bomb squad take it even slower. The train companies were already cancelling services left right and centre to avoid the area. It was a total clusterfuck and he was the officer responsible for making the call.

"Those grenades had better be real, otherwise Denham's gonna have my head," Ray said, imagining the look on his boss's face if it turned out to be a false alarm.

"Nah, they're real all right. I got a good look at 'em. Russian RKG-3 anti-tank grenades."

"How d'you know that?"

"There's that scene in American Sniper, where he has to shoot a kid and a woman who try to throw one at an American tank. These are the same and the box says it in Russian," said Andy.

Ray looked at him and smiled,

"You do know some weird shit. But it still doesn't mean they're real. They could be fakes."

"Who'd make a box full of fake versions of an obscure Russian anti-tank grenade?" Andy asked.

"Fair point," Ray conceded, "But if they're real, where the hell did he get 'em from? It's not like you can phone up Deliveroo. He'd need serious connections and I don't believe Titheridge has them. He's too dull and middle class..."

"He's got a kill room with a bucket of hands," Andy pointed out.

"Yeah, but he'd still need someone to fix this for him.

So, who's he working with?"

Andy shrugged, but then had a flash of insight,

"Maybe he's logged it in his little book?"

"Oh yeah..." Ray's eyes lit up, "Yeah, I like that!" he cried, giving Andy a playful punch on the shoulder.

They'd got up to the cordon and Ray beckoned Emma over to them,

"Yes, guv'?"

"Everything secure up here?" Ray asked.

"Yep," Emma replied, looking up at him eagerly, "The public have turned up, but seem to be no trouble. Now we're just waiting on the bomb squad."

"Good," Ray liked Emma White, she was clear and efficient and had an indefinable something about her,

"Now, here's what we're going to do... I'll brief the bomb squad when they arrive. They'll be in charge of the crime scene from that point, but I want you here with the CSIs ready to go in when they've finished."

"Where will you be?" Emma asked.

"Me and Andy have to pick something up in Peckham. We don't know how long it's going to take, so just in case this is resolved while we're gone, you take charge – got it?" Ray said, looking into her bright, brown eyes.

"Got it. And the press?"

"Say nothing."

"Right, guv'," Emma looked very happy. This was real responsibility and the fact that Ray was trusting her with it made her feel great. She'd move heaven and earth to repay his trust.

"Aha!" Ray cocked an ear – there was the sound of distant sirens,

"Here they come. I'll tell Belinda you're in charge while we're away... but one piece of advice..."

"What?" Emma looked at him quizzically.

"If she asks you to come down and have a look in the fridge, don't."

Half an hour later, Andy was driving across town towards Peckham Rye while Ray lounged in the passenger seat. As ever, the bomb team had acted like they were the only adults on the scene and patronised everybody they could, but now Ray and Andy were away from the crime scene and out in the sunshine of a summer's day. With the warm wind blowing in through the open windows, they were able to process what they'd just experienced.

They hardly spoke for the first ten minutes of the drive and it wasn't until they'd got to Dulwich that Andy broke the silence,

"Well, that was nice."

Ray smiled.

"Always good to face evil and come out on top," Andy said with satisfaction.

"Is that what you think he is – evil?" Ray asked.

"Yeah. What would you call him?"

"Sick."

"Really?" Andy sounded surprised.

"Yeah. I don't believe in evil," said Ray, settling himself into a more comfortable position in the passenger seat. The pronouncement had a finality about it, but Andy wasn't about to let the comment go unchallenged,

"Really, really?" Andy asked as he swung the car into Dulwich Grove and drove up the tree-lined hill towards a crossroads where they got stopped by the lights. Just behind them on their left was a posh girls' school, while just ahead of them on their right was a posh co-ed. This was the land of the Range Rover. There were lots of very well-spoken people in that neighbourhood. Andy gave Ray a sideways glance to see if he was serious or just stirring it to pass the time. Ray was staring steadily ahead and his profile was inscrutable.

"Yeah," Ray said without moving his gaze from the road ahead.

Andy shook his head and laughed.

"All right," he said, "I'll bite – what makes you not believe in evil? We see evil shit every bloody day!"

"No, we see *shit* every day," Ray replied, "Just because we see acts of violence and meet violent people, that doesn't prove the existence of some deeper force driving it all."

"So, you're saying that Mister Brian Titheridge – kill room, bucket of hands, confessed to sixty-eight murders – ain't evil?" Andy asked, pulling away from the lights and continuing on towards East Dulwich.

"Of course he isn't," Ray said, turning towards Andy, "People add 'evil' on afterwards as a simple way of explaining nasty stuff. I'm not saying that his chopping people up and leaving their heads in fridges stuffed with each other's genitals isn't bad. I'm not saying he shouldn't be stopped. I'm just saying that he's a sick man who needs psychiatric treatment. And I don't believe he's been moved to commit violent acts by a nebulous evil power."

"Ooh, 'nebulous', that's a good word. Is that one of them words of the day that you've got to try to slip into a conversation?" Andy smiled.

"No, that would be 'snide', like that remark," Ray replied evenly.

Andy broke off to negotiate the traffic through the centre of East Dulwich. It was always bad through there. Ray stared across at the large, Victorian townhouses that were separated from the main road by fifty yards of park and thought, not for the first time, that it must be a lovely place to live. Especially in summer. You'd be right near all the pubs and restaurants, but with all those cool plane trees and greenery between you and the traffic. Andy drove up past the houses,

"So, what are you saying – everyone who kills should go to the nut house instead of prison?"

"No. Not all murders are the same. There's a world of difference between Titheridge's butchery and a crime of passion or someone who kills during a robbery."

"What if somebody plans out a murder in detail before doing it?" Andy asked.

"That just proves they're devious and meticulous. It's the motive that interests me. If there's no logical reason for killing, then I'd say they're most likely mentally ill. Greed, passion, revenge, envy – they're all things that can lead people into believing that murder is the logical thing to do. But there's nothing logical about hacking up total strangers. Let alone sixty-eight of them. That's not normal. There's a sickness there. And in my opinion, that's all there is," said Ray.

While Andy turned right to go up the hill along the edge of Peckham Rye, Ray looked over at the large park that gave the residents of that poor part of London a beautiful green space to enjoy. Yes, Peckham had its million-pound townhouses, but most of it was poor. Ray loved the way that across a lot of London, richer people had to live in fairly close proximity to poorer neighbours. There were some very exclusive areas in London and some total shitholes, but generally, even the richest boroughs had their share of poverty. And here, rich and poor had been able to enjoy a really great park since the late nineteenth century.

"Anyway," Ray sighed, "It don't matter what I think. It all depends on what twelve members of the public and the judge in the courtroom think. I'll bet my flat Titheridge gets sent to a secure hospital for the rest of his life."

"Diminished responsibility?"

"Yeah. Once they see his scrawls all over the kill room, they'll decide he's as nutty as squirrel shit."

"At least we got 'im, eh cap'n?" Andy beamed as he saw Ray's face cloud momentarily and then break into a smile.

"I'll give you cap'n! I'll have you keel-hauled for insubordination, you cheeky sod."

"That's more like it! We should be happy!" Andy exclaimed, "We've caught an insane fucking serial killer at the scene - tons of evidence, complete confession, bish-bash-bosh! And I, for one, am going to celebrate with six pints of craft lager, followed by the dirtiest kebab I can find. Interested?"

"No!" Ray snorted, "I've got a real life. I'll go home, kiss my wife and daughter, ask them about their day and have a couple of glasses of Primitivo, or possibly Nero d'Avola with a nice plate of pasta."

"Wow! That sounds exciting. I wish I had a real life," Andy said, slapping on the sarcasm.

"Yeah well, it's better than lager and kebabs. What's that old saying..." Ray reached into a dim memory, "A man is as old as his arteries – so in your case, you're forty-two, going on ninety."

"We're here!" Andy said, ignoring the grim truth and pulling up in front of a nineteen-thirties terraced house with a tile-hung frontage and a neat front garden.

They got out of the car and walked up the path to the house, between beds of roses on either side that were well past their best but not yet looking sad. The house was a purpose-built maisonette and the porch ahead of them had two doors. The floor of the porch was of deep red quarry tiles, which ran up the walls on either side for about three feet, before giving way to white painted stucco. Both doors were original, with central stained-glass panels depicting what looked like lilies. The brass plate covering the doorstep of Titheridge's flat was buffed to a high shine.

"That's a good sign," said Ray.

"What that this isn't going to be a rat infested cack hole like his lock-up? I bloody 'ope so!" Andy replied.

"All the same, let's stay sharp. Last thing we need now we've got him, is to cock it up with a procedural misstep," Ray said and, as he turned the key in the lock, they both put their game faces on.

It turned out that Titheridge had the downstairs flat and the door opened into a light and airy entrance hall. They could see through to the kitchen beyond, which was flooded with light from a big window looking out to the back garden. Ray closed the door and they stood and listened for a moment. The house had a pleasantly solid silence about it. It was the silence of thick carpets and well-upholstered furniture. There was no particular smell. Somewhere within – probably on the mantlepiece in the front room - there must have been a carriage clock, because Ray could hear a light but regular ticking. He looked at Andy, who nodded and did what he did best,

"This is the Police! If there is anyone here, please show yourself," he said loudly, but without bellowing.

The silence seeped languidly back in around them.

"Alright, let's do a sweep." Ray said and they went through the door to their right.

Thankfully, the flat was much smaller than the lock-up and, some questionably chintzy furniture aside, was perfectly pleasant. Once they'd looked through the front room (to Ray's satisfaction, there *was* a gold carriage clock on the mantlepiece), they went through to the kitchen/diner.

It was large and well-kept, but both of them looked at the fridge with a certain degree of suspicion.

"I'm opening it on three," said Andy, looking to Ray for confirmation. Ray nodded.

"Three!" Andy blurted and pulled the door open.

Ray looked with relief at the fridge, neatly stacked with ready meals.

"Oh my God – it's worse than I thought," Andy gasped, "He shops at Lidl!"

"I wouldn't relax yet," Ray warned, "The freezer could be full of feet."

Andy opened it up without ceremony.

"No, just more ready meals," he said.

"Okay, come on," said Ray and they took their search to the rest of the rooms.

The small spare bedroom was comfortable, but yielded nothing other than an extension of the chintzy theme from the sitting room. Meanwhile, the bathroom had clearly been fitted in the 1990's and needed updating. That left the master bedroom. When they opened the door, they were greeted by the faint smell of lavender. The room was spotless and the bed neatly made. In fact, everything was very neat. The shirts in the wardrobe were pressed and the three suits in there were still in their plastic dry-cleaning bags. The chest of drawers was filled neatly with pants, socks, T-shirts, casual trousers and pyjamas.

"He must have someone who cleans the place and does all his linen," Ray said, because this neat little world was so totally at odds with the lock-up.

"Yeah, I can't see a man who nails intestines to the wall keeping a place this spick and span," Andy agreed.

"Right, let's see if he was telling the truth about this notebook," said Ray, walking over to the bedside table and opening the top drawer. There were just three things inside – a black A4-sized notebook, a red and gold Waterman fountain pen, and a packet of black ink cartridges. Ray took the notebook and opened it. He flicked through the neat pages of perfectly legible writing until he got to the last entry. He skimmed the page and said,

"Alfred Standish,"

Andy gave him a confused look.

"The bloke on the operating table who'd had his eyes pulled out is – or was – Alfred Standish of fifty-three Mercer Road, Burgess Park."

"Yeah, I know Mercer Road – some nice Victorian houses down there. Pricey. How d'you know it's him?"

"Let's just say that Mister Titheridge has been very detailed about how he captured him and what he did with him afterwards," then he began to read aloud,

"*Undressed him and strapped him securely to operating table. Brought him round with smelling salts before cutting first hole for his purification. Standish a screamer. Kept looking at me angrily afterwards. Couldn't get hard for the purification ceremony because of his angry look. Ordered him not to look at me, but to no avail...*"

"Oooh! 'No avail'? Nice to have a killer who uses such flowery language," said Andy.

Ray continued,

"*Decided to pull out his eyes by hand. Difficult and messy. Left one V hard. Had to get up on table with knees either side of his head. When it finally gave, momentum took me off table. Standish unconscious again. Stuffed sockets with rags to staunch bleeding. Took a Viagra and waited for Standish to regain consciousness. In agony when he came round. Screamed throughout first purification, which I completed to my satisfaction. Big load...*"

"Fuck me! That's disgusting!" Andy cried. Maybe he'd pass on that dirty kebab after all – stick to peanuts, crisps and booze.

"Shall I keep reading?"

"Please don't! In fact, why don't I check out the garden while you have a nice read of that? Who knows, maybe that bloke's eyes are in the shed?"

"Yeah, go on," said Ray, "But you're going to miss some great stuff – there's four more purifications to go."

"Happy to miss 'em, thanks all the same!" Andy replied over his shoulder as he went out the back door.

The air was fresh in the moderate breeze that had blown the rainclouds away and Andy took in a few good lungfuls. The kitchen door opened from the side of the house onto a sandstone-coloured patio, which ran around the back of the house. He wandered out and saw an expensive-looking, metal table and chair set. The garden sloped up from the house, and a two-foot red-brick wall acted as a buttress against the edge of the well-mown lawn. In the middle of the wall, four steps with a shallow pitch led up to the grass. Stepping stones of the same colour as the patio led in a meandering line up to the far end of the garden about sixty feet away. Up there, in the shade of an ornamental fruit tree, stood a moderately new shed. The sunshine totally bathed the south-facing lawn and patio. Andy luxuriated in its warmth as he closed his eyes and tried not to think of Titheridge, his lock-up or the late Mr. Standish. He breathed slowly again. He loved police work, loved the thrill of danger on a day like today, really loved the chance to legitimately punch someone's lights out, but finding the sort of nightmare they'd found earlier... that he could live without. He exhaled calmly, opened his eyes, shielded them from the glare and took the yellow brick road up to the shed. He very much hoped that the eyes would be elsewhere.

In the kitchen, Ray sat at the four-seater wooden table and immersed himself in the mind of Brian Titheridge. As he'd expected, it was a mind that was very sick indeed.

"*March 25th. Saw one today,*" Ray read, "*Strolling along the South Bank without a care in the world. Followed him to a flat in Butlers Wharf. Hung around rest of day waiting and planning. Man clearly lives there. Went to LJ and got van. Returned to BW around 10pm and posed as delivery driver. Tasered target and got him into van. Took to LJ for purification. Very talkative. Lots of good leads. Dismembered and moved remains to SH for acid bath. Fed tongue to next door's cat. That's the end for Henry Talbot of Butlers Wharf!*"

Ray blew out between his lips and used his tongue to create a staccato 'twhaugh twhaugh' rhythm. SH? Could be shorthand for a place name. He assumed LJ was Loughborough Junction. SH... Streatham Hill? Sydenham Hill? Selhurst? None was a million miles from Loughborough Junction. He could have a garage, house or lock-up in any of them. Ray flipped through the pages. Some were very detailed about the acts he performed. He clearly enjoyed inflicting pain on his victims and, unfortunately for them, he was very imaginative.

As Ray read on, he wondered if he would be different afterwards. He couldn't unsee or unthink the images conjured by the neatly written words on the pages before him. Did each fresh realisation that a man had inflicted these dreadful acts on other human beings somehow diminish Ray's own humanity? Was Ray slowly being dragged into the darkness by these and a hundred other crimes he'd investigated? Was his light of humanity being dimmed? He hoped not, but he acknowledged that over time any faith he'd once had in 'humanity' would be radically changed. Maybe that faith had always been wrong? He'd been brought up to believe that deep down there was good in everyone. What if that had been hopelessly naïve? Were children, if left to themselves, naturally hierarchical, cruel and fascistic as William Golding had proposed in Lord of the Flies? Ray certainly remembered having to take abuse from children at school which would have seen any adult sacked from their workplace. So, if children were capable of unfairness, violence and vindictiveness, why did anyone think that adults should be any better? For a moment, Ray stared unseeing at the notebook. He was a policeman, but he was no angel. The illegal push dagger clipped to his belt proved that. He had desires and appetites that weren't necessarily positive – the sort of desires and appetites that high-achievers seem to be prone to. The desire to possess, to dominate, to constantly prove himself the best, and an appetite for excitement, for pleasure and for more – more of everything. But he was trying to balance those desires and appetites so that he could be a good husband, father and detective. Although he didn't believe in 'good' and 'evil', he understood how over time people could be warped into something they hadn't previously been by the harshness of their surroundings or the vicious behaviour of people around them. What concerned him was that perhaps reading these pages wasn't so much snuffing out some of his inner light, but releasing some of his inner darkness.

The sound of the back door opening made Ray start,

"You all right?" asked Andy.

"Yeah, fine. It's just... this ain't light reading," Ray replied, wafting the notebook, "Anything in the shed?"

"No, thank Christ!" Andy was VERY pleased to have found nothing more sinister than a pair of shears in the shed.

"Well, I know one thing," said Ray, brightening, "I know where Titheridge got his grenades from."

"Where?" Andy asked, pulling out a chair and sitting down next to Ray to look at the notebook.

"Russian fixer called Alexei Ukhov. According to this, our Mister Titheridge caught up with Ukhov at a lock-up over in Silvertown. Tasered him, and was just about to drag him out to his van when he noticed some boxes. Thought their contents might come in handy, so he took 'em. It says here that he's also got a box of Kalashnikovs and five thousand rounds of ammunition for them."

Andy whistled in respect,

"That could've kept him in bodies and blood for a while..."

"Yeah."

"And presumably mister Ukhov met a painful end."

"Oh yeah!" Ray said, firmly, "Yeah, Titheridge really went to town on him. Did his usual thing of making lots of holes in Ukhov that he didn't have before they met. Then, after he'd had his way with him in those new holes, he did that to him..." and Ray pointed out the relevant part of the page, then watched the look of disgust on Andy's face as he read what Titheridge had done next.

"Holy fucking shit!" Andy said when he'd finished reading, "Oh fuck! Fuck!" and he put his hands to his cheeks and stared at the notebook,

"He really didn't like him at all, did he?"

"No," Ray replied.

"Christ on a fucking bicycle!" Andy was genuinely shaken by what he'd read,

"You don't really think he did that do you?" he said, looking to Ray in the hope that it couldn't be true.

"Why would he lie in his own journal?"

"You mean he could've done that to us and all we had to defend ourselves was a fucking tennis racquet?"

Ray nodded in reply.

"No! If that's the way things are going, I might have to get a different job!" said Andy, pushing the book away and getting up from the table. He was not a happy bunny!

"Anyway," said Ray, closing the notebook and getting up himself, "We got what we wanted. Best go back to the lock-up and see what's happening. I'll put in a call to get some uniforms here to secure the crime scene. Come on," and Ray led the way back to the car.

Half an hour later, they were in conference with the commander of the bomb squad team,

"They're real all right," said Bob Hughes, a short, thick-necked man with a soft Birmingham accent,

"About fifty of them and each one's designed to blow through the armour of a main battle tank. If they went off together..."

"Bye-bye Loughborough Junction," said Andy.

"Exactly. But here's the good news," Hughes said, pulling his eye protector up and resting it on the front of his helmet,

"Unless some idiot pulls the pin on one and chucks it back into the box, they're perfectly safe."

Ray gave him a look that questioned that statement.

"Obviously safe within the bounds of unexploded ordnance. Same goes for the crate of ammunition."

"Next steps?" asked Ray.

"My team are going to have to sweep the entire place," Hughes said.

Andy groaned inwardly – the lock-up was huge and full of junk. A full sweep of it could take all bloody night. His longed-for pints of lager and dirty kebab receded further into the distance. Ray picked up on the slump of Andy's shoulders and had an idea.

"So basically, that's pretty much it until tomorrow," it was a statement, not a question.

"Realistically, yes," Hughes nodded.

"So, I can let the crime scene investigators go and we can go and start interrogating our suspect, leaving you in charge of the scene?"

"Yes, although when we're done..." Hughes began, but Ray finished the sentence for him,

"We'll leave some uniforms here and they'll secure the crime scene when you're finished. Then Belinda and her lot can come in tomorrow and collect evidence to their hearts' content. Sound like a plan?"

"Perfect," said Hughes with a smile, "Right..." he continued, pulling his eye protectors down, "No rest for the wicked," and he gave them a wave as he walked stolidly back towards the lock-up.

"Neat footwork!" Andy said, his face a picture of relief.

"Yeah, yeah, you're not out of the woods and into the pub yet," said Ray, "We've still got an interrogation and a suspect to process, so we'd better get our skates on."

Within ten minutes, Ray had briefed all the relevant parties.

"We'll be here bright and early in the morning," Belinda beamed as she leant out of the passenger window of her van.

"Thanks, Belinda. Depending on how our interrogation goes, you might not see me tomorrow,"

Belinda made an inarticulate noise of disappointment,

"But don't worry," Ray added, "You will be in the capable hands of DC White, here," he said, patting Emma on the shoulder.

"Marvellous!" said Belinda, giving Emma a friendly smile, "See you tomorrow," and then to her driver, "Onward!" and the van pulled away with the other just behind it.

The crowd of gawkers had thinned but, as a uniformed officer put the tape back in place across the top of the lane, a shockingly thin Indian man prowled slowly along the boundary. He was wearing an overlarge, double-breasted grey pinstripe suit and a pair of garish orange trainers. He must have had a serious deformity or injury, because his right leg stayed ramrod straight with each step. This created a cartoonishly pronounced limp and made the process of walking painfully slow as he contorted his upper body to compensate for the deficiency of his right leg. As he walked up and down next to the tape, he kept repeating one phrase over and over again in a thick Indian accent,

"Nutter! Fucking nutter!" he said, then grinned, flashing a mouthful of white, but crooked teeth.

"Nutter! Fucking nutter!" grin.

"Nutter! Fucking nutter!" grin.

His beady eyes darted about as he spoke and sometimes he seemed to say his phrase directly to whoever had caught his eye. Then he caught Ray's eye,

"Nutter! Fucking nutter!" he said, grinning.

Ray didn't like the way the phrase or the toothy grin made him feel.

"Who the hell is that?" Ray asked Emma quietly as the man continued his laboured perambulation along the line of the police tape.

"Just some local eccentric, guv'," Emma replied, but the way her eyes narrowed and took on a venomous look told Ray that the bloke had got under her skin, too. Emma suddenly realised her look had been noticed and she deliberately brightened,

"Sorry, that's all he's been saying for the last hour and he's getting on my wick."

"There's always one at a crime scene like this. Fuck knows where they seep up from, but they always appear. He's harmless. Just try to tune it out," said Ray, although as he watched the man turn at the far end of the cordon and then start limping back towards them repeating his mantra, he wondered whether that would be possible over an extended period of time. He really was strangely unsettling. Everything about the cadaverous man was wrong. The elements of the almost sing-song delivery of his single unpleasant phrase; his grinning teeth; his intelligent, darting eyes; and his excruciating way of walking – all combined to create a caricature that was so over the top, that Ray wondered if he was putting it on.

"Well anyway, ignore him," Ray said, turning his attention back to Emma, who was looking up at him, her eyes eagerly awaiting his orders,

"You get the uniforms organised and we'll see you back at headquarters in a while."

"Yes, guv'," Emma said and turned to get on with her tasks.

Ray watched her for longer than was strictly necessary.

"Nutter! Fucking nutter!"

The phrase, delivered from just behind him, broke the moment and shook Ray out of his reverie,

"Right Andy, let's go!" he called and left the weirdo hobbling up and down his new domain.

Chapter Six

Disappearing Act

"What d'you mean Titheridge hasn't arrived?" Ray couldn't believe what the desk Sergeant was telling him.

"I'm sorry, sir, but he hasn't come in," Sergeant Reese replied evenly. He could see Ray wasn't happy, but what could he do? He couldn't produce a prisoner out of his hat.

"What the fuck?" Ray was bewildered.

"Must still be at the hospital," Andy ventured.

"I s'pose... sorry about losing it, Sergeant," Ray said, turning his attention momentarily to Reese, who nodded back. Every officer snapped at their colleagues from time to time, so Reese thought there was no point in feeling annoyed about it.

"I'll give 'em a call," Ray said, walking away towards the stairs and taking out his phone.

By the time Ray had got to his office on the fourth floor, he was incandescent. He threw the door open, shouting,

"How the fuck do they have no record of him at the sodding hospital?"

Andy, in his wake, had no answers.

"This is apocalyptically bad!" Ray cried, "Fuck fuck fuck!" he was pacing up and down frenetically now,

"I just don't see how!" he said, his throat constricted with rage, fear and confusion.

Andy, who had become a passenger on the Ray Ennis anger express, shrugged and tried to look sympathetic.

"Fuck!" Ray slumped into the chair behind his desk, rested his elbows on it and put his face into his hands,

"We arrest the most prolific killer since Harold fucking Shipman and now there's no trace of any of either him or his police guard? Shit! I don't even remember the name of the Constable, do you?"

"No," said Andy, who was ashen faced. This looked like a monumental, career-ending cock up. And he'd be going down, too.

"I don't even know where to start with this!" Ray's exasperation snapped him into an upright position. As he stared into oblivion, his brain was spinning like a flywheel,

"Okay, here's what we're going to do... I'll report this to the boss and if he doesn't sack me on the spot, we're going to have to pull all the CCTV footage we can and track that bloody ambulance. No way it's disappeared without trace. And then..."

Ray's phone rang. He pulled it out and glanced at it with a grimace,

"It's the Chief,"

"Bollocks!" said Andy.

The ringtone went through its first cycle and started the second,

"You going to answer that?" Andy asked.

Ray blew out slowly and looked at the phone like it was a gun he was about to put to his head.

"Fuck it!" he said and answered the call,

"Hello, Chief, there's something I need to..." Ray listened. So did Andy,

"I don't know how to..." another pause, "But I think you need to hear what I have to..." pause, "All right, I'll be there in two," and Ray ended the call.

"What?" Andy searched Ray's face for answers, but all he found was confusion,

"Chief wants me upstairs right now. Not you, just me. Won't say what it is, won't let me get a word in."

"Shit," Andy said – none of that sounded good, "Want me to come with you anyway for moral support?"

"Nah..." Ray stood on legs that were wobbly from the sudden burst of adrenaline, "I'm a big boy. I can take care of myself," and he walked with deliberate firmness towards the door. He didn't want Andy to see he was shitting it.

"Listen, whatever happens," Andy said, "I'll put myself forward for half the blame. I know you're the senior officer an' all, but we are a team. Collective responsibility," and he looked at Ray with genuine affection and concern.

"No worries. This'll be fine," Ray winked and then he was gone.

Chief Inspector Charles Denham was a heavy-set man of about sixty, with thinning, greying hair, but a thick, black moustache. He was sitting solidly behind his desk in a sixth-floor corner office with a lovely view across south London when Ray knocked at the door,

"Enter!" Denham called, although his private school accent made it sound like 'Entah'.

The door opened and he could see that Ray was on edge, but desperately trying to control it.

"Sit down, Ennis," Denham said, indicating the chair across the desk from him.

"Thank you, sir," said Ray in a voice he hoped sounded firm and bright.

"Any idea why I want to see you?"

"Something to do with the Titheridge case?" Ray ventured.

"Yes, you could say that," said Denham, looking carefully at Ray.

Fuck!

If Denham wasn't coming straight to the point, then this was bad. *Really* bad. Ray had seen Denham in action many times and he wasn't a man to mince his words.

"It's all my fault, sir. I should never have let Titheridge out of my sight. But I have a plan..."

"I'll stop you there," Denham said firmly.

Bollocks!

Ray prepared himself for the end of his career. He almost laughed out loud in hysteria. This should have been the high point of his professional life so far and yet, here it was crashing to the ground.

"You're probably wondering where Titheridge is..." the look on Ray's face told Denham that was the case, "Well, I know," Denham smiled.

"You know?" Ray was in shock.

"Yes. Right now, Brian Titheridge is in a helicopter en route to a secure facility in... actually, I can't tell you precisely where, because you don't have the necessary clearance, but it's a long way out of London. The point is, he's safely in custody."

"Not lost?" Ray could hardly believe it.

"Not lost," Denham confirmed.

"Oh, thank fuck!" Ray gasped, then quickly added, "Sorry, sir."

Denham smiled,

"I thought we'd lost him..." Ray began, but Denham held up a hand,

"It's all right. No explanations necessary. But there is one thing - I'm afraid that although he's in custody, he's not in *our* custody."

Ray looked questioningly at Denham,

"The Metropolitan Police... in fact the Police Service itself is no longer involved in this case. Don't ask who's running it now, because I don't know, but everything from crime scene investigation, to interrogating Titheridge, to prosecuting the case has been taken over by another department of state."

There was a moment of silence as this news sank in.

"We're completely cut out?" Ray asked.

"Yes."

"But it's our case. We did everything. Without our work there wouldn't be a case and he'd still be running around killing random people!" Ray protested hotly. Now he knew he wasn't getting fired, he'd regained his composure.

"I know. Frankly, I think it's a bloody disgrace, but there's nothing we can do – other than hand over any and all files and evidence related to the case," Denham gave Ray a meaningful look.

Ray sighed, produced an evidence bag containing Titheridge's notebook from his jacket pocket and handed it to Denham.

"Thanks," said Denham, putting it into his desk, "I'll see this gets to the right people."

"What, so that's it? Me and my team just walk away and forget it ever happened?"

"Yes."

"Will they take our statements?"

"Only yours will be necessary. It has been requested that you set up a meeting with this person," Denham picked up a card from his desk and handed it to Ray. The cream-coloured card felt expensive and, aside from the writing, it was unadorned. It read,

Elizabeth Russell
Regulator
HM Treasury
1 Horse Guards Road
London
SW1A 2HQ

***

"The Treasury?" Andy exclaimed, ten minutes later, "What've they got to do with anything?"

"Beats me," Ray shrugged as he slumped into the chair behind his desk.

"And there isn't even a phone number on it. Let alone an email address," Andy continued, turning the card over in his fingers.

"I know," Ray laughed, "It's like, hello! This is the twenty-first century calling! Put down the carrier pigeon and step into the present day."

"Elizabeth Russell – Regulator for the Treasury. What does that even mean?"

Ray shook his head. After a long and difficult day, this was all a bit too perplexing.

"Sounds like she's got thick glasses and wears a lot of tweed," Andy mused.

Ray smiled.

"On the bright side, your meeting with Denham could've gone a lot worse," said Andy.

"Oh, so much worse!" Ray agreed, taking the card back and putting it into his wallet. Then he remembered something and fixed Andy with a serious look,

"Yeah, all this stuff about the Treasury and Elizabeth Russell, that's just between you and me, right?"

"Alright," Andy loved a bit of cloak and dagger nonsense.

"No, seriously," said Ray, "Denham was very clear that only you and I can know about the connection to the Treasury."

"It sounds weirder every time you say it out loud," Andy replied, "But don't worry, your secret is safe with me."

"Thanks."

"When are you going to see her?" Andy asked.

"Might try to get it over and done with tomorrow, but there's something I want to do first..."

Andy recognised a wicked gleam in Ray's eye,

"I want to go back to Loughborough Junction for one last look."

"If you're looking for those missing eyes, you can count me out," Andy said firmly.

"No, nothing like that. I want to see what's so different about this case that means we can't handle it. Something might occur if we're at the scene."

"Won't it be crawling with Elizabeth Russell's investigation team?" Andy asked.

"We'll cross that bridge when we get to it, but are you in?" Ray said, fixing Andy with a fervent stare.

"Yeah, I s'pose. Hang on, though, how early d'you want to be there?"

"Seven-ish?"

"Right, in that case I'm off," said Andy, pulling on his jacket,

"If I'm going to get six pints in and a halfway decent night's sleep, I need to start!"

"Drinking on your own... tragic!"

"Who says I'll be on me own?" Andy said enigmatically.

"Go on, you sad bugger!" Ray laughed as Andy went for the door.

***

The one advantage of the sudden ending of the Titheridge case was that Ray was able to get home by seven fifteen. As he walked home from the bus stop on Streatham High Road, he wasn't even that angry about what had happened. Anger was pointless because it was out of his hands. And whoever had the Titheridge case, the fact that he was off the streets remained unchanged. It was a glorious, sun-soaked evening and Ray was going to spend it with his wife and daughter without any worries about work intruding. The evening was too beautiful for work! And yet, as he walked, thoughts swirled...

How can we square Titheridge's playroom with his meticulous notebook? Is he like Colonel Kurtz from Apocalypse Now? Is his mind clear, but his soul mad?

Ray concentrated on his thoughts, rather than enjoying the bustling sights of Streatham High Road. Pub and bar customers had spilled out onto the pavements and the restaurants were full of families finishing their dinners, preparing to make way for those not encumbered with children to dine later in the evening. Commuters, disgorged from the latest train to arrive at Streatham Hill, were heading to their homes. Some hurried, keen to swap their work clothes for something cooler. Others sauntered, happily taking it all in, allowing the sights and sounds and smells of the busy street to wash over them. Maybe they used that walk home to slough off their daytime masks so that they could arrive home more like the people they truly were than the people they were expected to be in the big, bad world beyond their front doors?

Ray walked through it all,

And where does Elizabeth Russell and the Treasury fit in? The Treasury... that's strange. Why are the bean-counters interested in a sadistic serial killer?

He was hardly noticing what was happening around him – until he reached the end of his road. Just as he was about to turn down it, he saw someone who stuck out from the crowd. About fifty yards further along the High Road, stood a man who was apparently not enjoying the evening. He was a fairly big man, maybe in his mid-sixties, with lank, grey-white hair falling straight down the sides of his head to his shoulders. The thinning hair on top of his head made his choice of growing out the rest of his hair seem odd. He was wearing an overtight honey-coloured trench coat with the straining buttons done up to his neck and he was standing with his arms straight down at his sides with his fists balled. His big, moon face was set with staring blue eyes and his lips drawn back from his closed teeth. He was breathing heavily, sucking the air in and out through his gritted teeth as if he was... seething. That was it! He was standing in the middle of the pavement on a lovely summer's evening, balling his fists and seething at the world.

"Poor sod," Ray said aloud as he turned into his road. It was a fairly pleasant road that ran down the side of the hill with smart two-storey Victorian terraced houses on either side and the occasional silver birch planted in the pavement for variety.

Ray arrived at his house, which looked much of a muchness with the rest of the houses on the street. Red brick, with white painted heavy stonework around the large sash windows. The front door was set into a small porch, the front of which was ornately designed with white pillars apparently supporting a white decorative arch over the top. The path between the road and the door was tiled in a busy Victorian design in blue, russet and white.

The Treasury... a bucket of severed hands... Titheridge ripped out the man's eyes... The Treasury... it's like so many Treasury predictions and reports, something isn't adding up...

The low front wall was topped with two feet of cast iron railing and the space between it and the house was used for the wheelie bins of the two flats within. Ray and Vicky had the ground floor flat. He opened the front gate and went to the door. Had he paused on the street and looked up the hill, he would have seen the man in the trench coat standing, still as stone, and fixing him with his furious glare, his watery blue eyes brimming with rage and his ragged fingernails cutting into the palms of his hands as he balled his fists with all his strength. Oblivious, Ray opened the front door with its Victorian stained glass and stepped into the communal front hall.

The door to his apartment was on the right and the stairs up to the first-floor flat were straight ahead, with a rather ugly fireproof security door at their top. The area where the downstairs corridor of the original house would have run along the side of the stairs had been bricked off and it was part of Ray's flat. There was a small communal table for letters and parcels by the front door and Ray idly flipped through the post. Nothing for him or Vicky. She'd probably taken it in earlier. He opened the door to their flat and went in,

"Hello!" he called.

"Garden!" Vicky called back from the depths of the apartment.

Ray hung his jacket on the coat stand by the door and sauntered along the corridor past the doors to the master bedroom, Chloe's bedroom and the bathroom. The corridor opened into a large kitchen/diner/living area with a light grey natural stone tiled floor.

Where is Titheridge right now?

Beyond the large L-shaped sofa at the far end of the room, floor-to-ceiling folding doors fitted across the full width of the room and opened onto the garden. The doors were drawn back. Beyond, in the postage stamp of a back garden, Vicky was lounging in a comfy chair next to a round table. She had a large glass of Prosecco in her hand and the bottle was in a cooler on the table next to her.

I hope Titheridge is somewhere unpleasant!

"What are we celebrating?" Ray asked, bending down to kiss Vicky. She wanted to linger on the kiss, but Ray straightened up,

"So, what's the occasion?"

Vicky dredged up a carefree smile, held up her glass and said,

"The end of the rain."

Ray laughed,

"Any excuse!" and he poured himself a glass and sat in the chair next to her. The Prosecco was wonderfully chilled and was a perfect palate cleanser from the day,

"I don't want to talk about my day," he lied. In fact, that was all he wanted to talk about, but devices to cut holes in people for sex wasn't really family fare.

Internally, Vicky breathed a sigh of relief. That must have been the reason Ray had ended their kiss. Maybe there'd been something unpleasant at work.

"So, what happened in your world?" Ray asked, looking at Vicky, and she talked him through what the psychologist had said. She was in a black T-shirt and pink running shorts (which she'd bought when she'd decided to go on a health kick but never used for actual running). She had curled her legs up onto the chair so that, from where he was sitting, he could see an enticing expanse of buttock at the top of her slightly heavy thighs. He liked that. In fact, he loved her curves and, contrary to the notion that men are incapable of multi-tasking, he was quite able to calmly ogle his sexy wife while paying attention to what she was saying. Almost.

He was a senior partner in the firm and threw it all aside to kill people... he clearly had a mental breakdown, but why? Is the 'why?' the key?

"Well, we kind of thought that didn't we?" Ray said when Vicky had finished her assessment of the meeting with Thalia Moncrief.

"Yeah, but it's good to have a diagnosis so we can get her all the help we can," said Vicky with a sharpness in her tone.

"No, no, no..." Ray soothed, "I'm not saying it's not justified and necessary..."

Although he had said exactly those things when Vicky had first suggested getting Chloe checked out.

"I'm with you on this," he said.

Now, after months of wrangling.

"What I mean is that as parents we knew deep down this was the likely outcome."

Well, *she* had noticed it and had brought it to his attention a dozen times before he'd started taking it seriously.

"Anyway," she said brightly, "The psychologist loved her and says she's gifted."

"Wow!" Ray's face broke into a wide grin.

It was at this point that Chloe appeared from the bathroom to join them.

"Hello, my gifted girl!" Ray cried and opened his arms.

Chloe ran forward and jumped onto him for a big cuddle. She was already in her PJs and she felt soft and warm against him. He wondered whether there was anything in the world better than this. No. Not even close. He gave her a big kiss and quizzed her about the tests. Having been as silent as a clam for most of the day, Chloe opened up in her father's arms and babbled about what she'd done and what she thought about it all. Listening to her, Vicky smiled, but couldn't help feeling that it would've been nice for Chloe to have opened up to her like that. Or at all. Ah well – dads and daughters! Vicky thought that if she wanted a connection like that, she'd need to have a son.

"What's for dinner?" Ray asked.

"Ordered Chinese. Should be here in half an hour," Vicky said and before Ray could jump in, "Yes, kung pao chicken and sweet and sour deep fried pork balls with egg fried rice for Mr Greedy."

Ray smiled at her,

"Sounds perfect!" it wasn't quite the rich pasta and bottle of Primitivo he'd envisioned, but it would do nicely.

"Want a hand or two of Uno before dinner?" Vicky suggested.

"Oooh, yeah!" Chloe cried, bouncing up and down on Ray.

"Squashing me's not going to help!" Ray groaned, "Go and get the cards!"

"Okay!" she said, using Ray as a springboard to leap away before running into the house.

The cards and games were kept in a box built into the area under the bay window in Ray and Vicky's bedroom. The room looked out onto the street and during the day a set of 'one way' blinds were always drawn down. These let light into the room and allowed anyone inside to see out, but didn't let people outside see in. As Chloe romped into the room, the blinds were down and she went straight for the box under the window with the sort of complete focus children never seem to have for their homework. Snakes and Ladders, Monopoly, Hungry Hippos – aha! Finally, her fingers found the packet of Uno cards and she pulled them out and shut the box, but as she straightened up, her breath caught in her throat and she stood, transfixed. Standing outside the front gate was a man in a trench coat. His face was fixed and seething as he stared at the front door like he was trying to see through it. The man was strange and frightening. Chloe thought he looked like he might try to break the door down. What did he want? Why was he there? He seemed to be bursting out of his coat in anger, but worst of all was what surrounded him. He stood in the golden evening and yet it was as if he was stepping out of a man-shaped black hole. The entire area for about two feet around him was an impenetrable black. Chloe had never seen anything like it in her life. Her instincts screamed at her to run, but her legs were stuck in concrete. She stared at the wide face. It was blotchy pink and white, but a mass of broken veins showed red on the cheeks and nose. She saw how the fat on his neck bulged out over the top of the buttoned collar of his dirty white shirt, saw the sweat beading on his forehead and jowls, saw the little, crooked teeth through which he was dragging breath. And then slowly, as slowly as a nightmare, the big, round face turned towards her and he was looking her in the eyes.

How could he see her through the blind? It wasn't possible.

"Run, Chloe, run!" voices in her head screamed, but she could do nothing. He was holding her in his basilisk gaze, suffocating her with the hate and anger he was emitting. She had stopped breathing the moment she'd seen him and more than a minute had passed since. And now, as his eyes bored into her, he raised his right arm and pointed with his index finger. It aimed right at her heart and she could feel a pressure against her ribcage, hard and focussed like a finger end. Then his lower jaw opened and his face contorted in a silent shriek. Chloe heard nothing. It was as if he was silencing the world around him with this empty-mouthed cry. Worst of all, the darkness around him was growing and seeping towards her. First it engulfed the gate, then the wall and now it was blotting out the light in the room. There was something in the darkness. Something terrifying. It had seen her and it wanted her with such a fierce longing that it bordered on rage. It was feeling for her through the darkness and its desire was fixed on one thing – it wanted to taste her, to suck her into the darkness and savour her youthful sweetness forever.

Something in Chloe kicked in and she released a shrill scream, which broke the man's hold on her and she pelted out of the room, back to the garden and into Ray's arms in floods of hysterical tears.

"What? What happened?" Ray struggled to cling onto her. She seemed to want to simultaneously hide in his arms and escape past him.

"Have you hurt yourself?" Vicky had leapt from her chair and was trying to look into Chloe's face.

Chloe was making incoherent noises as Vicky went through the usual parental concerns from wasp attacks to choking, but this was something beyond all that. Chloe was desperately gulping in air and the rational part of her that was trying to tell them what had happened was being stopped by the shock of what she'd seen. Instead of words coming out, great sobs were convulsing her body until she was finally able to choke out,

"Man!" and point in the direction of the front of the house. Ray was up instantly and putting Chloe into her mother's arms, then running through the house, palming his second push dagger as he went. The flat was empty, so he opened the door to the front hall – nothing there, and the front door was firmly shut. Ray pulled it open, coiled for whatever might be there. No one. He stepped outside and checked the front areas of his and next door's house, but they were clear. In another second, he was through the front gate and scanning first down and then up the street. There seemed to be no one down the street, but as he looked up towards the High Road, was that the tail of a honey-coloured trench coat disappearing around the corner? Ray blinked. There was nothing there. Just to be sure, he jogged up to the top of the road and looked in the direction he thought he saw the coat go. Nothing of interest – just the same scene of people going home after work or socialising outside the bars and cafes. No strange man seething on the corner or hurrying away. Ray had a good look up and down the High Road, then went back to the flat. A final look around and then in he went, locking the doors behind him.

"Well?" asked Vicky, who was standing in the garden holding Chloe in her arms.

"Whoever it was, he was long gone by the time I got out there," Ray said before taking his glass of Prosecco, draining it and pouring another.

"You didn't see anyone suspicious in the street?"

"It's Streatham – half the people out there look suspicious," Ray replied, "But forget out there, what about you, Chloe? Are you alright?"

"Yes," her voice was small and when she turned towards him, her face was puffy from tears and being buried in her mother's shoulder for so long.

"Why don't you tell us what happened?" Ray asked.

Chloe gathered herself. She didn't want to think about the man she'd seen, but she knew she needed to tell her parents about him. Slowly, she told them what she had seen and described the man. As she spoke, she exactly described the strange bloke Ray had seen near the top of the road. Ray kept his expression neutral. He nodded along, making it clear he was full of sympathy and support, but he didn't admit that he had seen the very same man earlier. It was weird and he didn't want to unduly worry his wife and daughter. The fact that Chloe's description of the man was perfect... that was puzzling! Who was he? Had he simply followed Ray from the

High Road? Or had he seen Chloe and Vicky earlier and then come sniffing around? *No, it can't be that.*

Ray dismissed the thought and stuck with the idea that the man had followed him. He had, after all, made eye contact with the bloke. Ray knew that sometimes that's all a person in turmoil might need to start following someone.

But none of that explains the darkness seeping towards her...

Again, Ray dismissed it. She'd been talking about auras since she'd been a toddler and Ray set no store by it. Maybe it was part of her visual stress? Whatever, Ray wasn't about to start looking for a man with a black aura around him, but he would keep an eye open for that strange man in the trench coat.

Vicky, meanwhile, couldn't make sense of it. Maybe the day had taken more of a toll on Chloe than she'd let on? Maybe the three-hour psychological assessment had simply been too much? Yes, Chloe had visual stress and yes, she talked about auras around people, but this sounded like a full-on psychotic episode. Especially since Ray had found no one outside. Perhaps Chloe had misconstrued what she'd seen? Could the light from the setting sun have got into her eyes and confused her, and then her imagination just ran with it? Vicky was in a quandary.

"Well, whoever he was, he's gone now and you're safe here with us," Vicky said, giving her daughter a cuddle,

"But just to be on the safe side, do you want to sleep in with us tonight?"

"Yes, please," Chloe smiled faintly.

"Good job we got that Euro King," Vicky said to Ray, who looked up to the heavens and said,

"Praise to the Gods of Ikea for delivering us an enormous bed."

All three of them smiled and the mood was lifting. Would it really be right for Ray to ruin all that by admitting that he had seen the man that Chloe had described? No, it wouldn't. It would overcomplicate everything. Ray would keep silent - even if that meant giving Vicky a false sense of security and effectively leaving Chloe hung out to dry and sounding like a crazy kid. In a couple of days, Ray would talk to her alone, tell her that he had seen the man, but not go into details. He could apparently take Chloe into his confidence, say that he'd been protecting Vicky, because he'd thought she'd overreact. Yes, that might open a channel of communication between him and Chloe, one where she would feel grown-up and extra special. And Vicky? What she didn't know couldn't harm her. Or make her go off the deep end. She had that habit... yes, the less she knew, the better. Yes, that was the way he'd play it...

The sound of the doorbell made all three of them jump,

"It's the bloody Chinese!" Vicky exclaimed, with a hand on her rapidly beating heart.

"I'll go," said Ray and on the way to the door, he grabbed his wallet.

"Come on, you can help me set the table," said Vicky, heaving Chloe off her and going into the kitchen. She thought some hot food and the physical mundanity of setting the table, eating and clearing up were exactly what they needed to calm them and put the strangeness of the last half hour into some sort of perspective. Chloe trotted in after her and took the cutlery from her mother, then set the table in the garden. It was warm, safe and filled with the sound of birdsong, and Chloe quickly found that the image of The Man was fading into the background. Vicky brought everything out on a tray and they piled into the dinner until they were all a bit overstuffed.

Why did Titheridge leave his job to start a murder spree?

After eating, Ray's mind went back to it like a tongue to a bad tooth. As the evening drew in around them and the air cooled, Ray's mind was turning the Titheridge case over and over. He was only half listening to Chloe and Vicky prattling about TikTok reels...

What's the Treasury angle? And since when did they take over police cases? Is that even legal? Wouldn't they need a court order or the permission of the Attorney General? And why? Why are they interested?

Finally, Vicky shivered and suggested they go inside. Ray put his thoughts aside and together they cleared the remnants of the food away and bundled onto the sofa to watch The Croods, which was one of Chloe's all-time favourite films. She was one of those children who really lived the films she watched, and she couldn't help but bounce up and down on the sofa at all the exciting bits, squealing when the jeopardy got too much for her.

Once she'd calmed down after the film, gone through her bedtime routine and kissed Ray goodnight, Chloe snuggled down into the middle of her parents' big bed.

"Are you *sure* we can't get a pet?" Chloe asked. It was the usual question after watching The Croods and seeing all the cave people ending up with their own animals.

"No, because we'd have to leave them alone in the flat and that wouldn't be fair," said Vicky gently.

"But a cat wouldn't mind. I think I'm a cat person – just like daddy Crood."

"Yeah, but they had grandma there to look after things when everyone was out hunting," Vicky said, thinking she'd shut that door firmly.

There was a pause as Chloe thought for a moment,

"Then why doesn't granny Ennis move in with us and then we get a cat?" she asked.

No bloody way! Vicky liked her mother-in-law, but... hell no!

"Because she's got grandpa Ennis to look after..."

"He could come too. They could sleep in my room and I could sleep in here with you and Ray and Mister Fluffles."

"Mister Fluffles?"

"That's what I'm going to call the cat."

Wow! Somehow Vicky had let this get horribly out of hand!

"I think what we need is some sleep and then we can think about it tomorrow, yeah?"

"Okay," Chloe said, putting her thumb into her mouth and lying on her side. Then, just as Vicky was leaving, she added,

"We can invite them to stay in the morning."

Vicky laughed and said,

"Nighty-night. Love you."

"Love you, too."

Chapter Seven

In The Dark

It was still dark when Chloe swam out of sleep and became aware of her dad gently snoring next to her. She was curled around him and she felt warm and safe. Behind her, she could feel Vicky breathing evenly. Chloe wanted to drift back to sleep, but there was a problem. She had an insistent urge to wee and it wasn't going away. What to do? She didn't want to wake her parents up, but she knew she couldn't get through the night without going to the loo. She carefully disentangled herself from her dad and lay flat on her back between her parents, listening to them as they slept and the noises of the night. Somewhere in the distance, cars were passing and... was that a bird singing? Didn't all the birdies go to bed at night? It definitely sounded like a bird. She would have to ask Vicky about it in the morning. There was a slight creak from a settling beam in the house, but it didn't worry Chloe, because it seemed like a natural sort of noise for the middle of the night. Even the house was snoozing. However, all these thoughts didn't take away the gathering urge inside her. She realised that she would have to pick her way out of the bed, so she wouldn't wake up Ray and Vicky, then summon up her courage to go down the hall to the bathroom. She didn't like that idea. She found the corridor a little scary during the day, let alone in the dark in the middle of the night. Maybe she could wake Vicky up and ask her to go with her?

Chloe lay for minutes as she swayed between being a big girl and doing it all herself, and waking her mum up so she wouldn't get scared. She listened hard - nothing but her parents in the depths of sleep breathing evenly. No, she wouldn't wake them up. She'd be a big girl and go on her own. Anyway, her eyes were accustomed to the dark now, so she'd be able to do it. All it would take was a little bit of bravery. Eep Crood, the brilliant cave girl, would do it, and so would Chloe! Hardly breathing, she slipped out of the top of the thin summer duvet and worked her way down the bed. Her dad stirred and she stopped, waiting and hoping that he wouldn't wake up. After a few seconds, he started snoring in a slightly different pitch and Chloe continued her quest. It seemed to take an age to get to the end of the bed, but when she made it, she swung her legs out and felt for the floor with her feet. Then she gently put her weight on them and hoped there wasn't a creaky floorboard. All good. Now she was up, half the battle was won. She simply had to creep across the room and down the hall.

The windows had heavy curtains to keep out the streetlights, so the room was very dark, but Chloe's young eyes were coping. As she moved across the room, she could see shapes in various shades of dark grey. There was the chair with discarded clothes on it; there was the shape of the fireplace on the wall; there was the half-closed door... then she stopped. What was *that* shape? Her heart skipped and then started pounding. There was a large, black shape in the space between the back of the door and the wall. It was darker than anything else in the room. What was it? Then the hairs stood out all over her and she was frozen. The black shadow was the exact shape of the man from earlier. The Man was *in the room*! And she knew he was there for her. Now she distinctly heard the quiet hiss of air being drawn and then exhaled through gritted teeth. Chloe wanted to scream, wanted to run, wanted to do anything but stand and watch in wide-eyed terror as the black shape slowly peeled itself from the dark wall behind it and moved towards her. The patch of total blackness seeped noiselessly across the darkened room and, although it was the shape of The Man, it seemed to be only the black void of his shadow. Where was his physical body? She could hear his hissing breath, feel his bulky presence and sense his hatred and anger but there was something else. She knew that he wanted to do things to her. Things that she didn't want or understand. Things that would hurt her forever. She was terrified by how much he wanted her, but, as the shape of him oozed towards her, however hard she looked into the blackness, she couldn't see *him*. Like before, she was stuck fast. Nothing would work and now the darkness was looming above her.

She looked up into void that was the shape of The Man and it felt like he was covering her in a heavy blanket of black velvet. He was smothering her and she was struggling to breath. Her parents were only three feet away, but they'd might as well have been on the moon. Then she was caught up in his overpowering scent. It was musty with a sour note of unwashed crevices after days of heat. Chloe stopped breathing altogether with the smell stuck in her nose as the total darkness closed around her. All sight and sound disappeared into that impenetrable void. Something told her that if she didn't act, she would die. She didn't want to die! Could she move? Everything felt so heavy. So very heavy. She was suffocating. With her last ounce of will, she kicked out hard at the velvet blanket of darkness. She kicked again. And again. Then she was falling backwards into nothingness, but she had one last kick in her...

"OW!" Ray cried out as he got a sharp kick to the back of his head from the heel of a child. Suddenly, he was wide awake and feeling for the bedside lamp. It clicked on to reveal the flailing feet of his darling daughter, who had somehow turned herself around in the bed so that her head was stuck under the duvet at the wrong end. Ray grabbed a flying foot and pulled, so that Chloe slid up towards him enough that he could uncover her.

"Hey, wake up!" he urged as loudly as he dared without waking Vicky. He gave Chloe a shake and she woke up like someone coming back from the dead. Her eyes flashed open and she dragged in a great lungful of air, then realised where she was and immediately scrambled into his arms and started crying.

"Shoosh... shoosh," he soothed, holding her close, "It's alright... were you having a bad dream?"

Chloe nodded and said,

"The Man was here in the room and he tried to take me into the dark forever."

"What man?"

"The Man!" Chloe said loudly, and suddenly Ray understood.

"Wassup?" Vicky mumbled blearily.

"Bad dream," said Ray.

"No, it wasn't a dream," Chloe insisted, "He was here."

"Where?" Ray asked, pointing to the empty room.

"There!" and Chloe pointed to the area behind the door.

"But there's nothing there now, is there?" Ray asked.

"No," Chloe admitted.

"Good. Then we can go back to sleep."

"Can I go to the loo first, please? And can we leave the hall light on?"

"Yeah, no worries," said Ray.

"Shall I do the honours?" asked Vicky, "I need to go anyway."

"Want Ray," Chloe said firmly, with her thumb planted in her mouth.

"Okay, looks like you're the winner. I'll follow you," Vicky said to Ray, who rolled his eyes at her while Chloe's head was over his shoulder.

Even a Euro King bed isn't quite big enough for two adults and a seven-year-old to sleep together in total comfort. Especially if said seven-year-old has had a fright and wants to cling to someone. Ray spent what was left of the night with Chloe wrapped around him one way or another and, as the darkness petered out, he found himself pushed right to the edge of the bed with one butt cheek over the side. Finally, he gave up on sleep and silently eased himself out of the bed without waking Chloe. He looked at his watch in the shaft of light from the hall – five to six. It had been a broken seven hours, but he could cope. He took his phone, turned off the six-a.m. alarm, quietly gathered his clothes and left his two favourite girls sleeping. Ray dressed in the kitchen while waiting for the coffee to brew. It was already a glorious day and, as he walked out into the garden with his coffee, Ray couldn't help but be energised by the warmth, the scents in the air and the singing of the birds in the block of gardens. Now his brain had woken up, it was off and trying to solve three puzzles at once. First was the weirdness of the previous night. Even in the bright sunshine of a glorious morning, there was something about Chloe's nightmare and

The Man he'd seen on the High Road which lingered unpleasantly. Second was the Titheridge case – he wanted to get another look in that railway arch. And third was the owner of the business card he was turning over in his hand. Yes, he certainly wanted a well-chosen word or three with this Elizabeth Russell.

By seven, he and Andy – looking somewhat the worse for wear – were getting out of their car at the top of the lane that ran down to Titheridge's lock-up.

"No cordon," said Ray. He had expected at least a line of police tape to be strung across the end of the lane. Andy shrugged and they started walking.

"Ever get deja-vu?" Andy asked, looking at Ray with bleary eyes.

"At least it's not been raining this time," Ray smiled.

Or had it? As they approached the far end of the lane, the puddles in the potholes were still full of water. Funny! It had been a warm afternoon and a clear night. And the water was greyish.

"Notice anything?" Ray said.

"Aggregates," Andy replied simply.

He was right. There was a sprinkling of sand and gravel that hadn't been there before.

"And rubble," there was brick and concrete detritus scattered across the lane.

"Shit!" Ray said, staring in amazement.

The lock-up before Titheridge's had a large van parked in front of it, which obscured their view of the front of Titheridge's place until they were almost there. Now they could see the front. Instead of a bricked-up arch with a steel door set into it, the entire frontage had been demolished and removed.

"What the fuck?" Ray's exclamation was strangled by surprise.

The two men stopped and stared, hardly believing what they were seeing.

Yesterday, the lock-up had been filled with old junk. What they were looking at now was a great, empty cavern. Andy rubbed his eyes. No, he still couldn't make sense of it.

"Where the fuck's it all gone?" his voice rasped after a night of heavy snoring.

Ray started forward, peering down into the gloom.

"Everything's gone! How the hell? There must've been tons of crap in here. How could they do it?"

Ray couldn't imagine how many men and trucks it would have taken to clear that space overnight. A lot. It must've been a big operation, but who could organise that so fast? Not the police, that was for sure. Then his mind made a connection and his heart sank.

"Oh, you know what?" he said, taking out a torch,

"What?" Andy followed suit, but his brain was still very much at home, cradling a cup of sweet tea in bed.

"Sand, aggregates, water – what do they make?" and Ray moved quickly through the empty railway arch down towards Titheridge's 'playroom'. Andy was lagging behind. His stomach wasn't quite ready for fast movements. Ahead, he saw Ray stop and look down at the floor.

"Fucking concrete!" Ray pointed at the floor as Andy arrived.

Where there should have been a trap door leading to a room full of evidence to convict a prolific and vicious killer, there was a rough square of wet concrete in the floor.

"Still soft as shit," said Ray, "If you stood on that, it would be goodbye Andy."

Andy looked at it, but couldn't quite compute it.

"They've filled our crime scene with concrete," said Ray, running a hand distractedly over his bald head.

"Why would they do that?" Andy couldn't make head nor tail of it.

"I've got lots of reasons, but none of them make any sense," said Ray, pacing away from the concrete square,

"Why they've done it doesn't concern me as much as who 'they' are," he said, turning back to face Andy,

"Who would take an active crime scene and fill it with concrete? Apart from anything else, who has the manpower to do all this overnight? Who?"

Andy tried to think, but only one answer came,

"The army?"

"Bingo," said Ray, "Only the Royal Engineers could do something like this with zero notice. But who are *they* working for?" Ray suspected that the answer was on the expensive business card in his pocket.

"Right..." he said, trying to think what to do next,

"So, someone's taken Titheridge somewhere. I was assured that the crime scene would be investigated and now it's full of concrete. I was also assured that Titheridge would be prosecuted. A bit hard if you bury all your evidence..."

All the evidence? No, this wasn't all the evidence. Belinda and her team had been taking photos and collecting unpleasant goo in pots, perhaps they might still have...

"It's all gone," Belinda Warburton said in her bluff, no-nonsense way.

It was half past eight and she had just arrived at her office to find Ray and Andy waiting for her.

"All of it?" Ray asked, hoping that she'd kept copies of something.

"All of it," she said, hanging her jacket on a hook on the back of her office door. It was a drab, cramped room and, even though Andy was sitting down, he seemed to take up a lot of the available space.

"Some very polite techs were waiting for us when we got back yesterday," Belinda continued,

"They had official clearance to take everything, so I had to let them do it. And they spent a couple of hours making sure there was nothing left on our computers, either... is he all right?"

Belinda indicated Andy, who was still looking very pale, even for him.

"Lager and kebabs," said Ray. Belinda nodded,

"Here, take a couple of these, they'll perk you up," she said, fishing in the top drawer of her desk and throwing a plain, white box of pills to Andy. He pressed a couple into the palm of his hand,

"What are they?"

"Trade secret, designed with medical students in mind. Keep the packet, you look like you need them more than me," she smiled as he knocked them back with some water from a bottle he took from his jacket.

"Anyway, what's the problem?" Belinda asked.

"Nothing much, just that the railway arch has been totally cleared and your kill room is full to the brim with setting concrete," said Ray, watching for Belinda's reaction. She looked at him in total confusion.

"What?"

Yes, Ray was sure she was genuinely surprised,

"Not only that," he continued, "But we've just come from our boss and he says it's not a problem. He says everything's been taken in hand and that we're not to worry."

"Which, in itself, is rather worrying," Belinda nodded.

"Just a bit," said Ray, "Who can we trust?"

"Each other," said Belinda firmly, "And the good thing is, you've got an ace up your sleeve."

"What?"

"Me," Belinda said proudly, "You see, I have what some people call a 'photographic' memory. I can recall with perfect clarity everything from that crime scene. So, if you need to check any detail or need any information from that scene, you've still got it."

Ray smiled. He'd always liked Belinda, but now he realised what a true star she was.

"Thanks, that means a lot," he said, "Although we've been told to drop everything to do with the case. We shouldn't have even been at the lock-up today. So, I don't see how we're going to make use of your superpower," and then he looked her in the eyes,

"But thanks. That really means a lot to me."

Belinda smiled back at him. It was good to know they had an ally.

By the time they got back to Ray's office, Andy was already perking up.

"There must be some sort of amphetamine in these," he said, shaking the box of pills, "I feel great!"

"How can you feel great after what's happened?" cried Emma, rushing in to see them,

"Sorry to barge in, sir, but I just heard about the Titheridge case."

"Yeah, it's crazy," said Ray, "But you didn't notice anything odd after we left?"

"No. Everything was... normal. Once the bomb squad packed up, I organised the detail to secure the crime scene and that was it. Everything by the numbers. But when I came in this morning expecting to go back to the scene..." and she left the sentence unfinished.

"So that means they must have done it between about seven last night and seven this morning," said Ray with a degree of awe in his voice.

"Done what?" Emma asked and Ray told her about the empty railway arch, the newly filled kill room beneath it and the fact that the leadership team seemed all right with the whole thing. Ray watched as her pretty face went through the same emotions as Belinda's. This was a surprise to her, too. That was good. Ray was beginning to work out exactly who he could or couldn't trust, and Emma was on the right side.

Once they'd discussed the ins and outs of the situation, Emma had an idea,

"You know, I've got a close friend who works... well, let's just say he works in 'intelligence',"

Ray and Andy looked at each other – that would be a euphemism for MI5 or MI6,

"And I could ask him – off the record – if he's heard anything about this. Something this big would definitely make waves," and she looked to Ray with her direct brown eyes, hoping he'd say yes.

"Good idea," said Ray. He loved Emma's eagerness, "You do that and Andy's going to call an old army mate of his to see what he knows."

Emma looked supremely happy about being able to help. She smiled and said,

"What about you, guv'? What's your plan?"

"I've got a contact," he said enigmatically, "And I think I'll go and meet them now."

Chapter Eight

The Regulator

Within the hour, Ray was walking up the steps to the entrance of The Treasury, facing St James's Park. The grand, imperial solidity of the building was designed to make the visitor feel small, and the bright sunshine on the white stone hurt Ray's eyes. He was glad to get inside and marched over to a comfortingly airy reception area.

"Can I help you?" smiled one of the receptionists from within the oval of white desk surrounding her and her colleague.

"Yeah, I, er... I'm here to see this person," and he handed the youngish red-headed woman the card he'd been given. She scanned it and gave it back to him,

"Do you have an appointment?"

"No, but I'm Detective Inspector Ray Ennis, Metropolitan Police and she has requested to see me," he replied, showing his ID. As someone who saw very senior members of the Government, Parliament and the security forces on a daily basis, the receptionist wasn't particularly impressed, but she was professional enough not to let it show, and smiled at Ray saying,

"Let me see..." before looking at her computer screen and tapping away at her keyboard, "Yes, she is here today. If you'd like to take a seat, I'll get someone to come down for you."

"Thanks," said Ray and he walked across the highly polished stone floor to wait on one of the uncomfortable chairs by the wall.

The receptionist made a call and spoke in hushed tones, casting a couple of glances across at Ray during the conversation. She put the phone down, caught Ray's eye and held up two fingers, while mouthing 'Two minutes'. Ray nodded and smiled. The receptionist went back to doing whatever it is that receptionists do when there's no one to receive, and Ray stared into space. What did any of this have to do with the Treasury? It was baffling. Yes, Titheridge had been a partner in a big accountancy firm, but surely that wasn't the link? The minutes passed and Ray was no closer to working anything out, when a very smartly dressed man in his early thirties strode across the airy reception area towards him. He looked very fit and his light grey suit was perfectly cut to accentuate his physique. He was olive-skinned with dark hair in an 'on-trend' style and was good looking in a classically Mediterranean way,

"Detective Ennis?" he asked in a middle-class London accent.

"Yeah, that's me," Ray replied, rising.

The man held out his hand,

"Oliver Fernsby, I'm Ms Russell's executive assistant,"

Ray shook the offered hand. It was dry and strong.

"Right, let's get you a security pass," and they went back to the main desk, where the woman Ray had spoken to did the honours.

"If you'll follow me," Oliver said and led the way across the reception area towards a door on the far side. As they went, Ray noticed that both the receptionists were watching Oliver Fernsby quite closely.

Oliver held the door open for Ray and said,

"Apologies, but we don't have a lift to our part of the building. It's a bit of a faff, but I suppose it all adds up in the daily step count."

"Fine by me," said Ray and he followed Oliver down two flights of stairs to a long corridor with a high, arched ceiling. Everything above the deep, blue carpet was painted in a rich cream from the walls to the doors and the wood panels around them, to the unused picture rail. There was a sense of solidity, tradition and caution about the place. This was a serious place of serious business. They walked to the very end of the corridor, which must have been a good fifty yards, and Oliver opened the cream-coloured door, allowing Ray through first.

Ray was expecting an ante room to an office, but instead, the door opened into a dimly lit, round, cool and echoey chamber, in the centre of which was a cast iron spiral staircase. This, Ray did not expect.

"Sorry," Oliver looked apologetic, "I realise it's a bit odd to go down before we go up."

Ray shrugged in a 'what can you do?' way.

Oliver smiled.

Ray looked up at the stairs spiralling up towards a circle of light from the roof. There was something odd about it. Then it struck him,

"Hang on, these stairs don't access any floors on the way up."

"No," said Oliver, "Only ours. We're the only people in the building who use them."

"Lucky you!" Ray said.

"Follow me," Oliver smiled, then started the noisy climb up the metal stairs. As he followed, Ray couldn't help thinking that the staircase was absolutely in keeping with the card he'd been given and the lack of telephone number or email address. Of course there wasn't a lift, and of course the staircase looked two centuries old, and of course they only went to one office. Fortunately, the building had been constructed at a time when people felt that six floors were more than enough, so it only took a couple of minutes of clanking up the metal stairs before they finally arrived at the top.

Now they were right under a dome of frosted glass, which bathed the top of the stairwell in diffused light. Their footsteps on the iron walkway that led from the top of the stairs to a heavy oak door ahead of them reverberated down the six floors like it was a huge well. Ray looked over the edge, immediately wished he hadn't, and turned his attention to the door ahead of them. It was carved with an array of what Ray presumed were heraldic symbols, and the words 'Office of The Regulator' were painted on it in gold leaf. Oliver took out a security dongle and waved it at a pad next to the door. There was a deep click and he ushered Ray into a comfortable office that wouldn't have looked out of place in the 1910s. To the right of the door there was a large mahogany desk inset with red leather across the top. Behind it in the corner was an ornately carved standard lamp with an elegant, fluted shade in gold with red dragon designs. On the desk were the usuals – computer, mouse, keyboard, In tray, Out tray and a landline phone. However, it was an ancient candlestick style phone with separate ear and mouthpieces. The walls were lined with bookshelves and any parts that weren't, were panelled in dark wood. There were no windows in the room and the only natural light came from a skylight in the ceiling above the desk which, like the one above the stairs, was of frosted glass. The diffused light gave Ray the feeling of being somehow under the sea. To the left of the door, four leather club chairs were positioned around a highly polished round wooden table. On the far wall, there was a well-stocked drinks cabinet, a small fridge, a water cooler and a small sink set into a discreet black marble worktop. Directly across the office from the entrance, there was another door. That would be the office of Elizabeth Russell.

Ray realised he had been somewhat awed by the grandeur of the building and the strangeness of the way they had accessed the office. He needed to pull himself together and remember why he was there. He was angry and he wanted answers, but before Ray could say anything, the other door opened and a tall woman of about thirty, wearing a black shirt and scarlet trouser suit walked through,

"Detective Inspector Ennis, a pleasure to finally meet you," she said, striding towards him with her hand outstretched,

"I'm Elizabeth Russell," and she shook Ray's hand firmly. She had bulky silver rings on every finger, which made her handshake heavy. Her left hand was also sporting a big silver ring on each finger. As Ray looked at her, he was mesmerised by her features and seemed to hear his voice replying to her greeting as if someone else was replying for him. She had the whitest skin of anyone he'd ever seen. It seemed almost translucent, as if she had never been in the sun. She had angular features, with high cheekbones and a narrow, straight nose. Her lips were full and naturally very red, while the lines around the corners of her mouth were suggestive of an easy smile. Strangely, given the fact that she couldn't be much more than thirty, she had white hair in a short, side swept pixie cut, but Ray was lost in her large, violet eyes. They were so remarkable and so calming that for a moment he forgot where he was and what he was doing there. His anger and his need for answers had been diffused like the sunshine through the skylight. Then she blinked and suddenly sound and awareness rushed back in.

"Sorry about the stairs," she said in a Yorkshire accent that had been very much softened by years of living in London, "But on the plus side, very few people come and bother us up here," and then she became conspiratorial,

"Between thee and me, that's very rare in the Treasury. There are more meddlers in this building than in the rest of Britain put together."

Ray smiled in spite of himself.

"Okey-dokey, come on in," she said, indicating for Ray to follow her into her office, then she stopped,

"Deary-me! Where are my manners? Drink? Tea, coffee, cordial, something stronger? The sun's bound to be over the yardarm somewhere!" and her face broke into a big smile revealing perfect, white teeth.

"Water's fine, thanks," said Ray.

"Okay, Oliver, this is your time to shine – one water for Detective Ennis and one Lapsang for me. And a plate of bickies. The posh ones. Right, follow me!" she cried expansively, marching into her office with Ray trailing in her wake.

The room was a good deal larger than her assistant's with a very high ceiling, so that the big oak desk on the far side seemed rather lost in the space. The desktop was inset with green leather and, apart from a brown folder and a fountain pen, it was empty. No phone, no computer, nothing. The left side of the room was dominated by a great, round window, which must have been twelve feet in diameter and looked out over St James's Park. The base of the window was level with the floor and the view towards Buckingham Palace was stunning. Two easy chairs and a low table had been placed in front of the window to enjoy it. Meanwhile, the three other walls were covered in maps and charts, some of which were modern, others of which looked as if they had come from different times and cultures. Aside from a selection of maps of the world, there were star charts, maps of the seabed, astrological charts and even maps of the moon and Mars. Against the wall opposite the window, ran a long, wooden bench covered in all sorts of antique equipment, amongst which were three antique globes. One looked like a cartographical globe from long ago, one was brass with an array of designs etched into it, and Ray was pretty sure the third was a spherical astrolabe. In the corner between the window and the desk, there was a large, brown leather-covered day bed scattered with cushions and what looked like a couple of bearskins. In the opposite corner there was a large, round table covered in green baize with eight high-backed chairs around it. Ray had never seen an office with a poker table in it before and the incongruity snapped him out of his reverie. What the hell was this place? Who the hell was Elizabeth Russell? And why the hell was she involved in the Titheridge case?

"Take a seat," she said, indicating the chairs by the window and sitting in the one that faced towards the door. Once Ray had sat down, she said,

"I'd just like to say, I'm really sorry about this Titheridge thing. I realise that you've done all the legwork on it, so having it taken away from you must be annoying..."

Ray wanted to say that yes, it was bloody annoying and showed no professional courtesy, but he was spellbound by her eyes again. They seemed to take away the need for anger. And their colour was like nothing he'd ever seen. Then she blinked again and, in that split second, he noticed that her eyelids were tattooed. The right had what he recognised as the symbol for the meditative sound 'Om', and the left was tattooed with a pair of crossed spears.

"Detective Ennis?"

Ray snapped out his reverie and regained his composure,

"Yeah, I can't say I'm happy about it, but that's not what worries me. We had a crime scene that was going to convict that monster and now..."

"It's full to the brim with concrete," she finished.

"Yeah. What's that about?"

"I'm afraid the Titheridge case is... how can I put it? Not ordinary," Elizabeth Russell's voice was beguiling.

"No, it's funny how sixty-eight murders lift a case above the mundane," Ray said and his voice was like a rapier, which, rather than parrying, she immediately wrapped in silk,

"I mean, it goes beyond the bounds of regular crimes and into a realm where regular policing methods are somewhat redundant... ah! Here's the tea! Come on, Oliver, I'm gasping!"

Now Ray had to wait for the rigamarole of tea being served before he could respond to her enigmatic statement. By the time Oliver had left the room and Elizabeth Russell had proffered the impressive selection of biscuits, Ray was champing at the bit.

"What do you mean by 'regular policing methods are somewhat redundant'?" Ray asked, sitting forward in his chair.

"You saw Titheridge's playroom," Elizabeth Russell replied calmly, "You saw what he did. Well, our Mister Titheridge has been targeting some very dangerous people. They're not the sort to play by what one might call the usual rules of engagement."

Ray thought about the Russian fixer Alexei Ukhov. She was right. If Ukhov's associates were ex-Russian military, they wouldn't care who they had to go through to get their revenge and their methods were savage.

"To be honest," she said, having sipped her Lapsang Souchong into which she'd carefully stirred three sugar cubes, "It's something of a miracle Titheridge is still alive," and she couldn't help but sound impressed.

"Well, he's invisible, so that makes it easier for him,"

"True..." Russell mused.

"So, you've spoken to him?" Ray said, looking at Elizabeth Russell with narrowed eyes.

"Of course," she wouldn't be very good at her job if she hadn't.

Ray decided to be direct,

"Are you in charge of this whole operation?"

"Yes, but you must understand that I've taken control of the case for the safety of you and your family," she said firmly.

"You really think they'd target my family?"

"Oh yes," she was sure of it, "For example, has anything odd happened to you in the last day or so?"

"No," Ray lied, but the spectre of The Man in his trench coat loomed up out of his memory and stood there, seething at him.

"Good," Elizabeth Russell seemed relieved, "Because if Titheridge is right – and I'm taking you into my confidence here, this doesn't go beyond this room," and her violet eyes seemed to pierce his soul as he nodded in agreement, "If Titheridge is right, then there is a potentially extensive secret network of ruthless and very dangerous people working in this city. Their leader has no regard for human life. In fact, he enjoys killing and has been doing so very regularly for some considerable time and using his network to cover his tracks."

"No, wait a minute, wait a minute – are you saying you believe any of what Titheridge says?" Ray exclaimed.

"Yes," she replied and took a sip of her tea.

"But he's a madman. Have you read his logbook?"

She nodded briefly.

"He's a sadistic killer," Ray continued, his voice rising, "One of his victims was a primary school teacher and before putting her out of her misery, he snapped off all her front teeth with a pair of rusty pliers and left her strapped to that operating table in a pool of her own piss for two days. He beat her to death with a brass crucifix, for fuck's sake!"

Ray's outburst broke over Elizabeth Russell like a wave, but once he'd finished, she was as unmoved as a great rock,

"Yes, we are investigating Linda Hammond."

"You're investigating her murder?"

"No, we're investigating her. Her background, who she knew, what she did..."

"But she's the victim!"

"Not according to Titheridge," Elizabeth Russell looked at Ray imperturbably.

"So, you're accepting the word of the serial killer that his victims all deserved it?"

"What you need to understand," Elizabeth Russell said, carefully putting down her cup of tea, "Is that Titheridge has told me certain information that I already know to be true beyond any shadow of a doubt. I am therefore moving forward with my investigation on the basis that Titheridge could be right about everything."

"I can't believe it!" Ray exclaimed, "I can't believe you're seriously taking his side."

"This isn't about sides, this is about public safety," Elizabeth Russell shot back, "You should be happy..."

"Oh, really? About what? Having all the evidence to convict a murderer buried in concrete, or finding out that he's being looked after and listened to by the Treasury? And what has the fucking Treasury got to do with any of this?"

"You should be happy," she replied with consummate grace, "That he is off the streets and that we are working to ensure that a much more sinister group of people is rounded up and put out of action. As to the role the Treasury plays in all of this..." she looked into space for a moment, considering her next move,

"It is what it is," she sighed, "The Department of The Regulator of The Treasury has been neutralising threats to the state for over three hundred years. The reason you haven't heard of us is because, as the oldest branch of Britain's Secret Services, we are – by definition – secret. Usually, we plough our lonely furrow but sometimes, as in this case, our work cuts across that of other security branches. This is the first time we've crossed paths with the Met in twenty-five years. It certainly took your Commissioner by surprise. I got the impression that he had to phone the Home Secretary before he believed me. So, that's why we are involved in your case."

Ray didn't look very happy with the explanation. Elizabeth Russell felt it was time to build bridges,

"The reason I hoped that you would come to see me is because I have a lot of respect for you and wanted to explain the situation to you personally," she said with a warm smile.

Ray seemed a little mollified, but a question occurred,

"How can you have a lot of respect for me when you don't even know me?"

"I know of you," she said, getting up and going over to the desk to pick up the folder on it, which she brought back,

"Yes, this is your file. You are having a stellar career and part of my job is to keep an eye open for talent – hence the file."

"So, you're not spying on me?" Ray said in a way that made it very clear he thought she was.

Elizabeth Russell laughed at the thought and the serious look on Ray's face,

"Oh, good Lord, no! I don't have time for anything like that! The likelihood of you becoming the sort of threat that we have to deal with in this department is vanishingly small. No, it's simply that you have a skill set which could be very useful to us if you ever wanted a change – now, don't worry..."

Ray had started a defensive response,

"I'm not trying to... what's that ridiculous footballing phrase? 'Tap you up'. No. I was thinking maybe a few years down the line..."

Ray didn't know what to think. He'd come to give her hell about ruining his case and now she was practically inviting him to join the Secret Service.

"I'd have to think about it," said Ray, "What's the pension like?"

"Very generous," she smiled – especially the disability and widows and orphans pensions,

"Although I have to admit I'm also rather interested in your DS."

"Andy?" Ray cried, incredulous.

"Of course! He's fifty percent of your team."

"You do realize he's failed in his last three attempts to get promoted."

"Yes, but we like people with grit."

"He's certainly got that," Ray smiled, "And some of it isn't even between his ears."

Elizabeth Russell laughed, then said,

"But seriously, you're a very effective team. I think you could thrive here at some point in the future."

Ray seriously doubted that.

A silence settled on them in which they looked at each other. She was enjoying her view. Ray was an impressive man. Clearly clever, a good leader, tough and not unpleasant on the eye. Meanwhile, Ray looked at Elizabeth Russell in her perfectly cut, black open collared shirt and scarlet suit, with her white hair, tattooed eyelids and fistfuls of silver rings, and decided she was unlike anyone he'd ever met. Her intelligence, her humour, the relaxed sense of power that seemed to pulse around her...

"May I ask a personal question?" Ray asked.

"Shoot."

"Why do you dye your hair white? Is it to lend you more gravitas?"

This caught her off-guard. Of all the questions he could have asked, she hadn't expected that.

"Er... I don't. This is its natural colour."

"If you don't mind my saying, you seem a bit young for white hair."

"I don't mind at all. It turned white suddenly."

"Why?"

"I got a bit of a shock."

"Must've been some shock!" said Ray.

"Oh, it was..." she replied and, just as her mind began going back to the moment, she reigned it in,

"May I ask you a question?" she returned,

"Yeah."

"What did Titheridge say to you about his actions? Did he give any details?"

Ray wondered for a moment whether to keep his cards close to his chest, but with the case out of his hands, what did he have to gain? He'd be honest with her, but wouldn't mention the fact that the conversation with Titheridge had been recorded on his phone.

"Yes, in fact he wouldn't shut up once we'd caught him."

Elizabeth Russell laughed. It was low and strangely infectious,

"He has been somewhat loquacious since we purloined him from you," she said, "But he seems to have lost some important details. I think being caught was a shock to his system."

Ray was glad – that fucker deserved a shock or two, preferably from an electric chair,

"Like I say," he continued, "Titheridge babbled on. Most of it was nonsense..."

"What sort of nonsense?" Elizabeth Russell sat forward in her chair and her gaze was hungry.

"Stuff about being the only person able to stop *him*," Ray could see the hope in those violet eyes, "But he didn't say who this mysterious person was."

"Bugger!" she cursed in frustration.

"Then there's the invisibility thing – did he tell you about spending thousands of pounds on it?" Ray asked.

"No, he was just proud of the fact that *they* couldn't tell that he could see them."

"So, he didn't mention the Druid?"

Elizabeth Russell used infinite control to give no sign that this was the jackpot,

"No," she said and Ray was blissfully unaware that he was in the process of handing over the Crown Jewels.

"He said he spent a long time tracking down a Druid in Europe, then paid him thousands to create an amulet and thousands more to have it surgically implanted."

"Did he say what it was, or where?" Elizabeth Russell asked, making it clear that she thought it sounded like nonsense,

"No."

"We'll x-ray him and see whether he's talking rubbish," she sounded like it would be a waste of time, but internally she was tipping her hat to Brian Titheridge. That's the way to do it! Don't take the time and effort to create an amulet and then risk losing it. No, Mister Titheridge really understood the danger he was in and how to stay safe. Well done, that man!

"Was there anything else?" Elizabeth Russell said with an eagerness that suggested that she was looking for something else.

"Just that he'd killed sixty-eight of them and that there were many more walking the streets, and that we were inconveniencing him."

That sounded about right.

"Pity," she said with a crestfallen look, but inside she was very satisfied with what Ray had told her. Having said that, it wasn't all good news. This confirmed that she had an incredibly dangerous foe to deal with. She was deeply concerned for Ray's safety and she gave him a hard look,

"And you're quite sure nothing strange has happened to you since you arrested Titheridge?"

This question again! He'd have to play it carefully.

"Define strange."

"You know... strange. Out of the ordinary. Have you felt like someone is following you, or had an odd sense of dread, or has anyone close to you had an inexplicable incident?"

"No," Ray said without hesitation.

"Good... Okay... because if you get on the radar of the people Titheridge has been dealing with, it will end very badly," and the gaze she levelled at him seemed to weigh him down.

Ray felt the need to leave and decided bluntness was the best move,

"I need to go, but before I do, I need to get things straight."

"Fine."

"The Titheridge case is over for me, but you are handling it and will see that justice is served and that he never gets out, right?" and he looked her in the eyes. They didn't waver as she replied,

"Absolutely. We will do our utmost to ensure the public's safety."

"And justice?"

"We will see justice is done," Elizabeth Russell replied, holding his eyes with hers.

"Good," said Ray, rising, "Then I'd best be off."

Elizabeth Russell also rose and led the way to the door, which she started to open, then paused,

"Promise me one thing," she said,

"If I can."

"If anything inexplicable happens, however small, please let me know."

"I will," again the lie came all too easily.

Elizabeth Russell held out her hand and, as he shook it, she said,

"And remember nothing about this department..." and she paused, looking into his eyes, "...Can be discussed with anyone who hasn't signed the Official Secrets Act."

"Of course," Ray nodded – yeah, like anyone would believe the Treasury had a department of spies!

"Well, thanks for trekking all this way to visit us and please come again if you have anything you want to discuss," she smiled.

"Is there any way I can email or phone you?" asked Ray, "Trekking's all well and good, but technology saves a lot of time."

"Certainly. If you give Oliver your mobile number, he'll ring you and then you'll have the number for his line,"

"You don't have a phone?"

"No. They don't agree with me. Neither do computers," she said, raising her eyebrows.

"All right then. Thanks for an interesting hour. Good to meet you!" said Ray as he crossed the outer office to the door being held open by the ever-efficient Oliver.

"Oh, hang on! I think I may have something of yours," Elizabeth Russell said, and she felt in her jacket pocket as she crossed the room,

"We took it out of Titheridge's leg," and she opened the palm of her left hand to reveal Ray's push dagger, looking spotlessly clean.

Ray looked at it in her hand, then looked her in the eyes.

"There's no judgement here. We understand that sometimes you have to do what you have to do," she said neutrally.

"Thanks," Ray smiled, taking it from her, "These are getting harder to find," and he slipped it into its sheath on the back of his belt.

Elizabeth Russell gave him a knowing smile, turned on her heel and strode back towards her room,

"And remember – anything out of the ordinary, let me know!" she called over her shoulder, then closed her door and was gone.

When Oliver got back fifteen minutes later, he found his boss lounging on his desk.

"Well?" she asked, leaning forward. She knew that Oliver had listened to the whole conversation via the bug under the coffee table.

"Inflexible and angry. Not sure it's the right combo for us."

"Mmmm," Elizabeth Russell mused, "He does have a very red aura. But the flare, charisma and determination..."

"He's got a closed mindset. Do you really think he could ever come round to understanding our work here?"

"Maybe. He might surprise us..." she paused and considered their conversation, "I love the way he lies so easily."

Oliver laughed,

"I knew it! You can never resist a good liar!"

"But he looked me right in the eyes and lied so smoothly about not having anything strange happen to him. It was very impressive. And you know what a useful skill that is – especially out in the field. Christ! We have to lie all day out there."

Oliver conceded the point with an inarticulate grunt, then said,

"I wonder what *has* happened to him since he caught Titheridge?"

"Good question. I hope for his sake that these people haven't noticed him."

"Should I get someone to watch his house?"

"Not yet. We're too understaffed with Jones still in hospital, and Smith and Brown out of the country. Let's see how this plays out first."

"Gotcha. You going back to see Titheridge now?" asked Oliver.

Elizabeth Russell sighed,

"Yes, for all the good it'll do."

"How could he have killed so many of them and still know so little about them?" Oliver wondered aloud.

"Because he's just a gifted amateur," she said, "And his mind is a bit cracked. Even under deep hypnosis, he won't describe the thing he saw.

And I'm not going to push him, because I think it would shatter him," she hopped off the desk and began to pace up and down the room,

"Think about it... his only 'method' has been to wander around the City, waiting to spot one of these people. Then he hunts them down and ccchhhhh," she drew her finger across her throat,

"The fact that he's done sixty-eight, is an indication of how big this network is. But maybe, just maybe he can give us some information about this Druid. Once I've pumped him for that, I think that'll be it for the interrogation."

"And then what? Happy pills and carpet slippers in a sanatorium?" Oliver asked.

"What? And waste all that raw talent? No," Elizabeth Russell shook her head, "Tomorrow, we hand him over to the trainers."

"Really?" Oliver was surprised.

"Oh yes. We're going to take that gifted amateur and help Brian Titheridge turn pro."

Chapter Nine

Thin Ice

Vicky was awoken by a hand flopping across her face. She grimaced and gently moved Chloe's hand and arm back to where they belonged. Vicky got up noiselessly and looked at her daughter. Chloe was lying in the middle of the big bed with her arms and legs spread wide in a star shape. Give them an inch...

The clock looked at her reproachfully – past ten and only just getting up! Tut, tut! Vicky ignored its accusation. This was the summer holiday. They could stay in bed all day if they wanted – although she'd never tell Chloe that, or they wouldn't be able to get her out of bed until the start of next term. Chloe's arm flopped back to where Vicky's face had been and, after a moment, the absence of the face was noticed and Chloe began to stir.

"All right, sleepyhead?" Vicky asked softly and Chloe looked up at her through the dissipating fog of sleep.

"D'you want tea?"

"Mmmm," Chloe nodded.

"Okay," said Vicky, but as she turned to go, Chloe said,

"Let me come, too."

"Still don't want to be alone? Come on, then," and Vicky took her ankles and gently pulled her to the end of the bed, then took her hands and heaved her onto her feet.

"Follow me!" and she led the way down to the kitchen.

Some children are either totally awake or unconscious. For them, it's not so much sleep as a simple recharging of the batteries. When the morning comes, they switch on – often far too early for their parents' liking. Chloe wasn't one of those kids. It wasn't until she'd finished breakfast and was halfway through her second cup of tea that she fully woke up.

"So, it's a beautiful day," Vicky said, clearing away the breakfast things,

"What shall we do? Drive over to Dulwich and picnic in the park? Walk in the woods at the top of the Common? What about a swim in Brockwell Lido?"

Chloe considered the options. They all sounded very bright and sunny. A bit too bright and sunny!

"Can we go skating?"

"Ice skating on a sunny day like this?" that seemed contrary, even for Chloe.

"It'll be nice and cool in there," Chloe said.

"But you need sunshine for vitamin D," Vicky protested.

"But it's good exercise," Chloe countered.

"So's swimming,"

"Yeah, but the pool will be packed, but the ice rink might be empty," Chloe replied.

Vicky damned whichever gene had given Chloe such a grasp of logic.

"All right, but we'll have to walk there," Vicky said.

"Deal," Chloe smiled and they shook on it.

***

The homeless woman, bundled up in multiple jumpers and coats, stopped on the pavement to wipe sweat from her face. She was a somewhat round woman in her sixties with dull, brown, puffy eyes, dark red hair sticking out at odd angles from under the black shawl covering her head, and a face that always looked livid and swollen as if she'd been recently beaten up. She cast an accusatory glance at the hot sun high above, then set off along Streatham High Road once more with her distinctive rolling gait. She was carrying two large plastic bags full to bursting with clothes and possessions, but her most remarkable feature wasn't the way she walked, the many clothes she wore or the fact that she carried her world with her. No, what scared little children, made older children point and adults look away from her, was her beard. It wasn't a few long hairs on her chin that she didn't control, but a beard that covered her entire jawline in three or four inches of hair. Even the hairs themselves were unsettling, because they were a random mixture of red and black, so that the overall effect looked wrong. And, of course, she made no attempt to tame them, so they stuck out in all directions. It was all wild and unruly and, because she wore too many clothes, she sweated heavily. The result was a smell that hung around her in a hideous pall of stale sweat and rotting cauliflower. All of this was her armour, forged over years of living on the streets. Her name was Penelope and a very long time ago - before she had met The Man - she had been a cellist in a prestigious London orchestra. Once she had been sensitive, talented and loved. However, Penelope had long since disappeared. Now she was simply known as Bag Hag.

Today, she had a job to do. The Man had business elsewhere and she'd been tasked with keeping an eye on Wondergirl – the brat of some copper that The Man had his eye on. Was she really the great prospect The Man thought she was? Bag Hag would soon see for herself, because she was now about two hundred yards from the end of her road. But here was the problem – the brat could apparently see the darkness to which Bag Hag and The Man had given their lives. If she didn't want to be noticed, she'd have to play it very carefully. Fortunately, there was a bus stop with a bin to the side of it that gave Bag Hag a perfect line of sight to the end of the child's road. The bus stop would give her cover and the bin would give her the excuse to loiter there, rootling through it. Nothing quite like sifting through a bin to make you almost invisible in London. People either looked away in revulsion, or in guilt that anyone should be reduced to such behaviour almost a quarter of the way through the twenty-first century.

Very occasionally, someone would come and offer to help her with money or food, but that was rare.

And so, in the baking heat of the sun, with sweat running off her scraggly eyebrows, Bag Hag hunched over the bin while keeping one eye out for the wunderkind. Of course, trawling through bins wasn't what it used to be. Back in the nineties, you could find some choice pickings, but by the noughties, bags of dog poo had started appearing in bins. Now, it seemed like half of the stuff in public bins was dog poo. On the other hand... she'd hit paydirt already. There, sitting on top of a bag of dog doings was half a Marks and Spencer egg and cress sandwich, still in its package. She picked it up and gave it a sniff – a bit whiffy, but it would do. She munched it contemplatively. Yes, there was definitely an underlying shadow of dog bowel in there, but it was a warm egg sandwich from a bin, so what else could she really expect? Once she'd finished it, she went back to sifting through the bin. She was so engrossed that she didn't even notice she was humming the scherzo from Beethoven's third cello sonata. The man who had been at the bus stop when she arrived moved to the other end of the shelter and checked his watch – why did they always take an age when there was a weirdo around?

Forty minutes later, Bag Hag had almost exhausted the secret delights of the bin when she saw a woman and a child arrive at the junction she'd been watching. The woman looked ordinary, but the child! A golden light shone all around her. She was radiating psychic energy like a burning brazier. Bag Hag wanted to reach out and draw some of her energy towards her, just to taste the sweetness that she knew must be there, but she stopped herself. If the child had any awareness, she would feel her energy being drawn off. Bag Hag couldn't risk that, so she shuffled further behind the shelter so that the child wouldn't spot her. Mother and daughter turned in the other direction and walked southwards towards the unforgiving sun riding high in the cloudless blue. Bag Hag collected her bags and started rolling after them. As she looked ahead, she was calculating what she could use as cover along the way. Yes, that dark shop doorway would do, and that phone box... those parked cars, the telephone junction box, that builder's skip. After that, there were a few trees in the central reservation between the dual carriageways that would work in her favour. So long as they didn't walk too quickly...

Up ahead, Chloe was regretting not taking Vicky's advice to wear a baseball cap. The sun was dazzling her and, as they walked along the side of the wide ribbon of asphalt, the heat coming up from the ground was doubling the effect of the sun above.

"You okay with the sun?"

Vicky had noticed Chloe wince and could feel that she wasn't happy through her hand as she held it.

"It's fine," Chloe lied, and Vicky smiled to herself. This would be part of Chloe's learning experience, that sometimes (or more often than not) her mum was right about things and should be listened to.

"Are you going to skate?" Chloe asked as they worked their way along the busy High Road.

"Depends. Do you want me to?"

Chloe considered for a while. Vicky would be bound to try to teach her, even though she wasn't much better at skating than she was. That was the problem with having a teacher as a parent – she seemed unable to stop teaching!

"No, it's okay if you don't want to," Chloe replied at last.

"And you'll be okay doing it on your own?"

"Yeah."

"All right, if that's the way you want it, I'll get myself a coffee."

They arrived at a crossroads and had to wait for the traffic light. Now that they were motionless and silent, Chloe noticed a funny feeling. It was a sort of dread. Like she was being watched. She looked over her shoulder and immediately stiffened – was it The Man?

"Are you all right?" Vicky asked, feeling the change through her daughter's hand.

Chloe peered across the road at the dark shadow in the doorway under the awning of a shop. It was as black as the darkness around The Man, but the shape was all wrong. Whoever that was, was short and round. As Chloe looked harder, she wondered whether it was a simple trick of her eyes. The shaded depths of the shop doorway would be dark and, after walking in the dazzling sun, her eyes would make the darkness even blacker.

"It's nothing," Chloe said, looking up at Vicky with a half-smile.

"All right..." Vicky was unconvinced, but then the lights changed and the moment passed,

"Come on, we've got the light," Vicky said and led the way across the road.

In the shop doorway, Bag Hag breathed a sigh of relief. That had been close! Well, the child was everything The Man had made her out to be and more! She seemed to be not only able to see Bag Hag's aura, but feel her presence, too. Yes, she would be perfect for their needs... well, for someone's needs, anyway! But this made everything that bit more complicated. She'd have to be even more careful. The Man had been very specific about not being seen. And you didn't want to get on the wrong side of The Man - unless you enjoyed being given the Last Rites. She waited until mother and daughter had walked away, then slipped out of the doorway and followed. Now she had to spot every possible doorway she could use and make sure that she didn't get so close that the child could feel her. She muttered imprecations under her breath as she tried to keep pace with the pair. Why couldn't they have stayed at home and made her life easier? Her legs were already aching from walking faster than she was used to and the combination of heat and wearing too many clothes was chafing her between her legs. She began to feel that whatever The Man had planned for the child, she bloody well deserved it!

Fifteen minutes later, Vicky and Chloe walked through the automatic doors of the sports centre and into the cool, air- conditioned reception area. Bag Hag watched them go in and immediately looked around for somewhere to hunker down that had a view of the entrance. Not easy! The road had widened to six lanes and on the side opposite the Sports Centre, large, five storey housing blocks were set back from the road. There was a big, grassy area in front of them that offered no cover. The only place nearby was the red brick church next door to the Sports Centre, but there was no way she was going near that. The thought of Christianity made her physically queasy. Was it an allergic reaction to something so different to the faith she now had? Or had she once been a Christian? Did the proximity to the church make her feel guilty about the choices she'd made? Did it matter? The fact was, she wouldn't go near the place. She looked around and then she saw the perfect spot. Further up the road was the memorial to those who'd fallen in the First and then the Second World Wars and there, in the little garden around it, was a vast cedar tree. Its flattened canopy of dark, evergreen branches cast such dense shade beneath it, that even on a sunny day, her darkness would be hardly distinguishable from the shadow of the tree. Plus, it gave her a long, but clear sightline to the exit of the building. Yes, that would do nicely! Bag Hag lumbered off in her rolling way, but not before she'd spat on the ground in the direction of the church. Fuck Christ! She'd found the way, the truth and the darkness.

By the time Vicky had got her coffee, Chloe had been skating for about ten minutes. The staff at the coffee shop weren't really what you could call motivated. Half-asleep, would be more accurate. If ever there was a case for people to get high on their own supply, it was the zombies in that coffee shop. Vicky moved carefully, trying not to spill her drink as she worked her way up through the stands around the impressive Olympic standard rink. She settled herself on one of the cold, plastic seats, placed her coffee on the seat next to her, got her big, hooded fleece out of her bag and put it on, then topped it off with a red woolly hat. Once she was settled, she sipped carefully from the cardboard coffee cup, which was steaming heavily from the small slit in the plastic lid.

"Holy shit!" that was BAD! Dreadful coffee. A total con! Vicky suppressed the urge to go back and give them a piece of her mind and instead waved at Chloe. She looked like she was having fun, skating around moderately well and even having the confidence to wave back. That was good.

In fact, all of this was good. After what had happened yesterday and last night, they needed a bit of normality.

Normality. That was a laugh. What about their lives was 'normal'? As Vicky sat in the almost empty stands, watching the thirty-or-so people skating about, and drinking her dire coffee, she wondered whether anyone married to a detective had a 'normal' life. The fact was that Ray's job came first, second and third, with Chloe in fourth and her in a distant fifth. And if they'd owned a cat, she wondered whether she'd even be in fifth. There was always something more urgent, more important than them. Compared with the crimes Ray worked on, Vicky's worries and concerns always seemed so small and irrelevant. But they weren't. Creating a healthy family home was important. Without it, what was the point in life? However many crimes Ray solved, there would always be more. That would never end, but Chloe's childhood would. She'd grow up and then that magic time would be gone. Ray couldn't see that the most precious part of his life was slipping through his fingers. One day, he'd finally look up from what he was doing and Chloe would have left home. Then there would only be Vicky. And what would happen after that? Ten years of marriage had seen them slowly grow apart. Now it felt like they were trying to high-five each other but kept missing. How would they be in another ten years?

Vicky finished the coffee with a grimace and crushed the cup in her hand as she thought about the responsibility she had for where her marriage was. It wasn't the first time they'd struggled – they'd known each other since school, so they were bound to have had their difficult times, but Vicky's actions had been the cause of their greatest test. She'd had a 'liaison' three years ago. It had been one of those things. Ray had been working too hard and not giving her any time or attention. Vicky had felt unattractive, unappreciated and unloved. It wasn't like Ray was the only one with a job. She'd been working too. Chloe was in pre-school and Vicky was juggling work with running the house and doing ninety-five percent of the childcare. But no, Ray's work was so fucking important. It was as if he didn't really come *home* at the end of the day, but more like he was coming back to a hotel. He'd eat, sleep, wash, (very) occasionally have sex, and then head back to work. His interest in Vicky, Chloe and in their family had been zero. So, when William, the P.E. teacher at the school she'd been working at, had made her feel noticed and sexy, she'd responded. Looking back, Vicky had never intended it to be anything serious. Poor William had been little more than her way of trying to get Ray's attention. She and William weren't discreet, so it was inevitable when Ray found out. Of course, he had been furious, but when he had arrived home, all he'd said was,

"I know about you and William. I'll be at my mum's until the weekend and then we'll talk."

When the weekend had come around, they'd talked it out. She finished it with William and she and Ray started couples counselling. After two weeks, they made love. It was piquant, bordering on the aggressive, and re-forged their bond. Looking back, it was funny, but what Ray had found most annoying was the fact that William was a gym teacher. For some reason, that had stuck in his craw the most. That and the way no one ever shortened William's name. He was never Bill, Billy, Will or Willy. Always William. Ray hated that. As for Vicky, even though she'd got Ray's full attention (at least for a while), she'd borne a sliver of fear ever since. The fear that one day Ray would do to her what she had done to him. Maybe that was part of the problem now? Maybe she could sense that he was cooler towards her? Was it simply the work, or was there something more – or someone? Vicky looked down at her tummy and grasped her spare tyre through her jumper. That didn't help, either. Here she was getting frumpier while Ray seemed to get fitter and better looking with age. And rather than making her feel lucky at having bagged a keeper, it only made her feel more insecure. Shit!

Maybe Ray's current distance was simply down to work? Maybe all the things she was insecure about had nothing to do with it? But whatever the reason, it didn't change the reality – their spark was gone and he was starting to treat the house like a hotel again. And the worst of it was, she was having to play a role she never wanted – the hall monitor. She was the one having to constantly corral Ray and Chloe; she was the one who had to be on top of Chloe's education and development and lead Ray by the nose through it; she was the one who had to stay ahead of their finances; she was the one who had to run everything. She'd never wanted any of that. She'd wanted to be the cheeky lover, the playmate and drinking buddy. The friend with loads of benefits. Not the bloody hall monitor! She smiled bitterly. A hall monitor without authority. And it was worst in the bedroom. She was the one who had to initiate intimacy, but she didn't feel like she had any right to. At least, not since William.

And now, here she was again, having to push Ray and Chloe through the process of seeing the educational psychologist. Ray didn't have the first clue how screwed up the state system was when it came to children with special educational needs and disabilities. It might take years to get a diagnosis, by which time most kids who needed help hated school more than anything. Why couldn't Ray take an interest and support her? Why did it always have to be a struggle? She wanted desperately to get back to their light, loving friendship, but his lack of interest in vital things like Chloe's development meant that she was having to be a nag out of necessity. How could she rebuild their love life when she wanted to grab him and scream into his face that he needed to step up. And then there was Chloe. Had the meeting with the educational psychologist set something off to cause the nightmare? She couldn't even be sure that Chloe had really seen the man she'd claimed to. There'd been no one out there when Ray had checked. But why would she have made that up? Vicky would keep a close eye on her over the next week and then report anything odd to the psychologist at their next meeting. That was all she could do. No, in fact, there *was* something else she could do - she could have some fun with her daughter.

Out on the ice, Chloe was enjoying herself - even though there were some bigger boys in ice hockey skates charging about, dodging in between the other skaters, Chloe knew they wouldn't hit her. They were all too good. The people you had to watch out for were the ones who didn't know what they were doing and looked like newly born deer, tottering on unsure legs. When they fell – and they did always fall – they'd reach out for anyone or anything nearby and that was when they could get you! Apart from avoiding them, she loved the feeling of being out on the ice – the cool air flowing around her, the speed, the feeling of almost being weightless as she glided across the smooth surface. That's what she liked to do most – get up a bit of speed and then just glide. She also felt safe out there, because on the ice under the white lights, she'd be able to see The Man and his aura coming a mile away. Since she'd seen him, she had been afraid. And even if Vicky and Ray said he wasn't real, she knew he was. He was real and he would keep coming for her until he finally took her. She knew that. But how could she tell her parents? Grown-ups were so difficult! They ignored what they didn't want to believe. They disbelieved on purpose. Why did they do that? Without their help, how could she protect herself? Could she pretend to be ill until they went on their family holiday to Norfolk? No. Vicky would insist on taking her to the doctor and then everyone would get cross. The only thing she could do was keep on the lookout and try to avoid situations where The Man could catch her.

When Chloe and Vicky finally emerged from the Sports Centre, Bag Hag had fully recovered herself after the walk down there. She'd been sitting in the shade of the great cedar tree and watching the little birds flitting about the cenotaph and the garden of remembrance. She hated the little birds and had spent much of her time shooing them away. So, when she saw the mother and daughter emerge, blinking, into the bright sunshine, Bag Hag was glad to be able to leave, but annoyed with them for making her wait around to be hassled by twittering birds. She stared daggers at Chloe's back as the pair walked away, but instantly regretted it. The brat immediately turned to look behind her, causing Bag Hag to duck back into the dark shadows. She waited, and then the child was led away by her mother. Bag Hag let out a long sigh. That had been close! Wow! She was amazed. The child was so powerful! She had sensed Bag Hag's intention even at two hundred yards. How powerful might she become with the right training? The Man needed to be told that there was more to this one than the others. Usually, they took people who were only just tapping into their psychic powers, but this girl was already on the road to controlling it... but how far had she got? An unpleasant smile writhed across Bag Hag's mouth. It might be fun to test how much control the child had. The Man's instructions were that the child shouldn't see that she was being followed. What Bag Hag had in mind was much more fun than that.

"Tapas?" Vicky asked. It was the last throw of the dice. Since leaving the Sports Centre, she'd offered Chloe the choice of every possible restaurant the High Road had to offer for a nice lunch. So far, nothing had been right and Vicky was starting to get a teensy bit tetchy. The fact was that she wanted to have a light lunch in a halfway decent restaurant and she was damned if Little Miss Picky was going to take that away from her.

"Will they have those prawns in garlic?" Chloe asked.

"Of course," Vicky said brightly – this was the first positive response she'd had.

"All right then," Chloe said.

"Great! Let's head up to the usual place now," Vicky smiled, thinking of the family-run tapas bar at the other end of the High Road, and of their very passable, perfectly chilled house white that would go nicely with said prawns.

Now that they had a definite goal, they picked up their pace slightly and fell into silence, thinking about the cool restaurant and what they might have.

"Of course, you do know that he's going to eat you," Vicky said.

The sudden remark took Chloe by surprise.

"What?" she asked, turning to Vicky.

"The Man will come and take you to *him*. And *he* will eat your flesh and your soul," Vicky said, smiling.

Chloe shook her head and looked at her mother again. Everything seemed normal. They were walking along and Vicky looked happy and relaxed.

"What?" Chloe stammered.

"Yes, yes, *he'll* eat you. No doubt about that," Vicky was looking ahead towards where they were going as if she'd done nothing more than comment on the weather, then she chuckled,

"I once saw *him* peel a child. Peeled the little boy like a satsuma. Only, instead of juice squirting out, it was blood. Who knows, maybe *he'll* peel you?" and she gave Chloe a broad, beaming smile.

Chloe felt like a frog was leaping about inside her chest as her heartbeat went haywire. What was happening? Why was Vicky talking like that? Should she run? Yes, she needed to get away... but no! No, there was something else. It was that feeling. That feeling of dread and of being watched, but this time it was much stronger. And suddenly, she knew. She didn't know how or why, but she knew that someone was in her head. Someone was making her imagine Vicky saying all these horrible things. Vicky would never say any of that, but someone nasty would. And that nasty person had somehow got into her head and was there right now. Instinctively, Chloe knew that she had to get them out of her head immediately – otherwise they might read her thoughts or try to make her do something she didn't want to. She stopped dead in the street, closed her eyes and let out a silent scream with every ounce of her being.

"You all right?" Vicky had lost her grip on Chloe's hand the moment she'd stopped and now she was looking at her daughter, who was standing ramrod-stiff with her eyes closed and her fists balled at the sides of her body.

"Chloe?"

No response.

"Chloe! Are you all right?"

Suddenly, Chloe opened her very blue eyes and looked at her,

"Sorry," she said.

"What was all that about?" Vicky looked worried.

"I swallowed a fly and I could feel it in my throat. It was horrible!"

"Oh, you poor thing!" and Vicky laughed in relief as she hugged Chloe to her,

"Do you still want to go to the restaurant?" she said, when the hug was over.

"Yeah," Chloe said with genuine enthusiasm.

"Okay, then," Vicky replied, taking her hand and setting off. As Chloe walked with her, she had a spring in her step. Far from feeling frightened or violated that some nasty stranger had been inside her head, she felt energized and happy. She had forcibly thrown the evil presence out of her head. And not only that, but she also knew that they would not be able to get inside her head again. She could feel a new energy all around her as if she'd been powered up. It was strange and exciting at the same time. She had done something spectacular – or at least, she thought she had.

Three hundred yards behind them, a small crowd was gathering at the door to a betting shop. A fat, stinking old vagrant woman had collapsed. It was probably a mixture of drink and the heat. Poor old biddy. And she must've hit her face when she fell, because her nose was bleeding. Hands helped her to her feet, but then she batted them away. Huffing and puffing, she picked up her bulging plastic bags and hurried away as fast as her bulk would allow her.

Chapter Ten

Some Body

The thing about Mexican Dave was that his name wasn't Dave and he wasn't Mexican. It was a name bestowed upon him by the clientele and staff of the homeless shelter he'd been frequenting for the last five years. He'd turned up one day, wheeling his battered racing bicycle and wearing a dark blue shell suit, a pair of black leather brogues without socks and a sombrero. In the intervening five years, nothing had changed. He still had the same clothes, the same thin black hair emerging from under the sombrero, the same Desperate Dan sort of a face with its black stubble and huge lower jaw, and the same grin that revealed his total lack of upper front teeth. He didn't talk much but when he did, it was almost impossible to understand what he was saying thanks to his lack of teeth and his outrageous Scottish accent. Anyone from Scotland would have been able to spot that it was fake, but who was going to call him out on it? No one. And he knew it. Besides, he wasn't a problem and, as far as the staff and clientele of the homeless shelter were concerned, he was OK. Yes, he was eccentric and, yes, he talked a load of twaddle, but it was harmless twaddle and he didn't put any noses out of joint.

About three hours after Ray had finished his meeting with Elizabeth Russell, Mexican Dave left the hostel near Tottenham Court Road with a cheery wave and an incomprehensible farewell to the woman on reception. He hopped on his bike and started pedalling down the Charing Cross Road as if his life depended on it. It was hot and sunny, and within a minute, sweat was starting to bead on his forehead under the sombrero.

The whole area was crawling with tourists, gaping at sights which ordinary Londoners ignored, turning the pavements into a nightmarish kaleidoscope with their garishly coloured foreign clothes and backpacks.

"Oot the way, yer foreign swine!" Mexican Dave yelled as one of the verminous tourists stepped blindly off the curb and into his path with their mouth gaping stupidly at yet another 'sight'. Mexican Dave wished his bike was fitted with machine guns at the front and a flame thrower in the back. That would clear the way!

"I didn't vote for Brexit to allow you illegal aliens in!" he bellowed as he swerved around another of the foreign rats. The 'illegal alien' only heard a roar of garbled nonsense before catching a blur of sombrero, gleaming black eyes and a huge jaw before the madman on the bicycle was gone. And anyway, Mexican Dave hadn't even voted in the referendum, because 2016 had been one of the years he'd lost to... well, when he thought about it, he couldn't even remember what he'd lost that year to, but he supposed he must have been having fun.

Soon he swung away from Trafalgar Square and down to The Strand, which was also awash with evil tourists. Whatever happened to Britain for the British? Within fifteen minutes of weaving in and out of tourists and traffic (and swearing at both of the twin evils), he was crossing the river at Waterloo Bridge and the front of his sombrero folded upwards in the wind. The rough string that held it to his head was tight under his enormous chin and his mouth was like an open, black letterbox, heaving in great gulps of air as he pumped his legs furiously. He ought to change gear, but he didn't. He found the feeling of almost pedalling too fast exhilarating. There was something about being on the ragged edge that made him happy. So, when he slammed on his brakes and skidded to a halt to avoid being hit by a truck coming around the roundabout off Waterloo Bridge, he cackled with laughter. Even though he was a remarkable sight, hunched over his handlebars with his sombrero down over his eyes, nobody really noticed him. The tourists were too busy with 'tourist crap', while native Londoners didn't see him at all. Like most big city dwellers, Londoners are very good at ignoring anyone who might be mad, because they've got better things to do with their time than get hassled by crazy strangers. Everything about Mexican Dave screamed 'crazy' and it was like an invisibility cloak that allowed him to charge around the city unnoticed and unmolested.

He adjusted the sombrero, looked to the right and pedalled into the traffic to the usual sound of blaring car horns as he totally failed to judge their speed and almost caused an accident. But he didn't care. He sped off as if nothing had happened, leaving angry drivers in his wake. At the crossroads near the Old Vic theatre, he ran the red light and froggered his way through the traffic screaming across in front of him. Five minutes later, he was causing similar mayhem around Elephant and Castle before he was spat out into the relative calm of Newington Causeway, cycling north back towards the river. He huffed and puffed his way through Borough, crossing two cycle routes, either of which would have given him a safer and more direct route to London Bridge, but he'd ignored them. Given the choice of the safe route or running the risk of death around Elephant and Castle, Mexican Dave would always choose the latter. He took a right just before London Bridge and a minute later was half crashing to a halt as he arrived at Hay's Gap, where he wheeled his bike the twenty yards to the riverside walk which linked London Bridge and Tower Bridge.

Pushing his sombrero to a jaunty angle, he walked along, grinning toothlessly at every individual he could in the slow-moving river of tourists clogging up the footpath. Their eyes always slipped away from his to look at anything other than the mad bloke in the sombrero. Within a minute, he'd reached the far side of the entrance walkway of London Bridge City Pier. He wasn't interested in the comings and goings of the Thames Clipper boats; he had come for the show on the tidal beach next to the pier. He stopped and looked over the edge of the riverside walk. Down below, two men whom he knew to be Detective Inspector Ray Ennis and Detective Sergeant Andy Harper were in close discussion with a big woman. Nearby on the beach, a large, square-sided tent had been set up to stop idlers from seeing what was going on down below.

"Spoilsports!" Mexican Dave shouted in his thick, fake Scots accent, before ducking back behind the wall when Andy looked up in his direction.

"Nutter! Fucking nutter!" came a familiar voice from behind him and Mexican Dave turned to see Roaming Rohit, the Nawab of Newington, limping towards him, grinning as always. He always made Mexican Dave laugh, even though his English was limited to one catchphrase. Like Mexican Dave's name, Roaming Rohit's catchphrase had been bestowed upon him by others. It had been the one English phrase he'd heard over and over again after his family had cast him out and he'd had to rely on the state social security system. He'd heard the phrase everywhere from homeless hostels, to the Job Centre, every hospital he'd ever washed up in and the occasional police station – they'd all labelled him as a 'fucking nutter'.

"Here, Rohit yer lame duck bastard. Wha's goin' on?"

Rohit joined him and simply said,

"Nutter! Fucking nutter!"

"That bad, eh? Does anyone else know?"

"Nutter!" Rohit said firmly.

"Oh, shite! Noo' we's all in fuckin' bother, ain't we?"

"Fucking nutter!"

"Aye, ye got that right, laddie!"

Mexican Dave lifted up the front of his sombrero and scratched his sweaty head.

"Right, I gotta plan. You sit tight here an' keep an eye on things. I'll go an' tell the Princess what's happened."

"Nutter! Fucking nutter!"

"Aye, good point. They did see you yesterday,"

"Fucking nutter!"

"How the fuck are ye goin' tae see the Princess? By the time ye limp over to the meetin' place, they'll have made an arrest, brought the case to court, secured a conviction, seen it overturned in the Court of Appeal, appealed that appeal, got another conviction an' put oot a press release about how his death in custody was accidental."

"Nutter!"

"It can't be helped, pally. If we want tae get the word oot today, we's gotta play to our strengths. Mine's speed, yours is..." at this point, Mexican Dave stopped. What was Rohit's strength?

"Yours is being a total nutjob."

"Fucking nutter!" Rohit agreed and then Mexican Dave was off, wheeling his bike through the crowd until he could get to a road and then he'd pelt off like a madman, which he felt was just about right.

Down on the narrow beach of sand, gravel and centuries of accumulated filth, Belinda Warburton was telling Ray and Andy what she'd found so far.

"It's the torso of a man, probably no older than thirty. I'd guesstimate that he's only been in the river since last night and that he was killed sometime yesterday evening. But these are preliminary observations, not set in stone," she added.

"Right," Ray sighed, shifting his feet so that he didn't sink into the damp sand and pebbles of the beach,

"So, we want to pull all CCTV footage from every bridge across the river upstream from here to... Richmond weir?"

"Doubt he's come that far," Belinda said, "He can't have been in there more than fifteen hours."

"Better do it anyway, just in case."

"Right," said Andy, "And which bridge do you want to take?"

"Huh?" Ray was confused.

"For the sweepstake. I'm bagsying Chelsea Bridge," Andy said, getting his marker down first.

"Fiver on Battersea," said Belinda, "Good bridge for dumping a torso off."

Ray gave her a look of rebuke.

"But it is," she protested.

"We're not taking bets on which bridge he got slung off," said Ray flatly, "After what happened yesterday and this morning, we want to do this one by the book and show the powers that be what good detective work looks like."

"All right," said Andy, "No bets," but he winked at Belinda behind Ray's back. There would be betting, but Ray wouldn't know about it.

"Okay, thanks, Belinda. You'd better get back to it so you can vacate the beach before the tide comes in."

"I'll let you know if anything major turns up," she said and hurried back into the big tent.

"Fuck me!" Ray said, staring across the river towards the 'Walkie Talkie' building that loomed up out of the smaller buildings of the City of London. He'd walked out of Elizabeth Russel's office and straight into this mess! He'd love to think that it was some sort of conspiracy; that he and Andy had been chosen for this new case because of some shadowy reason; that the minute he'd left her office, Elizabeth Russell had been on the phone to his chief to ensure that he'd hand this case to them to keep them away from Titheridge. Ray smiled. The thing that conspiracy theorists always seemed to have a blind spot for, was luck. The reality was, that the main reason he was standing there was simply because the body had washed up on the south side of the river. Had the currents and tides been different, it would have washed up a couple of hundred yards away on the north bank and be causing problems for a totally different police unit. But no. Here it was on the South Bank and firmly in his lap. On the plus side, at least it would stop him brooding on the Titheridge case. He took a deep breath – traffic fumes, a whiff of sewage and the scent of wet stones. There was something strange about his meeting with Elizabeth Russell: he was very fuzzy about what her office had been like or the details of their meeting. He had impressions rather than defined memories. He thought that the meeting had gone well and he felt he'd got closure. He knew that Titheridge was off the streets and going to spend a long time behind bars. He knew that Elizabeth Russell was a very capable – and gorgeous – woman, but didn't seem to have the specifics of their talk at his disposal. But he felt all right with that. It didn't seem to matter. He knew that all this was strange, but he was comfortable with that, too. Weird!

"Are we off, then?" Andy broke Ray's reverie.

"Yeah, let's get back and organise ourselves. We need to be ready for whatever Belinda turns up," Ray replied and they started to walk across the narrow beach to a set of stone steps up to the riverside walk above them.

"I heard back from my army mate," Andy said in a tone that told Ray nothing had come of it.

"And the bad news is?"

"They had no idea who put in the call to clear the railway arch and fill the basement with concrete. They just got orders and the timeframe in which to complete them."

Ray trudged towards the steps and cracked a rueful smile. Why was he at all surprised? Emma's contact had flatly denied all knowledge about any of it and then warned her that if *he* didn't know anything, it would be better for her career to leave it well alone.

"I s'pose it's not our problem now, so no need to lose sleep over it. Best to crack on with what we've got in front of us," he said as he started up the steps.

"Nutter! Fucking nutter!"

Ray heard it loud and clear.

"Hang on," he said, turning to Andy, "Did you..."

"It's that bloke from yesterday," Andy confirmed.

"What the hell's he doing here?" Ray said, quickening his pace and jogging up the steps with Andy at his heels.

When they got up to the busy riverside walk, there were plenty of tourists, but neither of them could spot the distinctive cadaverous owner of the voice they'd heard.

"You go that way, see you back here in ten," Ray indicated to the left and Andy hurried off into the crowd of people flowing downstream towards Tower Bridge, while he turned right and pushed his way upstream towards London Bridge.

Ray barged his way through the crowds, scanning faces, dodging in between people, muscling dopy backpackers out of the way. Everything was a jumble of faces – every shape, every colour, some bright eyed and eager, others tired and overstimulated by Big City sightseeing. But all he wanted to see was that stick-thin body painfully contorting itself as it hobbled away. As he half-jogged through the crowd, he had an unsettling feeling. There was no way the cripple could have got away from them. He must have been close when he'd spoken and yet it was as if he'd melted away into the paving stones. After five minutes, Ray stopped. The man hadn't come this way but, as he turned to go back, Ray had a creeping sensation in his gut that he couldn't shake off. The one thing he could remember clearly from his meeting with Elizabeth Russell was her insistence that if anything strange happened, he should get in touch. And this was strange. To have the same crazy turn up at two serious crime scenes in two days was not normal. Especially when the crazy in question could only move at about one mile an hour. Ray shook his head,

"Come on, mate, get it together," he muttered.

The likelihood was that Andy would be back at the meeting place holding the 'nutter' by the collar. Nothing bizarre, just an ordinary case of some weirdo getting about a bit. Then they could find out who he was and advise him to mind his own business. Yeah, that would be it.

It wasn't. Ray returned to find Andy empty handed and bemused.

"No luck?" He said as Ray approached,

"No."

"I don't get it," Andy said, shoving his hands into his trouser pockets,

"He must've been right here and there's no way he could outrun us, so where the hell is he?"

Ray shrugged.

"Weird!" Said Andy. He was right. It was another weird thing, but Ray was not about to buckle and go running to Elizabeth Russell. Sod it! Sod the 'nutter' and sod these feelings of disquiet. He would throw himself into some good old fashioned police work and everything would turn out fine.

"Come on, we've got a case to work," he said.

Chapter Eleven

The Princess

By the time Mexican Dave cycled through the Victoria Gate into the north end of Hyde Park, he was a hot, sweaty mess. He wished he looked better, because he was going to meet a lady, but there was nothing he could do beyond pulling over, taking off his sombrero and wiping away as much sweat as he could. When he'd finished, he replaced the sombrero and waited in the sunshine. It was a glorious day to be in the park and he was glad to see that the traffic on the road snaking through it was almost solid. That would make it easier for him to keep up with the Princess when she arrived. He'd already pedalled like fury for six miles across town to arrive at the rendezvous on time, so he felt that he deserved a bit of a breather. It wasn't easy being the messenger of a God. Somewhere in the jumbled mess of images and information that passed for his mind, the name 'Hermes' bubbled up. That's what he was – Hermes, only with a battered old Bianchi bike instead of winged boots. As he stared about him, his big, crazy eyes defying passers-by to catch their gaze, Mexican Dave wondered briefly what his life had been like before Krowos had changed it forever. Krowos, the Lord of Dimension, the Bringer of Pain, the Destroyer of Hope – the only god manifested on this earth. He did not need faith to believe in Krowos. He had seen *him*. He had seen the shattering horror of a god and had fallen on his face in terror. In that moment, the truth of his total insignificance had filled him so that all his pride, arrogance, self-importance and sense of self had been instantly flushed out. He was nothing more than a speck, an ant that could be crushed at any moment, but rather than obliterating him, Krowos had shown him an ineffable secret of the universe. All the bonds tying him to reality had snapped and he had plunged through galaxies of stars, great nebulae and the inter-stellar void into an alternate space and time far beyond the capacity of the human mind to comprehend. He couldn't describe what Krowos had shown him because it made no sense. And when he had returned to earth a moment, or a lifetime later, his old life had gone and there was only Krowos.

As Mexican Dave stood straddling the crossbar of his bike, surrounded by the beauty of Hyde Park, he strained to think of anything before Krowos. From somewhere came dim images of a woman hugging him and a child playing in a pink paddling pool on a sun-browned lawn in a back garden. Were they people he had known, or had he dreamt them? He couldn't be sure. There was only one sure thing in his life now – the power of Krowos. It was a power that could give untold pleasure and unimaginable pain. Again, images flickered across his mind. He was in a pink room, kneeling on a large, heart-shaped bed and giving it hard to a beautiful young woman from behind. The light brown skin of her ample buttocks rippled with his powerful thrusts as he gripped the soft excesses of her flesh in his calloused hands. Then other images appeared. Images of torn and broken limbs in a pit of misery with a soundtrack of screaming. Were these memories, or...?

The sound of a revving V10 engine broke into his daydream and he looked up to see a red Audi R8 Spyder with the roof down slip into the park. A beautiful young woman with light brown skin was behind the wheel. Mexican Dave could only see her top half, which was barely covered by a sport's bra struggling to keep things contained. He didn't count the big, dark shades and grey Chicago Bulls baseball cap as clothes. Her stage name was Shiny Starrr, and she was one of Britain's most successful pop singers. She'd hit the top of the charts with her first single aged just seventeen and now, at twenty, she had more than enough money to retire. Of course, she wasn't about to do that - she had too much work to do for Krowos, whom she'd been serving since she was sixteen. As she approached, Mexican Dave slowly moved off and, when she came alongside a few moments later, he increased his speed to match hers.

"All right, Princess?" he called in his inexplicable attempt at a Scottish accent.

"Good, yeah," her voice was sharp, with a Tottenham twang,

"What'yer want?"

Mexican Dave looked across at her. Below her slim tummy, a pair of canary yellow hot pants were the only other item of clothing on her. She had broad hips and the hotpants were as strained as her bra. Mexican Dave looked hard at the fleshy thighs emerging from the shorts. Yes, it wasn't a dream, he *had* been in there.

"Stop staring and start talking! I can't be arsed to drive around again if you don't tell me every'fing."

"Aye, right. We got a problem. Last night's sacrifice has washed up on the South Bank and the coppers are on it."

"Fuck! Marco is such a useless arsehole!" Shiny spat, "E's got one fucking job to do after the ceremony an' 'e can't even get that right."

"An' it's one of his slaves, so..." Mexican Dave didn't need to finish the sentence – Shiny's quicksilver mind had already got way beyond it.

"The filth'll 'ave 'im in days. Fuck!" Shiny could see an annoying time ahead. She was in the middle of recording an album, but she had to break up every day by getting to this rendezvous bang on three pm, and she had to spend her nights trawling the clubs for fresh meat for Krowos – all while running a massive Instagram feed to influence her young fans towards the darkness of the only god on earth. The last thing she needed was this sort of aggravation.

She looked at the corner ahead where the road dog-legged before going over the Serpentine and her heart sank. There, standing like a statue and glaring straight at her was The Man. In spite of the sunshine, his overtight, honey-coloured trench coat was buttoned up to his neck and, as always, he was breathing through gritted teeth and balling and unballing his fists, held down to his sides. This would be more aggravation. She checked her rear-view mirror and indicated that she was pulling over.

"Get out the way!" she shouted at Mexican Dave, who slowed so that she could pull ahead and then stop. The Man looked slowly from Shiny to Mexican Dave and back again. Shiny wanted to shout at him to hurry up and get into the car, but she knew better than that. If you tried to hurry The Man, he'd fuck you up. That, rather than vanity, had been the real reason for her highly publicised 'nose job' at eighteen. Eventually, in his own good time and ignoring the angry horns of passing cars, The Man opened the door of the car like someone who'd never done it before and got into the seat painfully slowly. Shiny indicated and pulled back into the traffic as The Man stared straight ahead, breathing angrily through his teeth. Shiny started talking immediately,

"We're gonna have to summon *him*. Marco's sacrifice has been found by the police."

The Man placed his large, blotchy pink hand over Shiny's perfectly manicured petite hand which had been resting on the automatic shift stick. She wanted to pull away from his touch. It was greasy and always made her feel dirty, but she left her hand there to be the conduit. After a moment, she felt words forming in her mind, as The Man took over her internal monologue,

"Which policeman is in charge?"

Shiny had no idea,

"Who's in charge of the police investigation?" she called to Mexican Dave, who was cycling alongside them as they drew to a halt in the middle of the Serpentine Bridge.

"It's that black fella who our friend here went to see last night," Mexican Dave replied.

"Interesting!" the word formed in Shiny's mind whether she wanted it there or not,

"His daughter saw me last night."

"What?" Shiny said in genuine surprise.

"What? What did he say?" Mexican Dave asked.

"Shut it!" Shiny ordered, as more words started forming in her mind,

"Oh yes, she saw me. She's only about seven, but she's so full of power! Krowos will love consuming her. She will be delicious. And her father is a cauldron of anger and passion… he could very easily become one of us. You must summon Krowos tonight and inform him of the policeman and his delicious little daughter. He will also be able to direct you as to what to do about Marco's mistake. As for the little girl, I am keeping her under observation. The mother might have to go."

"Okay," Shiny replied, out loud to the voice in her head. It was always strange talking to The Man. It was like having a conversation with herself, but with no control. That wasn't the worst of it. When The Man was in your head, he could leave things there. Things that could be excruciating. Yes, in four years, Shiny had learned to respect and fear The Man almost as much as Krowos. She was utterly repulsed by him, but inexorably drawn to his immense power.

"If we're doin' this behind Marco's back, you'll 'ave to come tonight to make the numbers," Shiny said to The Man, who nodded.

"Right, Mexican Dave, you're gonna have ta get on yer bike and round up Tiger Lil, Pete Le Meat, Plain Jane, The Captain and The Boss."

"Right! See yous later, Princess!" Mexican Dave shouted as he peeled off to the left down a cycle path through the park, leaving Shiny and The Man in the car. She got to the south exit of the park and carried straight on across Kensington Gore and down Exhibition Road. She was intending to swing past Harrods, up to Hyde Park Corner, then back to the recording studio off the Edgeware Road.

"Where d'you want me to drop you off?" she asked, glancing across at The Man, whose face was hidden by a curtain of lank, grey, sweaty hair. Horribly, he turned his face to look at her, breathing hard through his yellowed teeth as his watery blue eyes bored into her and words arrived in her head,

"I'm staying with you until the ceremony," and now the edges of his mouth turned upwards in an unsettling grin. Shiny felt a twisting in her gut. Christ! That was the afternoon – and her – well and truly fucked.

Chapter Twelve

Body Talking

Around seven that evening, Ray, Andy and Emma were in the mortuary with Belinda and she was talking them through her findings,

"This is all rather unpleasant," she said with a grim smile,

"Can't be sure of the precise cause of death, but there are no signs of poison or drugs. It's either decapitation or the loss of the other limbs. And there's something very odd going on here. The arms and legs haven't been cut off, they've been torn off. Needless to say, the amount of force required to do that is immense."

Ray and Andy looked at each other. Great! Why should it be simple? Emma looked at the shape under the white sheet and wished Ray hadn't insisted she join them.

"The head wasn't cut off, but it wasn't ripped off, either."

"What, so it just fell off?" Andy felt belligerent about the strangeness of the last forty-eight hours. He didn't want or need any more, thank you very much.

"It would be preferable if it had," said Belinda, casting her gaze from one to the other of them,

"Because in my professional opinion, the bruising and jagged cuts are consistent with a bite from a very large animal."

Silence.

Ray gave Belinda a look that suggested she should expand on her statement.

“A wide mouth with lots of triangular, sharp teeth. Like a shark’s teeth. Whatever made this wound was about three feet across and had the force to cut straight through the neck in one go.”

She let that sink in.

Emma shifted uneasily, not taking her gaze from the corpse.

“So, you think there’s a shark in the Thames?” Asked Andy.

“Highly doubtful,” Belinda replied, “This wound could have been made by a large bear trap. If his head had been put in a device where the jaws of the trap could be triggered, then that could sever the head in this way...”

“Great!” Ray exclaimed, “We’re either looking for Jaws or bloody Jigsaw!”

“Who?” Belinda looked confused.

“He’s a horror movie character who kills people with elaborate devices. And I’m pretty sure one was a bear trap,” said Ray, looking to Andy and Emma for confirmation. Andy nodded,

“Yeah, probably. Sounds like the sort of thing he’d do.”

Emma dragged her eyes from the shrouded corpse to look at Ray and nod in agreement.

“Well, that’s fucking great!” Ray cried, “I think I preferred Titheridge. Nice, normal serial killer.”

“There’s more,” said Belinda and Ray looked at her reproachfully, “I’m sorry, but there is,” she said.

“Sorry,” Ray held up his hand in apology, “I’m on edge. What else can you tell us?”

“I think there might be a ritualistic element to this,” she said.

“How so?”

“I’ve taken a look at the stomach contents and this person’s last meal was a barley porridge with flax seeds, false flax, knotgrass and pale persicaria.”

Andy and Ray looked at her blankly, while Emma was again staring fixedly at the body.

“Those were also the main constituents of the last meal of Tollund Man,” Belinda explained, “He was found in a peat bog in Denmark in the nineteen fifties and is believed to have been the victim of a ritual sacrifice.”

"So, you think there's a link to a case from the nineteen fifties?" Andy asked.

"No," Belinda shook her head, "His body was *found* in the nineteen fifties. He was sacrificed around three hundred and eighty BC," and she looked at them as if to say 'Put *that* in your pipe and smoke it!'.

Ray thought hard for a few moments,

"The ingredients of this porridge, are they easy to find?"

"You can find barley and flax in most health food shops, but you'd really have to work hard to find some of these other ingredients."

"And it's too much of a coincidence that our guy would just happen to have eaten a very similar meal, which means this is deliberate," said Ray, "And if it's deliberate, someone is copying an ancient ritual."

"Not quite," said Belinda, "Tollund Man was hanged, not torn limb from limb with his head apparently bitten off."

"Yeah..." Ray said slowly, while his mind worked furiously, trying to make sense of it.

"But there's more," said Belinda, and now her eyes twinkled impishly,

"You remember the unfortunate recipient of Mister Titheridge's attention from yesterday?"

Ray was never likely to forget it and he nodded at her.

"Look here," Belinda said, pulling back the sheet covering the body. Andy and Ray craned forward, while Emma simply stared, her brown eyes widening at the sight of the horrific, jagged marks around the stump of the neck. Belinda pointed to the victim's chest and there, above the heart, a symbol had been cut into the flesh. It was a squashed rhombus, like some sort of long crystal, on a diagonal slant and cutting through the middle of a horizontal figure of eight which resembled the symbol for infinity.

"This symbol was tattooed above the heart of the man in Titheridge's kill room," said Belinda.

Ray tried to recall it, but there had been so much to process and the victim had been covered in so many symbols cut into him by Titheridge, that he couldn't picture it in situ,

"Are you sure?" Ray asked.

Belinda tapped the side of her head,

"Photographic memory," she replied, "I'd bet my house on it."

"Could this be one of Titheridge's victims?" Asked Andy.

"Only if he was out and about killing and dumping the body into the river last night," Belinda stated bluntly.

Ray silently cursed Elizabeth Russell. If she hadn't interfered in the case, they'd have known that Titheridge couldn't have committed this crime, because he'd have been in their custody. But as things stood, the time from the moment Titheridge was taken to the hospital was a blank.

Ray sighed,

"I can't see anyone letting Titheridge out of their custody so he could do this," he said reluctantly.

"But there must be some link to Titheridge. That's not something you see every day," said Andy.

"Ah, but this body has something the other one didn't..." Belinda began, and Emma looked distinctly unsettled by the likelihood of more bizarre revelations,

"This poor fellow's been branded," Belinda continued, turning the body slightly to reveal a burn scar in the middle of the left shoulder blade. Ray, Andy and Emma looked at the 'XIII' symbol.

"Roman numeral for thirteen," said Ray.

"Unlucky for some," Belinda observed with a raised eyebrow.

"Hang on..." Andy looked like a bulb had switched on in his head, "I recognise that. Ten years ago, I did a stint in a special unit to break up human trafficking gangs, and one of them branded all their 'products' with that symbol."

This took them all by surprise and Emma gave Andy a look of reappraisal,

"What happened to the gang?" Ray asked.

"We thought we'd broken them up. The two ringleaders got life sentences and there must've been half a dozen others that went down for it. I s'pose some of 'em could be out now."

"Where were they based?" Asked Ray.

"Mmm, yeah," Andy mused, "City of London, then over the river into Borough and down the Old Kent Road to New Cross, out to Eltham, Rochester, Canterbury and Dover. They had safe houses and drop-off points all the way along the A2. Vicious fuckers."

Ray looked at Belinda,

"Any chance that this bloke has been kept as a slave for the last ten years?"

"No," she replied, "He was branded maybe a few months ago," and she swept the sheet back over what was left of the body, which Emma was still looking at thoughtfully.

"Right," said Ray, clapping his hands and rubbing them together briskly – this was exactly the sort of police work that would get him back to himself,

"Andy, you get Emma up to speed on your old people trafficking gang,"

"Sure thing, hotshot," said Andy, whose face broke into a smile when he saw the flash of annoyance cross Ray's features.

"And then you," Ray continued, looking down at Emma's eager face, "Will have the task of finding out where all the old members of the gang are."

"Will do," she said brightly.

"I'm going to start reviewing all the CCTV footage from the bridges up the river. When you've finished briefing Emma, you join me," Ray said, looking to Andy, who gave him the briefest of nods in reply,

"Thanks, Belinda. Always a pleasure to see you, if not some of the company you keep."

"Don't knock 'em," Belinda replied, "They might not be pretty, but at least they're quiet and they never try to steal my lunch from the communal fridge."

***

"How was your day?" Ray asked as he pecked Vicky on the cheek. He sounded tired.

"Pretty good," she replied as she finished washing the lettuce for the big Greek salad she was making,

"Chloe went skating and then we had lunch at the tapas bar over the way."

"Oooh, nice!" Ray nodded, stealing a couple of cubes of feta cheese that Vicky had diced and left in the big salad bowl,

"Oi! Hands off!" Vicky smiled, "Hungry?"

"Starving! Lunch was a bag of crisps and a Curly Wurly I found in my desk. How's Chloe today?"

"Pretty good. Still a bit shaky after the nightmare and seeing that man, but otherwise good."

"Good, good..."

So, the same symbol was tattooed on the man in Titheridge's playroom and cut into the torso from the Thames...

"I think we need to talk about Chloe later," Vicky continued.

"Yeah, sure..." Ray said, looking out into the garden,

But what's the link? Is there a link? There must be a link...

"It's not like anything bad happened today, but I feel like there's a change in her."

"Mmm-hmm," Ray nodded,

The CCTV should give us something. All we need is a foothold...

"Anyway, we'll talk later," Vicky said as she heard the loo flush.

"Okay,"

The arms and legs were ripped off... how do you do that?

"Ray!" Chloe squealed as she ran over to him and gave him a hug.

"Hey, beautiful, how was your skating? Did you do anything new?"

"I skated backwards a bit," she said, smiling.

"Backwards! That's great!"

Not cut off, ripped off...

"Come and look at the painting I did," she said, taking his hand and pulling him out into the garden, where a big piece of paper was on the table, held down with a stone on each corner.

Ray looked at the colourful daub of a unicorn riding a rainbow to a distant field.

The torso and Titheridge's victim had the same symbol on them...

"What is it?"

"Duh! It's a Brexit unicorn – and those are the sunlit uplands!" Chloe said proudly.

Ray cast a glance at Vicky, who shrugged,

"After a glass of wine at lunch, I might have got into a Brexit conversation with Mel."

"Ah!" Ray understood. Mel and his brothers ran the tapas bar and, being Spaniards who had built lives and a business in London, they always had some choice words to say about Brexit to those customers who they knew were sympathetic to their position.

"Well, I'm sure your unicorn will have fun in the sunlit uplands," Ray smiled.

After dinner and a bit of TV, Chloe went to sleep in her parents' bed again. Vicky would have preferred her back in her own bed, but Ray didn't mind. He thought it would be cute to have her in there again. Once they were alone, Vicky outlined ideas for how they could make sure Chloe could get the best out of the Special Educational Needs and Disability service that her school offered. And, although Ray engaged, he was never proactive. He was preoccupied with thoughts of the wounds on the torso in the river and what could possibly have made them. He didn't even notice the growing sharpness in Vicky's tone, or the peremptory nature of the kiss she gave him before going to bed.

The arms and legs were ripped off...

Chapter Thirteen

Krowos

Unlike The Shard, The Walkie Talkie, The Cheesegrater or The Gherkin, the office block that was the London headquarters of Global Actuaries Ltd had no name. Its twelve storeys of steel and glass displayed no innovative design, had no quirks and the building wasn't even brutal or ugly enough to elicit a negative response from passers-by. It was as bland and anonymous as the number crunching that went on within. It had been built in the 1990s to replace an equally uninspiring office building, which had been constructed in 1946 after a Nazi bomb had levelled its dull, Victorian predecessor. In fact, the site had been occupied by architecturally nondescript buildings since before the Norman Conquest. Anyone rewinding through time, looking at the dull nature of every structure that had ever been built on the site, might even conclude that someone didn't want any attention to be brought to that particular place. It was on the southern side of Candlewick ward in the City of London, a few hundred yards from London Bridge and only a couple of hundred yards from the Monument to the Great Fire of London in 1666. During the day, the area was all hustle and bustle. By midnight it was empty. Very few people lived there and after midnight most of the buildings were the lonely fiefdoms of nightwatchmen.

It was just after midnight when an electric black cab ghosted east along Cannon Street with a shimmering 'zzwing'. There wasn't much traffic, so the cab didn't have to wait to make the turn down the narrow road that separated the Global Actuaries Ltd building from its neighbours. The narrowness of the road and the height of the buildings either side of it gave the cabbie the feeling that he was driving into a fissure in the earth. Tommy was a big man – six foot and the better part of twenty stone. The vintage 2001 blue XXXL Millwall FC shirt that he was wearing barely concealed his large gut, which brushed against the steering wheel as he turned the corner. He smiled as he went into the dimly lit ravine – if there was ever a road that seemed like an entry to hell, this was it. How true it was! Especially for one of his passengers. In the back, Shiny Starrr lounged across the main seat. Opposite her, on one of the pulldown seats that faced backwards, sat The Man. Meanwhile, between their feet on the floor of the cab lay Harry, a seventeen-year-old who Shiny had picked up in a club the previous week. He was bound and gagged and covered by a black blanket. He lay still, because his struggles earlier in the journey had been met with punches, kicks and warnings of much worse if he didn't shut the fuck up.

Tommy pulled around to the back of Global Actuaries Ltd and positioned the cab as close to the door as he could. Shiny got out and pressed the intercom,

"It's me," she said, and a moment later the back door clicked and swung open.

Shiny held it and signalled to The Man. He got out of the cab in his deliberately slow way, then turned to grab Harry's feet. He slid him across the floor of the cab as if he weighed nothing, then eased him out and carried him, bundled in the blanket, towards the door. There was no need to hurry, because there were no security cameras covering the back of the building. Within seconds, Harry was inside.

"Thanks, Tommy! Laters, yeah?" Shiny smiled as she waved to the cabbie from behind the closing door,

"See you, Princess," Tommy replied, and the last view he had of Harry was The Man standing him up and taking the blanket off him. He looked young, disorientated and afraid. Then the door clicked shut. Tommy lit a cigarette and pulled away. As he turned right to go back up to Cannon Street through another ravine between the buildings, he thought about the boy and what was about to happen to him. It made his pulse quicken. One day, he would be part of the inner circle and he would be able to witness a sacrifice. The Man had told him that one day it would be so. And The Man was always right. All Tommy had to do was fulfil all that was required of him, and then... his hunger would be satisfied.

Over the course of the next hour-and-a-half, Tommy brought four other people to the back of Global Actuaries Ltd. The first was an elegant Chinese woman in her late fifties, who was the only person Tommy had ever met who smoked using a cigarette holder. He knew that she owned a string of restaurants, but not because she had told him. In three years of driving her and the other members of the inner circle to and from the office building, she had hardly spoken to him. The others had told him about 'Tiger Lil' and the brutal way she had built her restaurant empire. But even though she never talked to him, he didn't mind. After all, what were they going to talk about - recipes for sweet and sour pork balls? Tommy's next passenger was a handsome but tough-looking man of about thirty-five. He was an English aristocrat of the old school – terribly well-spoken with a cut-glass accent, who always tipped even though the ride was free, and who always enquired after Tommy's wife and family. In short, he was a gent. Normally, Tommy didn't like toffs, but this one was a Captain in the Household Cavalry and an expert sniper with a string of confirmed kills in some of the world's most dangerous places. That made him all right in Tommy's book.

Twenty minutes after delivering 'The Captain', Tommy was back with an ordinary looking man. He was of medium build with short brown hair that was going grey. Tommy reckoned he was probably about sixty and nothing about him seemed remarkable. He didn't even possess that spark or twinkle that special people always seem to have. So, why was he in the inner circle? The answer was simple. Pete Le Meat was the biggest trader in Smithfield meat market. He understood the appetites of Londoners better than anyone and that instinctive understanding extended to the rarefied appetites of Krowos. He knew how to satisfy the cravings of a god and was able to bring fresh sacrifices from any part of the country through his extensive meat supply network.

The final drop-off was Plain Jane. She was the trickiest one of the lot. She looked like the sort of friendly, cardigan-wearing, slightly befuddled post-menopausal woman you might expect to see organising a village fete. The reality was that she was a ruthless TV executive, who had access to a huge pool of young actors and presenters, most of whom would do almost anything for their big break in television. The entertainment industry has always been a beacon for those running away from broken families, those trying to erase their pasts to create new futures, and those who are alone in the world. Plain Jane was expert in targeting the most vulnerable, befriending them, ensuring that they would not be missed and then offering them to Krowos. Her mumsy, middle-class, bumbling bonhomie somehow made the eventual betrayal all the more vicious.

"Thanks, Tommy," she said as she heaved herself out of the back of the cab,

"I'll see you later," and then she swept her unkempt hair away from her face and moved in close to Tommy's open window,

"You'll have noticed that Marco isn't with us tonight..."

Tommy nodded,

"There's a very good reason for that," Plain Jane said with a knowing look,

"I wouldn't be surprised if next time you come here, you'll be the passenger and someone else will be doing the driving," and she smiled at him before going to the door and pressing the intercom. A few moments later she was inside. Tommy's heart was beating fast. So, that's how things were! Marco was out and he might be in. As he drove away, he realised that this could be the most important night of his life, and his mind was filled with fanciful imaginings of what it might be like to be one of the exalted servants of Krowos.

As the door closed behind her, 'Plain' Jane Hardiman blinked in the hard light reflecting off the scuffed white walls of the large service entrance. The hall must have been about twenty feet by twenty, with the stainless-steel doors of a large service elevator straight ahead. Set in the same wall, but in the right-hand corner, a set of double doors led to the main stairwell up into the building. In the centre of the wall to her right, a set of double doors opened onto the stairs to the basement and sub-basements. To her left, a service window was set into the wall with an unlit room behind it. Jane turned right and walked through the double doors and down the stark concrete stairs. Her kitten heels clattered loudly as she walked down four levels. It always amused her that however sparkling and opulent a building might be, as soon as one got to the basement stairs, every building was pretty much identical – dusty concrete, harsh lighting and a vague smell of damp. Unlike the simple push-bar exit doors of the basement and sub-basements A and B, the door leading to sub-basement C required an electronic key fob to open it. Jane wafted her fob at the panel on the wall, the door clicked and she opened it.

It was like entering the spa of a hotel. The floor went from dusty concrete to large Indian sandstone tiles, the lighting was mellow and the walls were a deep terracotta. Also, it was hot. It was always hot and, as usual, Jane immediately broke into a sweat which started on her upper lip, beading between the downy hairs that were the legacy of menopause. Straight ahead down the corridor, there was another security door, although this one looked more sophisticated than the previous one. Halfway down the corridor to the right, a wide archway opened into a large changing room, from which she could hear a couple of muted conversations. Jane clacked down the corridor – she hated being the last in, because it made her feel like she was holding everything up, even though their arrival times were outside their individual control. As she went through the arch, the conversations, inevitably, stopped and everyone turned to look at her.

"Hello," she said in her ever-so-friendly tone that never failed to calm even the most skittish actor or presenter,

"I won't be long," and she bustled over to the wall on the left of the door, where each member of the inner circle had their own arched recess with shelves to house their goods and chattels during the ceremony.

"No need to hurry," said Pete cheerfully in a voice made hoarse by years of smoking and shouting in Smithfield market.

Jane smiled back at him, but internally she was thinking that it was all well and good for him to say there was no hurry, but he was already changed and good to go.

He was standing nearby in a billowy crew neck white cotton robe with a pair of leather sandals on his feet. Otherwise, he was unadorned. He looked more like a hospital patient than someone about to summon a god. The other members of the inner circle were all dressed in the same, simple way. Even Shiny, who was taking her turn as high priestess for that ceremony, had no fineries and none of her usual bling. Unlike the invisible gods of the Abrahamic religions, the Hindus and others, Krowos was uninterested in fripperies. *He* had only one requirement for his ceremonies – blood. Aside from Jane, who was quickly divesting herself of her clothes, the only person in the room who wasn't wearing a ceremonial robe was The Man. He was standing on the other side of the room near the entrance to the elegant shower area, and he was naked. He stood, staring hard at Jane and seething. His body was pink, blotchy and hairless, with thin legs supporting a body that was stouter than it ought to be. Most of his fat was held on his belly, and the skin was taught and shiny. Like the buttons of his overtight coat, the skin of his tummy looked like it might burst at any moment. And yet, seen from behind, he hardly looked overweight at all.

Jane glanced at him and hoped that she hadn't done anything to annoy him. Even though he was a ridiculous figure when naked, with his thin arms and oversized, livid face adding to the general oddness, Jane knew the strength The Man had. If the urge came upon him, he could kill them all and even the good-looking Captain of the Household Cavalry wouldn't be able to save them. Then Jane noticed the one part of The Man she'd tried to blank out – he had a raging hard-on. A quick look at the Princess, Tiger Lil and The Captain confirmed her worst fear. All three of them had a defiled look of grubby shame about them. And it seemed like she was next. This didn't surprise her. At some point, everybody got fucked by The Man.

Tonight was just one of those nights. As always, Jane had mixed feelings about it. She was thoroughly repelled by The Man, but he was the best sexual partner she'd ever had. He could do things no one else could, but afterwards she was always left with the nauseating knowledge that she had let that creature inside her. Jane paused for a moment with such thoughts swirling in her head before taking off her knickers. Then she slipped them off and, before she could get into her ceremonial robe, The Man started to move towards her.

"Um... can I quickly go to the loo first?" Jane asked, but the look in The Man's eyes said 'No'. Whatever she needed to do, she could do it with him.

He stood directly in front of her, staring into her soul with his terrifying, blue eyes and breathing hard through his foul teeth. She was enveloped in his eggy breath and fought the urge to throw up. Not that her doing so would have stopped him. No bodily function put him off his stroke. He stretched out his right hand and put it on her left shoulder,

"Turn around and bend over," said the voice in her head and she complied. Jane felt the blunt end of his average-sized cock fumbling for an entrance, so she reached back to guide him. Against logic and every instinct she had, the touch of The Man had instantly made her wet and ready for him. Then, as he began to grind into her, he unleashed his true talent. The Man could do much more than simply communicate directly with someone's mind when he was touching them. He could stimulate any and all of their nerve endings to deliver unimaginable pleasure – or pain. Within seconds, Jane was a bucking, screaming alley-cat, caught in a firestorm of feral arousal, while the other members of the inner circle watched in grim fascination. They all knew the feeling of total helplessness and indescribable pleasure as The Man possessed every atom of her being. It was delicious liberation and bitter enslavement. None of them was surprised when Jane's bladder let go as The Man powered into her.

The show only lasted about five minutes, but it was more than enough. When The Man pulled out, Jane fell to her knees, sobbing hysterically. The other members of the inner circle moved away to give her space to recover herself, as The Man walked across the room and slipped on his ceremonial robe. While Jane was still on her knees, a fit-looking man in his fifties with neat salt-and-pepper hair walked through the archway into the changing room.

"Everything's ready out there," said the man who Mexican Dave called The Boss. His name was Simon Montague and he was the CEO of Global Actuaries Limited. He looked down at Jane,

"No hurry, though," he smiled, revealing his very white, very even teeth. Although he hadn't been the recipient of The Man's favours that night, he had experienced it often enough to have sympathy for Jane. The aftermath was always discombobulating, but it was much better than if The Man was angry with you. He had experienced that only once... Simon Montague closed his mind to the memory of the moment, but could recall the weeks it had taken to get over the shock.

Once Jane had got up and slipped into her robe, the group fell in behind Shiny and they processed down the corridor to the door at the far end. Shiny placed her hand on the screen next to the door, which scanned her fingerprints. After a moment, the door opened and they walked into the large, empty room beyond. It was dimly lit by red LEDs set into the ceiling and its rough walls were clearly ancient, with numerous depictions of human sacrifice carved into them. Above the old, nail-studded wooden door on the far side of the room was the same symbol of the elongated crystal through the centre of an infinity loop that had been tattooed on the chest of the man in Titheridge's 'playroom'. Being inside the room always gave The Captain the feeling of being in a submarine, because of the lighting and the constant hum of air being circulated by large, unseen fans. Shiny led them across the flag stoned floor, grasped the thick, round loop of twisted iron that was the handle of the wooden door and opened it. A stench of rotting flesh flooded out from the room beyond.

***

Harry Naylor's world had imploded three days earlier. He had been at a club, dancing and having a good time with some mates, when everything had started going swirly. He distinctly remembered wondering if someone had spiked his drink, but that was the last thing he'd known. When he'd woken up, he'd found himself in a basement room with nothing but a mattress on the floor, a sink and a toilet. He was fitted with a metal collar around his neck, which was attached by steel wire to a rail set into the ceiling. He quickly discovered that he could lie on the mattress and reach the toilet and the sink, but he couldn't quite reach the door. He had shouted himself hoarse in the first three hours and then a slot had opened at the bottom of the heavy security door and a tray with a bowl of some sort of weird porridge and a cup of water on it was shoved through. Before he could shout for help or remonstrate with whoever was there, the slot had closed. And that had become his world. No explanations, no sign of his kidnappers, just blank, faceless silence. Then The Man had arrived. And the pain had begun.

Now, Harry was standing naked with cable tie handcuffs attaching his hands to a chain behind his back. The chain was set into the top of an ancient stone monolith, which was covered with images of a nightmare creature feasting on humans. Harry's mouth was shut tight with duct tape and tears were streaming down his face as he desperately tried to scream for help with the last of his failing strength. The room was huge and round with only one door, which was made of old wood, studded with nails. Around the edges of the room, flaming torches in steel holders were the only source of light, and their flickering flames gave him glimpses of the horrific carvings on the walls. In the centre of the room, there was a large, round hole, which must have been about thirty feet wide. The whole floor was tiled in white and sloped gently towards the central hole, the edges of which were tiled like an expensive swimming pool so that the drop off into darkness was curved and smooth. There were three other monoliths at equal intervals around the room, each with a chain set into the top. Tonight, Harry was the only prisoner. Alone in a room that exuded terror.

What was in the pit? He looked at the stark delineation between the white of the tiles and the black of the hole. He didn't want to know. Whatever it was, it stank. Harry had to concentrate hard to stop himself gagging. If he threw up now, the gaffer tape over his mouth would surely make him choke to death on his vomit. What *was* in the pit? The darkness of the hole was unnatural, as if it was absorbing light like blotting paper. Did it matter? He couldn't see any way out. He was going to die right there in that stinking room. But WHAT WAS IN THE PIT? He couldn't stop his mind from coming back to that single, terrifying thought. Then the door opened.

A group of people in white robes trooped in, led by someone Harry recognised – that singer! What was her name? Something Starrr. It was on the tip of his... all thought stopped when he saw The Man. Harry involuntarily emptied his bladder. The sound of his urine splashing against the tiles seemed amplified by the near silence of the room. The Man leered at him. He clearly enjoyed what he saw. Yes, there was nothing quite like a naked young person with a glistening, beautiful body who was terrified to the point of pissing themselves... The robed figures formed a semi-circle on the far side of the hole in the floor so that they had a full view of Harry. It was as if they expected something to come out from the void below. Once they were all in place, the singer stepped forward and, to Harry's horror, she drew a large, ornately decorated knife. She walked towards Harry, who started thrashing and moaning, desperately begging for mercy, but only making inarticulate noises through the duct tape.

"Krowos!" Shiny Starrr cried out and the suddenness of it made Harry stop struggling against his restraints.

"Come to us," Shiny called out, "Accept our gift and advise us!"

Before Harry knew what was happening, Shiny stepped forward, ripped the duct tape from his mouth and slashed at his right forearm with the blade. Harry yelped in pain, but Shiny ignored him, carefully holding the dagger so no drops of blood were lost from it as she walked towards the hole. At the edge, she held the dagger at arm's length with the tip down. Slowly, Harry's blood ran down the gleaming blade, finally forming an ever-bulging drop. Shiny watched it carefully and, just before it had grown too fat to cling onto the blade, she called,

"Krowos, take this taste and come to us!"

Then the drop of blood fell into the silent, black void.

Shiny quickly moved to the far side of the hole to join the others and watch and wait. It made no sense to Harry. What the hell did the woman think she was...

Then a sound came from below.

It was a deep, resonant snort. The sort of sound a mastiff or a Great Dane would make. But whatever was down there sounded *much* bigger than that. The guttural growl which followed snapped Harry to his senses and he struggled with all his strength against the cable tie handcuffs. His instinct told him that he had to get out – even if that meant ripping off his hand to do it. As he pulled, the plastic of the cable tie dug deep into his left wrist and he saw blood dripping to the floor. Yes! That was the way. He had to tear through his own flesh and run. He was screaming and shouting, one moment pleading with the people in the robes, the next cursing them. All of them were looking at him and smiling horribly. Yes, they all enjoyed this part – the last burst of hope, which would inevitably be extinguished. There was another deep growl and, as Harry started thrashing like a hooked gamefish, there was the feeling of something big climbing up towards the top of the hole. The harder Harry struggled, the faster the thing in the hole climbed until, at last, there was a 'whumpf' that Harry felt more than heard. It was as if something massive had arrived and its bulk had caused the air in the room to compact to make space for the behemoth. Harry felt a pressure all over him and was finding the air difficult to breathe. And yet, there was nothing there. Harry looked at the robed figures and they were all staring as if they, too, were trying to see if something had joined them in the room. All except The Man. His watery blue eyes were fixed on a point just in front of the hole and the look of awe and horror on his face showed that he did see something. And that it terrified him.

Pete Le Meat stared at the scene of the lad tied to the rock. He was now still and trembling, knowing that something had emerged from the void, but not being able to see it. Pete wasn't sure which gave him more pleasure – when the sacrifice couldn't see Krowos, or when they could. The ones who couldn't see the Lord of Dimension always entered this pool of calm. They knew that something was terribly wrong and that Death had entered the chamber, but their physical senses told them that nothing was there. This calmed them and allowed the fading embers of their hope to kindle once more, just before they were utterly and spectacularly extinguished. Pete always wanted to laugh in this moment. When you already knew what was going to happen, seeing this brief glimmer of hope was brilliantly hilarious. And then there were the ones who had the gift or curse of extra-sensory perception. They could see exactly what came out of the darkness and they always screamed. Sometimes they stood paralysed with their gaping mouths emitting no noise at all, even when all the veins on their necks were standing out as they strained to vocalize their terror. They were the ones Krowos enjoyed the most, because only *he* could hear them. But whether they screamed aloud or not, they saw what few people had ever seen – a god. Most of them instantly lost their minds. To be faced with absolute truth was simply beyond the limit of most human brains. In a world of lies and constructs – society, religion, the financial system, love, family – seeing truth was a sledgehammer blow to the face. Here was the truth that showed them everything they had ever thought or believed in was nothing but smoke – insubstantial nonsense that obscured a reality they couldn't comprehend. Pete wondered what would happen to him if he, a believer, could see Krowos.

Tiger Lil watched the young man with eager, hungry eyes. No carnal experience came close to this in giving her pleasure. She could not see Krowos, but she could sense *him*, sense *his* power, and in a few moments the boy would experience it in all its excruciating glory. Tiger Lil looked hard, drinking in every detail – the terror in the boy's eyes, the clean muscular lines of his naked body, the rivulets of sweat across his taught stomach that ran into the neat patch of black hair above his genitals. Tiger Lil felt the bloom of pleasure in her own loins as if an expert tongue had circled her clitoris. This young man was perfect. The unseen god was sniffing the air. Lil could feel it. What would *he* do? What would...

Suddenly, the boy was lifted off the ground as if by a great hand. His arms strained behind his back as the cable tie cuffs held him to the now taught chain. Lil stared as every muscle and sinew in the boy's shoulders tensed to breaking. Then there was the squeal of pain as the unseen hand pulled the boy away from the chain, snapping the cable tie cuffs, which cut to the bone of his left wrist. As the chain clattered to the floor, the young man's blood spattered across the white tiles. That pleased Krowos. Oh yes, that excited *him*. Then the frenzy and the inhuman screaming began. Krowos went at the lad like a greedy person faced with an array of tempting treats. First, the lower half of his left arm disappeared, leaving the bloody stump of his elbow spraying blood. Then his right leg was pulled out to the side and twisted. There was the dull crack of his hip dislocating and the stomach-churning sound of ripping tendons and skin as the leg was torn off. It hung momentarily in the air next to its former owner, whose eyes were clouding with shock and the rapidly closing curtain of death. And then the leg was gone. Blood poured from the wound, but none of it was falling on the floor. It was being consumed by Krowos. With a grunt of pleasure that all *his* servants felt, the other leg, the genitals and lower torso disappeared as if bitten off in one great mouthful. The boy's entrails slipped down and out of the stump of his torso. Some splattered onto the floor, but his intestine was drawn out of him as if it were a length of spaghetti being sucked up by a messy child. When it was down to the last couple of feet of oesophagus, the ribbon of bloody flesh became taught. It seemed to be cut cleanly and the remnant snapped back into the body.

With a cracking of bones and sinew, the head was pulled off what was left of the body and it hung in the air. The once handsome face had contorted with the final agony of life ripped from it and the sightless eyes had cried blood before the release of death. The head disappeared, then first one arm, what was left of the other, and finally the distorted remains of the upper torso. All that was left to show that Harry Naylor had ever existed was a splattered pile of scarlet viscera on the stark, white tiles. And now they had come to the moment that The Man always feared the most. He could see it, but the others merely felt Krowos turn to look at them. Now was Shiny's time. She was the priestess; she would be the conduit for the one true god. She stepped forward and put out her hands with the palms facing upwards. After a moment, her eyes rolled back into her head, displaying only the whites. She turned to face the others and began to speak in a voice so deep and resonant that they felt it in their souls.

Chapter Fourteen

Swings And Roundabouts

The next day dawned with a glittering sun and a blue sky that seemed to go on forever. Of course, when Vicky and Chloe got up around nine, Ray was long gone.

"So, I've heard that they've finally re-opened the playground on the Common," Vicky said while making Chloe's toast,

"Wanna take a look?"

"Yeah!" Chloe said happily. After pushing the unknown stranger out of her mind the previous afternoon, she was feeling supremely confident. It was a glorious morning and she wanted to be out in it. They had breakfast, then they caught the bus down to Streatham Common and it wasn't long before they were getting off at a stop next to a wide stretch of grassland that swept up the hill and away from the main road. About five hundred yards up the slope, mature trees marked the beginning of the woodland that crowned the hill. The new playground was down near the main road, where the ground was level. It was only half past ten, but the place was already awash with kids running around laughing, screaming and revelling in the sunny day.

"Okay, so you go and knock yourself out – not literally, I don't want to spend the day in A&E – and while you're having fun, I'm going to get myself a coffee," Vicky said.

"Okay," Chloe smiled.

"And stay in the play area, or you won't get an ice cream," and Vicky gave her the serious look she always deployed when she wanted information to be taken seriously.

Chloe gave her a thumbs up and ran off to find something to play on.

What Chloe wanted to do was get on the swings, but they were busy. Why were swings always busy? Because they're ace, of course! Should she go and play on something else, or wait patiently for her turn on the swings? It was a tricky call. She knew how adults were impatient and had short attention spans, constantly moving from one activity to another, so if she did other stuff and then queued for the swings, there was a chance her mum would come over and announce they had to leave before she'd got on. No, she couldn't take that risk. She would stand enjoying the sun until it was her turn. It was almost ten minutes before she got her go, but the wait was fine. She was able to breathe the air and enjoy the way the green of the Common led up the hill until it seemed to touch the blue of the sky. Why was the sky blue? She was sure she'd been told, but couldn't remember. Anyway, now it was her turn on the swings.

When it comes to the great inventions of human history, most people point to things like the wheel, the lightbulb, the steam engine or the aeroplane. And yet, is there anything that can give such instant, unalloyed joy like a swing? Chloe got on, walked herself backwards to get the seat as high as she could and then pushed off. For the first few swings, she worked hard to get the momentum and then she was free! Suddenly only a small amount of extra effort would push her higher and faster, and with every swing she got that joyous feeling of weightlessness and that moment where she seemed to leave her stomach behind. Her face broke into a wide smile and then she was laughing. One moment, she was at the top of the backswing, looking down eight feet at the ground below; then she was swooping down at the ground at high speed; then being catapulted into the endless blue; then falling back to start it all again. A large poplar, which had been allowed to grow wild, stood about five yards on the other side of the fence marking the boundary of the play area. It was magnificent and gave shade for anyone wanting a picnic. As Chloe swung herself higher and higher, she felt like if she let go at the top of the swing, she'd be able leap high into the tree's branches. It was amazing. Chloe felt released - released from the control of parents, from the control of teachers and even from the bonds of earth and gravity. She was the mistress of her universe.

She swooped up to the top of the swing's arc, legs and arms straight, face to the heavens and the infinite blue. Then she dropped back through the arc, folding her legs under her and putting her arm, shoulder and stomach muscles into getting even more out of the backswing. She got to the top and looked down at the poplar ahead of her. That was when The Man stepped out sideways from behind the tree. And time stopped. While Chloe was frozen at the top of her backswing, high above the ground and unable to move, scream or even breathe, The Man raised his arms as if he wanted to catch her. In that moment, a darkness that was like the gateway to a void in space and time opened up. Unlike before, it didn't spread towards her, but opened in a large circle around The Man. Then he stepped to the side, so that he was clear of the great, black hole in reality. Chloe was still held at the top of the swing's arc and even though she was trying with all her might to use her newfound power to break free, she could only watch in horror as The Man grinned and pointed to the centre of the void. Then a sly voice sounded in her head in perfect sync with his red, cracked lips,

"Krowos is coming!"

And The Man nodded with a grin of unspeakable knowing.

Chloe wanted to close her eyes, to make it all go away, but she couldn't. And she didn't understand. What was Krowos? Who was this hideous man? What was he pointing at? And then Chloe saw it. Right at the centre of the darkness, there was a tiny point of light that was slowly getting bigger. Chloe could only watch as realisation slowly dawned. It wasn't a growing point of light. It was a thing that was scrabbling out from the void and getting closer and bigger with every passing moment. As it came, Chloe felt as if the air was tightening around her. Now it was big enough to see that it was some sort of animal scuttling towards her on many legs, which were flailing unnaturally fast, as if the creature was overcome with a madness to get to her. Why couldn't she close her eyes or look away? Now it was close enough for her to start seeing details. It had a plump, white, maggoty body that bulged and rippled sickeningly as it moved. And as it came towards her, Chloe could see that the legs weren't legs at all – they were more like the tendrils of a plant. They were fat and flexible, slick and slimy, so that as they haphazardly thrashed while scrambling towards her, viscous ooze flicked out from them. Behind the hellish creature, a thick cord trailed out from the rear end of the maggot's body. Chloe fought to close her eyes but couldn't and had to keep watching as the monster stampeded towards her.

The head and face were like those of a horribly warped human baby. The head was bloated, yellowish-white, hairless and without ears. It was heavy and out of proportion with the rest of the body, jerking this way and that as the tendril legs drove the thing towards her. But it was the face that caused Chloe to let out a silent scream. It had chubby cheeks and a protruding, bulbous forehead, but no eyes. Instead, at the point which should have been right between the eyes, the face was dimpled in, as if the thumbs of two great hands had pushed hard into the doughy, forgiving flesh. This distorted the entire face, so that the nostrils of the short nose didn't point down but faced forwards. Then there was the mouth. Three times wider than a normal mouth with thin, grey lips that barely covered the horrific array of shark-like teeth. And as the thing scrabbled out from the darkness, the mouth was snapping and salivating so that slime dripped from the fat chin.

Chloe still couldn't look away and had to watch as the thing got bigger and bigger and bigger until finally the eyeless face almost filled the black hole The Man had created. Tendrils gripped onto the edges of the dark hole and pulled the fat head through and into Chloe's world. The great, jowly face looked up at Chloe and the mouth with its sharp teeth grinned at her.

"Krowos!"

A voice boomed inside her head.

Then The Man clicked his fingers and suddenly Chloe was hurtling downwards on the swing as her internal scream erupted from her. She swung down, then up towards Krowos and, to her horror, she was losing grip on the swing. Her butt was slipping forwards and her hands seemed unable to hold on, and then she was thrown off the swing and she was flying forward straight towards the fat, babyish face. The huge mouth opened and the sharp teeth prepared to bite through her. She was screaming and waving her arms to stop herself, but she was falling into the ravenous jaws, which snapped across her midriff in a fountain of blood.

***

All of Ray's happy images of sleeping alongside his child were shattered by the scream. He shot bolt upright and fumbled for the light. In the first seconds of dazzling glare, he was able to assess that there was no danger in the room, and yet Chloe was screaming and writhing on the bed. Vicky had also been torn out of sleep and the look of shock on her face at seeing her daughter was the same as Ray's,

"Chloe! Chloe, wake up!" Vicky shouted, shaking her hard by the shoulder, but it was no use. Something in the dream wouldn't let her go.

Ray was now standing looking on as his daughter convulsed on the bed, emitting the most piercing shriek he'd ever heard.

"Shall I throw water over her?" he shouted to Vicky, who was shaking and had that disorientated look of someone who'd been dragged out of sleep.

"No. I'll have to change the sheets. Let's try to get her up."

And then they were manoeuvring Chloe to the edge of the bed, shaking her and trying to get her to stand. The screaming wouldn't stop but she was still asleep. Ray had a terrible feeling in his lower gut exactly like the one he got when he knew violence was about to kick off.

"Slap her!" he shouted to Vicky.

"Really?"

"It's that or the water."

"Okay..."

Vicky braced herself for the feelings she would have afterwards, knowing that she'd slapped her daughter, but this was frightening.

SLAP!

Vicky smacked the flat of her hand across Chloe's face with more force than she meant to.

"Shit!"

But it worked. Chloe's eyes opened and the scream turned to racking sobs. Vicky immediately hugged her tightly.

"It's all right," she said gently, "Everything's all right. It was just a dream."

"But... it... was... so... real," Chloe sobbed.

"I know. Sometimes dreams can be like that," Vicky said, "But look – here we are all safe in our room. Nothing scary here."

Chloe's breathing calmed down as she looked around the familiar room. Her parents were with her and she was safe. And yet...

"I saw that man again. He was in my dream."

"What man?" Vicky asked.

"The man I saw outside the window. The one Ray went to look for. He was there with a monster from the dark," and Chloe started to get agitated again.

"Hey, hey, stay calm, sweetheart," Vicky said, stroking her daughter's hair again.

Chloe was thinking about that thing from the dark and how it had torn her to pieces. The pain had been so real!

"Shall we try to snuggle down again? Before we do, do you need the loo?"

"No, it's okay," Chloe said in a small voice.

"Right, let's try to get back to sleep," Vicky said, fluffing Chloe's pillow and inviting her to snuggle onto it. Ray got up and went to the hall, switched the light on, half closed the door and came back to bed.

After a few minutes of fidgeting and trying to get comfy, it was clear none of them were falling asleep and Vicky whispered,

"Do you want to make a Chloe sandwich?"

"What's a Chloe sandwich?" Chloe said quietly, turning her head to look at her mum in the half-light of the room.

"Well, what happens is that Ray lies on his side facing out of the bed, then you lie on your side and snuggle right up to him and then I lie on my side and snuggle up to you. And that's a Chloe sandwich," Vicky said, giving Ray a sideways look that made it clear this was an offer he couldn't refuse. He smiled back at her. Yes, she'd sold him as part of it, but he was okay with that.

Chloe thought about it carefully. She'd be totally protected if anyone – or any thing - came to try to get her. They would have to get through her parents first and she couldn't imagine anyone being able to do that.

"Yes, please, I would like a Chloe sandwich," she said in a voice that was small and still vulnerable after her nightmare.

"Okay, then, let's do it," said Ray and he lay on his side.

Chloe eased herself into position against him and he could feel her heartbeat against his back. Then Vicky moved into position and lay her arm across Chloe and onto Ray.

"See you in the morning. Love you," Vicky said and the others responded in kind.

There was something soporific about the position and soon their breathing calmed down as they fully relaxed. Incredibly, Chloe was the first to fall asleep. Vicky could almost feel the moment it happened and she smiled to herself when she realised her daughter had dropped off. All she had to do now was fall asleep herself, but it wasn't quite so easy. Vicky lay there thinking about how unpleasant the incident had been. She'd never seen anything like it. What could have set Chloe off on such a vivid nightmare? Could she and Ray have handled it better? She couldn't imagine what else they might have done, but the memory of slapping her own daughter like that was unsettling. And although Ray had listened to her plans for Chloe and getting the most out of the school, she'd got the distinct impression that his mind had really been elsewhere. It was just like before. How could she turn their relationship around? Questions went around inside her head, but gradually each one span off into the darkness until there were no questions left and she slipped into sleep. In the end, only Ray was left awake. He wasn't happy. Something was seriously off and he couldn't grasp exactly what. He looked at it logically. Chloe had been fine until this week. Yes, she had visual stress; yes, she struggled with writing and reading; and yes, she saw auras which other people didn't see, but this week she'd gone off the deep end. What had changed? The child psychologist. Before Chloe had gone in there, she'd been happy-go-lucky. Now she was having screaming nightmares. Why had Vicky insisted on getting her checked out?

But those were vague thoughts. What really kept him up was work. What the hell was going on? He felt that he wasn't seeing the big picture. There was something between Titheridge, Elizabeth Russell and the torso in the river, but what? He felt like he was going around and around the edge of something, but however hard he tried to get to the middle, he seemed to be pushed away. He couldn't shake the feeling that Ms Russell of the Treasury was playing him. Well, in the morning, he'd get ahead of things. He and Andy would check through the CCTV footage from the bridges across the Thames, then they'd go and see Belinda's contact about the torso's stomach contents. And Emma was bound to come up with something about the brand on the body. Yes, he could rely on Emma to deliver. Finally, Ray slipped off into sleep with thoughts of Emma looking up into his face to give him some good news.

Chapter Fifteen

Seven Dials

Ray awoke from his broken and troubled sleep feeling like he'd been put through a mangle. He gently kissed Vicky and Chloe without waking them and then dragged himself into work. Fortunately, the morning went like clockwork. Andy had fully briefed Emma the previous evening on the trafficking gangs and she had launched into her research with gusto. Then Ray, Andy and a couple of unlucky constables had reviewed the CCTV footage from the bridges over the Thames. Although they'd found no evidence of bodies being slung off any of the bridges, it had been a bit of simple, honest work. And it told them that whoever dumped the body in the river wasn't totally stupid, because they'd done it away from the security cameras that filmed almost everything the Great British public did. Once they'd finished watching the last of the footage, Andy got up from his chair and stretched.

"I'm getting a coffee," he announced, "Anyone want a coffee?"

"I thought you'd never bloody ask!" Ray exclaimed, "I'll have a cappuccino and a double espresso."

"Right. What about you two?" Andy looked at the constables, one of whom shook his head, while the other indicated that his bottle of water was quite sufficient.

"Saves me money. Meet you back here?" he said to Ray.

"No, I'll see you back in my office."

"Amazeballs," Andy yawned and sloped off, while Ray tasked the two constables with the fun job of reviewing all the available CCTV footage from the north and south banks of the river between London Bridge and Wandsworth.

When Ray got back to his office, Andy was lounging and sipping his coffee,

"What now, hotshot?" Andy asked as Ray opened the lids on his two drinks.

"Now we fuel up," he replied, using a biro to push the froth of his cappuccino aside to see if there was enough room for the espresso. There was, and he poured it in, then carefully stirred it with the biro as he continued,

"Then we get off our arses and meet up with Belinda's expert in ritual sacrifice," and he brandished a piece of paper at Andy,

"I've got a full list of our torso's stomach contents and she assures me that if anyone can help us, it's this Professor Jenkins."

Andy brightened up,

"Which university are we going to? I hope it's King's. I like King's. Great student bar."

"According to Professor Jenkins' secretary, today is his day off and we'll find him in his shop," Ray said, then took a grateful sip of his espresso-cino.

"An academic running a shop? What sort of shop?" Andy asked – this sounded fishy already.

"I don't know," said Ray, "But I can reveal that it's called – and you're gonna love this – it's called 'Esoterica'."

Andy exploded with laughter,

"Esoterica! What's he sell – canned bullshit?"

"I'm guessing it's items of an esoteric nature?" said Ray, silently thanking God for coffee.

"So, literal cans of literal bullshit," Andy replied, "And you really think this charlatan's going to be able to help us with our ritual killing?"

"That's what Belinda says. Apparently, he's a friend of a friend."

"And where will we find this friend of a friend bullshit vendor?" Andy asked.

"Seven Dials – Monmouth Street," Ray said.

"Of course! Where else but that hub of rigorous intellectual activity. Yeah, as leads go, this sounds like a banker!" Andy laughed.

And now Ray had said it out loud, it did sound ridiculous.

"Plus side," said Andy, "I think The Crown is a Greene King pub, so at least we can get a halfway decent pint after, to wash away the lingering taste of..."

"Bullshit?" said Ray.

"You got it, chief!" said Andy, raising his cardboard cup in salute to Ray's genius.

***

Certain activities and circumstances seem to persist in particular areas of big cities, no matter how the march of time changes the world around them. The area of St Giles in the Fields in London has always attracted the sick, the destitute and the darkness that follows in their wake. Since it was between the ancient City of London and the City of Westminster, St Giles was deemed the perfect place for a leper colony. For four hundred years until the mid-fifteen hundreds, lepers had a haven there and, after that, those stricken by poverty could not resist being drawn to the area. During this time, the crossroads at St Giles' Circus was the site of a gallows, where witches, criminals and traitors were hanged. One such damned soul was Sir John Oldcastle, who was hanged and set on fire as he was hanging – though not before he had cursed the King, the executioner and the ground on which he died. Eventually, Tyburn, at the far end of Oxford Street, became the favoured place of public execution, but the condemned would stop at St Giles for a 'St Giles Bowl' – a final drink before their death. The Great Plague of sixteen sixty-five started at St Giles, which became the site of a large plague pit. In the eighteenth and nineteenth centuries it became famous as 'the rookery', a pestilential warren of filthy slums where misery piled on misery for those unfortunate enough to call it home. Even when the slums were torn down and modern buildings took their place, St Giles was a hub for the homeless and a beacon for the damned, with the serial killer Dennis Nilsen working in the local job centre.

It was also a centre for the occult and, around the Seven Dials, shops dealing in magic, mysticism and astrology flourished from the nineteen sixties onwards. 'Esoterica' on Monmouth Street was one of those shops. As Ray stood looking at the window display of crystals, dreamcatchers, 'magic' wands, scented candles and all the usual paraphernalia of pseudo-occultism, he seriously began questioning Belinda's recommendation. After Ray had spent a few minutes contemplating the nonsense in the window and enjoying the sunshine, Andy trudged down the street towards him,

"Parking round here is next to fucking impossible," he complained, wiping the sweat from his forehead, "It's not Seven Dials, it's seven circles of hell."

"I thought there were nine circles of hell?" said Ray.

"This adds up to nine if you include New Oxford Street and Shaftesbury Avenue," Andy said bitterly.

"All right let's be calm. We got work to do... and tuck your shirt in - I don't want you embarrassing me in front of the professor," Ray replied, opening the door as Andy struggled to shove as much of his shirt back into his trousers as he could.

Inside, they were unsurprised to find the place stank of incense. Ray thought about the stalls near Brixton station with their colourful arrays of different types of incense that all smelt the same, no matter what weird and wonderful ingredients were supposedly in them. The shop itself seemed a relic of the twentieth century. Unlike other shops in the neighbourhood that used modern ideas of light and space to display their wares without overloading the senses of the customer, the décor in Esoterica was dark and the place was like a jumble sale. Items seemed to have been piled onto any available surface with little apparent rhyme or reason, while every inch of wall space was taken up with heaving bookshelves. As Andy closed the door, an electronic chime rang in a room in the back of the shop and then they heard the sound of someone approaching. A thin man in his late forties with a bushy black beard pushed his way through the curtain of beads in the back doorway,

"Hello, can I help you?" he asked in a deep baritone voice.

Andy said nothing. He was staring at the man, who was wearing an ill-thought-out combination of a baggy T-shirt with a print of a Marijuana plant, VERY short cut-off jean shorts revealing thin legs covered in black hair and a pair of brown crocs with beige socks.

"I'm Detective Inspector Ennis and this is Detective Sergeant Harper. Are you Professor Jenkins?"

"Ah, yes! And I believe you're here to talk about ritual sacrifice," he said with a gleam in his eyes as he rolled the words 'ritual sacrifice' around in his mouth,

"I'd offer you a seat, but..." and he indicated the cramped shop full of clutter.

"Standing's fine," Ray smiled, "And thanks for helping us. I'm afraid I can't go into too much detail, because of the ongoing investigation, but we'd like your opinion on these ingredients," and he produced the piece of paper and handed it to Professor Jenkins, who looked down the list. As he did so, he made confirmatory noises at certain entries, then smiled and grimaced at a couple of others before finally looking back at the two men.

"Yes, this is an extensive checklist for what we would expect to find in the stomach of someone sacrificed during the late Iron Age. I'd say it leans more towards the European tradition than the British."

"In what way?" Ray asked.

"No traces of mistletoe, such as the mistletoe pollen found in the gut of Lindow man."

"Lindow man?" Ray inquired.

"The body of a man who was clubbed on the head, garrotted and had his neck broken before being dumped into a peat bog sometime between two BC and a hundred and nineteen AD. He's named after Lindow Moss, which is the peat bog where he was found up in Cheshire."

Andy and Ray looked at each other: the professor might look a bit bonkers, but he spoke with a quiet authority.

"But it's not what's similar about these ingredients to those of other sacrificial victims that draws my eye, it's the differences. Yes, flax seeds, barley, pale persicaria – yawn, yawn, yawn," he continued, miming a great yawn,

"But this list contains nettle, yarrow, sage, rosehip, calendula and, tellingly, dandelion root and buckthorn berries," but although his eyes glinted with the spark of enlightenment, Professor Jenkins could see that the two policemen were still in the dark.

"Those are all purifying herbs. Most of them are anti-inflammatory, some are diuretic, calendula will make you sweat like crazy and, if either of you were women, yarrow could stimulate your menstrual flow."

Andy and Ray looked at each other.

"Then, of course, dandelion root and what are sometimes known as 'purging' buckthorn berries will clear out your bowels in double-quick time," the professor concluded.

"Okay, so this is a good cleanse. So what?" said Ray.

"Other human sacrifices have not been cleansed in this way and a number have been found to have ingested materials with psycho-active properties. Like mistletoe or ergot. But *these* ingredients would leave a person very clean inside. After this lot, I doubt you'd have much sweat, urine or faeces left in you... Hm!" the professor chuckled, "It's almost as if..."

"As if what?"

The professor pondered for a few moments and then said,

"Put it like this, if you went fishing tomorrow and caught yourself a big, fat carp, you wouldn't want to eat it right away,"

"Why not?" Andy asked.

"Because their guts are full of mud and all kinds of oomska. So, what you do is take your carp home alive and release it into a cool, freshly drawn bath. Leave it in there overnight and it'll empty all the crap from its bowels into the water. Then you can eat your carp without all the muddy, nasty bits. If this," and he held up the piece of paper,

"Is anything to do with human sacrifice, then it would lead me to wonder whether the sacrificial man or woman was going to be eaten afterwards."

"Oh..." Ray had not been expecting that.

"Yes, someone who'd been fed all this would be purified spiritually and physically. Their flesh would be pure. If I'd gone to all the trouble of putting this shopping list together and feeding it to someone, I don't think I'd be wanting to waste all that pure flesh after the event," the professor said with a faraway look in his eyes and his deep voice resonating within the small shop.

Ritual killing and possible cannibalism! Ray sighed internally – this case was getting better and better!

"Is there any evidence of cannibalism in your case?" the professor asked.

Only if the arms, legs and head are the first bits on the barbecue!

Ray put that thought aside and soberly replied,

"I'm afraid we can't comment on the case itself."

"Of course. Of course – yes, you just said that. Sorry."

"Not a problem," Ray waved away the apology, "But how difficult is it to get these ingredients?"

"Some of them are a bit specialist, but most of them are within the reach of even the amateur forager – especially now that the internet is there to tell people how to do it," Professor Jenkins replied,

"You'll also find a lot of them in some of the shops around here. You know what this area is like for astrology, folk remedies and so on."

"Can you give us the names of the shops?" Andy asked.

"Certainly. Although I wouldn't bother trying all of them. The two that I'm pretty sure carry all these ingredients are The Herbalist and The Dead Zone,"

Ray and Andy looked at the professor quizzically,

"Yes, I know," he said, "The Dead Zone sounds ridiculous and, believe me, it has even more ridiculous décor, but they do know their stuff," and then Professor Jenkins gave them the addresses, while Andy noted them down.

"But the bottom line is, you can find any of these within spitting distance of London. Although there is one thing I would say..." and he looked thoughtful before continuing,

"This doesn't feel modern."

"How do you mean?" Ray asked.

"Some people might direct you towards druids to ask them what they think about all this..."

"Druids? Like in Asterix books?" Ray's entire knowledge of druids was drawn from Asterix.

"No – and that's precisely the problem," said the professor, and his deep voice filled the room as he became steadily more agitated,

"The ancient druids, who are likely to have been in charge of the sacrifice of Lindow Man, were utterly destroyed by the Romans. And because they only kept their history by word of mouth, all their knowledge disappeared with them. Any druids you find today are modern druids - basically an eighteenth-century re-boot with no real connection to the druids annihilated by the Romans. As far as I'm concerned, they're a bunch of poseur hippies who have no idea what they're doing, but who would be happy to waste your time with their neo-pagan charlatanry."

After the professor finished, the shop became still once more, but the air seemed charged like a heavy afternoon after a peel of thunder.

"Thank you very much for that warning, professor, and thank you for your time today," Ray said, shaking him by the hand.

"My pleasure, and if I can be of any more help in your case, please don't hesitate to call my office," the professor replied, before shaking Andy's hand.

Ray went to the door and opened it, then part closed it again as he turned and said,

"Oh yeah, Belinda sends her regards."

"Thank you. Yes, dear Belinda. Such a brilliant mind – such deliciously gruesome anecdotes at dinner parties!" the professor smiled with a wicked gleam. Ray and Andy smiled back and then stepped out into the street. Once they were a few yards away, Andy said,

"Shit dress sense, but I quite like him."

"You're weird. You do know that don't you?" Ray replied.

"Watch it, or I'll slip some yarrow in your tea and sit back to watch the crimson tide drown you."

"Nice," Ray said, "Good to see that the sensitivity training hasn't been lost on you."

Andy gave a little bow of thanks.

"Now, come on," said Ray seriously, "Let's try one of these herbalist shops he recommended and see what we can find out. Where's the nearest?"

"Neal Street," said Andy.

"Great. We'll go back to the top of the street and round the corner."

"That's not great at all," said Andy, shaking his head.

"Why not?"

"Cos the pub's the other way."

Chapter Sixteen

The Herald Rides Out

When Mexican Dave got word that Ray would be in Seven Dials around one o'clock, he had dashed straight out of the homeless shelter in the heart of St Giles and hopped on his bike to pelt across town to Candlewick and the offices of Global Actuaries Ltd. After the ceremony the previous night, the Word had come down that Krowos, the Lord of Dimension, wanted to see Ray for himself. The god wanted to size the man up. Although this wasn't unknown, it wasn't a regular occurrence. Usually, new nominations to the inner circle were assessed inside the temple. If Krowos liked them, everything was fine, if he didn't, then he would simply devour them. But there were times when the god heard about someone and wanted to see them in action. Ray was being accorded that privilege. Now they knew exactly where he would be, Mexican Dave would have the honour of leading the way and announcing the god's presence to the people. He thought this was a great day indeed as he freewheeled down to the back door of the building, jumped off the bike and pressed the intercom,

"Hoots, mon, it's me!" he cried in his dreadful approximation of a Scots accent, and the door opened.

Given the circumstances, he didn't have to stand on ceremony and, after plunging down the basement stairs two at a time, he crashed through to the circular chamber and marched over to the edge of the gaping black void of the hole. He stretched out his left arm, pulled up the sleeve and used his pen knife to slice into his skin. He didn't need much blood, just enough to attract the god. He squeezed and the drops fell into the darkness. Then he heard the sound of movement and he stood back from the edge. Although Mexican Dave worshipped Krowos, he didn't fully understand how *he* worked. He knew that inside the temple, no human could stand against the god. Krowos could crush anyone who was inside the temple. However, outside the temple, Krowos could only physically touch those who could see him and, since the only people who could see him were those blessed with extra-sensory perception, that meant that over ninety-nine percent of the population were out of the god's reach. While Krowos ate most of the people who could see him, some (such as The Man and Mexican Dave himself) were spared, given a scintilla of the god's power and allowed to serve his needs. This service usually involved kidnapping, killing or physically abusing those who couldn't see the god and therefore those whom the god couldn't touch. Mexican Dave, The Man, Roaming Rohit and others were, almost literally, the hands of a god. However, hand of a god or not, Mexican Dave knew that Krowos might accidentally crush him as he emerged from the pit if he didn't shift his arse and get out of the way.

As always, the emergence of Krowos from the pit filled Mexican Dave with awe, fear and the feeling that he was on the winning team. He could feel, more than hear, the god's instructions and Mexican Dave led the way up through the building to the back door. This simple act revealed another aspect of Krowos that Mexican Dave couldn't understand. Even though the god stood over ten feet high, he was able to pass through the stone and steel of the building. And yet, when it suited *him*, Krowos could pick up physical objects, like a block of stone, or a car. Mexican Dave couldn't fathom it. This was in a large part because of another aspect of Krowos' power – almost everyone who saw him instantly lost their minds. Only those who had some sort of spiritual protection, or who had perfected their psychic powers could look on Krowos and maintain their sanity. Mexican Dave emerged into the sunshine, adjusted his sombrero so that it wouldn't come off as he rode ahead of the god, and got on his bike.

"Make way for Krowos, the Bringer of Pain!" he shouted as he emerged from the narrow side road and turned left into Cannon Street. Naturally, every person who noticed him immediately disregarded what he said as nonsense. You don't get truth from idiots cycling around wearing sombreros. In fact, moments after he had passed, almost all the people who heard him couldn't even remember what he'd shouted.

Michael Tanner was having a lovely lunch. Admittedly, he was sitting at his desk, but he had a nice view of Cheapside and enjoyed the way the sunshine lit up the gold embellishments of the big, square clock on the side of the building at the end of Ironmonger Lane. Also, he had a proper club sandwich – a double-decker with carved turkey, smoked back bacon, heritage tomatoes, lamb's lettuce and plenty of mayonnaise. He'd just taken a big bite and was revelling in the taste sensations when he saw a man in a sombrero cycling down the street. Bit odd, but then it was Lond... his pupils instantly became like dinner plates, his mouth (full of food) fell open, the sandwich dropped to the desk and his bladder let go. What was *that*? What *was* that? WHAT WAS THAT? The thing was there in the middle of the street! Why wasn't everyone running? Didn't they see it? It paused momentarily and looked over its shoulder right at him and then he started laughing. The suddenness of his loud, harsh laughter made Suzie at the next desk spill her latte,

"Blimey, Michael!" she exclaimed, grabbing some tissues to blot the coffee on her desk. She was about to have a go at him, but when she turned around, she stopped.

Michael was laughing, but his face was a twisted nightmare of anguish and despair. Tears were rolling down his cheeks as he laughed and laughed, staring fixedly out of the window.

"Michael, are you all right?" she asked, but he kept on laughing and now each loud 'Haaa' was drawing out into a primal cry. Half-chewed sandwich was falling from his mouth and his face was going red as he strained out each laugh. Finally, he ran out of breath and drew in air with an even more disturbing, drawn-out 'Huuuuuuurgh', before laughing again.

"Michael?" Suzie cried, getting up and going to him. She clicked her fingers in front of his face and shook him by the shoulder, but he could only stare and laugh. With every passing moment, the laughter was getting more strained and every vein in his neck and face was fit to burst through his taught skin.

"Er... I'll get help!" Suzie said and grabbed her desk phone to dial reception.

Michael didn't really hear her trying to explain what was going on and that they needed a First Aider and maybe the defibrillator. All Michael could hear was the screaming of his own blood rushing through him as his heart beat at two hundred BPM. He didn't even know he was laughing. All he knew was what he'd seen, and what he'd seen had destroyed reality. Everything was wrong! Everything he'd ever been taught, everything he'd ever thought – all of it was nonsense. In the moment when the thing had looked over its shoulder at him, everything that had tethered him to a universe that he understood had snapped. Now he was floating in the chaos of truth, while the thing continued its journey west along Cheapside. Externally, Michael was still shrieking with the laughter of utter despair – loud, abrasive and the stuff of nightmares. It was a blessing when the catastrophic cerebral aneurysm hit. Michael stopped laughing as suddenly as he'd started. Suzie turned and looked at him, at his empty eyes staring at nothing. Then he crashed face first into the desk and slumped to the floor.

Angel Ibeh was near St Paul's Cathedral, waiting to cross the road where New Change meets Cheapside. She was nervous. The job interview would start in about an hour, but her guts were already twisting themselves into knots. It wasn't even like the job in advertising data analysis was that amazing, but she really wanted the higher pay. Should she say that in the interview? Of course not! Pull yourself together, Angel!

"Make way for the all-seeing Master of Reality!"

The shout made her look. She didn't even see Mexican Dave. She only saw Krowos, swaggering towards the junction. Her last word was,

"Shit," and then she quite deliberately stepped out in front of the truck that had sped up to catch the light before it changed. She couldn't live in a universe with that thing in it. Angel stepped out so late that the driver never even saw her. In the blink of an eye, her body was crushed, dragged, broken and spat out of the back of the truck. The cab following it slammed on its brakes and two seconds later, three cars had piled into it.

As Mexican Dave led the Destroyer of Hope from Cheapside onto the A40, he laughed loud and long. Yes! Yes, you worms – tremble before the one, true god. And he laughed uproariously when they got to Holborn and a man threw himself out of his office window. Best of all was the look on the face of the woman who was about to go down the stairs at Chancery Lane tube station. She had seen Krowos just as she was about to take the first step down. The double look of shock as she simultaneously realised that everything she'd ever known was wrong and that she was falling headlong down the stairs... fuck, that was priceless! Then she was gone, falling down two flights of stone stairs which had solid brass inlaid to protect the lip of each step. By the time she reached the bottom, she had broken her right shoulder, her jaw, her left ankle, three ribs and her neck. Sadly, for Allison Fitch, she didn't die that day.

By the time Mexican Dave took the left turn onto Shaftesbury Avenue, three people were dead and four had gone insane. It was one of the best days of his life and he shouted,

"All praise the mighty and powerful Krowos, Lord of Dimension!"

A few people turned to look at him briefly, but none of them saw the god in their midst. Mexican Dave cackled. If only they knew, they'd all be pissing their pants and then begging him to put in a good word for them with the god. The lights changed and he led the way to the point where Neal and Monmouth streets meet. He indicated for Krowos to stay where he was, while he checked out the shop to see if they were still there. After pushing off, he was able to freewheel to the shop. Yes, there they were, talking to some bearded weirdo. He turned to look back to the end of the street and gave a double thumbs up to his one, true god. Now was the time for stealth, so he wheeled his bike a little way down the street and took off his sombrero, so that it hung down behind his back. After a few minutes the two men came out of the shop and started walking up the street straight towards Krowos. Mexican Dave gesticulated wildly to indicate that these were the men they had come to see. Krowos nodded and concentrated on Ray. Yes, there was something there, a real strength of purpose. Krowos could understand why his servants had recommended this man. Yes, a man like this might be very, very useful.

Chapter Seventeen

Florence

Florence Gichuru had been working in 'The Herbalist' on Neal Street for five years since moving to Britain from Kenya. She came from a small town about twenty miles inland from Mombasa and she, like all the women in her family, had been born with The Gift. Ever since she could remember, she had been able to feel and see things that her friends couldn't. As a girl, she had made friends with the spirit of a little boy, who had died falling out of a tree and whose spirit had somehow tethered itself to the life energy of that tree. He didn't understand why he was there and he was lonely, so was very happy that Florence could see and hear him, but he was always a little sad, because he knew that he shouldn't really be there. Eventually, Florence and her mother had helped him transfer to the spirit world and she had felt a burst of joy and peace at the moment of his passing.

However, The Gift also opened up a darker world. She quickly discovered that many spirits that do not pass on are mean and unpleasant. They are often held here by their own avarice, their anger at dying or their hatred of those that have outlived them. She remembered the old woman who haunted the crosswalk at the end of her road. All that the average person felt when they were standing at that crosswalk was perhaps a chill in the breeze, but Florence could see and hear her. If anyone came by, the woman would shout and swear at them, cursing their life and bemoaning her death. But she reserved her worst curses and threats for Florence, because she knew she could see her. Over time, Florence had got used to such beings, although when she'd moved to London she hadn't been quite prepared for the sheer number of them. But all in all, she was chilled out and used her Gift to supplement her income at the shop by holding seances. Her time at 'The Herbalist' had been a happy one and she was proud that the stock they offered was the real deal – unlike some other shops in the neighbourhood that she could think of. The shop itself was a positive space in which to work and a lot of thought had been put into making it an intriguing and fun place to visit. Everything was neatly laid out from herbs, to books, to specialist tools for witches and those interested in the arcane arts.

Florence was sorting out the orders for the next month when the bell on the door of the shop rang. She looked up from the computer and her breath caught in her throat. What was THAT? Two men had entered, but she couldn't take her eyes off the creature that was bending down to look at them through the window. Involuntarily, she clutched at the protective amulet she wore on an amber necklace beneath her jumper and said a prayer to her ancestors under her breath. She could sense the thing outside feeling for her soul. Somehow, it saw her as a threat and it was trying to break down her defences, but she was strong and stood firm, then one of the men started talking at her,

"Hello, I am Detective Inspector Ennis of the Metropolitan Police, this is Detective Sergeant Harper. Would you mind helping us with an enquiry?" Ray said, smiling his most friendly smile.

The woman behind the glass-topped counter looked to be in her early thirties and was very pretty, but seemed overcome by dread at seeing them.

"Miss?" Ray said as Florence stared past them at the entity that was squatting outside the door. Then she realised that it couldn't come in. Her protection was too powerful. The dread faded from her eyes and a serene look came over her, then she shook her head slightly and looked at the two men,

"I am sorry. You must think me very rude," she said in her Kenyan accent that delivered each word with a precision that left a distinct space between each one.

"Sorry if we startled you," said Ray.

"It is not you, it is what you have brought with you that has shocked me," she said, looking over Ray's shoulder with her big brown eyes.

Ray looked confused, then half turned to see Andy standing behind him,

"Would you be more comfortable if my colleague remained outside?"

Internally, Andy was hoping she'd say yes, because he'd be straight down The Crown for a pint.

The woman behind the counter smiled broadly and replied with a chuckle in her voice,

"No, it is not the man with you. It is the other..." and she indicated toward the door with her head.

Ray and Andy both turned to look, but could see nothing but the street and shoppers wandering up and down. Andy turned back and Ray gave him a 'WTF?' look. Andy gave the slightest of shrugs and then Ray turned back to the shop assistant. She gathered herself and began,

"I think we have started on the wrong foot. I am Florence Gichuru. I am a herbalist and medium. How can I be of assistance?"

"We're investigating a case and wanted to know if we could get any of these ingredients here," said Ray, handing the list over to Florence.

She started to read it, but kept looking up at something behind the two men. Andy felt a vague shiver run down his spine. Things were getting a bit weird and he wasn't sure he liked it.

"Sorry, but I am finding it difficult to concentrate with that 'other' out there. Can we go into the back where we can sit and talk?"

"Of course," Ray replied.

"Great. I'll lock the shop and then we can have a drink," said Florence, coming around the counter and walking over to the door. She was wearing a pair of sky-blue linen trousers, flip flops and a light jumper in rainbow colours that looked like it had been knitted at home. She approached the door carefully, holding onto something next to her chest under the jumper, and pulled the top bolt as if she was afraid something might burst through the window at her. All the while, she was muttering under her breath.

"We've got a right one here," Ray whispered.

"Giving me the creeps!" Andy whispered back, while Florence turned the store sign to 'closed' and quickly stepped away from the door.

"Good. Now we will not be disturbed. Follow me, gentlemen," she said as she led them through an archway into the back of the shop.

On the far side of a stock room that had a set of stairs down to a basement, there was a cosy little kitchen with a table big enough to seat four at one end. Florence motioned for the men to sit down and said,

"Tea? Coffee?"

Ray and Andy looked at each other. They were of the same mind.

"Tea please," Ray replied, "Milk no sugar for me, and a dash of milk and three sugars for my colleague."

"I'm not sweet enough already," Andy quipped, but it was lost on Florence, who had flicked the kettle on and was now staring out of the back window into the small courtyard beyond.

"Anything wrong?" Ray asked.

"Nothing," Florence replied and got three mugs down from the cupboard. She didn't notice the hairline crack in the handle of the mug she was using for her coffee, because she was too preoccupied with the thing that was now sitting in the middle of the courtyard watching them intently.

"So, that list?"

"Yes, sir," Florence replied, pronouncing 'sir' as 'sah'. She had another look at the list,

"Yes, we have all of these things here – except buckthorn berries. It is not the season yet and we are out of our supplies of freeze-dried berries. I would have to order these in, but we will have them back in stock in the autumn."

"Do you have any customers who might have purchased all of the items?" Ray knew this was a punt, but why not?

"I think I would remember a shopping list like this," Florence said, pouring the boiling water onto their tea bags and her instant coffee. Then she turned back to Andy and Ray,

"May I say something?"

“Yeah, ‘course,” said Ray.

“The crime you are investigating must be very serious. That thing would only come out if it was very serious,” and she pointed towards the courtyard.

Mad as a brush. Those were the words going through Ray’s head, while Andy made a mental note to watch her very carefully when she was putting anything into his tea.

“Do you see something out there now?” Ray asked, although he already knew the answer.

“Yes, but there is no point in you looking for it. You do not have the sight.”

“How convenient,” said Andy in a low voice.

“It is not convenient; it is very fortunate for you. If you are unprotected and can see it, I am sure it would kill you,” and Florence took the bags out of the mugs and prepared their tea.

“But you are protected?” Ray asked.

“Yes, I have powerful magic,” said Florence as she brought the mugs of tea and coffee to the table. She sat down and reached into her jumper, pulling out a necklace of amber beads, with a black stone amulet on it. She showed it to them on the flat of her palm. There were designs and what looked like words carved into it. Once they’d had a good look at the amulet, she put it back down her jumper,

“While I wear this it can do me no harm.”

“But what is ‘it’?” Ray asked, unable to resist.

“I do not know. It looks young and not yet fully formed, but it is powerful and it is hungry.”

“For what?”

“For you,” Florence said, looking directly at Ray.

“Me? Why me?” asked Ray.

“I do not know. Perhaps it sees you as a threat? Or perhaps you have something it wants. I thought it was interested in me, but it is clearly you it wants.”

Ray had had just about enough of this bollocks and said,

"And is it interested in DS Harper?"

Andy scowled – the last thing he wanted was to be dragged into this madness.

"That I cannot say, but you must take this seriously. If a creature like that is after you, it will get you in the end."

While Ray had to restrain himself from snorting with derision, Andy found Florence's conviction about what she was saying very persuasive. He wasn't sure whether it was simply the effect of having tea on a hot afternoon, but he was suddenly feeling sweaty.

"Listen, if I can tell you something about your case, will you take me seriously?"

"Yeah, I s'pose," said Ray.

"Take my hands," Florence ordered and he reluctantly did so. Florence closed her eyes and evened out her breathing, then said,

"Relax and think about your case."

Ray looked over at Andy and rolled his eyes. Andy smirked.

"Making faces does not help," Florence chided, opening her eyes and giving Ray a hard stare.

"Sorry, I'll try to relax."

"No need. I found out what I wanted."

This threw them.

"Like what?" Andy asked, incredulously.

"You have part of a body and you are wondering if it is linked to a previous case where the victim was also badly mutilated."

"Blimey!" said Andy before he could stop himself.

Ray looked at Florence. What the hell?

"Neat trick," he said, roughly extricating his hands from hers.

"No trick," Florence replied calmly, "I am able to read a person's feelings and sometimes it comes to me as images. The images from you are grotesque. That room..." and she shook her head and swore in Swahili.

Silence.

While Andy looked gobsmacked, Ray became more alert and wary. How could she know about the room? Or was she simply playing them? Was she using the classic 'psychic' tricks of picking up on body language and verbal cues to tell people what they hoped to hear? She might have worked out from their demeanour that they were investigating a murder, or looked at the list and recognised the significance of the ingredients. Beyond that, what had she said that couldn't apply to any murder scene? Two mutilated bodies, grotesque images, a horrible room – they could all simply be percentage gambles. Lots of bodies are mutilated in some way, most murder scenes are grotesque and most murders happen indoors... in rooms. Before Ray could speak, Florence said,

"I can see you are sceptical, but you must believe me – there is an evil power at work in your case. Sometimes it acts for itself, but at other times it uses people to do its work."

For some reason, Ray's mind went straight to The Man in the honey-coloured trench coat. He didn't like what he saw and closed his mind to it.

"Getting back to our list, is there any way to check your records to see if someone has bought all these items over time?" Ray asked.

"That would be very hard. And anyway, if you were a criminal, would you use your card to pay for anything that might relate to your crime?"

Ray shook his head. Of course not! It would be cash all the way.

"Fair point," he said, then pushed his chair back and stood up,

"I'm afraid we're going to have to go."

Andy stood up, too, but not before he'd looked ruefully at his mug of tea, which was still three quarters full.

"You will not stay to finish your tea?" Florence sounded a little bit hurt.

"Sorry, but we have other enquiries to make," Ray insisted and he led the way out of the back parlour and into the main body of the shop. He didn't see Florence looking out of the back window as if something had just climbed up the side of the building. She breathed a small sigh of relief and followed the men to the front door, which she unbolted.

"Thank you for your time," Ray said.

"You are welcome," Florence smiled.

"Sorry about the tea," Andy said, and Florence was about to happily reassure him that it was all fine, when her eyes fixed on something in the street. Andy looked – there seemed to be nothing out of the ordinary.

Florence pushed past Andy and grabbed Ray's arm. Hard.

"You must be careful!" she said forcefully, "That thing is following you and it won't stop until it gets what it wants. It is like a big baby. It wants food; it wants toys; it wants to satisfy its hungers – and if it doesn't get what it wants, it makes everyone's lives a nightmare. It will make your life a nightmare!"

Ray looked at the genuine concern in her eyes – she really believed all this nonsense,

"Well, I, er... I'll be extra careful," he stammered.

Florence let Ray's arm go and gave a frustrated snort,

"You may not believe in this thing," she said, staring hard at the great creature which was now standing on the other side of the street waiting for them,

"But it believes in you!" and with that, she closed the door on them, locked it and hurried back to the relative sanctuary of the kitchen.

"They're all fucking mad round here," said Ray. In the bright sunshine of the July afternoon, Andy agreed with him, but while they'd been in the dingy kitchen, he had felt something. Maybe it was Florence's personality and conviction or the dismal surroundings, but Andy had felt distinctly uncomfortable and... oppressed. It was as if a blanket of doom had been thrown over him. Now he felt as if it had slipped off. The sun was out and he felt normal again... well, almost. Deep inside, he had a nagging feeling like they were being watched and that whoever was watching them bore them ill will.

"Here's the plan," Ray declared, "Check out the other shop the professor mentioned; swift half in The Crown; back to headquarters to see what Emma's come up with."

"Works for me cap'n!"

Chapter Eighteen

What Goes There?

The moment Oliver stepped into her office, Elizabeth Russell knew something was terribly wrong.

"Something's happening out there. I've heard five ambulance call outs in the last ten minutes. Three accidents, one suicide and an apparent heart attack," and as he spoke, he walked straight over to the map of London on her wall,

"They start here at the eastern end of Cheapside and head west down the A40."

"How far has it got?"

"Last call was from outside Holborn tube."

"The well-trodden path from Newgate Prison to St Giles and Tyburn."

"Yes," Oliver had seen the route's significance immediately.

"Well, I'd better get out there, then. I'll start at Marble Arch and work my way east," she said as she rushed out of the office.

Within five minutes, she was cycling fast down the Mall, then sweeping up past Buckingham Palace to Hyde Park Corner and on up through the park to the Marble Arch. Like Mexican Dave, she was an arresting sight to those who noticed her – a tall, elegant woman wearing a cream linen trouser suit and a stylish cycle helmet thrashing her Electra Cruiser Lux with its fat, three and a half inch tyres up Park Lane. She finally swung round Marble Arch and stopped at the end of Oxford Street to catch her breath. She had a straight view of just over a mile down Oxford Street to the Centre Point office block at Tottenham Court Road. In between large gulps of air, she assessed the situation. Everything looked normal. There was nothing to see... but no. Somewhere on the far side of Centre Point, there was a darkness hanging just above the buildings. That would be where the action was. She checked over her shoulder to gauge the traffic, then heaved the heavy bike forward and pedalled hard towards God only knew what.

"Shit the bed!"

Elizabeth Russell pulled up at the corner of Neal Street and stared at what looked for all the world like a huge umbilical cord in the middle of the road. It was about two feet thick, pus yellow, slimy and, to her nose, stank like a latrine at the height of a dysentery epidemic. None of the shoppers or tourists going about their business could see or smell it. Lucky them! It trailed from the top of Shaftesbury Avenue and headed off out of her field of vision down Neal Street. Elizabeth Russell regarded it with an academic eye. Beneath the reeking, slimy skin, she could see huge veins of a thick, blueish-grey liquid, pumping sluggishly towards whatever was around the corner. Well! This was a new one on her. She was going to have to be careful. She took off her helmet and parked her bike, then sidled up to the corner of Neal Street. She took a breath and, with her heart racing, cautiously edged her head around the side of the building.

"Fuck me!" she gasped, whipping her head back around the corner and flattening herself against the wall.

"Fuck... me!" she repeated, her sparkling, violet eyes wide with fear as she tried to regain control of her breathing. Seeing the huge creature squatting in the middle of the street was like being dumped into a barrel of freezing water. It wasn't simply the fact that the beast was hideous with its bulbous, distorted baby head, fat, maggot's body and its slimy tendrils that seemed to have minds of their own as they swished and waved around it... but the hatred it was radiating was almost overpowering even for her. No wonder all those people had been killed and injured on its journey across town. Just the sight of this thing would be enough to scramble the brain of most untrained psychics. And yet, for all its size and obvious strength, it didn't seem capable of harming any 'normal' people. In fact, the people wandering around the street were not only blissfully unaware of the presence of a truly terrifying monster in their midst, but they were also able to walk straight through it as if it wasn't there. Intriguing!

Elizabeth Russell drew a deep breath and looked around the corner again.

"Crap!" she said. The 'whatever it was' had disappeared from sight, but its trailing cord led up the side of the building and over the top of the roof above 'The Herbalist'. Even though it wasn't in the street, she still darted back behind the corner to think. If the creature couldn't interact directly with most people, then the likelihood was that it had at least one person with it as a servant. She had another quick glance around the corner. Yes! The mad looking man with the bicycle, the sombrero and the black aura all around him. So, *this* was what Titheridge had been up against. Elizabeth Russell felt a bloom of warmth in her chest for him. He'd been an ordinary accountant with latent psychic abilities, but somehow, he'd managed to stay sane when he'd seen the creature, and then shown the strength of character and cunning to wage his own private war on its servants. He might not be stable now, but he was an impressive individual and clever enough to have realised that he'd be no match for the creature itself. Good old Titheridge!

After her initial shock, Elizabeth Russell was calming down. She had another good look at the street, fixing the image of Mexican Dave in her mind. Then the beast started clambering over the roof of the building. Sweet Jesus, it was hideous! The sight of it made her catch her breath. Elizabeth Russell stood very still as the creature looked all around and carefully sniffed the air. She could only hope that all her magical protections would make her look like just an ordinary person with zero awareness of the supernatural. The beast pointed its dreadful face straight at her, then looked the other way and scuttled down the side of the building and sat with its back to her, watching the front door of The Herbalist. So, it couldn't see that she could see it. That was very good indeed. And the same went for the man with the sombrero. Even though he'd looked right at her, all he'd seen was an ordinary person. Of course, she wasn't giving herself enough credit – Mexican Dave had seen a very beautiful, stylish, intelligent-looking woman standing at the corner, but he had ignored her, because she clearly had no psychic powers.

Elizabeth Russell watched as Ray and Andy came out of the shop. So, that was it! The creature was interested in Ray Ennis' new 'torso in the river' case. Or maybe it was interested in Ray and his partner themselves? Ray probably fitted the type that might become an acolyte – tough, powerful, a man of action. But maybe it was attracted to Ray's partner – what was his name? Oh yes, Andy. There was something about him that could be attractive to a creature like that. To Elizabeth Russell's trained eye, Andy was clearly open to ideas of the occult. He might even be one of those people who was a late bloomer and suddenly developed psychic abilities later in life. Whatever the reason, the creature and its acolyte followed Ray and Andy as they walked towards the other end of Neal Street. She would follow them to observe, but there was little she could do beyond that. She needed more information before she could even start thinking about how to destroy this thing. And if there were more casualties that afternoon, that would just be bad luck. She ducked back around the corner and fetched her bike. At over forty pounds in weight, it was a big lump of metal to lug about, but its fat tyres and robust frame were perfect for the rigours of cycling in London. And anyway, it kept her fit and strong. She watched and waited for the bizarre group ahead of her to get a bit further away, then she set off after them. She was intrigued by the great black pall that surrounded the creature. It was more than simply evil. It had a very inter-dimensional feel to it. Yes, that could be it. If this thing spread its time between more than one dimension, then that could explain how it had been able to go under her radar. Maybe it wasn't here all of the time? But if it wasn't here, where did it go? And why did it need this unwieldy umbilical cord? With these and about a thousand other questions swirling around her head, Elizabeth Russell followed her new Public Enemy Number One as it joined the tourists enjoying Seven Dials on a sunny day.

***

Florence Gichuru walked into the kitchen and heaved a great sigh. Those men had no idea of the danger they were in! Why were people so closed off to the supernatural? It was so frustrating. She looked at her watch and decided she'd take ten minutes to gather her thoughts and finish her coffee, then she'd re-open the shop. She sat down at the table and took a sip – a bit cold! She got up and put the mug into the microwave for forty-five seconds, gave the coffee a quick stir and sat down again. She could see from the steaming liquid that she'd probably given it too long, so she waited and thought about what she'd do later. Maybe a spiritual cleansing bath? Yes, after seeing that thing today, her spirit needed cleansing. After it had tried to psychically dominate her, she felt as if unwanted hands had been feeling her all over. She picked up the mug and had just brought it to her lips when the handle snapped off in her hand. In a split second, her jumper was covered in hot coffee and she leapt up with a cry of shock and pain. She went straight to the sink and turned on the cold tap. Then she quickly pulled the jumper up over her head, but she was moving too fast. She didn't notice that part of her necklace was caught in the weave of her jumper and in her haste, she wrenched the necklace apart, sending the amber beads cascading to the quarry tiles of the floor below. The amulet! She could feel it fall and, although she desperately grabbed at it, the amulet hit the hard floor and shattered. To her, the sound was like a thunderclap.

The look of shock on Florence's face turned to terror a moment later. The creature! It was back, and she watched, frozen, as it scurried down the side of the building and into the courtyard, turning its bloated, eyeless baby face to leer at her. She stood watching in nothing but her bra and trousers, utterly defenceless. A terrifying grin split the creature's face, displaying its sharp teeth. Now, it could touch her, now it could defile her body, now it could taste her soul. She turned to run, but the back window smashed in and a slimy tendril whipped around Florence, pinning her arms to her sides and crushing her. She was trying to scream, but nothing was coming out, then the tendril picked her off the ground and smashed her face down onto the edge of the sink. Her mouth exploded in a burst of blood and shattered teeth. Her head lolled, dazed, then the tendril threw her across the room, with her arms and legs flailing helplessly. The impact with the wall hammered the breath out of her in a mist of blood, and she crumpled to the floor, semi-conscious. Now she was incapacitated, Krowos could take its time. It came into the room and loomed over the defenceless woman.

Florence was struggling for breath and looked up at the creature that was blurred by the blood in her eyes. Oh God! Its eyeless face was staring into her soul. A number of slimy tendrils slithered towards her across the floor, but she couldn't move. A wave of revulsion hit her as the first tendril touched the bare skin of her left foot and slipped up the inside of her trouser leg to spiral around her calf and up her thigh like the stalk of a bean plant. The other tendrils did the same with her arms, other leg and her throat, then lifted her off the ground and up the wall until she was almost touching the ceiling. The hideous, eyeless face slowly came in close and its fat tongue licked up her half-naked body from her stomach to her face.

"Oh yes, I will absorb your power and feast on your sweet, sweet soul!"

The voiceless words emerged in her mind and, although they had no tone, Florence could feel the sly greed of their intent. Then the pain began. Heat was building up in the tendrils that were gripping her until it became unbearable and she started to silently scream. With the intense heat came sharp, jolting bursts of blue sparking agony so that Florence involuntarily convulsed as she was held high against the wall. The thing was draining her of her psychic powers and the torment made her beg for death. She could feel her soul being sucked away and now everything was becoming disconnected. She could also feel the creature's frustration. It wanted to do so much more to her, to defile her in ways beyond her imagination, to rip and tear and split her over hours before finally eating her body and soul... but it was away from its sanctum, it didn't feel safe and it had other business to attend to. No, it would reluctantly have to end this now.

Suddenly, Florence was thrown face-first to the cold, tiled floor. She groaned, but before she could move, the tendril around her throat constricted and pulled her head back. As her back arched, another tendril pushed down hard on her lower spine, pinning her to the floor. Her head was slowly pulled back and the sinews started to strain. In a last frenzy of life, Florence clawed at her throat, trying to loosen the creature's grip, but it was hopeless. With a horrible slowness, her head was pulled back and her spine arched further and further. She was gurgling in agony and her eyes looked as though they might burst from her straining face. And now the creature's distended baby face was right in front of hers and smiling in triumph. Her back kept arching over and every tendon was stretched to breaking, bones grinding, joints cracking. Slowly, slowly the force increased across every bone and every joint until one of them inevitably...

An instant after the sudden, dull crack, Florence's body folded over backwards, both hips dislocated, her broken spine ripped through her intestines and her life was gone. The face stared sightlessly up at the ceiling, framed on either side by the soles of her feet. Krowos savoured the sight and the last sweet taste of her, then scuttled away. The sound of water running into the bloodied stainless-steel sink filled the lifeless room.

Chapter Nineteen

The Dead Zone

Ray and Andy had been in 'The Dead Zone' for ten minutes and they were not enjoying it. The shop was designed like a gothic nightmare with dismal lighting, black painted walls, imagery of witchcraft and devil worship everywhere, and death metal playing over the speaker system. The man and the woman who were the two members of staff were both dressed in black, heavily tattooed, pierced all over and wearing badly applied makeup. On top of that, they had been borderline aggressive when asked about the ingredients list. Finally, Andy cracked,

"You know what, guv'," he said, turning to Ray, "I think I can smell marijuana," and he sniffed at the air.

"It's incense," said the woman behind the counter coldly.

Ray sniffed the air, too. The man who had been leaning against the back wall trying to look as uninterested in proceedings as he could, squirmed slightly and glanced through the door at the back into the room beyond.

"Incense? Well, that's what you say, but I can't be sure," Andy continued, "I think we need to call this in. Get a warrant to fully search these premises with the sniffer dogs. What do you say, guv'?"

"Yeah, call it in," Ray replied.

As Andy pulled his phone out of his pocket, the man said,

"Hey, there's no need for any of that. Give me another look at that list and I'm sure we can help."

Andy and Ray exchanged a look, then Andy showed them the list again.

Ray's phone went off and he took it out of his pocket. It was Emma.

"It's headquarters," he said – mainly to intimidate the annoying shop assistants – then he stepped outside the shop and took the call.

"Emma, what's up?"

"I think I've found our man, boss," Emma's voice sounded excited down the phone.

"Great! Who is it?"

"Bloke called Marco Fabbri. Went down for three years as part of the people trafficking gang that branded their goods with the Roman numeral thirteen. Got out early for good behaviour, kept his nose clean for a couple of years, then disappeared. Re-surfaced four years ago running his own clothing company out of a place near Burgess Park..."

"Right on the gang's old route out through South London to Kent," Ray smiled.

"Exactly!" Emma sounded triumphant, "The company's doing okay. Not making losses, not making big profits... in other words, not attracting anyone's attention. It's just ticking along nicely."

"And it's the perfect front for his old line of business," said Ray, "The only question is, is anyone else investigating him?"

"Ahead of you, boss," said Emma proudly, "Already checked and you'll be pleased to know that there are no ongoing investigations. Even the Inland Revenue aren't interested."

"Emma, you are a fucking star!" Ray said with a broad grin.

"Thanks, boss," Emma replied. She was sitting in the office in front of her computer and she couldn't help blushing at the compliment.

"I love it!" said Ray, "Now, don't go out and get pissed tonight, because I want you on your best form tomorrow when you, me and Andy pay mister Fabbri a visit. Yeah?"

"Yeah, of course!" Emma could barely contain her excitement, "Thanks, boss!"

"Thank you, Emma, that's really good work."

Ray put his phone away and turned back towards the shop. He was grinning again - that was a good break. Now they could make some progress! Emma was worth her weight in gold. She was a great team player but was confident and dedicated enough to be left to her own devices. And now it looked like she'd come up trumps. The image of her eager face looking up at him to receive orders came into his mind and he felt a burst of warmth towards her. Ray walked back into 'The Dead Zone' with a spring in his step and found the bloke behind the counter talking Andy through the various ingredients on the list.

"Had any customers in by the name of Marco Fabbri?" Ray asked.

The look of surprise quickly followed by concern on the woman's face told him that they had.

"No," she lied badly.

Ray gave her a withering look and then turned to the man.

"Well?"

The man's shoulders slumped in defeat.

"Yes," he said, "He's a regular."

"And let me guess, over the last couple of weeks he's bought everything on that list," Ray's stare could have melted lead, so the lanky streak of piss standing behind the counter didn't stand a chance.

"Yeah, but there's no crime in that. None of this stuff's illegal," he stammered.

"No, it isn't," Ray conceded, "But what he might have used it for is. So, you two have a choice – tell us everything you know about Mister Fabbri right now... or come down to headquarters to make statements under caution."

The man and woman looked at each other and then did the sensible thing.

Forty-five minutes later, Andy and Ray walked out of The Dead Zone and the transition from Stygian gloom to bright sunshine made them both shield their eyes.

"What a tit!" Ray laughed, shaking his head as they walked back to their car,

"He paid for the stuff with his own credit card. He's either too dumb to understand or too arrogant to care."

"Wouldn't surprise me if it was a bit of both," Andy replied,

"Fabbri always was an oily little shit. The one thing he's had on his side so far is luck. In the original case, he only went down as an accessory, but we had evidence that he'd raped at least a dozen of the women who'd been trafficked. Trouble was, none of them would press charges or give evidence against him.

"Lucky boy," Ray said dryly.

"Not any more. That skidmark's luck just ran out."

"Question is, who's behind him? Somebody this stupid isn't going to suddenly pop up with the organisation and the money to set up a legitimate clothing business."

"Not unless he won the lottery."

"So, who's in the shadows? And what interest do they have in human sacrifice?" Ray wondered.

They walked in silence for a minute, not noticing the bloke with the sombrero and bicycle who was following twenty yards behind them.

"There wasn't any evidence of human sacrifice in the original case, was there?" Ray asked.

"Nah. Just the usual kidnapping, rape and murder you'd expect from scumbags like Fabbri," Andy said and then, for no reason he could figure out, he shivered.

"You all right?"

"Yeah, just got a funny feeling like someone dropped an ice cube down the back of my shirt."

"Probably 'cos we're going past that shop we were at earlier," Ray pointed to The Herbalist, which still had the 'Closed' sign in the window.

"Probly," Andy agreed, "Anyway, what was that about ritual sacrifice?" he continued, trying to shake off the weird feeling of cold.

"Why would Fabbri get involved in human sacrifice now and jeopardise his entire operation?" Ray asked.

"Why would he join a people trafficking gang in the first place? Maybe it's as simple as... he's a scumbag and he's not the sharpest tool in the box?" Andy said – he remembered Fabbri clearly from the previous case. He'd hated him then and he hated him now.

"That would make it simpler, but maybe he's been forced into the human sacrifice thing by the person who's bankrolling him. His business would be a perfect front for finding people who might be here illegally – people who are impossible to trace."

"Yeah," Andy nodded, "But whoever's running Fabbri hasn't taken into account how stupid he can be..."

"Like buying all those herbs on his credit card..." Ray interjected.

"So stupid!"

"So, all we have to do now is work out who's really running this racket," Ray said, but even as the words came out of his mouth, he knew that it would be easier said than done.

He was still turning the problem over in his mind three hours later as he walked home from the bus stop. Streatham High Road was bathed in the golden light of another glorious evening and as Ray looked at the people standing outside the pubs and bars, he decided it would be good to stop thinking about work. He was getting nowhere trying to second guess Fabbri's motives or who might be behind him. If he put his mind to being with his family and maybe have a couple of beers, there was the possibility that the answers he was looking for would be there in the morning. Yes, that was a sound plan. That was what he needed. A nice, normal night in... then, just as he was about to turn down his road, Ray saw The Man in his buttoned-up trench coat. There he was, standing in the middle of the pavement at the corner of the next block, allowing people to rush around him like water as he stared at Ray and seethed.

"Mother fucker..." Ray said under his breath, then he shouted,

"You! Stay there! Police!"

The Man held Ray's eyes for a moment, then turned on his heel and walked around the corner to the right and down the hill away from the High Road. Ray sprinted after him as soon as The Man turned to walk away. He rounded the corner expecting to have significantly closed the gap on the slower, older man, but he was already about a hundred yards away and on the other side of the street at the corner of a small road running parallel to the High Road. He was standing like a statue in his ill-fitting coat staring at Ray and seething.

"Stop!" Ray ordered, locking his eyes onto The Man's watery blue stare and starting to run towards him. The Man turned on his heel again and walked around the corner and down the side street.

Ray put on the afterburners and his feet pounded hard down the hill towards the corner The Man had vacated. Using only peripheral vision to gauge the traffic, he sprinted across the road, but when he got to the corner, The Man was nowhere to be seen.

What the fuck?

Ray slowed to a jog and continued in the direction The Man had taken. Maybe he'd gone into one of the houses or had ducked behind a front wall. As Ray jogged on, he tried to look over the low front walls of the houses he was passing. Nothing on this side of the street, but for all he knew, the bloke had swapped sides and was hidden over there. And then Ray saw him.

No! No, this was all wrong.

The Man was standing over a hundred yards up ahead at the far end of the road staring at Ray. His lank hair and long arms held straight down seemed to elongate him, but he didn't seem tired. He was simply standing there seething in his tight trench coat and staring at Ray as if everything wrong in the world was his fault.

What the absolute fuck?

Ray slowed his pace and walked towards The Man, keeping eye contact and narrowing the distance between them with every step. It was like a stress dream where Ray was trying but failing to catch a criminal. Only this wasn't a dream. This was real and happening. Now he had closed the gap to about fifty yards. Surely, he could chase down this old, overweight man? Forty yards. Ray had only seen him walking, but he couldn't possibly be able to outrun a fit young man like him? Thirty yards. Ray was returning The Man's fierce gaze and thinking about what he was going to do when he caught him. Twenty yards. Ray slowly took his set of handcuffs from his pocket. Without breaking eye contact, the old man turned his body and started walking around the corner, his head turning further and further round and back to keep his eyes locked on Ray until snap! The Man's face turned away and he was around the corner, heading down the hill again.

As soon as The Man moved, Ray burst into a sprint and it was a matter of seconds before he was at the corner. The Man should have been less than twenty yards away, but he was gone. The street, which ran straight down the hill for a couple of hundred yards to a T-junction at the end, was empty. Ray skidded to a halt and wiped the sweat away from his eyes. No, the street was still empty. Ray's chest was heaving from the exertion, but as he walked down the hill, he got his breath back. This was impossible! The old bloke couldn't have disappeared... but then, he shouldn't have been able to outrun Ray either, and yet here Ray was, alone in the street. Ray stopped and looked carefully at the junction almost two hundred yards away. Empty. This time the old man wasn't standing there waiting for him. So, where the hell was he? Ray shook his head as if to clear his thoughts. This was fucked up! He turned to go back up to the High Road and stopped in his tracks. There, at the top of the street where it joined the High Road, stood The Man. Ray couldn't believe it. It defied reason! He'd just seen that fucker walk *down* the hill, but there he was at the top, staring down at him. He must have been seventy-five yards away. How did he get there? It wasn't possible. It just wasn't possible! How could that weird old bloke, who showed no signs of exertion and just stood there with an unchanging expression of seething anger on his face, have possibly got up there?

And then, for the first time, something changed. The Man's mouth, which had always been open in a sort of oblong to reveal his clenched teeth, very gradually changed into a horrible grin. It was full of menace and delight and knowing. The Man's body turned ninety degrees back in the direction of Ray's house, but the grinning face still stared Ray down. Then the feet started walking and...

Ray was sprinting. This time he didn't bother going after The Man. He ran back the way he'd come, staying away from the crowded High Road until he absolutely had to. The Man's look had made it clear that he had one intention – going to Ray's house. As he ran, his thoughts were as much of a blur as the houses flashing past him. Chloe must have seen The Man on that night a couple of days ago. She had exactly described the bloke Ray had seen earlier that evening and yet he'd pushed it away because it was too odd. And now he was in a waking nightmare, running himself ragged after a shadow. All he could feel was a wrenching sensation in his gut and a sense of guilt at being so bloody stupid. When he finally had to run up to the High Road to get back to the top of his own street, he didn't even look for the weird old man. His focus was on getting home. The fact that his street was empty when he rounded the corner was of no consolation. Ray had a sudden surge of speed for the final sprint down the hill to his front door. He was puffing from exertion as he took out his keys. Something wasn't right here. Yes, the door was shut, but something wasn't right. He happened to look across at his bedroom window. The blind was pulled slightly to the side and, in the gap between it and the window frame, he could see the face of The Man leering out at him with that vicious grin on his face and a horrible glitter in his eye.

"No!" Ray screamed as the blind fell back into place and The Man disappeared.

Ray fumbled with the lock, threw the door open and was doing the same with the inner door in a couple of seconds. How had The Man got in the house? Ray was through the door and inside in a frantic blur, almost tumbling into his bedroom. He stared about him, his chest heaving, but no one was there. Not behind the door, not under the bed, nowhere!

"Ray?" It was Vicky calling from the garden, "You all right?"

Ray ran to the entrance of the kitchen and stopped - there were Vicky and Chloe sitting in the garden enjoying the last of the sunshine. Vicky stiffened on seeing Ray so agitated.

"I'm fine," Ray panted, "Just stay there."

Chloe went over to her mother and held onto her.

"It's fine, it's all fine," he lied, "Just give me a sec'..." The Man clearly wasn't back there, so he'd be either in the bathroom or Chloe's room. Ray surreptitiously took the boning knife out of the block on the counter, sidled out of the kitchen and closed the door behind him.

After the blurred frenzy of the chase, everything was suddenly very still. Ray's chest was heaving, but his other movements were careful and calculated. First, he would shut the inner door to the flat. As he did, he was able to keep an eye on the other doors. Now, if the man was in the house, he was kettled between the front door and the kitchen door. Ray then moved back down the corridor, so that he could clear the bathroom first, then Chloe's room and thus flush anyone away from his family at the back of the house. As he moved, he kept the knife ready just in front of him to thrust into any potential assailant. The choice of the boning knife was no accident. There was a selection of knives in the block, including a large carving knife, but none of them would have been right. All the others had blades that were wide and could be bent or deflected if they hit a rib, but the boning knife was narrower and thicker – perfect for piercing deep into flesh. The bathroom door was open and the shower curtain was drawn back, so it was the matter of a couple of seconds to check it. Ray moved along the corridor and stood for a moment outside the closed door of Chloe's room. He took a breath, then burst in. Nothing. Aside from toys, books and clothes it was empty and there were no places for anyone to hide. Ray knew that there was a spare mattress under the bed, so nowhere to hide under there either. And then he was in the corridor again and stalking towards his and Vicky's room. Still nothing there. He scanned the room from the corridor and could see no one. The only place The Man could be was the one place he hadn't checked - the built-in wardrobes. Fuck! Ray blew out his cheeks and opened the doors with speed and precision, keeping the knife ready to thrust. All clear. However, he didn't uncoil. He went out to the external front door with the knife at the ready, had a quick check up and down the empty street, then closed the front door and closed and locked the inner door.

"Well?" Vicky asked when he came back into the kitchen.

"It was nothing, sorry," he replied, placing the knife back into the block in such a way that she couldn't see what he was doing.

"Doesn't seem like nothing," she said, looking at him with a piercing gaze.

"The last few days have been weird and I haven't had nearly enough sleep. I'm jumping at shadows... are you both okay?"

"Yeah. We got back from swimming around five and since then we've just been chilling," Vicky said.

"Sorry," said Ray, shaking his head, "I didn't mean to worry you. My bad for going off the deep end," Ray added, hoping that would be an end to it,

"What's for dinner? I'm starving!"

Then, while Vicky described the chicken and chorizo jambalaya she was going to make, Ray cracked open a beer and took a long slug of it. Vicky was talking and he was nodding along, but his mind was elsewhere. He didn't know how he felt about what had just happened. Hell, he didn't really *know* what had just happened. This was a weird end to a generally successful day... but everything else that had happened had been real. He couldn't be so sure about the last ten minutes. Who the fuck was that man? At some point tomorrow, he'd get someone to check the database and see if anyone matching his description came up. But how could the old man have outrun him...? Ray couldn't make sense of it. And all the while, Elizabeth Russell's request for him to get in touch with her if anything out of the ordinary happened kept bubbling up. And this was out of the ordinary. Plus, there was Chloe's experience and her subsequent nightmares about The Man. Kids had nightmares. Nothing strange about that. They had nightmares about strange people they might have seen. Again, perfectly normal. Kids usually didn't need to be slapped to be woken up from a nightmare. That was not normal. What had just happened was not normal. Should he go running to Elizabeth Russell like a little boy who'd scraped his knee? No. Fuck that. Ray decided to push it all aside. He needed a night of normality, a night of calm, a night where he could recharge his batteries, and that was precisely what he was going to do.

***

Much later that night, after Ray had achieved all his goals, Elizabeth Russell walked through the door of her office like a hurricane making landfall.

"Up, Oliver!" she cried as she marched through her assistant's office and into her own.

Oliver grunted as he jumped out of one of the leather club chairs and stumbled after her. When he got in, she was already standing with her hands on her hips, looking at the map of London on her wall. She looked somewhat ruffled around the edges and her cream linen trouser suit was grubby and creased, with an oil mark on one trouser leg where she'd caught her bike chain on it.

"This is a big one," she said as Oliver joined her,

"And I mean that literally. It must be twenty foot long from arsehole t'beak."

"It's got a beak?" Oliver exclaimed.

"No! That's a phrase. Haven't you ever seen Withnail and I?"

Oliver looked at her blankly and with the blurriness of shattered sleep.

"It's a brilliant film. When this is over, watch it online. Now come on, keep up," she said briskly,

"Point is, we've got what appears to be a twenty-foot-long inter-dimensional monster with an umbilical cord that can easily stretch from Seven Dials to London Bridge. And it had a wander round town today."

"Holy crap!"

"Close, but no cigar. Unholy crap - that's what it stinks of. I tell you, if that's what its dimension smells like, then it can fuck off back there. But right now, its umbilical cord seems to be attached right about here..." and she took a red pin and pushed it into the map.

"It's a company in Candlewick called Global Actuaries Limited, and I want all the information you can pull on them by nine. I need to be able to pay them a visit later tomorrow,"

"D'you mean later today?"

"What's the time?"

"A quarter past three in the morning," Oliver replied.

"Yes, then in that case, later today... fuck! I totally lost track of time. You see, I followed them from Seven Dials..."

"Them?"

"Oh yes, it's got a madman in a sombrero with it."

"Sombrero..." Oliver said out loud as he scribbled it down.

"So, they left Seven Dials – oh, but can you guess who was there, too?"

Oliver puffed out his cheeks and narrowed his eyes as he tried to imagine, but finally gave up.

"None other than our Detective Inspector Ennis – and this creature has a real hard-on for him. You know, it wouldn't surprise me if we aren't the only group trying to recruit Ray Ennis."

"They want his soul?"

"Yes, but more specifically in the case of this thing, it needs his body and his mind."

"How so?"

She quickly explained her theory about the creature only being able to touch those who could see it.

"Weird," said Oliver, who was still struggling to slough off the deep sleep he'd been dragged out of.

"And as if that wasn't enough, there's a bonus – Ennis's Sergeant Harper has latent psychic powers that he doesn't even know about," Elizabeth Russell said with a glint in her eyes.

"How do you know?"

"When he walked through the umbilical cord on Monmouth Street, he flinched. I saw it clear as day. Everyone else on that street was wandering through it like it wasn't there, but Sergeant Harper looked like he'd been doused in cold water... anyway, that's all tangential – here's what's really important... so, I followed them back to their place in Candlewick and ensconced myself in a little corner with a view and observed. Lots of comings and goings. The first one was a fat cabby, who went in, then came out twenty minutes later without a passenger."

"Getting orders?" Oliver suggested.

"Probably, because I then watched him come back a few times during the evening with various passengers, who all looked like vagrants. One stick-thin Indian man, a very unpleasant looking old man in a trench coat and one woman who I swear had a beard."

"Interesting collection."

"Indeed. And then the cabbie took them away one by one. Oh yes, I also need all the information on a black cab, number 66666."

"Really? That's his cab number?"

"I know!" Elizabeth Russell said with a tone halfway between incredulity and respect, "You've got to admit, that is quite stylish."

Oliver nodded, but then became serious,

"But is there a Christian aspect to this?"

"Nah," she replied firmly, "I'm guessing there's only space for one god at this particular party and he doesn't sport a beard and a long white robe."

"What does it look like?" Oliver asked, kind of dreading the answer.

Elizabeth Russell described the thing, then added,

"Actually, you really ought to see it. Good practice for when you finally graduate to field work. If it goes walkabout again, I'll take you with me," she smiled.

"I look forward to it immensely," Oliver said without emotion.

"Drink?" Elizabeth asked, walking over to the cabinet in the corner near the vast day bed.

"Best not, thanks. Work to do."

"Good point! I need you sober as a judge. You don't mind if I...?"

Oliver shook his head. He was hardly going to say no to his boss having a drink!

She threw some ice into a cut-glass tumbler and poured herself three fingers of Monkey Shoulder scotch and another three of Drambuie, then gave it a stir.

"On the plus side," she said as she came back to the map of London, "No one else was unfortunate enough to see this thing on its way back home."

"Thank goodness for that," said Oliver.

"But there was another casualty. I heard a scream this afternoon in Seven Dials and it was while I didn't have eyes on the monstrosity. I suspected it had done something nasty and I was right. On my way home, I broke into The Herbalist on Neal Street and found one of its former employees folded in half backwards. There was a smashed amulet on the floor..." she didn't need to say any more. Oliver was already there.

"All very messy, all very unpleasant," Elizabeth Russell continued, "So, I want a clear-up team on this one and I want them to feed this info back to Ennis and Harper by close of play tomorrow."

Oliver gave her a questioning look.

"I mean today. Come on, you know I mean today," and then she took a long, luxurious sip of her now delightfully chilled drink.

"Oh yes!"

That felt good!

"Now, what else? I need archives to search for any occultist activity in Candlewick going back as far as they can. We need to know if this thing has a history or whether it's a recent intruder to our little world. Also, if there are any other examples of days like today – a crop of deaths or people going mad – I want to know about them."

"But presumably you'd remember something like this?" Oliver said.

"True," Elizabeth Russell mused as she took another pull at her drink, "I don't, so with any luck we've got ourselves a newbie, but I'm not always in town, so I might have missed an incident or two. Worst case scenario is, it's been here a long time and has grown some deep roots into our reality. In which case digging it out might... be... tricky."

"Not very likely though, is it?" Oliver asked hopefully.

"You'd be surprised at how slippery some of these things can be. I think we should count ourselves lucky that it needs this umbilical cord. Fuck knows what it would get up to if it was running free about the town," and then she contemplated the map and the room fell into silence, punctuated only by the clink of the ice in her glass.

"Anything else?" Oliver asked after a minute.

"No, that's it for now – oh, actually, send a message to Titheridge from me 'Mate, you've got balls of steel' with a double exclamation mark."

"Got it."

"Said it before, I'll say it again - that bloke should get a fucking medal!"

Chapter Twenty

The Gangmaster

It was only nine-thirty in the morning and Marco Fabbri was already having an excellent day. For him, one of the perks of running an operation that involved people-trafficking and modern slavery, was easy access to vulnerable women. Some of them would do anything for their freedom and that morning, little Naz had done everything he'd told her to. A smile played across his thin lips as he eased his Range Rover out of the driveway of his detached five-bedroom house in Brockley, Southeast London. When he got back later, he'd continue where he'd left off. He turned left on to Lewisham Way and drove in the heavy traffic towards New Cross. It was slow going and was likely to be worse when he got onto the Old Kent Road, but he didn't care. Unlike his over-worked, under-paid staff, he didn't have to clock in on time. Today was an easy day. Turn up, check in with his team to make sure everything was running smoothly, have a good lunch and then home around three for a swim and fun with Naz. As a naturally lazy person, he loved days like this. Overall, he was a fairly unremarkable man: forty-five years old, five feet ten, fairly fit looking with an olive complexion and a thick head of dark hair that was all his own. He wasn't good looking, but he wasn't frightening either. Just an ordinary looking man driving a nice car to work.

However, it wasn't Marco Fabbri's physical attributes that had got him into Krowos' inner circle. He was very good with numbers, he'd always been popular with other criminals, he had always been lucky and when, on occasion, his luck had run out, he had always kept his mouth shut. These were useful attributes, and the clincher was the fact that he had an array of contacts which could keep up a supply of untraceable sacrifices for the only god he had ever believed in. There was no doubt that the last four years serving Krowos had been the best of his life. He already had the next three sacrifices lined up and he was sure that the Lord of Dimension would love them. Like that glorious summer's morning, there wasn't a cloud on the horizon… or was there?

His 'factory' was no more than a low-rise, prefabricated, grey little production facility, and when he pulled into the car park next to it, there was a car that he didn't recognise. It was suspiciously ordinary, which meant there was a chance it was an unmarked police car. Part of him wanted to turn right around and bolt for the coast. He could be in France long before the police could find him. He could easily continue his work from there. But another part of him, the lazy part, pointed out how hard it would be to start up again. Maybe it wasn't even the police? Maybe it was a visit from Customs, the Inland Revenue or Border Force? He knew this facility was clean as a whistle, so why be afraid? They couldn't have anything on him, so why not see what they wanted and run rings around them? He sat in the car with the engine running for about two minutes until the lazy side prevailed, then drove to the far end of the facility and reversed into the last parking space. He turned the car off and sauntered along the length of the building to the main entrance.

Sure enough, he was hardly through the glass double doors before his receptionist was up out of her seat with a look of concern on her chubby face,

"Mister Fabbri, the police are here. I showed them into the conference room. I hope that's all right?"

Cheryl's features were set in the sort of look a dog gives their owner when they think they've done something wrong.

"Don't worry, Cheryl, you did the right thing. Did you offer them a drink or anything?" he said cheerily in a soft south London accent.

"Ooh, no, I didn't think to," she said, flustered.

"Don't worry, come with me," he smiled and he led the way through a door to their right, up a flight of stairs and along a short, dull corridor. He opened the door at the end to find Ray and Andy standing on the far side of the large table in the functional conference room that had a plastic, unused smell to it. Andy was looking out through the large internal window at one end of the room which gave a view of the entire shop floor below where over a hundred men and women were busy sewing T-shirts together. A door next to the window led onto a gantry that crossed the entire workspace to a fire door at the far side.

"Good morning gentlemen, I'm Marco Fabbri, how can I help you?" He was smiling and looking relaxed, but Ray noted a shiftiness in his eyes.

"Mister Fabbri, I'm Detective Inspector Ennis and this is Detective Sergeant Harper. We'd like to ask you some questions, please."

"'Course. Always happy to help the police. Can Cheryl get you any tea or coffee?" Fabbri was all smiles and hospitality. Andy was buying none of it and watched him closely. One thing was clear – the man didn't remember him.

"No, we're ok, thanks," Ray replied.

"Okay. Just my usual coffee Cheryl."

Cheryl nodded and left them to it.

Fabbri sat down at the end of the table and indicated for Ray and Andy to do the same. They did so, sitting next to each other to his right.

"We know who you are and what you've done," said Ray bluntly, "Just wondering if you were doing it again."

Fabbri gave an ironic 'Ha!' and shook his head with that weary look that old lags had when they were faced with their past for the nth time.

"I run a legitimate business here. I've left that world far behind."

Andy gave him a hard stare and said,

"Really? Because this washed up in the river this week," and he produced a large photograph of the torso, which he pushed across the table towards Fabbri.

He looked it over coolly.

"Well, that is a tragedy, but I don't see what it has to do with me."

"Recognise this brand?" Andy said, pushing a photograph of the back of the torso with XIII branded onto the left shoulder blade.

"'Course I do. That's the old gang's brand, but I'm telling you, it's nothing to do with me. I turned my life around in prison and now I'm legit."

As Fabbri spoke, his mind was going twenty to the dozen. Was there anything that could link him to the body? How the fuck had it washed up? What if they went to the house and found Naz chained to the towel rail in his bathroom? How'd he explain that? No way the little bitch would keep her mouth shut. And besides, she was chained to the fucking towel rail. Christ! And there was coke and weed in his bedside table. Shit! Why hadn't he driven straight to the coast when he'd seen their car? Fuck! And what about the body? He racked his brain for details of the night it was dumped. He was pretty sure he couldn't be linked to it, but he kicked himself for getting Frank and Joey to dump it. Even with his very fucking clear instructions, they'd screwed it up. If he got out of this, he'd make sure that the rest of their lives were short and painful. But he had to play it cool. Just play it cool. He mustn't allow them to take him in, because if they scratched the surface... he thought of Naz again. Fuck!

"Thing is, you're the only member of the old gang that's out and still in London," Ray said, looking straight through the man, "You haven't even left your old patch."

"What, it's a crime to live south of the river?"

"That body was branded this year," said Andy.

"Not by me," Fabbri replied blandly.

The door opened and Cheryl came in with a steaming mug of coffee. Andy quickly gathered up the photographs while Cheryl walked across the room and carefully placed the mug of coffee on the table in front of Fabbri. Even though they would never have admitted it, Ray and Andy were both thinking the coffee smelled great.

"Are you sure you don't want one? Cheryl adds hazelnut syrup..." Fabbri offered, and Cheryl smiled proudly at them.

Andy and Ray both shook their heads.

"Okay, thanks, Cheryl."

She nodded and left them to it.

"But you can see how this looks, can't you?" asked Ray after the door clicked shut.

"Do you think I'd be stupid enough to use the same brand?"

"Stupid or lazy – take your pick," Ray replied.

Fabbri's face revealed nothing, but he was internally flaying himself with the word 'lazy'. It wouldn't have been difficult to get a new brand made, but he just couldn't be bothered at the time. Shit!

"I'm neither, because it has nothing to do with me," he said smoothly.

"Yeah, you keep saying that," Andy replied.

"And I'll keep on saying it, 'cos it's the truth," and he took a sip of his coffee. Damn, that was good!

"Really?" Ray asked.

"Yeah, really," Fabbri said.

And then the air became charged with tension. All three of them felt it. Ray and Andy prepared to make their move. Fabbri tried to look relaxed by sipping his coffee again. So good! Such a pity if he couldn't finish it.

"I tell you what," Ray began, "Why don't you come..."

Fabbri flicked the mug deftly and the spray of scalding liquid caught both cops across the neck and chest.

As Ray and Andy reacted in pain and surprise, Fabbri was up and running for the door on the far side of the room. He was at the end of the table and shoving open the door to the gantry before the other two were out of their chairs. Twenty feet below him, the open plan factory floor was full of workers bent over their sewing machines. The sound of his running feet on the metal above made some of those who weren't wearing headphones look up. As he ran, he pulled out his phone and hit the number he needed.

"I'm getting out. I'll contact you when safe!" he panted, but before he could hit the button to turn it off, the policemen were through the door and on the gantry. He'd have to shift it! He slammed the bar on the fire door at the far end of the gantry, pushing through it and onto the metal landing at the top of the fire escape outside. Who the fuck? There was a woman standing there and he stumbled into her before he knew what was happening.

"Stop!" she shouted as he shoved her backwards, knocking the wind out of her, but as he started to scramble down the stairs, she stuck out a foot. That was all it took. He didn't even have time to cry out before he tripped face first down the metal steps. His nose exploded on the edge of the third step and then his momentum threw him over, so he got a blur of sky, then a crack across his spine. He tumbled over again and the cold metal of the next step smashed his left eye socket. There was a spray of blood as he continued to fall head over heels. The back of his head cracked on the edge of the next step and now he was falling sideways with his head in empty space as he rolled down the last steps towards... the white burst of light as the back of his neck hit the metal upright of the handrail at the bottom of the steps was the last thing he knew. His phone tick-tacked across the concrete, thrown from his dead hand. Then there was a moment of stillness.

Ray burst through the fire door and in an instant, he clocked that both Emma and Fabbri were down.

"Get her!" he shouted as he ran down the stairs. Then, after a few steps, he slowed – Fabbri was very still and staring sightlessly into the blue above them.

"Fuck!" Ray swore, but then he saw the phone and he was running again. He jumped the body and was at the phone in a second,

"Please, please, please..." he prayed as he got to it,

"Yes!" he shouted – the phone was on and unlocked! He picked it up and could barely contain his joy that the last number called was right there on the screen. He took out his own phone and quickly photographed the screen with the number, then looked back up the stairs where Andy was bending over Emma,

"She all right?" Ray called.

"Winded!" Andy called back.

"The fucking phone's unlocked and I've got the number he was just calling!"

Andy stood up,

"You little beauty!" but then Andy wiped the elation off his face as the factory foreman ran around the side of the building.

"Call an ambulance!" Ray ordered and the man turned tail to run back to the office.

Ray could hardly contain his joy at getting Fabbri's phone seconds after his last call.

"This," he said, brandishing the phone as he walked up the stairs to where Emma was sitting, "Is going to blow this case wide open..."

But his smile faded as he noticed the look of misery on Emma's face,

"Sorry, Em – are you all right?"

"Yeah," she said, staring fixedly at Fabbri, "Just a bit woozy."

"She's going to have a bit of an egg on the back of her head," said Andy, "Probably got a very mild concussion. Ironwork isn't the most forgiving surface," and he clanged the metal rail with his knuckle.

Ray could see her unblinking gaze was on the body at the bottom of the stairs.

"Hey," he said gently and, when she didn't react, he knelt on the step below her to put himself between her and Fabbri,

"It's okay," he said, looking into eyes that were full of emotion,

"It was an accident and it's not your fault."

"But I tripped him," she said, replaying the moment. It *was* her fault.

"It must've happened in less than a second," Ray soothed, "You probably stuck your foot out instinctively."

"And anyway," said Andy, "It's just bad luck he ended up like that. The odds were in favour of him getting away."

"Yeah, I guess," Emma said quietly.

Andy looked down at Fabbri. That was the problem of having a career built on luck rather than judgement – when your luck finally turned bad, it could be catastrophic.

"These things happen in this job," Ray said, looking deep into her eyes, "And I'll make sure you get all the emotional support you need, okay?"

Emma started to nod, then winced.

"Mental note to self, don't nod when you've just bashed your head."

Ray smiled and Emma smiled weakly back.

"I think you're going to be all right. And my report will show you did your job brilliantly."

This made Emma's face light up as she felt a wave of respect and affection for him. Seeing that on her face gave him a pang of something, too. It was simultaneously nice and unsettling. He didn't want this to get weird, so he stood and held the phone out to Andy,

"You look after this and make sure it doesn't switch off."

"No problem," Andy took it and started looking for games.

Ray turned and viewed the scene. It wasn't pretty, and it would cause him a headache, as the death of any suspect should – even when they'd got what they deserved. The fact was that he, Andy and Emma weren't vigilantes. There were rules in place to protect the public and ensure justice, and the three of them would be put through the process. But they'd be fine. This was an accident and the truth would out. He sighed,

"I know it doesn't feel like it now, but this is a good day," although Fabbri's sightless gaze begged to differ. Ray looked up into the blue summer sky as the wail of sirens approached.

***

Four hours later, Ray and Andy were sitting in the elegant corner office of the CEO of Global Actuaries Limited. On the other side of the desk, Simon Montague looked relaxed and immaculate in an expensive grey suit that almost matched his hair. To his left, and slightly set back from the desk, sat Prunella Hemphill, the company's senior lawyer. She sat with a pad and pen poised on her lap as she looked the policemen over with sharp eyes.

"And you say this..." Simon Montague fished for the name,

"Marco Fabbri," Ray said evenly.

"That this Marco Fabbri had my phone number?"

"Yes, sir," Ray replied.

"Well, I can't imagine how he got it. I certainly didn't give it to him."

"But he had it all the same, and not only that, it was the last number he called before he died," Ray was staring Montague down, but his relaxed attitude didn't waver.

"Again, I really don't know why he would do that," he replied, "I'm not denying that I did get a call from a number I didn't recognise a few hours ago. I thought it was a scammer, so I picked up, but didn't say anything."

"Why would you do that?" Andy asked.

"Because automated cold calling systems disconnect after a couple of seconds if you don't say anything," Montague explained pleasantly.

Ray looked out of the window at the narrow view between buildings to the river. This man was very smooth. Maybe he could ruffle him a bit.

"Two hours ago, we went to Mister Fabbri's house. Do you know what we found?" Ray asked, casting his eyes back to Montague, who shrugged his shoulders,

"I'm afraid I have no idea."

"A woman called Naz Rahman, who was chained to a towel rail and who was being used by Mister Fabbri as a sex slave."

"That's awful!" Montague exclaimed with apparent horror.

"Doesn't it worry you that a man like that has your number?" Ray said, looking sharply at Montague.

"Of course it does!" Montague replied equally sharply, "Clearly, I'm the victim of some sort of data leak and I'm going to have to not only change my number but have our security team investigate the matter. It's highly unlikely that I'm the only person in the company this has happened to. What you need to understand is that our company trades on its reputation for unimpeachable integrity. Our clients have to be sure that they can fully trust us. Every day our cyber and security teams defend this company from all sorts of attacks from malware to attempted blackmail. Organised criminals and, I'm sad to say, some of our competitors would not think twice about hacking my number and selling it to unpleasant people to sully our reputation. And that is what I believe has happened here."

Ray and Andy sat silently staring at Simon Montague. He spoke fluently and with genuine feeling. He was the CEO of an international company that were known for their integrity and he came across as an honest man. And yet... a scumbag people-trafficker had phoned him as his last act on this earth. And where had Marco Fabbri got the money to set up his legitimate business? As they sat in the expensive office, it was clear that the money to set Marco up would be small change to an organisation like this, and they would be able to afford the sort of accountants who could make any links between the two companies disappear. Andy and Ray had the exact same feeling in their guts – the man was bent in some way, but was brilliant at covering it up. Ray decided on a new tack,

"So, you wouldn't know anything about a ritual sacrifice that washed up just across the river this week?"

Before Montague could reply, the lawyer stepped in,

"If you're accusing Mister Montague of murder, then you'd better have some very good evidence, otherwise I shall bring this up with the Commissioner in the morning," and Prunella Hemphill looked each of them in the eye, then continued,

"And believe me, you won't even be on traffic duty by lunch time."

Before Ray could reply, Montague interjected with his hands raised in a gesture of peace,

"Now, let's not get carried away," then, turning to Ms Hemphill, "It's all right, Pru, I'm sure that was an enquiry, not an accusation."

Ray said nothing to confirm or deny it, but sat there looking daggers at the fancy lawyer.

"Anyway, I'm perfectly happy to answer the question – all I know about the so-called 'Torso in the Thames' is what I've read in the papers. Your mentioning ritual sacrifice is the first I've heard about anything like that."

"No, it hasn't been released to the press," Ray replied.

"But presumably you know that this is a place of ritual sacrifice?" and Simon Montague was pleased by the confused looks on the faces of the two prying busybodies on the other side of his desk,

"We have a sacrificial chamber in this building. Would you like to see it?"

What the hell? Ray couldn't figure out what the man was talking about. Was this some elaborate attempt to throw them off course? He said,

"You have a sacrificial chamber?"

"Yes. Come on, I'll show you," Montague said, standing up and beckoning them to follow him.

Ray and Andy exchanged a look, then stood and followed him, with Prunella Hemphill bringing up the rear.

Montague led them out of the room to the lift, which took them down to sub-basement A. On the way, he explained,

"You see, our company has been on this site for about two hundred years. The previous buildings weren't nearly as big as this one, so their foundations weren't as deep. When we dug out the foundations for this building, we found something rather interesting."

The lift doors opened onto a reception area that was more like the entrance to a museum exhibit than something you'd expect to find in the sub-basement of your average business.

"Here you can see what the builders found," Montague said, waving a hand towards a couple of blown-up photographs on the opposite wall with explanatory text.

"Yes, it's the remains of a Roman temple. Obviously, we had to get archaeologists in immediately and this is what they excavated..." and Montague led them through a set of heavy doors into a very large, circular room with low lighting. A circular walkway above the excavated temple gave them a perfect view of it. The round walls below were covered in carvings and parts of the floor displayed the original mosaic tiling, with a large, stone table in the middle of the space. Meanwhile, on the wall next to the walkway were an array of large photographs of the excavation and copies of the most interesting carvings on the walls of the temple below.

"There are no prizes for guessing that the stone table was used for human sacrifices. That's according to the carvings on the walls, anyway," Montague continued,

"But two things particularly interested the boffins. First was the fact that although the Romans were a bloodthirsty lot, they didn't practice human sacrifice. Julius Caesar was apparently so horrified by the human sacrifices of the Celtic druids that he decided to wipe them out. So, the fact that the Romans built this place specifically for human sacrifice is very strange. The second thing that got the boffins all of a quiver, was the way that after the Romans left, the Britons, the Saxons and even the Normans continued to use this place for human sacrifice."

Ray listened, but was watching Montague's body language for anything that might give him away. Andy, on the other hand, was totally in his element and instantly engrossed in the story and the place itself. He knew that Roman, Saxon and Celtic sites cropped up all over the city when foundations for new buildings were excavated, but he'd never seen one this well preserved before.

"So, in a way, yes, this company does have a link to ritual sacrifice, but only through this excavation," Montague concluded, looking Ray in the eye. Ray looked back at him with eyes of flint. Montague was impressed. Yes, the others were right about this man – he was the real deal and would make a very good replacement for Marco if they could make him join them.

"Thank you for the history lesson," Ray replied, "You've certainly got an interesting place here."

"And it's open to the public for free every Saturday morning. It's part of our corporate outreach."

Ray crinkled his nose at the copy of a carving showing a priest pulling the heart out of a woman lying on the sacrificial table. Some outreach!

"But all this doesn't change the fact that a vicious criminal decided to phone you while he was running away from the police."

"As I say, I can't change that fact or explain it, but we are very happy to cooperate with the police in any way we can – aren't we, Pru?"

"Yes, of course," said the lawyer, although her look made it clear that their 'cooperation' would be like getting blood from a stone.

"Our security teams will be running their own investigations and I will personally make sure that all their findings are shared with your team as soon as we have them," Montague added, "Now, if you don't have any further questions for me, I would like to leave you in the capable hands of Ms Hemphill," and he offered Ray his hand.

Reluctantly, Ray shook it, saying,

"Thank you for your time, but we may need to talk to you again in the near future."

"Well I'm right here," Montague smiled, then he turned on his heel and left them with his formidable lawyer.

Twenty minutes later, Ray and Andy came out from the highly polished main reception of Global Actuaries Limited and into the dirty chaos of Cannon Street.

"What do you think?" Ray asked as they walked towards the place they'd parked the car.

"Articulate, intelligent, affable... bent." Andy concluded.

"You got that feeling too?"

"Yeah. There's something going on there that's all wrong, and I don't believe his story about a data leak. There's a connection between him and Fabbri – all we've got to do is find it."

"Good," Ray was very glad to have Andy at his side – his instincts were usually spot on,

"There was something about that man I didn't trust..."

"What man would that be?" said a woman's voice from behind them.

Chapter Twenty-One

Wheels Within Wheels

Ray turned around so fast he almost cricked his neck only to see Elizabeth Russell standing right behind them.

"What are you doing here?" Ray demanded.

"First off, it's a free country – I'm allowed to go where I like. Secondly, it appears that our investigations have crossed again... oh how rude of me, I should introduce myself – I'm Elizabeth Russell," she said turning her sparkling, violet eyes to Andy and holding out her hand.

He extended his hand in something of a daze as her eyes became his world,

"Andy Harper... good to meet you," and as he took her hand in his, he could feel a strange jolt of energy between them.

"Well, hello!" said Elizabeth Russell archly as she looked Andy up and down, then she added briskly,

"Come on, let's keep moving. We need to talk and I know just the place."

Even though Ray was annoyed by her sudden appearance, he found it difficult to say 'no' to Elizabeth Russell and soon they were sitting in a dark corner of a tiny, deserted basement bar on St Swithin's Lane with three pints of Camden Hells lager in front of them. She took a long sip of hers and sighed,

"God, that hits the spot!"

Andy couldn't take his eyes off her. Her beauty and aura of strength were incredible as she sat there in her perfectly tailored, black trouser suit. And she drank pints.

"Everything good at home? Nothing strange going on?" Elizabeth Russell fixed Ray with a conspiratorial look.

"No, all good," he replied briefly. He was pissed off with her already for butting into another case – the last thing he wanted to do was involve her in the odd things happening in his home life.

"Good," she smiled brightly, "Right, I'm sorry to carpetbag you like this, but I think the seriousness of what we've got here requires us to dump protocol and just talk to each other."

"Okay, I'm listening," said Ray. He had a bad feeling about where this might be going, but he would try to be diplomatic.

"I need you to lay off Global Actuaries Limited," Elizabeth Russell said bluntly.

"What?" Ray couldn't believe it. What right did she have...

"This is a vital part of my current investigation and I need Simon Montague to feel safe and happy. I take it you just met him?"

"Yeah. We both think he's bent," Andy said.

"Oh yes, as a nine-bob note," she agreed, "But I need you to leave him to me."

"Is it just our cases you want to steal or are you doing this to some other poor coppers?" Ray said bitterly.

"I know how it seems, but I need you to trust me..."

"Trust you!" Ray laughed.

"Yes, because I'm on your side. Anyway, you've got enough on your hands with the Marco Fabbri case."

"How do you know about that?" Ray didn't like this at all. How did she know so much?

"Okay, cards on the table," Elizabeth Russell said, laying her heavily ringed fingers flat on the table,

"I have complete, top-level access to anything I want. I knew what happened with Fabbri before he was cold. The way I look at it, you're on the verge of clearing up his human-trafficking network, so why don't you concentrate on that and leave Montague to me?"

"Because we think he's the one bankrolling Fabbri. Come on, Andy, back me up on this."

Andy had a gulp of lager, then said,

"Yeah, Fabbri was phoning Montague when he died. They're in it together."

"Yes, but it's not something you can do anything about," Elizabeth Russell said.

"Why not?" asked Ray, "If we can prove a link to Fabbri..."

"Montague is connected in places you can't imagine. Believe me, you will never be able to make anything stick. And if you try to, it might destroy your careers. Or worse," and she looked at them seriously.

"If we're putting cards on the table," Ray said, meeting her gaze with defiance, "Is this all wrapped up with Titheridge's murder of Alexei Ukhov? Have we been unwittingly picking away at an international arms-dealing network?"

Elizabeth Russell didn't want to try to explain the truth to them. If this arms-dealing angle gave them something they could understand and see that it was clearly beyond them, then she was glad to use it.

"Yes," she lied.

"Fuck!" Ray sat back angrily.

"Sorry, but I'm telling it like it is," she continued, lying easily, "And I'd rather do this face to face over a pint than by going to your boss and telling him that you need to back off."

Elizabeth Russell then took three large gulps at her ice-cold beer and looked from one to the other of them, lingering on Andy. He was looking at her strong, yet elegant hands, noticing that under each heavy silver ring, there was a tattoo.

"But you think you can catch him?" Ray asked.

"Yes," Elizabeth Russell was stating a fact, which covered Simon Montague, the other members of the cult and the creature they all served.

"What can you do to him that we can't?" Ray asked.

"Right now, nothing," she said, looking candidly at each of them in turn, "But when the time comes, I'll make Montague wish he'd never been born.

That you can count on. But I won't be able to do it if they get spooked by you."

"They?" Ray asked.

"Yes, 'they'. Simon Montague is not the top of the tree. Not by a long way," she said. Just from looking at Montague, she'd been able to tell he had no psychic abilities. There was no way he was running things for the creature,

"Montague's part of a network. Yes, he's important, but he's not the leader. And right now, there are other people in his network keeping an eye on him. I don't want anything to happen that might make them scatter. I want to catch the lot of them," then she downed the rest of her pint and looked at her watch – half past two,

"Too early for shots?" she asked, looking at them impishly.

"You are a piece of work," Ray said, staring at her.

"Thought so - too early..."

"Sod the shots!" Ray growled, "It's the way you keep sweeping the rug from under us. That's what's pissing us off, right Andy?"

"Yeah," Andy said, but as he looked at Elizabeth Russell, he couldn't honestly imagine what she could ever do to piss him off.

"I know this must be hard," she said in a conciliatory tone, "But your vital role in this will be made very clear to all the higher-ups. It'll be good for your careers. And you can look on this as a favour I owe you. If you ever need help from someone with real clout, I'll be there for you. Deal?" and she held out her hand to Ray.

He sighed, then finally, reluctantly said,

"Deal," and shook her hand, so heavy with silver rings.

"Now shots?" she suggested hopefully.

"Sorry, but we've got work to do. Come on, Andy, drink up," and the pair of them downed the remains of their pints and stood up.

Elizabeth Russell followed suit and said,

"Hopefully next time we meet this'll be cleared up and I won't be poaching a case from you."

"Yeah, that would be nice," said Ray coldly as he moved away.

Before Andy could go, Elizabeth Russell held his arm and stopped him briefly.

When Ray realised that Andy hadn't followed him, he turned back to see her whispering something into Andy's ear, before letting go of his arm. He walked across to pub to join Ray, while Elizabeth Russell picked up the three glasses and took them back to the bar, where she announced in a clear voice,

"Pint of Hells and a shot of Monkey Shoulder, please," as she turned to Andy and Ray to give them a cheeky wink. Ray shook his head and stalked out of the bar with Andy in his wake.

"So, what was all that about?" Ray asked when they got in the car and he could be sure that the Russell woman wasn't about to pop out at them from nowhere.

"What?"

"The thing that whatshername was whispering into your shell-like before we left."

"Oh, that," said Andy, colouring slightly as he drove the car out of the underground car park and into the bright sunshine, "Nothing really. Just inviting me out to dinner next week and giving me her home address."

"Do what?" Ray squawked. Did he hear that right?

"Yeah, see, she doesn't have a phone, so she told me to turn up at her place next Thursday at seven-o-clock."

"And you said yes?" Ray could not believe what he was hearing.

"Yeah, why not?"

Ray was so shocked, that he wasn't able to articulate the half dozen or more reasons 'why not' and ended up gesticulating while making strangulated noises.

"Look," said Andy, "I know that she's taking another case off us, but I think she's being straight and… well… have you seen her? She's stunning. And the way she looked at me… if I hadn't said yes, then you'd need to have me committed right now."

"And you don't think you're a little old for her?" Ray looked at Andy witheringly.

"I don't think so," Andy said, but now Ray had said it out loud, he wasn't so sure.

"Oh, come on, she can't be more than twenty-eight."

"So?"

"So, put it this way, if you filmed yourselves in action, it would be that niche porn... what's it called... grandpas fuck teens!"

"Yeah, maybe..."

"Definitely!"

"Yeah, but the point is, at the end of the day, those grandpas do get to fuck the teens, so... winner, winner, chicken dinner," Andy declared.

Ray exploded with laughter,

"And that's the way you 'win' an argument, is it?"

"Yes, it is," Andy grinned.

"You should try that next time you're giving evidence in court. I'm sure the defence would give up and change the plea to guilty on the spot. Or you could just say 'Boom!' at the end of your evidence, or 'Drop the mic!'."

They laughed, then gradually fell into silence and, as London drifted past the window, Ray thought about Simon Montague. He wanted to know more about him and if there was any possibility of a link between him and Fabbri's traffickers. For some reason, he just didn't believe Elizabeth Russell's story. He decided he'd get Emma to look into it on the quiet. She'd already proved her worth and he knew he could depend on her loyalty. Yes, they'd get back and dive into the paperwork on the Fabbri case, then he'd have a quick chat with Emma.

"You all right, Emma? How's the head?" Ray asked as he and Andy walked across the main, open plan area towards his office.

"Yeah, fine. A little tender, but I'll live," she said, gently rubbing the back of her head, "Unlike that woman you interviewed yesterday afternoon – Florence Gichuru – she was found dead this morning."

Ray and Andy both stopped in their tracks.

"Dead?" Ray couldn't believe it. Why would anyone...

"And not in a normal way," Emma added with a troubled look on her face, "Unless you call being folded in half backwards 'normal'."

"Jesus!" Ray exclaimed.

"Yeah, the uniforms said it was a real mess," Emma replied, "And the report from the medical examiner doesn't make for light reading either. Apparently, whoever did it used some sort of hosepipe to pin her arms and legs and then wrapped it round her neck to pull her head back... it's sick stuff."

"But why do it at all? It's the people at The Dead Zone who supplied Fabbri."

"Could it be a warning to the rest of the occultist community not to talk to us?" Emma suggested.

"No, it's too much of a risk. Whoever did this must have known they'd be bringing attention to themselves, but they went and did it anyway. Like they don't care. And besides, Fabbri didn't know we'd been sniffing around, otherwise he'd've fucked off last night instead of trying to do a runner this morning. So, who's done this?" Ray was genuinely at a loss.

"Andy – any thoughts?"

"Sorry, there's something about her being folded over backwards that reminds me of something I've seen before," he had the pained look of someone who has a word on the tip of their tongue, but can't pinpoint it,

"Bollocks! That's going to annoy me for the rest of the day. It is so familiar..."

"Okay, we can't deal with it now anyway, so let's sort out the fallout from this morning and maybe something will pop into your pretty little head later," said Ray, then the three of them went their separate ways.

Four hours later, Ray was about ready to head home, when Andy came knocking on his door with Emma following close behind.

"I think I've done everything I can for today," Andy said, "Still got most of the papers from Fabbri's home office to go through. I'll bet my house we'll get something useful out of it tomorrow."

"How about you, Emma?"

"I've cross-checked the details of around half the factory staff... so far they're all clean. I'll get through the rest in the morning. Wouldn't surprise me if all those factory staff were above board, though. Unless he was really stupid, he'd want to keep his front company spotless."

"Okay, well done both of you," said Ray, and he stifled a yawn. Repeated broken nights had really taken their toll.

"And you'll be pleased to know that I've remembered where I saw that thing about the body folded over backwards," Andy said.

"Where?"

"In the Crime Museum. I was in there a few years ago researching something for a case and... well, you know me, once I was there, I found myself going down various rabbit holes. There was a case sometime in the nineteenth century, where a man was folded over backwards. Anyway, I've booked myself in to take a look at the details tonight. I'll have something for you in the morning."

"Great!" Ray's face brightened, "Sounds like a fun evening."

"Okay, laters," Andy said and he walked out with a wave over his shoulder.

"Emma..." Ray began,

"Yes, guv," Emma's eyes were shining with hope that he'd have something special for her, too.

"I need you to do something under the radar."

"Yeah, totally," Emma said.

"Now, this isn't an order. You don't have to do it. Fact is, it's sort of against orders," Ray knew that Emma usually played by the book, so he crossed his fingers under the desk.

"What do you want me to do?" she asked and there was still an eagerness to please in her eyes.

"I need you to see if there are any links whatsoever between Simon Montague and Marco Fabbri. I'm convinced Montague bankrolled Fabbri's company, but I've been told we can't investigate it..."

"Who's stopping us?" Emma asked.

Ray thought for a moment, then said,

"Best if you don't know. That way if things go wrong and you get hauled in to answer questions, it'll be obvious that you were doing this purely on my orders with no idea that it was wrong. Anyway, it doesn't matter for the job I want you to do."

"Okay," Emma said, but Ray could see she was a bit crestfallen that he hadn't taken her into his confidence.

"What I need is for you to see when and how those two might have got together. Do they support the same football team? Are they members of the same golf club? Maybe they're involved with the same charities?"

"Could be that. Charitable giving is always a good smokescreen."

"Exactly! And it would give them a perfect opportunity to meet legitimately. Anything like that."

"Got it," Emma said with enthusiasm.

"And you're sure you're all right with this?" Ray searched her pretty features for signs of reservations.

"Totally, boss!"

"Okay, thanks. But remember, nobody else hears about this – not even Andy."

"No worries, boss. I'll be like a ghost."

"Thanks, Em'," said Ray and for a moment their eyes met, before hers slid away.

"See you tomorrow," she said and hurried out, leaving Ray to his thoughts of Montague, Fabbri, Titheridge, Elizabeth Russell, and exactly how they all fitted together.

Chapter Twenty-Two

Night At The Museum

When he was at school, there had only been two things that Andy Harper had really excelled at – rugby and history. Now he was in his forties, he'd hung up his rugby boots, but his love of history was still strong. The Crime Museum, once known as 'The Black Museum' had always fascinated him ever since he'd joined the force. It was in New Scotland Yard and wasn't open to the public. Even police officers needed an appointment to access it. Aside from the collection of death masks, hangman's nooses, murder weapons and other artefacts from Britain's most grisly crimes, the museum was also home to possibly the most extensive hoard of historical crime documents in the world. While The Metropolitan Police was established in 1829 and the Bow Street Runners in 1749 to protect citizens, the City of London had been policed by the City Watch since the 13th century. But there was more - papers and documents stretched back all the way to the Norman invasion. If there was one thing William the Conqueror liked, it was to know exactly what was going on and to write it down. The museum even had scraps pre-dating the Normans, including copies of Roman tablets detailing noteworthy crimes that had happened as far back as 47 AD.

So, after he had checked in with the duty officer and ensconced himself at a desk, Andy was able to roll his sleeves up and get stuck in. The research area was certainly conducive to concentrated study: it had no windows, subdued lighting and an air of seriousness, which reflected the information held there. Although Andy had a singular purpose, he had to ensure that he didn't get distracted by the fascinating history of crime in London. It had always been a violent city, where riotous crowds seemed ready to appear at the drop of a hat to cause mayhem, usually with apprentices doing most of the damage. Whether their targets were foreigners, as in the Evil May Day Riot of 1517, or falling wages and poor living conditions during the 1590s, or even prostitution during the Bawdy House riots of 1668, the apprentices always seemed ready to down tools and run amok for almost any reason. London had always been home to many gangs of criminals, which in the past had made some parts of the city no-go zones at night. The likelihood of making it across Covent Garden after dark in the mid-eighteenth century without getting your throat cut, had been low.

Against this rough and ready backdrop, London was regularly shocked by, and sometimes revelled in, gruesome murders. Jack the Ripper's whirlwind of mutilation in 1888 was simply one of many grisly cases that caught the public imagination down the ages. There were the Ratcliff Highway murders of 1811 in which two households within half a mile of each other were targeted just twelve days apart. In total, the killer had bludgeoned and mutilated seven men, women and children, with no discernible motive. Then there was the case from 1726 of Catharine Hayes, who murdered her husband with the help of two accomplices, both of whom were her lovers. They chopped off her husband's head, put it in a bag and threw it in the Thames, then dismembered the body, bagged it up and threw it into a pond in Marylebone. Of course, the head soon washed up, the rest of the body was found and Catharine's story unravelled. In the end, she confessed, claiming that the Devil had made them do it. When it came to her execution, she was burned at the stake, but the mechanism to strangle her before the flames engulfed her went wrong and she screamed horribly until the executioner dashed her brains out with a piece of wood. Delving further back into medieval times revealed a chaotic London of extreme violence with a murder rate twenty times that of the modern city. People needed little provocation before meting out violence - Roger Styward was murdered by two shopkeepers in 1326 for nothing more than throwing a bucket of eel skins into the street outside their stores.

There was so much opportunity for distraction, but Andy was disciplined. He had a vague idea of where he'd seen the article about the folded body, so he went straight into the archive and pulled out a small, plain cardboard box from one of the shelves stacked with similar boxes. He took it back to the desk, which had a microfilm reader on it. Andy opened the box and loaded the microfilm into the machine and then set to work finding the article he wanted. Against the light hum of the air conditioning, the only sounds were the quiet clunking and whirring of the microfilm reader as Andy searched, straining his eyes to read the old newsprint from long dead London magazines, newspapers and periodicals. It was old tech, but presumably the cost of digitizing the entire collection couldn't be justified, given the cuts to police budgets over the previous decade. Besides, Andy took pleasure from the mechanical noises, especially when he fast forwarded through the film and then decelerated to look at something more closely. There was something more real - almost more human - about the process when compared to scrolling through digitized documents.

"You beauty!" Andy declared after half an hour of searching. Yes! There it was! The Cheapside Horror. The article in The London Recorder from 1847 with its ancient typeface immediately drew Andy into a different time and place:

'Horror at Cheapside!

Authorities baffled and local people terrified by bloody murder.

In the early hours of Tuesday November 23rd, the body of John Henry Watkins of 106 Cheapside was discovered in his butcher's shop by Charles David Adams, an apprentice of the deceased. Mr. Watkins, a prominent butcher and supplier of meats to some of the foremost hotels in London, had been savagely beaten and folded backwards until his back was broken. Marks on his wrists, ankles and neck indicate that ropes were used to commit this heinous crime. However, it is clear that such a feat would require a number of men to perform the task, and yet no one was seen entering or leaving the shop at any time from its closure at 5 pm on Monday evening *to the discovery of the body at 4.30 am on Tuesday morning. The brutality of the crime is matched only by the mystery of who committed it, how it was done and why. The most alarming aspect of the murder, according to those who have seen the body of Mr. Watkins, is the twisted look of horror on the face of the victim, which has led the coroner to suspect that death was caused not by the breaking of his spine, but by heart failure induced by terror.'*

Andy sat back with a grim smile on his face. So, there it was, a nigh-on identical murder to that of Florence Gichuru, with no leads, no witnesses and no apparent motive. The case had stumped the authorities of the time and was left unsolved... unsolved... yes, that could by his 'in' to finding out if there were any other cases like this. Once Andy had copied the article onto the computer and saved it, he rewound the microfilm. The screeching whirr of the mechanism sounded horribly loud in the stillness of the room and when it fully rewound, the end of the film flapped about against the mechanism for a second or two. Andy looked around, fully expecting to see someone coming over to tell him off for making so much noise, but the room was empty. He replaced the film into its box and then put it onto the cart of items that had been viewed and which the staff would return to their correct places in the morning. He then walked back to the room where the films were kept with its rows of shelves containing microfilms. He was looking for... yes, there it was 'Unsolved Murders: Pre-1800'. After 1800, each century had its own microfilm of unsolved murders, but the one Andy had in his hand contained everything from 1799 back to the year dot.

As he walked back to the desk, he smiled to himself. The thing about murders in days gone by was that the authorities had been reluctant to let cases go 'unsolved'. Someone would almost always be found who at least vaguely fitted the bill of the murderer – even if that someone wasn't the perpetrator of the crime. They were often criminals who the authorities were glad to get rid of. England, far from being 'free' had been a place where even a child could get the death penalty for stealing anything over the value of twelve pence up until 1832. So, fitting up a known criminal for murder and giving the vengeful mob the catharsis of a public execution was an easy way of quelling the fears of the citizenry. This meant that the number of 'unsolved' cases were far fewer the further back into history you went. Maybe he'd get lucky and find something else?

He loaded the microfilm into the machine and started searching. This was when he was at his most vulnerable. Andy would have to try to ignore everything that didn't fit the pattern he was looking for... but it was so hard! Every case was fascinating in its own way and he had to keep stopping himself from falling into the story of every single one. He was able to get back as far as 1678, before a story drew him in. It was the murder of Sir Edmund Berry Godfrey, who was found impaled on his own sword at Primrose Hill in north London. Although it was supposed to look like suicide, his body was covered in bruises, there were strangulation marks around his throat and his neck was broken. The lack of bleeding from the sword wound also clearly indicated that it was made post-mortem - and not at the scene where the body was found. The question was, who had killed him and why...

"No!" Andy hissed, "Focus! Come on!" and he moved the microfilm forward.

Twenty minutes passed as he skimmed through London's strange, unpleasant and unsolved past. However, when he reached the 1536 murder of the MP Robert Pakington, he allowed himself a little time to revel in the story, because it was the first example of someone being murdered with a handgun in London. It had been a misty Sunday morning in November and Pakington was crossing the street on his way to church, when a shot broke the stillness. Many people heard it, but because of the thick mist, no one saw the assailant, and the murder was left unsolved. Was it a Catholic plot? Andy paused for a moment, imagining the misty scene and the shock and surprise of the local people as they realised that a killer was on the loose with a gun. He wondered whether they had a Tudor equivalent of Belinda, their brilliant medical examiner. He smiled as he imagined her in Tudor clothing, bossing the crime scene and telling people off for moving evidence. Then he shook his head, rubbed his eyes and got back to the job in hand. He spun the microfilm on, travelling ever further backwards through time. Was this all worth it? He was finding it interesting, but this should have been his downtime. Over the next forty-five minutes, his mind started wandering towards thoughts of a pub and a pint of London Pride. Then suddenly there it was.

"Fuck me!" Andy said loudly as he looked at a crude drawing of a man in medieval clothes who had been folded in half and whose arms and legs were clearly meant to be broken.

Andy read the copy of the original parish document excitedly. In 1306, a Lombard banker called Emilio Baldesio had been walking to his home in Candlewick when *'he was overcome with a great perturbation'*. He ran, screaming and crying out *'and exhorting both gentlemen and commoners alike to flee for their immortal souls'*. When he returned home, his servants later told the coroner that *'he was shaking and pale, with chattering teeth and soaked in sweat, as if afflicted with the ague'*. He had immediately locked himself in his bedchamber, refusing either food or to let anyone in. Later that night, his household was roused by a *'loud commotion'* and three of his servants ran to their master's bedchamber, which was still locked. Worried by the sounds of a struggle from within, the two manservants broke the door down as the housemaid watched. Inside, they found their master *'in a terrible fit of convulsions, in which he did rave and strain so hard as to break his own bones'*. Then, as they tried to aid their master, *'he did, with staring eyes and uttering nought but strangled noises from his gullet, bend himself full backwards until his back was broked'*. Baldesio's personal servant, who was one of the witnesses immediately ran to inform the watch that *'the Devil hath possessed his master and torn him asunder'*. When the authorities arrived, they were disposed to believe the servants, *'for two men and one serving girl of only thirteen years could not have the strength to break a man so. Only the diabolical power of the Devil himself could commit such sacrilege.'*

"Jesus!" Andy whispered to himself as he leant back from the microfilm reader. He didn't like the way the story made him feel and he couldn't help but look over his shoulder. The dimly lit, empty room behind him offered him no comfort. So, there *had* been another one, and this time it had been witnessed by three people. But the story was so... uncanny. He could only presume that the servants had murdered their master, probably with help, and then played on the superstitions of the time to palm it off as the work of the Devil. Otherwise... no... could they really have witnessed a man break his own limbs and back during a seizure? Surely it was impossible? And yet, what other explanation was there? Could they have stumbled onto something supernatural?

"Get a grip, Andy!" he said to himself out loud. There was something about being in that oh-so-quiet museum long after hours that encouraged the mind to start playing tricks on itself. Maybe he should call it a night? It was already knocking on eleven and there were plenty of places he could still get that drink... no. He would go through all the cases. He was already at the twelve hundreds. There wasn't that far to go before the empty chasm of the Dark Ages, and then he'd be into the Roman period and almost home and hosed. He took one last, wary look over his shoulder, then bent back to the microfilm viewer again.

After saving the section on Emilio Baldesio, Andy ran through the files on the microfilm. As he'd suspected, the further back he went, the sparser the information became until the great leap from the reign of Aethelred in 978 AD to 375 AD, when Roman rule in Britain was on the wane. Now he was looking at photographs of ancient tablets, accompanied by printed translations. He honestly didn't think there was anything else to come, but there was. In 124 AD, during the reign of the Emperor Hadrian, the body of a woman was found near a small shrine not far from the Forum: *'Record of the strange death of Julia the Diviner. Known to all in Londinium as a seer, Julia the Diviner was found on the nones of the month of Juno near the grove sacred to Krowos, god of the spring whose waters give power and protection to those whom Krowos deems worthy. Julia, that raven-headed perceiver of the invisible, had adjured citizens in the Forum to avoid the grove of Krowos, for she said he was a wicked god with nought but evil in his heart, that the Druids had shunned his place for fear of death, and that the gods of our ancestors would be displeased with any who might worship Krowos the Deceiver. Julia the Deviner also proclaimed on numerous occasions that Boudicca's destruction of the city was instigated by Krowos in return for a goodly supply of fresh human blood. Julia was found broken in two and drained of all her blood, although not one drop was shed upon the grass where she lay and no human footmarks were found. The only marks upon the ground were those of snakes, as if many snakes had come to that place. The priests of Krowos made an offering to their god to ease Julia the Deviner's passage to the afterlife and built her funeral pyre where she had fallen so that the god might better watch over her spirit.'*

"Blimey!" Andy said quietly. He had not expected that! The story was strange, but it was the image at the bottom of the Roman tablet that was deeply unsettling. Next to the word Krowos was etched a shape that he recognised. It was the diagonal crystal cutting through the centre of the symbol for infinity – the same symbol that had been cut into the torso from the river and the man in Titheridge's kill room. Andy felt a wave of disquiet envelope him from the back of his head to his face. What–the–fuck? What did this mean? Was this really something that had been happening since Roman times and was still going on? Or had some weirdos settled upon some ancient god and decided to bring back its cult? Either way, it was chilling. He quickly saved a copy to the computer and googled 'Krowos' on his phone. All the top hits were for an Italian Black Metal band, and after that most of the hits were for Kronos, the father of Zeus, who had castrated his own father, Uranus, with a sickle. However, he couldn't find anything on a god named Krowos. Weird. Shit, the whole thing was weird and honestly gave Andy the creeps. There they were, four identical murders down the ages. All unsolved, all shrouded in mystery and all hinting at some power greater than that of man. Perhaps it was because they were from less sophisticated times, but Andy found it fascinating that the last two clearly indicated the belief that the murders had been committed by some diabolical supernatural agent. What it was, nobody knew... but the

Lombard, Baldesio, had been broken before the eyes of three people... Andy googled 'epileptic fits breaking bones' on his phone and searched for half an hour – yes there were examples of people breaking bones, but that was usually from falling over or hitting themselves on hard objects during convulsions. Nowhere could he find anything about people convulsing so hard that they snapped their lower backs. So, unless the three servants had been lying and the truth was that they, along with three or four other men had broken Baldesio, then what had truly happened? Could they have witnessed a supernatural attack? And to cap it all, there was an ancient symbol being carved onto murder victims in the here and now...

Andy sat back in his chair and washed his face with his hands. What was he thinking? Was he really going to approach Ray and say,

"Morning, boss, I've cracked the Gichuru case. Yeah, looks like the murderer is an entity – possibly a god of some sort – that has murdered people in exactly the same way four times since the reign of Hadrian. Either that, or an ancient cult has been killing people in London for two thousand years."

No. That would be crazy. Ray would laugh him out of the office and put him down for a psychological evaluation. And yet... something deep inside him was squirming at the thought that the explanation was correct and that they were dealing with a being that had once been worshipped as a god. No! The likely explanation was that all the witnesses were unreliable and the investigators incompetent or lacking the technology and methodology to find the truth. Yes, that was it. But what about that symbol? Andy looked at his watch – almost midnight. He'd wasted a summer's evening trawling through nonsense when he could have been sitting in a pub garden. Even worse, he'd let the atmosphere of the Crime Museum and the fact that he was working late and alone get into his head. He was like someone lost in the vastness of the desert, seeing an oasis at every turn.

"Right!" Andy said firmly in an attempt to dispel the mumbo-jumbo that was weighing heavily around him. He got up, gathered his work, placed the microfilm on the trolley, turned off the machine, signed out with the duty officer and headed out of the building. He stepped out into the warm night and took a deep breath. That was better! The scent of London on a summer night – dissipating car fumes, cooling asphalt, hints of wet mud and sewage from the river and, somewhere deep in the mix, a dash of trees and flowers. He started along the Embankment towards Westminster Bridge. The jolly streetlights, the bustle of people going home after a night out, the trees lining the road, the glittering river boats and the great colourful Ferris wheel of the London Eye all lightened Andy's mood. Soon he had shaken off the strange feeling of disquiet that had gripped him so firmly in the museum. Yeah, he wouldn't mention any of his wild theories to Ray, just tell him about the three historical murders and see what he said. Even then, he could imagine Ray's serious face cracking into a broad smile and then laughing at the thought that Andy had probably come up with some supernatural explanation for it all. And then Emma and some of the others might weigh in... yeah, maybe this was all best kept to himself...

Chapter Twenty-Three

A Knight In Grubby Armour

Mexican Dave loved nothing more than an emergency, and they had one! Krowos was threatened. The police had violated the sanctity of *his* house by interrogating Simon Montague and now Krowos would have his revenge! Orders had been given, human chess pieces were on the move, and he had a quest: to slay a giant! Mexican Dave also loved to be overly dramatic and to do things with a certain style and panache. He spent the late afternoon taking a half-blunt hacksaw to the bottom of an iron railing outside a Victorian house that was due to be demolished in Camden. It was hot work and, as he sawed back and forth, sweat ran down from under the brim of his sombrero and into his eyes. In fact, the sombrero wasn't helping at all, because when he got in close to the railing, it butted up against it and sometimes folded downwards to obscure his view. He tried it hanging down on his back, but it always slipped round and got in the way. But he would not be defeated! There was no way he was taking the hat off completely. That never happened. Not when he was taking a dump, not when he was having a bath, not even when he occasionally got his rocks off with one of the half-dozen homeless women who were willing to shag for booze or drugs. And he wasn't about to start taking it off just because some bloody bit of ironwork was being a bitch!

Finally, around seven-o-clock, he cut through the last bit of the railing.

"Stitch that, you fucker!" he cried triumphantly in his dismally inaccurate Scottish accent. He stood up and held the piece of iron above his head like Aeneas brandishing his spear before his final, bloody conflict with Turnus. And then words came into his mind...

'Cunctanti telum Aeneas fatale coruscat,
sortitus fortunam oculis, et corpore toto
eminus intorquet.'

What did they mean? Were they Latin? Did he know Latin? Had he once studied Classics at Durham University? Or was it all a dream? Or was his life a dream since the day he first saw Krowos, and the god had opened the cosmic door to show him terrifying truths? Was understanding Latin one of the powers the god had bestowed upon him?

"Who fucking cares!" he cried wildly, brandishing the four-foot length of spiked railing again. Then he set to, filing smooth the blunt end and wrapping it in gaffer tape so that it wouldn't cut him. When he was done, he used the file to sharpen the pointy end to a vicious spike. Once it was all to his satisfaction, he hopped onto his mighty steed (well, his bike) and sped away, for he had a giant to slay!

As he manically cycled down from Camden to the river, Mexican Dave found himself ever more absorbed by thoughts of heroic battles. Was he Don Quixote, a knight errant doing good deeds astride his trusty steed Rocinante and about to face off against another recalcitrant giant? Or was he Aeneas, the great Trojan hero, set to do battle with Prince Turnus? To any bystander, Don Quixote was much nearer the mark. Like Don Quixote, Mexican Dave was bonkers and living in his own dreamworld. He cut a tragi-comic figure in his shabby clothes and ragged sombrero, riding his battered, rattling bike, trying to keep his balance as he navigated the traffic with a heavy iron bar in one hand, and a wobbling handlebar in the other. When he finally arrived on the embankment, he rested his bike against the trunk of a huge plain tree and propped his lance against it. Then he started to pace and talk to himself, sometimes in his sub-par Scottish accent and sometimes in a cultivated voice which spoke in Latin. Over the next three hours, he paced and chattered to himself as he fell ever further into the fiction that he was, in fact, Aeneas. Yes, bold Aeneas, fighting to avenge the innocent Pallas, who had fallen so ignominiously to the sword of the hot headed Turnus. And, as Aeneas, he would bring destruction to the malefactor with nothing but the steel of his spear and the strength of his right arm. So, by the time Andy stepped out of New Scotland Yard, Mexican Dave had wound himself up into a vengeful fury and, when he spied his enemy, he had to stifle a cry of triumph that the moment had finally come. He watched Andy walk along the Embankment, then take a left onto Westminster Bridge. Now was Mexican Dave's moment and, in his own mind, he made it heroic:

His bike was a rattling, rusty mess no more, but was transformed into a galloping steed, carrying him on its strong back to glory. They swept onto the bridge with the fury of storm clouds and, with the reins in his left hand, he held aloft his mighty lance. Yes, he was the legendary Aeneas, finally chasing down the cowardly Turnus. Now his strong right arm would deliver divine justice! Faster he galloped until he drew back his arm and took careful aim. His eyes flashed in triumph and his hand, suffused with godlike power, hurled the shaft. Its flight was true and it landed full-square in his enemy's back. Even as his foe fell, he pulled up his steed, which reared and neighed above the vanquished. And then the hero surveyed the scene of his bloody victory, before galloping off into the pages of history!

Naturally, the reality was rather different. Sweating, his sombrero flapping and his mouth agape, Mexican Dave pedalled madly after Andy. It was hard to cycle with the heavy length of sharpened railing in his hand, and it looked most likely that he'd crash the bike and impale himself, but somehow he made it onto Westminster Bridge. Here he had a stroke of luck – all the tourists were on the other side of the bridge, taking photographs of the Houses of Parliament at night. Andy was walking alone, giving Mexican Dave a clear run. He put on an extra burst of speed, which caused his sombrero to whip off his head and half throttle him with the string around his throat, but somehow Dave kept his balance and, as he got close enough, he launched the iron rod with a loud,

"Oooyah!"

The rod hit Andy to the right of his spine and he fell face-first to the ground, just managing to break his fall with his hands. Winded, dazed and in agony, he began to get up, but Mexican Dave wasn't taking any chances. He was off his bike in an instant, grabbing the end of the rod and, with a foot on Andy's lower back, pushing it into him with every ounce of his strength. Andy was shoved onto the pavement and felt a golden burst of pain through his chest as all the air was pushed out of him. As he panicked, he distinctly heard the tip of the rod striking the pavement under him, then everything went black. Mexican Dave picked up the bag Andy had been carrying, hopped back onto his bike and pedalled away, leaving Andy face down in a widening pool of his own blood.

Chapter Twenty-Four

A Day Out

It was already half-past ten the next morning when Vicky cocked a sleepy eye at the bedside alarm and groaned. She and Chloe had snoozed most of the morning away! Vicky turned and gave Chloe a gentle shake,

"Come on, sleepyhead, we can't waste the whole day in bed."

"Why not?" Chloe replied with the truthfulness of semi-sleep.

"Because there's a big, beautiful world out there and we've got to get out and enjoy it!" Vicky declared as she shrugged off the last vestiges of sleep and swung her legs over the side of the bed. She got up, walked through to the kitchen/diner and slid the back door open. It was deliciously warm outside and the sounds of lazy bees droning and birds singing in the gardens of the block made her smile. Their house was part of an unbroken terrace of houses that created an oblong around a centre of gardens. Their gardens were an oasis of green tranquillity inside a two-storey wall of houses which kept out the worst of the traffic noise. Even crafty foxes didn't have a way of getting through the barrier of houses into the calm interior, because the only way in was through the buildings. No, this was the realm of birds and house cats, which did their best to eat everything that came into their little world.

Vicky left the sliding doors open, put the kettle on and went to the loo while it boiled. When she'd finished, she called to Chloe,

"Tea?"

The inarticulate moan indicated that yes, a cup of tea would be most appreciated, thank you very much. Vicky smiled; Chloe was seven going on sixteen.

"Come on, cutie, get it while it's hot!" Vicky called once the mugs were on the table. After about a minute, Chloe stumbled into the room, shielding her eyes from the white light of late morning.

"You all right? Sleep okay?" Vicky asked as Chloe sat down.

"Yes, thanks," she replied and Vicky was glad to see that a couple of good nights' sleep seemed to have washed away Chloe's terror from two days before. Should she broach the subject? No. Why spoil a beautiful day?

"I've had an idea," Vicky said, and Chloe gave her a sideways glance. She didn't trust Vicky's 'ideas', because, being a teacher, her mother saw every day as an opportunity for learning something new.

"No, don't look at me like that," Vicky knew exactly what her daughter was thinking, "This'll be fun and I promise that you won't learn anything new at all."

Ha! A likely story. Chloe remembered the last time that promise had been trotted out and they'd ended up in some art gallery.

"I was thinking we could go to Borough, have a walk by the river, get some lunch in Borough Market, buy lovely, overpriced ingredients and come home and cook up a feast!"

There, that didn't sound too daunting, Vicky thought... and if the part of the river they decided to walk down just happened to include Sir Francis Drake's ship The Golden Hinde, Shakespeare's Globe Theatre and the Tate Modern Gallery, then maybe she could slip in a bit of education at the same time.

"All right," said Chloe with a smile born of ignorance of the vast number of learning opportunities that that particular part of London held.

"Great!" Vicky said cheerfully, "If you want, we could skip breakfast here and have brunch at the Market instead."

That was a step too far and Chloe's face became thoughtful,

"I don't like brunch. You don't get breakfast and you don't get lunch."

Vicky erupted in laughter. How could a seven-year-old come up with that?

"Okay," she said, and she was glad to see Chloe smiling too, "We'll have a light breakfast and a bigger lunch. Deal?" and she held out her hand,

"Deal," Chloe replied, shaking it firmly.

As they walked down the High Road towards the bus stop forty-five minutes later, neither of them noticed The Man. He was standing three hundred yards away on the other side of the road in the blazing sunshine, sweating into his tight, honey-coloured trench coat. He followed them, keeping that distance between them until they reached their bus stop. He stopped and stood like a statue staring at them, seething and balling his fists. The Man had a plan.

In the centre of Brixton, Bag Hag suddenly stopped sifting through the bin outside the Ritzy cinema and looked up Brixton Hill in the direction of Streatham. It was as if she had heard someone call her name and she looked up the hill with the concentration of someone taking complicated instructions. She nodded along until finally the message seemed to end. She turned away from the hill, picked up the plastic bags containing her life and walked towards Brixton underground station with her awkward, rolling gait. As always, the area around the station was crowded with beggars, buskers, people selling incense from small trestle tables, religious fanatics shouting the Word into the faces of passers-by, and ordinary folk just trying to catch the tube. Bag Hag wedged herself between a wall and a religious zealot, ensuring that she had a good view of the entrance to the underground station, and waited. The Man had given her a very difficult task. She had to follow the mother and daughter, who were already on their way down the hill on the bus. Bag Hag knew how tricky that could be! The way the child had unceremoniously thrown Bag Hag out of her mind had shown exactly how powerful the brat was. However, this time, Bag Hag had more flexibility. If the opportunity arose, she had permission to kidnap the girl. Even if that meant killing the mother. Bag Hag liked these instructions and she hadn't heard The Man sound so turned on by a prospect in a very long time, but they both knew that making a clean snatch would be hard. So, she would follow and watch them and bide her time, and then bam! Yes, that was the way to do it.

Within twenty minutes, Vicky and Chloe were hopping off the bus opposite Brixton tube.

"Busy today!" Vicky shouted over the noise of the bus and the traffic, as the crowd of humanity swelled around them.

"Keep a tight hold of my hand," and she felt Chloe's little hand grip hers harder. Good girl!

Then they worked their way through the streams of people going in different directions and made their way into the ever-busy station. The mass of stimuli bombarding Chloe worked in their enemy's favour, as she didn't even vaguely notice Bag Hag slip into the mass of humanity behind them and ghost along in their wake.

"What sort of food do you want for dinner?" Vicky asked as they rode down the escalator, "Indian, Italian, Chinese, steak and chips? They've got everything you can think of at Borough Market."

Chloe thought hard. What was she in the mood for? Was this one of those adult trick questions, where if she said 'chicken dippers and chips', Vicky would criticise her lack of imagination? Why did grown-ups ask questions if there was the likelihood they weren't going to enjoy the answers?

"Pasta," she said at last.

Vicky's face lit up,

"Good idea! We can think of what sauce we'll make when we get there and see what ingredients are looking good," she said as they got off the escalator and went to the platform they needed for the next train.

Since Brixton is the end of the line, there was a train waiting at the platform, slowly filling up with people until its departure time. There were still a couple of minutes before the train was due to leave, so Vicky and Chloe were able to choose where to sit. Neither of them saw the hairy face peeking around the corner of the entrance to the platform and watching them get on. Once they were inside the train, they didn't see

Bag Hag waddle her way onto the next carriage. Vicky and Chloe relaxed, talking about where they were going and blissfully unaware that there was a woman in the next carriage with kidnap and murder on her mind. Soon, the train pulled out and they were rattling down the tunnel on the way to Stockwell, the next station on the line, where they would change to the Northern Line and take it to London Bridge. After about a minute, the noise of the train screaming through the tunnel was too much for Chloe, who put her hands over her ears. Vicky gave her a little cuddle. She was a very sensitive child and that tube line was painfully noisy in places. Vicky had even found that it could drown out Motorhead played at full volume on her earbuds. Fortunately, the Northern Line wasn't so bad, so the rest of the journey would probably be fine.

In the adjacent carriage, Bag Hag watched the set of doors nearest her quarry. She wouldn't have much time between seeing them walking through the doors and being able to get off the train herself, so she was tense. The train slowed as it arrived at Stockwell and she saw the mother and daughter get up to stand near the door. Bag Hag heaved herself out of her seat and moved to the nearest door in her carriage. Other passengers studiously avoided looking at her, and one woman in her early thirties was holding her hand over her mouth so she didn't have to smell her either. Perfect. The doors opened and Bag Hag peeked out to see what the pair were doing. They stepped off the train and walked straight towards the nearest passageway to the next platform, which was the north bound Northern Line. So! That was their game. Bag Hag got off the train just before the doors closed and hurried, as much as she could, towards the other platform, where the next train was arriving. This would take careful timing! She waddled down the narrow passage and stopped before the platform, then bobbed her head out and back to see where they were. Yes, they were the equivalent of a carriage length up the platform. The train came to a halt and disgorged its passengers, then those waiting started to board. Bag Hag waited. She couldn't risk being seen. Then she made her break, but too late! The doors were closing. With a supreme effort, she darted forward and managed to get one of her plastic bags wedged into the sliding doors. There was a pause, then the doors opened and Bag Hag rolled onto the train.

"Stand clear of the doors please. Stand clear of the closing doors!" the voice of the driver crackled loudly through the train. He sounded peeved. If people were pissing about with the doors before lunchtime, what the hell would it be like in the evening rush?

Even though Vicky and Chloe only had four stops to go, they were glad to get a seat in the more crowded Northern Line train. The carriage was grubbier, the seats less padded and it all seemed to be older than the train they'd just vacated. Vicky looked around at their fellow passengers and decided that people always looked more miserable on the Northern Line than any other. But that wasn't going to dampen her spirits. She was going to have a lovely afternoon bonding with her daughter and that was that. For her part, Chloe was thinking about how she could get her mum to buy her some doughnuts. It was never easy getting treats out of Vicky, but she reckoned it might be possible. She seemed to be trying very hard to be chummy, so it might be easier to get what she wanted – especially when Vicky inevitably sprang something educational on her. Although the train was quieter than the last one, they didn't speak and just freewheeled through their own thoughts until Vicky nudged Chloe and said,

"This is us," as the train pulled into London Bridge.

They stepped off the train and were working their way down the crowded platform when Vicky said,

"Oh no, this is the way to the mainline station," and she turned them around in the crowd, "We need the exit for Borough High Street. Over there!" Vicky pointed at a sign high on the wall at the other end of the platform, but that wasn't what caught Chloe's attention. Somewhere in the crowd between them and the exit, she could see a black aura. In the jumble of adults, she couldn't see precisely who it belonged to, but it was there. She felt a shiver and saw the image in her mind of The Man pointing at her and the thing with the baby's head coming at her out of the darkness. She gripped Vicky's hand more tightly. She wanted to go home, but she knew she couldn't say anything. Vicky wouldn't understand and would think she was being childish. All Chloe could do was cling on tight and make sure that she didn't lose Vicky. Chloe watched as the black aura stopped moving towards them and started moving away. That was good, but she and Vicky were still going in the same direction as the person with the black aura. Even worse, Vicky was hurrying them along! Then Chloe realised her mother had been speaking the whole time,

"... so we ought to hurry up, or we won't be able to get everything done before the market closes. You never know what adventures could be waiting for us out there," Vicky finished, thinking of the new exhibition at the Tate Modern.

Yes, you never know, Chloe thought, losing sight of the black aura as it disappeared around the corner ahead of them.

Ten minutes later, Vicky and Chloe were walking along a cobbled street towards the river. Chloe was a bit more relaxed, because she hadn't seen the black aura since the station platform. Also, the crowds had thinned out, so she would be able to spot one more easily. Vicky was slightly more tense, because she knew exactly what was coming around the next corner...

"Oh wow! Look at that!" she exclaimed, trying her best to sound surprised.

There, in front of them in a small dock, was an old sailing ship from the fifteen hundreds. It looked like a mini version of a Spanish galleon with sails, rigging made of thick ropes, two crow's nests and a cannon pointing out through a hole near the front.

"This is the Golden Hinde," said Vicky enthusiastically,

"It's a replica of the ship Sir Francis Drake used to sail around the world between fifteen seventy-seven and fifteen eighty."

"Cool," said Chloe and she meant it. The ship was amazing to look at, and the fact that it seemed to have just been placed amongst office buildings, cafes and a pub made the sight all the more surprising.

"And on the way, they captured a Spanish treasure galleon and took so much gold and silver that when Drake returned to England, Queen Elizabeth the First knighted him on the ship."

"Why did she knight him?" Chloe asked.

"Because he was the first Englishman to circumnavigate the world..." Vicky wavered for a moment, wondering whether to add anything more, then decided that the truth was best,

"And because the Queen got half the proceeds of the voyage, so she was very, very happy."

"Even though he stole it from the Spanish?"

"Especially because he stole it from the Spanish. You see, England and Spain were sort of at war and they kept stealing ships and treasure from each other."

"So, he didn't get in trouble with the police?" Chloe asked, looking up at her mum.

"No," Vicky shook her head.

"Ray wouldn't like that," said Chloe, "He says all stealing is wrong."

"Well, yes, your father's right."

"Except when you give the Queen half of it," Chloe stated it like it was a fact.

Vicky laughed,

"Basically, yes. That's exactly how it is."

While Vicky and Chloe were enjoying the Golden Hinde, Bag Hag was busy organising herself. The incident on the platform, when she was following the mother and daughter and they'd suddenly turned around and started walking towards her, had shown how difficult it was going to be to stay hidden from the girl. Bag Hag needed help and, as she waddled a good distance behind the mother and daughter, she heard a voice close by,

"Nutter! Fucking nutter!"

"Ah, Rohit – just the man!" she said in a surprisingly mellifluous middle-class voice, turning to face the approaching Nawab of Newington, "Do you know the score?"

"Fucking nutter!" Rohit grinned, his white teeth standing out brightly against his dark skin in the sunshine.

"Good," Bag Hag said, "The little shit is stronger than The Man realizes, so we're going to have to go with Plan B and put Wilf, Smiler and Jaxx on them."

"Nutter!" he replied with a gruesome twinkle in his eye.

Bag Hag considered the trio for a moment. They were all older homeless people whose minds had finally cracked under the strain of a constantly shifting life with no safety net. Unlike her, Rohit, The Man and Mexican Dave, none of them had been touched by Krowos. This meant that they had no power beyond their own limited physical abilities, but it also meant their auras were clean. The girl wouldn't be able to spot them. Also, they were eminently malleable. All three were dancing on the edge of total mental collapse. All three had substance abuse problems. All three had been told that they might be needed and that the prize for success would be that they, too, would be touched by Krowos. And all three were willing to do almost anything for that. Yes, they were highly motivated and would do nicely.

"And Mexican Dave?" she asked.

"Fucking nutter!"

"Yes, he is, but where is he, Rohit?"

"Nutter!"

"Oh..." she said in awe, "Skewered him right there on Westminster Bridge?"

Rohit's crooked-toothed grin widened.

"I wish I'd seen him do it... Okay, so he's lying low. What about Tommy?"

"Fucking nutter!"

"Of course! London Bridge is his patch. Right, I need him here. I've got a plan."

After spending twenty minutes looking at the ship and talking about treasure, the Incas, Mayans and Aztecs, scurvy, the Spanish Armada and punishments like walking the plank and keel hauling, Vicky and Chloe continued their walk along the river path. Vicky was happy, because she'd got some education into the day, while Chloe was happy, because she could use the history lesson as leverage to get doughnuts later. They continued walking and had barely gone fifty yards when they arrived at the underwhelming ruins of what had once been a palace. While Vicky enthused about how the area had once been a palace used by the Bishops of Winchester, Chloe wondered how a couple of crumbling walls and some plants could really be a tourist attraction. Sometimes adults were stupid! Fortunately, after about five minutes, they walked on. However, within a hundred yards, Chloe got the horrible feeling that she had fallen into a terrible trap. Now they were at The Clink. This was the infamous prison whose name had become a slang word for any jail. Vicky was in her element, reading the notices about the history of The Clink, while Chloe smiled, nodded, oohed, aahed and plotted how to get doughnuts *and* ice cream out of this impromptu history tour.

Neither of them noticed the spectacularly hairy man wearing dirty grey jogging bottoms and a blue hoody sidling up to them. It was only when he spoke that they realised he was there.

"You don't wanna end up in The Clink," he said in a friendly West country accent through a bushy brown beard,

"Sorry! I didn't mean to startle you," he added, when he saw the looks on their faces. He didn't want to spook them... yet.

"It's just, you know – The Clink. Yer don't wanna end up in The Clink, do ya?"

"No, we don't," said Vicky, putting on the polite smile and tone that she reserved for mad people and elderly relatives. Chloe looked at the man and could see that while he looked a bit wild, with his mass of greasy, tumbling hair, his dirty and extremely hairy face, and grubby clothes, his aura was brown, not black.

"I've been all over and I never once ended up in the Clink," he said proudly.

"So, you've travelled?" said Vicky, trying to think of a way they could move on.

"Oh yeah, I travelled to Portsmuff," he replied, mispronouncing 'Portsmouth',

"Bournemuff, Weymuff, Plymuff..." and he paused as he ran out of easy places to name, then he had a brainwave,

"And Aberystwuff!"

"Wow!" Vicky was at a loss for words, but then thought 'fuck it' and decided they should just go,

"Well, it's been interesting to meet you, but..."

"Wilf. Me name's Wilf," he said.

"Hi Wilf, but we've really got to be going," Vicky replied and she was holding ever more tightly to Chloe's hand as she tried to move them away.

"I bet you've got a nice name," he said, turning his attention to Chloe, who looked up at him without fear or judgement,

"I bet your name is..." and he looked to the sky for inspiration, then fixed her with a sly grin,

"Chloe," he said.

It was as if he'd slapped both of them in the face. Vicky was amazed and a bit wary, but Chloe was instantly scared. How could this wild man have guessed her name, unless...

"Was I right?" Wilf said, grinning so that they could just make out some blackened teeth amidst all the hair.

"Er... no," Vicky lied, "Come on, Jemma, we've got to go – nice to meet you," and Vicky marched away with Chloe's hand very firmly in her grip.

"Bye, Chloe!" Wilf called after them, grinning and waving. Would the girl turn to look back at him? Yes! After about fifteen yards, she turned her head to glance back with a worried look on her face. Wilf's grin turned nasty and he winked when he saw Chloe's eyes widen. Then her head snapped forward and she hurried away, practically dragging her mother along. Wilf chuckled and melted into the scenery.

Vicky and Chloe walked fast through a tunnel under railway tracks and along past various pubs and restaurants until they got to the river walk. Vicky threw the occasional glance over her shoulder and was soon satisfied they weren't being followed, so they slowed.

"That was weird!" she said, looking at Chloe with concern, "You alright?"

"Yeah, fine," Chloe lied. It was very, very weird and she was definitely not alright.

They kept walking and soon arrived at Bankside Pier. Unsurprisingly for a sunny summer's day, there was a good crowd of people milling about, queuing for the sightseeing boats or trying to decide whether to spend their holiday money on a boat trip or something else. Amongst them, standing still but apparently scanning the crowd for someone he knew, was a heavy-set man with a big, bald head and an unutterably miserable look on his weary face. Smiler clocked Vicky and Chloe the moment they came out from the underpass of Southwark Bridge. He didn't do anything, but simply stood there watching them approach. The child was looking around her, vigilant for strangers who might want to do her harm. Yes, keep looking around little girl and eventually, you will see...

Chloe saw the bald man in the leather jacket fixing her with a hopeless gaze and she knew at once that something was wrong. He didn't have a black aura – his was brown, just like the other man – but Chloe had a feeling deep inside that he wanted to harm them. Just as Vicky was slowing down to take a closer look at the Globe Theatre, Chloe pulled at her hand and tried to drag her away – away from the man who was still watching them with his hopeless eyes.

"No, it's okay, we've left the strange man behind," said Vicky, "You should have a look at this, it's a replica of the Globe Theatre..."

"Is that bridge just for walking on?" Chloe butted in, pointing at the Millennium Bridge further down the river.

"Yes, it is," Vicky replied.

"Can we go on it first and then maybe come back here after?"

Vicky narrowed her eyes – what was this about? She made a quick calculation in her head that if they went on the bridge, then on the way back, they'd be in the perfect position to go straight into the Tate Modern art gallery.

"Okay," she agreed, and Chloe happily pulled her along towards the footbridge, leaving Smiler to watch them as they melded with the rest of the crowd. They'd soon be back, and then...

They walked not quite as fast as Chloe wanted along the busy river walk towards the grey bridge with its thick cables and walkway held up on V shaped supports across the river. After about a hundred and fifty yards, their pathway opened up to reveal the gigantic red-brick edifice of Bankside Power Station on their left with its great chimney towering hundreds of feet above them. Once a power station, belching toxic fumes into the heart of London, now it was the biggest modern art gallery in the city, and the Millennium Bridge led tourists from this temple of art straight across the river to St Paul's Cathedral. As Vicky and Chloe rounded the corner, an old woman got up from a bench shaded by silver birches and turned to face them. She was bent and wizened, wearing a filthy green coat in spite of the heat and she pointed her finger right at them. Vicky stopped and the old woman pointed and stared into their faces. The strange thing was that other people in the crowd didn't seem to notice her. They were walking past as if she wasn't even there. But Vicky and Chloe could certainly see her and she could see them.

"Sorry, can we help you?" Vicky asked. This was very strange and she didn't like it.

The old woman made no reply and the three of them seemed to be in their own world, paused within the motion of the world around them. The old woman's dark eyes were staring through Vicky and Chloe, and then her thin, heavily lined face twisted into something that began as a snarl until it finally turned into a shrieking laugh. The old woman was pointing right at them and shrieking with laughter, but everybody else was going about their business as if nothing was happening. And the longer the old woman laughed, the more disturbing it became. First it grew harsh, then angry and finally violent as she seemed to compress all her malice into the sound. After a few seconds of stunned silence and confusion, Vicky suddenly knew that this was all wrong,

"Come on!" she ordered and tugged at Chloe, who was transfixed by the sight and sound of the desiccated old woman whose laughter was like an attack.

Vicky walked very fast back the way they'd come, holding Chloe's hand very tightly. And now Chloe was scared. Vicky hadn't seen the other man, but they were walking right towards him.

"There's another one of them over there," said Chloe as she saw the man in the leather jacket, standing exactly where he'd been before and watching her with his melancholic eyes.

"What do you mean 'another one of them'?" Vicky asked, trying to pick out who Chloe was referring to.

"First there was the hairy man, then there was that bald man there,"

Vicky saw him and yes, he was staring at them without looking away,

"And then there was the old lady. They've all been watching us," Chloe insisted.

"What? Why would they be watching us?"

"I don't know," said Chloe, and she silently agonised over whether to tell her mother about seeing the black aura in the tube station. No, she couldn't say that – Vicky wouldn't go for it. Then she had a brainwave,

"Maybe it's because Ray's a policeman. Maybe these are bad people?"

That resonated. Vicky wondered what to do. Meanwhile, the man in the leather jacket with the disconsolate face kept his gaze on them both, especially Chloe. Vicky's brain was working hard – fight or flight? She wanted to confront him, maybe even cause a scene and shout that he was a 'paedo' before making a break for it, but what if he was some gangland killer out to terrorize a policeman's family? A stunt like that could easily backfire and put Chloe in danger. No, what they needed was a tactical withdrawal.

"Over here," she said, gripping Chloe's right hand and pushing her way through the crowds and back towards Borough Market. Vicky had other options, but all of them were down lonely side roads or alleyways. By going back to Borough Market, they could stay in the relative safety of the swarming tourists, and when they got through the market, they'd be on the main road, where she could hail a cab and they'd be safe.

One of the frustrations of living in a city that attracts lots of tourists is that moment when you need to get somewhere in a hurry, only to find your way blocked by a herd of ruminating zombies shuffling from one attraction to the next. As Vicky barged her way through the crowds, holding tightly onto Chloe's hand, she wanted to scream. Why couldn't they all just fuck off? As they approached The Clink, she looked out for Wilf and was glad that he wasn't there. Soon they were past the Golden Hinde and on the street that would take them down the southern side of Borough Market. But just as she was thinking they were home and dry, the crowds opened up ahead of them and there was Wilf, standing in the middle of the road waving at them,

"Hello, Chloe!" he called with a bright smile.

Vicky slowed and calculated.

"Hello, Chloe!" he repeated harshly with wild eyes.

They could go left and get into the market. Hopefully there'd be enough people between them and him to give them a chance of making it through to the main road.

"Hello, Chloe!" he screamed with all his anger.

Vicky pivoted left and dragged her wide-eyed daughter with her, plunging into the morass of humanity crammed into the space under the railway tracks that was Borough Market. Soon they were out of the sunshine and into the gloom, bustle and noise of the slow-moving crowds and market vendors. Even though the walls and great steel girders holding up the railway tracks were grimy from decades of pollution, the market stalls were jolly and brightly coloured. The scents of foods from around the world filled the space, but Vicky and Chloe had no time to notice – even when they went past a stall with fresh bread that smelled gorgeous. All they wanted to do was get through, but it seemed impossible! There were so many people! From somewhere nearby they heard an Indian man say,

"Nutter! Fucking nutter!"

When Chloe looked at where it had come from, her heart froze. Beyond a group of people, she could see the darkness of the void that surrounded someone very bad. She tugged at Vicky's hand to direct her away. It was just when she was having to make a choice where the main walkway forked to left and right. Chloe pulled her right. And now they were bumping their way through the crowd. For Chloe it was all too close-up, and she was lost in a forest of backs and stomachs. She couldn't see above anyone's shoulders to get an idea of where she was or where they were going.

"Ow!" she squealed as she took a sharp elbow to the side of the head from some dozy man in shorts with a Toronto Maple Leaves backpack. Normally, Vicky would have stopped and given him a piece of her mind, but she was keeping her eyes on the prize. She could see bright sunshine ahead and hear the sound of the heavy traffic on Borough High Street. Safety could only be about twenty yards away.

Bag Hag had heard Rohit's call and smiled when she saw Vicky and Chloe hove into view. Now was her time to shine! She barged through the crowd, using her bulk and stench as a battering ram, so that by the time her path intersected that of her targets, she was moving fast. She broadsided Vicky with the force of an enraged rhino. Vicky had all the wind knocked out of her, lost grip of Chloe's hand and fell to the ground. Chloe turned to see a terrifying face and an enormous shape scoop her up and drag her, screaming, away from her mother.

"Hey, you! Stop!" shouted the man with the Maple Leaves backpack. He might not have registered elbowing Chloe in the head, but he'd seen the weird woman deliberately charge Vicky.

His commanding voice drew attention to Bag Hag, who was still trying to make a break for the exit.

"What the fuck are you doing?" said a big man in butcher's overalls as he blocked her path.

"Help! I don't know this woman!" Chloe shouted and Bag Hag made the mistake of trying to cover her mouth with a filthy hand.

And now strong hands were grabbing Bag Hag and people were shouting over each other.

"Fuck off!" Bag Hag screamed, but then Vicky was there, and Chloe was in her arms and they were explaining the attack to the crowd. Angry faces turned on Bag Hag, but Vicky was keen to just get out.

"I'm sure it was just a silly mistake," she said, "Look at her. The poor old thing's mad as a badger. No, there's no need to call the police. My husband's a detective, so I'll talk to him about it," and, as she spoke, she and Chloe backed towards the exit and freedom.

Across the street, Tommy could see the commotion near the glass-fronted entrance to the market. Then he saw Vicky slowly backing out towards the pavement. This was his chance! He could arrive like a knight in shining armour and then they'd have the pair of them. Tommy pulled out into the traffic and, to a chorus of horns, executed a U-turn across the road. Yes! Vicky had her arm raised and was shouting,

"Cabbie!"

Vicky hoped the cabbie had noticed her and was overjoyed when the cab screeched to a halt in front of them,

"Could you take us to Streatham please?" she gasped and when the cabbie nodded, she opened the door and pushed Chloe in, then hopped in, slammed the door and slumped into the back seat. As the cab moved away, she put her arm around Chloe and pulled her in for a big hug. Chloe held onto her tightly and started to sob in relief that the nightmare was over.

Chapter Twenty-Five

Aftermath

When Andy didn't arrive for work by nine, Ray wasn't concerned,

"He probably got stuck down one of those rabbit holes in the museum. I'll bet he didn't leave until after midnight," he said to Emma, who was working at her desk. She turned her pretty face up towards him,

"Or stayed late and then found somewhere to drink after hours," Emma smiled, "He'll probably get here in about half an hour stinking of kebabs and garlic sauce."

Ray laughed – yeah, that sounded about right.

"So, how are you doing with Fabbri and Montague?" Ray asked, leaning in to look at Emma's screen. He caught the scent of her shower gel. It was fresh like a spring breeze.

"Nothing yet. I put in a couple of hours last night and found no shared interests or charities. Montague's in the sailing set down on Hayling Island..."

"On the south coast?"

"Yeah. Apparently, he's got a big house down there and he's off every Friday at three pm. Almost never spends a weekend in town."

"And Fabbri?" although as Ray posed the question, he suspected he knew the answer, and Emma's reply was unsurprising,

"I get the impression he didn't play nicely with others. Not a member of any clubs at all, didn't play sports, didn't even gamble. My guess – after finding that woman chained to his towel rail – is that he used all his spare time for sexually exploiting women he'd hand-picked from his trafficking.

When it comes to charity work, Montague does nothing – no links to any – but Fabbri was big on raising money for a number of play groups and nurseries across south London. You know, the type that help struggling families and single mothers to get low-cost childcare while the parents' work. He bankrolled a lot of events to promote the projects."

"Because he was such a delightful bloke," Ray said snidely.

"Yeah, and I bet he was lovely to his dear old mother, too," Emma smiled, "Anyway, the bottom line is, so far, these two are chalk and cheese."

Ray couldn't hide his disappointment, but he didn't want Emma to think that reflected on her,

"Great work, Em'. Tell you what, why don't you pivot towards the business side – see if there are any links there."

"Okay, Boss," she said, and her eyes were shining with his praise,

"Although, if these two are as slippery as we think, I doubt I'm going to find much without a court order allowing me to go through Global Actuaries accounts."

"Concentrate on Fabbri's side of it. He's dead, he's bent, so you can sift through everything with a fine-toothed comb."

"Gotcha!"

"Good one," Ray smiled and then he returned to his office.

It wasn't until after eleven that Ray showed real concern over Andy's whereabouts. He had spent the morning with his boss discussing the death of Fabbri and whether he and his team could have handled the situation better. Then, of course, there were questions about Florence Gichuru. All that had pushed Andy from his mind, but as he was coming back from his meetings, Ray realised that Andy hadn't replied to his earlier text,

'WTF? You coming in today, or what?'

When Ray walked back into the office, he fully expected to see the lovable lummox looking pale and bleary-eyed, nursing a coffee and a bunch of excuses, but no.

"Heard anything from him?" he asked Emma.

"No," she said lightly, but then noticed the concern on Ray's face,

"I'm sure he's all right," she added.

"Yeah," Ray said, looking distractedly into the distance. Normally, he wouldn't worry, but there was something about the last week that had been distinctly odd. And now he could hear Elizabeth Russell's voice in his head asking him to tell her if anything strange happened.

No!

He was certainly not calling her up about this. Andy was a grown man. He could look after himself... but if ex-Russian military were involved, could they have got to him?

His phone rang and he looked at the number – somewhere in London... should he? Yes,

"Hello? Yes, this is Detective Inspector Ennis..."

Emma watched Ray's face closely as he listened to the person at the other end of the line. Every muscle suddenly tensed,

"Sorry? Say that again," he said hoarsely.

And now Emma could see Ray's utter shock as the other person spoke,

"Yes... yes, I'll be right over," and he ended the call,

"Andy," he said, and Emma could see he was fighting his emotions,

"What's happened?"

Ray was already on the move,

"Someone attacked him last night on his way home. He's in the ICU at St Thomas'. I'm going to see him and find out what's happened. You stay here and get on with the case. Jesus!"

And then he was into the lift and gone.

"What you have to remember is that Sergeant Harper is very poorly," said Mr. Shah, a small, spare man who was the consultant in charge of the case. He and Ray were standing in the hallway outside the heavy, blue double doors that led into the Critical Care Unit. The light was eerie in the windowless space and seemed to wash the colours out of everything. Ray swallowed hard. He knew exactly what 'very poorly' meant in doctor speak – at death's door.

"The railing went through his lung and part of his liver," Mr. Shah continued in his perfectly cultured upper middle-class accent.

"Jesus!"

"But he's been very lucky. No arterial damage, and the incident happened only five hundred yards away, so we were able to get him in here very quickly."

"So, when did it happen?"

"Last night around midnight."

"Midnight? But why have we only just been informed?" Ray asked sharply.

"I'm afraid I can't tell you that," Mr. Shah replied evenly, "I save lives, I don't have anything to do with the admin side."

"Yeah, sorry. I didn't mean to... it's just a shock, y'know?"

"Of course. Now, we currently have him under sedation, but you can see him if you want. Are you in good health?"

"Yeah, I'm fine."

"Good. The last thing we need is anyone giving him an infection."

Ten minutes later, Ray was sitting, masked, gowned and gloved at Andy's side. Ray stared with wide eyes at his friend, who was surrounded with medical equipment and had two rows of three drips going into him – one set for each arm. Andy had been intubated and his breathing was being controlled by a machine that hissed and clicked next to him. The sound broke the silence of the bland room with its muted lighting, and Ray found that his own breathing synced itself to the machine, as if to help Andy breath. Ray felt tears welling,

"What the fuck, Andy?" he said gruffly, pushing down the emotions that were hell bent on bursting out of his chest,

"If you wanted a day off, all you had to do was ask – you didn't have to go to this extreme."

The hiss and click of the ventilator was the only response Andy could muster.

"I know you can hear me, so I want you to know that I'm gonna fuck up whoever did this to you. That's a promise, mate. A fucking promise!"

Ray could feel the tears rising inside him - the tightness of his chest, the constriction of his throat - but he wouldn't let them come. He fought hard and then said,

"Emma says hi. It looks like there's no connection between Fabbri and Montague. I wish I knew what you found out at the museum last night. Someone must think we're getting close to the truth, otherwise..." and he looked Andy up and down. It was incredible how someone so big and strong could be so easily reduced to the basics of life. Pierce even the toughest man in the right place and that's the end of him. Doesn't matter how fit and strong he is, you cut the right thing and he's fucked!

Ray didn't like where his silent thoughts were going, so he decided to think out loud about the case,

"But why come after you, not me? I'm the easier target – especially with my family to defend. And to do that in a public place... in fact on the bridge in London with the most surveillance, right next to the Houses of Parliament... that's bold. That's a real 'fuck you' move. That's..." Ray's mind turned to the logical conclusion,

"That's just what you'd expect from Russian ex-military. Big, bold and bloody. Yeah... this must have something to do with Ukhov. Fabbri's people wouldn't do this. They're probably all running for the hills right now. But a bunch of highly motivated, well-trained Russians trying to protect their illegal arms racket... this is their bread and butter. Yeah, that's got to be the angle... it's got to be..."

and yet...

Where did The Man fit in? He clearly had nothing to do with the Russians, but there he was. Every time Ray closed his eyes, he saw the face of The Man. It was from the moment he had turned back towards their flat when Ray was chasing him. The way he had turned his head with that hideous grin on his face... Ray couldn't unsee it. And Chloe was dreaming about him. Was any of that related to the case? It couldn't be. No, that was something else, something personal that he had to sort out, but it would have to wait. Right now, he would drop everything and put all he had into catching whoever put Andy in that bed.

"We're gonna catch 'em," he said firmly, then took Andy's right hand in his and gave it a squeeze,

"You get better, you lazy sod. I need you..." and that was when his emotions finally broke and the tears he'd been holding back came in a flood.

When Ray finally came out through the doors of the ICU, pulling off his gloves and mask, he was surprised to see Elizabeth Russell lounging on a chair in the waiting area. She got up as soon as he appeared and, as she approached, a penny dropped in Ray's mind,

"It was you, wasn't it?" his look was hostile, bordering on the aggressive, but Elizabeth Russell's response was disarming,

"Yes," she replied, meeting his hostility with absolute honesty.

"You admit that you kept the news of this attack on a serving police officer from the police?"

"Yes. My investigation is at a very delicate stage. I knew that this attack would bring a lot of media attention if it got out and I couldn't risk that," her tone was soft as a pillow. It absorbed all his anger and gave him little to rail against.

"But you could have told us."

"Yes, I'm sorry, but I needed time and space. It was a judgement call. Maybe I got it wrong."

"Did you tell anyone in the police service?"

"No," she replied simply.

"Fuck me! You are a law unto yourself, aren't you?"

"Sometimes, yes, but only when it's necessary. And in this case, it was necessary."

"Great. Good to know. So, aside from suppressing information, have you done anything useful like taken witness statements or had the crime scene investigated?"

"There were no eyewitnesses. Incredibly, out of the nineteen other people on the bridge at the time, none of them saw what happened and there were no cars passing. On the plus side, he was spotted less than a minute after the attack and brought straight here."

"And the crime scene?"

"I had a good look at it. There was nothing there."

"Oh! Oh, YOU had a good look at it, did you?" Ray exclaimed and then his tongue dripped with sarcasm,

"Thank Christ for that! That's much better than a team of trained investigators. Yes, I've often thought what a waste of time they are and that what we really need at the scene of a crime is someone from the Treasury."

Elizabeth Russell took it in silence and the expression on her young face gave no hint of how she felt about it.

"CCTV?" Ray asked, "You looked at that yet?"

"No," she admitted.

"Well, although I'm sure someone from the Treasury can undoubtedly do it better, I'll take a look at the footage myself. If that's all right with you."

"Yes, that's fine," she said, wondering when Ray's righteous indignation would blow itself out and allow her to get back to work.

"Good, right. I'll do that. And maybe I'll even share the information with you... Oh no, of course! You'll know what I've found out before I get up from my desk, because you have access to everything. What a fucking nightmare!" and with that, Ray stormed off.

Elizabeth Russell watched him go without any particular emotion. He was under stress and his points were all perfectly reasonable. She also knew that her youth and appearance riled older people. There was always the question in their minds as to how a woman in her late twenties could possibly be running a department of such power. But she couldn't help that, and she liked how she looked, so, quite frankly, they could all suck it. Then her mind turned to the attack and how she'd felt it the moment it had happened. That afternoon in the pub, she'd done more than just ask Andy out. She was sure that he had latent gifts which, if they were triggered by the case, could put him in danger of insanity or death. So, in those few intimate moments she'd forged a psychic bond with him, something that would alert her if anything serious happened. The moment that iron spike had struck his back, she knew – and she knew where he was. Fortunately, she was still at work and since the Treasury is only a few hundred yards away from Westminster Bridge, she was able to get there fast. Thirty seconds faster than the ambulance, in fact. Those thirty seconds saved Andy's life. She was able to channel her power and cast a spell to staunch the bleeding. Then she saw him safely into the ambulance, cancelled the imminent arrival of the police and called in her own clean-up crew. Since then, she'd been trying to search Andy's mind for clues as to why it had happened. Unsurprisingly, given the shock to his system, all she'd got so far was garbled nonsense. Now he'd had more time to rest, she would try again. Somehow, she knew that whatever was in that rough, handsome head of his, was essential to her job of dealing with the creature in Candlewick. She walked through the doors of the ICU as if it were nothing more than a pub or a restaurant. Without a thought for PPE, she walked down the corridor to his room, and as she went past the bustling doctors and nurses, not one of them noticed her. Elizabeth Russell entered Andy's room, sat by the bed, took his cool right hand in hers, bowed her head and slipped into his mind.

"Right, drop the Fabbri case!" Ray announced as he crashed into the office. Emma saw how angry he looked and worried what was coming.

"Emma, my office!"

She jumped to it, followed him in and closed the door.

"Andy's in very bad shape. Someone skewered him with a length of iron railing and left him for dead. Got him right through the lung and the liver."

"Oh my God!" Emma breathed, eyes wide, "What are his chances?"

"They don't know. Depends how much fight he's got in him."

"When did it happen?"

"Last night around midnight."

"But why weren't we told until lunchtime?" Emma couldn't understand why it wasn't all over the news.

"Someone doesn't want people to know," Ray replied and from his look, Emma gathered that he wasn't likely to tell her who that someone might be.

"Right now, he's in a medically induced coma and on a ventilator."

"Shit."

"Yeah..." Ray felt that Emma had pretty much summed it up perfectly, "But we're going to sift through all the CCTV footage from New Scotland Yard, up the Embankment to Parliament, across Westminster Bridge and anything we've got in the Waterloo area. We're going to see exactly who did this and nail the fucker to the wall. Got it?"

"Yes, boss! I'll pull up the CCTV footage now," and, after a brief look which confirmed their collective resolve, she left to put the plan into action.

Chapter Twenty-Six

'Twixt Cup And Lip

Tommy was yards away from completing the kidnap, but just as he was pulling across the road, another cab nipped in front of him and he was forced to drive away.

"Fuck!" he shouted, battering the wheel of his cab with the flat of his hands,

"Fuck! Fuck! Fuck!"

The plan was fucked and he was the one who'd fucked it!

"Fuck!"

As Tommy drove down towards Elephant and Castle, the ramifications of his failure hit home. Krowos was not a forgiving god. Krowos loved to punish. Tommy had fucked up and now he was probably fucked. He toyed with the idea of just driving from the Elephant to Kennington, straight down the A3 and out of London forever. Would he ever truly be safe from the anger of Krowos? He knew too much about the set-up to be left to his own devices, and he also knew that they were very efficient at tracking down anyone who escaped from the fold. No, it was pointless trying to get away. He'd have to man-up and hope that he was still in one piece afterwards. An image flashed through his mind of an old man who had tried to escape Krowos, but who'd finally been found twenty years later by Tommy, Rohit and The Man. The image was of The Man with a foot planted on the old geezer's chest as Rohit and he pulled yards of the old man's intestines out of him.

"Fuck..." Tommy sighed as he swung off left towards the Old Kent Road. He would circle around via Tower Bridge, go to the temple and present himself to The Boss. What would happen... would happen. As for the idea that he might get a promotion to the inner circle - well, that was fucked.

Meanwhile, Vicky and Chloe were holding each other in the back of the cab that had saved their lives. Chloe's face was buried into her mother's shoulder and Vicky gently stroked her hair until her sobbing subsided.

"You okay?" Vicky asked.

Chloe wiped the tears away from her red, puffy eyes and nodded.

"That was horrible, wasn't it?" said Vicky. Chloe gave a nervous half-sob-half-laugh,

"Yes."

"C'mere!" Vicky said and gave her a very big cuddle,

"I'm very proud of you. You were so brave!"

And now the significance of what had just happened hit Vicky and she had to choke back the tears. God! She had almost lost her daughter! It was unthinkable. And to have it happen in broad daylight in a public space – it made no sense! Who were those people? How could they know Chloe's name and why did they try to take her? By the river, Chloe had suggested that they might have something to do with Ray's work, but they didn't look like the type of people who would be connected with organised crime. They just looked like vagrants. Vicky normally would never use that sort of term, because she had great sympathy for rough sleepers or anyone who had fallen on hard times, but in this case there was something different going on.

"I'm going to phone your dad and tell him," she said, taking out her phone and hitting Ray's number.

It was only about ten minutes after Emma had left the room that Ray's phone started to ring. He crinkled his nose – it was Vicky. She almost never called during work hours.

"Hey, what's up? I'm quite busy right now..."

A garbled stream of words cascaded out of the phone and Ray was quickly saying,

"Hold on, hold on, slow down. I can't... I can't understand you... what about Chloe?"

"I think someone tried to kidnap her," Vicky said with force.

"What?" Ray couldn't believe it.

"Yes, just now in Borough Market. There were at least four of them."

"Four of who?"

"I don't bloody know!" Vicky snapped, "One of them was a homeless woman who knocked me over and tried to run away with Chloe."

"Where are you now?"

"In a black cab going home."

"Okay, good. That's good. Um..." Ray's mind was whirring, should he tell her about Andy, or would that just freak her out?

"I'm sort of in the middle of something..."

"And it's more important than your daughter almost being kidnapped?" Vicky said sharply.

"No, it's just..." Ray would have to tell her, or she'd be furious,

"It's just that someone tried to kill Andy last night and he's in intensive care at St Thomas'."

"What?" Vicky felt shock and fear in equal measure, "So, first someone tries to kill Andy and then just by coincidence a woman tries to kidnap Chloe? Please come home!"

"I will, I will..." Ray said quickly, instantly regretting telling Vicky about Andy, "But there's something I've got to finish up real quick, then I'll come right home. Okay?"

"Okay," Vicky said reluctantly, but she knew she'd be a nervous wreck waiting for him to get home.

"And you're sure this woman tried to take Chloe?" Ray couldn't stop himself from asking. If there was a sliver of doubt that Vicky was simply overreacting, he'd rather stay there and try to nail whoever attacked Andy.

"Ray, she ran into me full tilt and the next thing I knew she was trying to drag Chloe out of the market," Vicky's tone was harsh. Why the fuck wasn't Ray taking what she said as the truth?

"Okay, okay," Ray soothed, "Let's leave this 'til I get home. I can sort this out, yeah?"

"Yeah," Vicky sniffled.

"Okay, give Chloe a big cuddle from me and I'll be back as soon as I can. I'm sure you're totally safe now. Love you,"

"You too," Vicky said. Maybe it was the phone line, but Ray didn't think there was much enthusiasm in the reply.

Ray rang off and went to find Emma, who was at her desk on the phone requesting the CCTV footage from the bridge. She looked up at him and could see he wanted to talk to her, so she indicated that she'd only be a minute or so. Ray waited patiently and when she'd finished he asked,

"How's it going?"

"Well," she said brightly, "All the footage we need should be here within the hour, then it's just a case of watching it through."

"Yeah, and since we have an approximate time for the attack, at least that narrows it down. Now, I've got to go home..." Ray said.

"What's wrong?"

"Something happened to Chloe and Vicky in Borough Market."

"Are they all right?" Emma asked, looking concerned.

"I think so, Vicky says someone tried to snatch Chloe..."

"*Tried* to snatch her?" Emma asked, worried.

"Yeah, but it's okay. Whoever it was failed. Vicky and Chloe are both pretty shaken up. They're heading back home now."

"Whoa! That's kind of crazy. On the same day as Andy..." Emma left the thought hanging.

"I know how it looks, but I think it's just a coincidence. And anyway, you know what Vicky's like. She has a habit of going off the deep end."

Emma nodded sympathetically – she'd heard a lot about Vicky's sensitive temperament.

"So, if you don't mind trawling through that footage alone, I'll catch up with you later."

"No problem," said Emma with a reassuring smile.

"Thanks, Em'. See you later," said Ray and, as he walked briskly towards the lift, he re-iterated his thought that Emma was worth her weight in gold.

About forty-five minutes later, Ray reached home. The street looked quiet and perfectly normal in the afternoon sun, but what difficulties were waiting for him behind his door?

"Ray!" Chloe squealed in joy as he opened the door and, before he knew it, she had flung herself into his arms. He heaved her up and she wrapped her legs around him, holding him tight as he kicked the door closed behind him and carried her down the hall to the kitchen. Vicky was there and, even though it was only around two pm, she already had a large glass of chardonnay on the go.

"You took your time," she said with a viperous look in her eyes.

I'm working on a very important case and you're taking me away from it...

Ray's thought was a split second ahead of his reply,

"I was in the middle of London, in the middle of sorting out the Andy thing when you called," he said calmly, not wanting to mention any details of the attack in front of Chloe.

"I got here as fast as I could," Ray replied calmly. He didn't want an argument,

"Anyway, I needed time to organise for a couple of uniforms to come over later and take some details about the people who did this to you."

This seemed to mollify Vicky, whose eyes lost their venom.

"So, now you're both a bit calmer, tell me exactly what happened," Ray said, sitting on the sofa with Chloe on his lap.

Vicky came and sat in the armchair, took a large swig of her wine and began to talk.

For the next half hour, Ray listened carefully as Vicky told the story with numerous interjections from Chloe. Although he didn't smile outwardly, he was amused by some of the details that Chloe could remember,

"And there were bits of sausage roll stuck in his beard!" she exclaimed when they got to the bit with the man at the Clink.

But as the tale continued, it got darker and Chloe's additions more disturbing.

"Her eyes were black," she said when Vicky was describing the old woman who'd laughed at them, "And she hated us."

Ray was genuinely shocked by the story and, when Vicky had concluded, he said,

"That sounds frightening."

"Tell me about it," said Vicky, draining her glass and getting up for a refill.

"Don't forget we've got officers coming in the next couple of hours to take your statement," Ray pointed out.

"What, so I can't have a drink to calm down?" Vicky shot back.

"No," he said calmly, sidestepping the argument she seemed desperate to have, "I'm just saying reign it in until after they've finished, then we can split a couple of bottles."

"Okay," she said. That seemed reasonable and she poured herself a small one,

"So, who do you think it was? Has it got something to do with your case?"

"I dunno, maybe?" Ray said, then he turned to Chloe and said, "Hey, why don't you go and watch something on the iPad in your room?"

"Okay," said Chloe, then she took her opportunity to make some capital,

"And can we get lots of ice cream tonight?"

Ray laughed,

"Yes! If anyone deserves it, you do."

Chloe smiled and went to her room.

Vicky came and sat on the sofa with Ray, who waited to hear Chloe's door click shut and then said quietly,

"There's a possibility that Andy was attacked by some Russian arms dealers."

"Oh my God!"

"But I can't see how what happened to you can be a part of it. These Russians are very serious and dangerous men. They're not beggars or mad old ladies. If they wanted to kidnap you, we wouldn't be having this conversation now."

Silence filled the void as that thought sank in.

"So, what the hell happened today?" Vicky asked.

"I don't know," Ray replied, shaking his head. All the while, the voice of Elizabeth Russell was clear in his mind,

"If anything inexplicable happens, however small, please let me know,"

Ray pushed the thought aside.

"This was targeted. WE were targeted," said Vicky, looking hard at Ray, "They knew Chloe's name and they tried to take her."

Ray thought about who they might be, but the voice of Elizabeth Russell intruded again,

"If you get on the radar of the people Titheridge has been dealing with, it will end very badly..."

But it couldn't be the Russians. No, they would have gone in mob-handed, kidnapped his wife and daughter, and would already be sending him bits of them with a warning to back off. So, what the hell was the answer?

"This is all because of your job," Vicky said, bitterly.

"Hang on, we've got no proof..."

"Who would do this other than the sort of scumbags you deal with?" Vicky demanded.

Put that way, she had a point. But maybe there was another explanation? Something that Elizabeth Russell hinted at – something strange... No! Ray shook his head and tried again to shove the woman from the Treasury out of his thoughts.

"Well?" Vicky was getting wound up by Ray's silence.

"I'm thinking," he shot back, "Can't I have a second to think?"

"Fuck!" Vicky said, tilting her head back to look at ceiling, "It was fucking freaky, Ray. There was something really weird about those people. It was almost like they were possessed."

"Really?" Ray sounded sceptical.

"Yeah, really," Vicky said, looking at him, "Chloe was right – that old woman had nothing but darkness in her eyes. You know, in my job, I get to meet some pretty screwed up, angry teenagers, who are in gangs, carry weapons and do some scary shit... but what I saw in that old woman's face made all that seem like sunshine and fucking rainbows. There was something very, very wrong in those people."

"A lot of the homeless have mental health problems..." Ray began,

"No!" Vicky insisted, "There was something unnatural going on today. That's my gut feeling."

Ray put his hand to his face and slowly dragged it across his jawline – if she said anything like that to the uniforms, he'd look like a right tit.

"I don't think there's a supernatural explanation to this, so let's just keep to the facts we know," he said.

"But what other explanation is there?" she said, looking at him defiantly.

"I don't know, but I can guarantee it's not a supernatural one."

Vicky looked at him and then the penny dropped,

"Oh, I get it," she said, "You're afraid that if I say anything like this when they come to take my statement, you'll look stupid."

"No, I..."

"Oh, come on, be honest, Ray! If I say anything about people being evil or the supernatural, you'll get embarrassed."

"Yeah... okay, yeah, I will be embarrassed if you and Chloe give them some mad story about possessed vagrants going around Borough trying to kidnap people. Yeah, obviously that would be embarrassing." Ray said with a tinge of anger.

"Fuck's sake, I'm not an idiot," Vicky said, with equal anger, "I've met enough coppers to know that they don't want to hear about that stuff – *you* don't want to hear about it and you're bloody married to me. So don't worry, Chloe and I will be good little girls and give clear descriptions of the fuckers who tried to kidnap her, without any hints at anything unnatural. Okay?"

"I'm not the one being unreasonable, here," Ray said coldly.

"Maybe not, but you seem to be deliberately not registering the strange aspect of what happened today."

"Well..."

"Which makes it seem like you don't believe me and Chloe."

"No, it's not like that..."

"Then what is it like?"

"I'm just trying to find some rational explanation for it, that's all," said Ray, and he sounded tired.

"Good for you!" said Vicky, getting up to pour herself another glass of wine.

By six, the polite and helpful uniformed officers had been and gone. Vicky and Chloe had given them the details of what had happened - without any references to the supernatural - Ray and Vicky had put down their boxing gloves (aided by the fact that Ray had joined her in the demolition of the bottle of chardonnay), and Chloe was chilled after watching fun things on the iPad. Now they were working their way through a feast from Deliveroo including buckets from Kentucky Fried Chicken, a tub of Ben and Jerry's Phish Food and a tub of New York Super Fudge Chunk. Chloe didn't like what had happened earlier in the day, but this was pretty cool. Finally, once they were all stuffed, they fell back on a bit of routine to bring normality to the day. Even though it was still fairly early, Chloe put on her PJs and brushed her teeth, while Ray kept an eye on her and Vicky chose a book to read to her before she went to sleep.

"Where do you want to sleep tonight?" Ray asked as Chloe rinsed her mouth.

"Can I sleep with you, please?" she asked in a small, slightly embarrassed voice.

"Of course," Ray smiled, putting his arm around her and planting a smacker on the top of her head.

"Come on," he said and led the way to their room. Chloe waited until he had flicked on the light and then ran in and leapt onto the middle of the bed. She loved the enormous bed her parents had. One day, she would have an enormous bed and share it with three cats and two dogs.

Ray prepared the pillows for the extra passenger and then said,

"Right, get yourself in there."

Vicky arrived to see Chloe snuggling into her nest and sat on the edge of the bed. She showed Chloe the book,

"I think we're all in need of a bit of Matilda," she said.

"Who's Matilda?" Chloe asked.

"You're about to find out," Vicky replied.

Chloe liked the cover illustration of a girl with her hands on her hips standing on top of a teetering pile of books. Vicky and Ray took it in turns to read a chapter and, forty-five minutes later, Roald Dahl had weaved his magic over all three of them. Then, with their most precious and most favourite person in the world safely tucked into bed, Vicky and Ray went quietly back to the kitchen to clear up the massacre of dinner, leaving the door open so that the bedroom was partially illuminated by the light in the hall. They didn't talk much at first, both going through mundane tasks as they put things in the dishwasher and the bin, but slowly they started chatting. As they worked their way through another bottle of wine, the needle from their earlier conversation was gone and they talked about their upcoming holiday to Norfolk and whether they needed to buy anything for it. They were going to have two weeks in a static caravan near Cromer. It wasn't glamorous, but it was perfect for relaxing and doing fun things with Chloe.

"Maybe this year, you can even swim in the sea," Vicky said with a wicked grin.

"I've told you, the only way you're getting me swimming is if we're in Barbados and the sea is body temperature," Ray replied. He didn't mind paddling in the cool sea, but all this cold swimming nonsense was sheer insanity.

"Fine by me," said Vicky moving in close to him, "I prefer being able to see that hot body of yours on the beach anyway."

Ray raised an eyebrow,

"Well, I suppose that could be arranged," he said, pulling her towards him and kissing her gently. Slowly their kisses became deeper and her hand slid down to grip his firm backside. Yeah, she liked that. He kissed along her jawline and down the side of her soft neck, knowing how much it turned her on. The smell and feel of her was reassuringly familiar.

"Now, before we get too excited," she said, letting go of his fine ass, "We mustn't forget that we've got a guest in the bed."

"Fair point," he replied, "Maybe tomorrow?"

"Fingers crossed," she said, looking up into his eyes. They kissed again with warmth but without passion and disentangled themselves. Then they took turns in the shower and got ready for bed, finally slipping in on either side of their wonderful daughter and settling down to sleep. As Vicky danced on the edge of sleep, she thought that this was what life was really all about – enjoying simple moments of connection with people she loved. Meanwhile, Ray lay in the semi-darkness, listening to the other two sleep as he chased after elusive oblivion. Why the hell would homeless people try to kidnap his daughter? That was very weird. Maybe Vicky and Chloe had got it all wrong? Maybe it *hadn't* been co-ordinated, but simply a crazy woman doing something desperate? Yeah, but Vicky and Chloe seemed so sure... Ray lay there trying to rationalize the abnormalities away, until finally he also sank into sleep, with the images of Andy in the hospital bed playing like a slideshow on the walls of his mind.

Chapter Twenty-Seven

The French Connection

"Krowos?" Oliver Fernsby said with a look of confusion on his face.

"Yes," Elizabeth Russell replied, her violet eyes shining brightly even though it was after midnight and she'd had another very long day. She perched herself on the edge of Oliver's desk and continued,

"It's called Krowos and it's been lurking right here in Candlewick since before the Roman invasion."

"Where did you find that out?" Oliver asked. Although he was glad they could now put a name to the creature, he was baffled by how she'd come by it - especially since they'd spent the previous night trawling the secret archives of the occult without turning up anything.

"That policeman I was telling you about."

"Oh yes, the ruggedly handsome one with the strong hands and sensitive eyes?"

"Yes..."

"The one with the deep voice and the magnificent arse?" Oliver smiled.

"Yes, all right, yes, maybe I laid it on a bit thick yesterday," she admitted.

In fact, she hadn't stopped talking about him all night.

"Anyway, it turns out we were looking in the wrong archive. Should've been looking in the crime archive under unsolved murders," she said, "Are you going to eat that?" and she pointed at a lonely Oreo on a fine bone china plate. Oliver shook his head and she snaffled it.

“So?” he asked as she scrunched her way through the cookie.

“So, our Krowos enjoys folding people in half,” she replied, wiping the last crumb from her lip with an elegant fingertip, “And that’s how Andy found him. The first known victim of our creature, back in the time of Hadrian, was an unlucky lady called Julia the Diviner. Although some people might say she should’ve seen it coming.”

“Krowos...” Oliver mused, ignoring her joke, “That’s a proto-Celtic word for *blood*...”

“Yes... go on,” Elizabeth Russell said, encouraging her assistant to work it out for himself.

“Ah... okay,” he said, realising that this was a chance for him to show that he was ready for field work, “And that’s exactly what people have been feeding it for the last two and a half or three thousand years... and that’s helped it grow. Presumably, in return for blood sacrifices it has rewarded its followers with power?”

“Good boy, but...” she said, urging him to make connections.

“But...” Oliver thought hard... but what?

“But...” he said again, looking at the bookcase for inspiration, “It also needs psychic energy. Presumably to help it stay in our reality.”

“Give that boy an Oreo!” Elizabeth Russell exclaimed.

She hopped up onto his desk and swung her legs off the side like a child in a sky blue, tightly tailored trouser suit, as she warmed to the subject of their enemy,

“You want to know why I reckon I haven’t noticed it?”

“Go on,” Oliver said.

“Because it’s weak. It doesn’t have the power to fully cross into our dimension – that’s why it needs that horrible umbilical cord. You should see it – it’s fucking foul... anyway, that’s beside the point, so... it needs the umbilical cord to keep it anchored to its dimension. It’s effectively here and there at the same time, and it’s drawing some of its power from there and the rest from here.”

“But where’s it from?”

“Fucked if I know,” she said, with her Yorkshire accent thickening,

"Probably some nightmare void where everything's got tentacles and suck people's brains out through their eyes..."

"You mean it's from Southampton?"

Elizabeth Russell couldn't help but roar with laughter and Oliver smiled in slight embarrassment at making the quip.

"Yeah, exactly like Southampton," she laughed, "But seriously, the reason it's eluded me is because it's very careful to avoid getting noticed, because it knows it's weak. It's built up its network, it's worked in the shadows and it's fed and grown bigger. And that's another thing we've been lucky with – this thing's a slow grower. Been here, what, three thousand years and it's only twenty feet long... remember that fucker we had to blow up in Cornwall? That was fifty foot if it was an inch, and that was only an egg. Imagine if it'd hatched."

Oliver nodded - the Pencarrow case still gave him bad dreams and he'd only assisted there for a day!

Now Elizabeth Russell was back on her feet, pacing restlessly and making expansive gestures with her hands,

"So, we know its name, what it likes, where it lives, the fact that it's relatively weak – on a cosmic scale, anyway – and that its most likely weak spot is..." and she indicated to Oliver that he should finish her thought,

"The umbilical cord?"

"Bingo! But what to do?"

"Cut the cord."

"Exactly, but we can't just wander down there with a big pair of scissors, can we? Where can we – as the young military folks put it – get some intel on it?"

And she turned her brilliant eyes onto Oliver. His answers would tell her what he'd learned and whether he had it in him to make good decisions.

"Intel. How can we get intel on a three-thousand-year-old inter-dimensional being that has done a very good job of hiding..." Oliver mused. Yes, this was tricky, but clearly his boss had already got there, so the key must be in front of him. He thought about what they knew and then suddenly it struck him – the name! It had been named by people living in Britain long before the Romans arrived. They didn't have written history, but their history had been kept orally by...

"Druids!" Oliver cried with a look of triumph on his handsome face.

Elizabeth Russell stopped pacing and clapped him on the shoulder,

"Excellent! Oliver, phone Gaston!"

"Really? It's already after one in the morning over there."

"Oh, come on, he's French! He's probably up late stuffing a goose with a duck or something equally gallic. Come on, come on, get dialling," she said, clicking her fingers to spur him on. Oliver went to the candlestick phone and dialled the number that he knew off by heart. There was a pause as he stood there with the mouthpiece in one hand and the earpiece resting near the top of his jaw,

"Allo – Gaston? C'est Oliver Fernsby. Ca va?" there was a pause, while Gaston presumably complained about the lateness of the hour,

"Quel dommage," Oliver looked sympathetic.

"What, has his duck died?" Elizabeth said quietly and Oliver waved her away.

"C'est Elizabeth... oui, elle veut discuter... okay... elle est la," and he held the phone towards Elizabeth Russell, who took it reluctantly, holding the earpiece as far away from her head as she could while still being able to hear,

"Gaston, so kind of you to take my call, sorry it's so late, but I've got a minor crisis over here and you're the only man who can help," she said in fluent, if somewhat anglicised French.

"Elizabeth, you know I always have time for you... even at ten past one in the morning," Gaston replied in French delivered so smoothly that it was the aural equivalent of quaffing a chilled Sauternes on a hot summer's night.

"Oh, come now, Gaston, when's the last time you got to bed before four am?"

There was a pause.

"Fair enough," he replied, "How can I help?"

"I've got a spot of Krowos trouble," she said.

"Ah! Dear little Krowos. Is he still ugly?"

"Utterly repulsive. Stinks like shit, but he's all grown up now..." and Elizabeth Russell launched into a short, but detailed description of the situation.

"Oh dear!" Gaston sympathised when she'd finished, "I can see why you can't have that. And I suppose you want me to tell you all about him?"

Duh! She thought,

"If you could, that would be very helpful," she said.

"What can I say, we came across him first in twenty-eight forty-three, so four hundred and forty-three BC by the Gregorian calendar. He was about the size of a small cat and was attached by his cord to a rock in a small spring near the Thames. Fairly close to where they eventually built London Bridge. At first, we weren't sure whether to worship him or not, but it became clear that he wasn't of this earth and that there was something... sour about him. So, we ignored him."

"Why didn't you kill him and send him back home?"

"It didn't seem necessary and it seemed like a waste of energy. He was no threat and it would have taken precious resources to get rid of him – a silver bladed axe, for example. And then there was the toll the spell would have taken on its caster..."

Elizabeth Russell silently nodded. Sending something back to its own dimension was never simple, however physically small they might be.

"It seemed like a lot of fuss over nothing, so we left him to his own devices. You've got to remember that in those days, most of the action in what became London was south of the river. Obviously, we kept tabs on him, especially when his cult started to develop. Then, around the birth of Christ, he went on a growth spurt. In five years, he was suddenly the size of an English mastiff. And as an aside, maybe that's why he's come out of hiding now – he could be on another growth spurt. Who knows, he may even be preparing to close off his link to his own dimension and live here permanently. It sounds like his power has increased greatly."

"Maybe, but he still can't touch those who can't see him, so..." Elizabeth Russell began,

"Ah, but he can," Gaston interrupted, "Within about a hundred feet of his anchor point to his own dimension, he can touch anyone, whether they see him or not."

"Oh! That's good to know," she said. That would mean anyone entering the basements of Global Actuaries Limited would be in extreme danger.

"Anyway, where was I?" Gaston said, "Oh yes... So, we let him get on with it..."

"Even though people were making human sacrifices to it?"

"Hey, we were all doing it, so we could hardly judge him for that. Then the Romans came and decided to try and wipe us out, so we lost track of him. The only thing we knew was that for some reason, the Romans didn't mind him and accepted him as another god to worship. Big mistake."

"How so?"

"While a few Romans were worshipping him and making the occasional human sacrifice, Queen Boudicca made a secret pact with him. In return for some of his power, she offered to drown Roman London in blood and offer it all to him. How do you think she was able to mobilise enough forces to destroy Camulodunum, Verulamium and Londinium? She sacrificed eighty thousand souls to Krowos. In London, the historian Cassius Dio described how the Britons strung up captured noblewomen, cut off their breasts and sewed them to their mouths to make it look like they were eating their own breasts. Then they were impaled. That much is true. Cassius Dio then claims that human sacrifices and 'exhibitions of insolence' were made in the grove of their war-goddess Andate. That was wrong. Some of our brothers were with Boudicca's forces and saw the slaughter first hand – all committed in the grove sacred to Krowos. After that, we heard that his size and power doubled. But by that point, the Romans had all but wiped us out, so we quit Britain and took refuge in the forests of France."

"And he was able to continue growing and feeding on human blood," Elizabeth Russell said, more to herself than to Gaston, "But the question is, how do I excise him?"

"You need a blade that has been ritually forged, inlaid with the words of power and then blessed. The priest or priestess must cleanse themselves before the rite, and the words of power must be spoken before cutting the cord."

That all sounded like it might take more time than she had...

"But," Gaston continued and her ears pricked up, "Fate would appear to be with you, Elizabeth. Tomorrow night, the moon will be in the perfect phase to bless the blade. It can be ready by the following morning. If you have someone here by dawn the day after tomorrow, you could have it in London by car by mid-afternoon."

"Excellent. I'll send a helicopter, with a car as back up," Elizabeth Russell said with a smile. Yes, an army Wildcat could have it back in London in a couple of hours.

"And what sort of blade do you require – sword or axe?"

"Good question. Hold on..." and she put her hand over the mouthpiece as she turned to Oliver and said,

"What do you reckon for cutting this umbilical cord – axe or sword?"

"Well, I don't know. You've seen it, so you know how thick it is and what..."

"No! Which will make me look cooler?"

"Oh, definitely the axe!" Oliver said without hesitation, "Give you that Viking/psycho axe murderer look."

"Yeah," she grinned, then to Gaston, "Yeah, we'll go with the axe, please."

"Of course... and what will we get in return?" Gaston asked.

And there it was! Typical Druid – always looking for an angle.

"What do you feel would be equitable?" she replied smoothly.

"A proper return to Anglesey would be nice."

Silence.

"Elizabeth? Are you still there?"

"Yes, thinking about it..." she replied. Unlike the modern faux druids, who had been pratting about Anglesey since the early nineteenth century, the ancient Druids had only returned to Anglesey after the First World War. They had been able to access their sacred groves and rebuild their power, but they hadn't been allowed to make any human sacrifices there. And that's what Gaston meant by a 'proper' return. Elizabeth Russell pursed her lips – this was exactly why Druids had been hunted down through the ages by everyone from the Romans to the Catholics, and the Protestants to the Nazis. One minute, Druids were all 'please and thank you', and the next thing you knew they were setting fire to wicker men full of virgins. On the other hand, they were a force for good and placated beings that could wreak havoc on the human race...

"Five a year and they all have to be willing," she said at last. God! She could almost hear Gaston grinning at the other end of the phone!

"Deal," he said, "And, just for the record, all our sacrifices are willing."

"Of course," she said – willing right up to the point when the fires were lit, and then suddenly their enthusiasm mysteriously vanished. It was no way to go and, as someone with personal experience of being on the wrong side of a ceremonial burning, Elizabeth Russell felt a great deal of sympathy for them.

"That just leaves the words of power," she said.

"Are you ready?" Gaston asked.

"Shoot," she replied.

He spoke the words and told her the precise thoughts she had to have in her mind to carry them into the world beyond.

"Got it. Thanks, Gaston. Anything particular needed for the cleansing?"

"No, just the usuals."

"And will I need a ceremonial robe?"

"No. Anything clean will do."

"Great," she hated wearing robes. White ones didn't suit her skin tone and they all made her look frumpy. She'd wear one of her scarlet trouser suits. It would undoubtedly be ruined once she'd been inevitably sprayed by the gloop in the stinking umbilical cord, but that was the price she was prepared to pay to look good.

"Okay, Gaston. Thanks for all your help. Oliver will be with you by dawn the day after tomorrow."

"Good. And when can we start... you know..." Gaston left it hanging.

"Tomorrow if you want, but remember, the deal is five, they've got to be willing and I do have eyes on things."

"Excellent! Sleep well and good luck!"

"Bye."

Elizabeth Russell returned the earpiece to its cradle and put the phone down like it was something distasteful she'd just found in her hamburger.

"Right, did you get all that?" she asked.

"Of course," Oliver replied, "It's all taped automatically as soon as you lift the receiver."

"Yeah, sorry, I keep forgetting. It's because I hate them so much!" she said with a shiver of revulsion as she looked at the phone.

"I'm having a drink. Want one?" she said as she went to the drinks cabinet on the other side of the room.

"Not for me, thanks. Er... can I ask one question?"

She nodded, putting ice into a cut-glass tumbler.

"Did you just agree to the Druids making five human sacrifices a year on Anglesey?"

"Yes," she replied, pouring three fingers of Monkey Shoulder over the ice.

"But doesn't that sort of undo some of the good of eliminating Krowos?"

"I s'pose," she admitted, adding three fingers of Drambuie to the mix and giving it a quick swirl with a silver stirrer.

"Is that right or ethical?" Oliver ventured.

"Maybe not for the poor sods in the wicker man, but overall, absolutely. What you've got to remember, Oliver, is who our friends are. Yes, the Druids are weirdy, beardy buggers, but they have wisdom beyond this world and have been protecting humans from the terrors of the Beyond for over five thousand years. Plus, I can have a reasoned conversation with them. Krowos has killed more than five people this week – that we know of – and I'm pretty sure none of them wanted that. And can I have a reasoned conversation with it to ask it to tone it down a bit? No. It's a tough deal to make, but that's just the way of the world... Oh God, that's good!" she exclaimed after taking a sip of her drink.

"Now, come on – we've got a helicopter and a bloody fast car to requisition... and then there's the small matter of sending an inter-dimensional creature back to whatever abyss it crawled out of."

"Actually," said Oliver, looking somewhat subdued, "I think I will have that drink."

Chapter Twenty-Eight

Housekeeping

While Ray and his family slept, Andy lay drugged into oblivion and Elizabeth Russell plotted Krowos' downfall, the service entrance of Global Actuaries Limited was the centre of a lot of activity and Tommy was at its heart. Around nine pm, he'd presented himself to The Boss, Simon Montague, and told him of the failure of the kidnap.

"Krowos will not be happy," Montague said simply, "Come with me," and together they went down to sub-basement C. Montague opened the door with his electronic fob and Tommy was immediately struck by how hot it was in the terracotta-coloured corridor inside. They walked down to the changing room and Montague pointed to an arched recess in the wall,

"Take your clothes off and put them in there, then put this on," and he handed Tommy a white robe. As he and Montague changed, Tommy was thinking about how he'd never been so close to the inner sanctum. However, any excitement he had was more than overwhelmed by the terror that this would probably be the very last experience of his life.

"You might want to use the lavatory first," Montague said before Tommy put his robe on, "The last thing you want to do is piss yourself in front of a god."

Tommy's feet slapped across the tiled floor and, as he went, Montague wondered how the man was alive at all – he was so fat! Tommy's stomach bulged horribly and sagged down so that his genitalia were lost in great folds of flesh and, as he walked to the toilet, his fat arse wobbled with the effort. Montague couldn't even begin to imagine how someone like that went about wiping their arse. No way could he get it clean! He imagined that the tops of Tommy's thighs were probably hot and red from chafing, and his arse crack would surely by a hot, crusty mess. He idly wondered if The Man had ever done to Tommy what he'd done to the rest of them. If he had, it couldn't have been pleasant.

When Tommy returned, he put on his robe and Montague led him down the corridor and placed his hand on the scanner by the door. It opened and they went into the red room with its ancient walls. Even though Montague wasn't in trouble himself, he had to pluck up his courage to turn the iron loop of the handle on the final door. Tommy wasn't prepared for the stench of decomposition that flooded out and he immediately turned to be sick. Fortunately, he had the self-awareness to avoid puking down the robe. The smell of the half-digested steak pie and mash was lost under the fetor of the room beyond. Tommy wiped his mouth and looked apologetically at Montague, who smiled thinly,

"Don't worry – happens to most people the first time," he said and he beckoned for Tommy to go through the door. When it closed with a thunk behind them, Tommy suddenly realised how much trouble he was in. His mouth went instantly dry and he started to shake.

"Come on," Montague said quietly, taking Tommy by the hand and leading him over to the edge of the large black hole in the floor. There, the smell was so bad that Tommy had to concentrate not to collapse and fall in.

"Arm!" Montague ordered and Tommy held out his left arm. Montague took the bared arm in one hand, while placing the index finger of his other hand against the fat, yielding flesh. It felt sharp and Tommy realised that Montague was wearing a metal finger end with a sharpened tip.

"Krowos, Bringer of Pain, Destroyer of Hope come to us and pass judgement on your servant!"

He jabbed the sharp finger end into Tommy's arm and squeezed a couple of drops of blood, which fell into the void below them.

"I'd stand back now," Montague said, moving away to leave Tommy exposed in the middle of the room. There was a sound from below like a great beast stirring in its lair, and then a rapidly increasing feeling of pressure in the room making it harder to breathe. Tommy was gasping and put his hands to his head – surely it was about to cave in from the pressure? Then suddenly he felt a thick vine whip around his body and lift him into the air as if he weighed nothing. Tommy screamed. He could see nothing, but he could feel that vine wrapped around him, squeezing the air out of him.

"Silence!"

The voice within his head scattered all thought and the scream stopped in his open mouth as if someone had hit his 'mute' button. Now his face was set in a soundless scream. Another vine seemed to wrap itself around his left arm above the elbow to pull the unwilling limb out at ninety degrees to his body.

"Relax!" the voice inside him commanded and he could only obey. His left hand, which had been tucked towards his body, flopped limply down so that his whole arm was straight out to the side.

"Your loyalty will be rewarded, just as your failure will be punished," the voice announced inside Tommy's head.

From his vantage point, Montague watched as the section of Tommy's left arm from the elbow to the hand disappeared. There was a spray of blood, quickly staunched and then Tommy was flung across the room to land in a heap, wailing and nursing the bloody stump where his forearm used to be.

"You will bring the other failures to me tonight," Krowos' voice sounded in both their heads, "Then send me my captains."

"Thy will be done," said Montague, who was now down on his knees in supplication. Then, the painful feeling of pressure receded until all that was left in the room was the gut-curdling smell and the sound of Tommy crying. Montague got up and went to help Tommy to his feet. Incredibly, the stump of his arm was hardly bleeding and looked like it had been cauterized.

"You are a very lucky boy!" Montague said, leading him out of the chamber.

Tommy didn't look or feel very lucky.

Over the next four hours, Tommy's cab arrived back at the building with various passengers. First was Wilf, followed by Smiler and finally Jaxx. All three entered the building expecting to be rewarded. None of them left. Then, The Man, Roaming Rohit, Mexican Dave and Bag Hag all arrived separately. Montague, having witnessed what had happened to the others, was glad when The Man told him to wait in the antechamber. Even from in there, Montague could tell when Krowos had emerged from his pit. In the antechamber, the air seemed tighter and more oppressive. Montague stood patiently, bathed in the red light, trying not to imagine what might be taking place in the inner sanctum. After five minutes, a single, high-pitched scream, followed by the thud of something heavy hitting the door told him that Krowos had been angry with Bag Hag. A few moments later, The Man, Rohit and Mexican Dave emerged from the chamber, their white robes covered in blood.

"Dispose of what's left," The Man's voice said inside Montague's head.

He bowed,

"Of course. Are there any other orders?"

"Only for us. Your task is to ensure that the police are no danger to the company."

"Yes."

"We will eliminate the policeman in the hospital and ensure the girl and her father come here."

"And the mother?"

The silence in Montague's head told the whole story.

Chapter Twenty-Nine

Test Results

"Gifted children often have vivid dreams," said Thalia Moncrief, looking sympathetically from Chloe to Vicky as they sat in her functional but sunny office.

"The thing is..." Vicky hesitated and was careful to make her next words not seem like an accusation,

"Chloe has hardly had any nightmares before, but since the session here, she's had a number of them."

"I see," Thalia said, thinking about it. The sunshine lit up her golden ponytail and seemed to radiate warmth and friendliness around her.

"It is hard work. There are a lot of questions to answer on the day. Maybe it played a part in setting off the dreams, but I'm afraid there's no way to find out. If they keep happening, then you should go to your GP. They'll be able to help. Now, let's go through the results of those tests..."

Chloe half switched off as Thalia and her mum talked about the test results. She was more interested in watching the glittering fragments of dust gently falling through the sunlight from the window. Where did it all come from and where did it all end up? She'd heard her mum talk about dust bunnies – were they like real bunnies? Was that where all the dust went?

The next thing she knew, she and Vicky were back out on the street walking through the crowds enjoying the sunshine.

"Five Guys?" Vicky suggested and Chloe nodded enthusiastically.

She couldn't have been paying much attention to their surroundings as they walked, because they seemed to be there almost immediately. However, she was totally focussed when the milkshake came. It was incredible. She wished she could sit and drink it all day, but all too soon came the sound of the last bit of shake being sucked noisily from the bottom of the cup. Why did adults all hate that noise so much? It wasn't that loud and never went on very long. Older people were funny about things like that. After lunch, she felt drowsy. That must have been why the journey home felt so disconnected. They seemed to almost teleport from Five Guys restaurant to the tube station, then straight down to the platform without the need for escalators or stairs. Then they were rattling along in the screaming tube train, and the next thing, they were out of the tube at Brixton and fighting through the noisy crowds to catch a bus up the hill to Streatham. All she could remember of the journey was the sound of the double decker slapping into the overhanging branches of the trees that were heavy with leaves. She always felt sorry for the trees when that happened. Was it painful for them? She was sure it would hurt her if a bus hit her hand as it passed, so the poor trees must have been in pain afterwards.

It was only when they got off the bus that everything around her seemed to pull into proper focus. The sun was gone and it had clouded over with those big, black clouds that summer storms have.

"I don't like the look of those clouds," said Vicky, looking up at the sky, "We'd better hurry, because we don't have coats or a brolly," and she took Chloe's hand, walking quickly along Streatham High Road, which seemed to stretch out ahead of them forever.

They got to a traffic light and Vicky offered her the honour of pressing the button to cross, which she did. That was when she saw The Man about a hundred yards away. He had rounded the corner from one of the side roads they'd just passed and was walking towards them.

"Vicky, look – it's that man!" Chloe pointed and the fact seemed to anger The Man, whose eyes narrowed as he walked deliberately towards them.

"The man you saw? The one in your dreams?" Vicky asked.

Chloe nodded, staring in terror at The Man as he inexorably closed the gap between them.

Vicky looked around. The traffic was too heavy to dare crossing, so she started pushing the button on the traffic light in the hope that her insistence would make them change. And still The Man walked towards them. Vicky looked around. Maybe they should go to the next crossing? But it was hundreds of yards away, and what if he crossed first and cut them off from getting home?

"Phone Ray!" Chloe said, and Vicky reached for her...

"Dammit! The bloody thing's out of battery..."

"Vicky, let's go!" Chloe was tugging at her arm, her eyes fixed on The Man, who was now only thirty yards away and closing.

Vicky seemed rooted to the spot with indecision and The Man was getting closer and closer, and the lights wouldn't change, and there was no break in the traffic.

"Vicky!" Chloe yelled.

The Man was right there! He was just a few yards away and now he was holding out his right hand to grab Chloe. Then the lights changed and, just as he snatched at her, Vicky pulled her away and they were running across the road. The Man followed without changing speed, so Chloe and her mum were able to widen the gap between them.

"It's okay, it's okay," Vicky was saying as she dragged Chloe along, while she kept looking back at The Man and his hate-filled eyes,

"We'll get home, lock the door and I'll call the police from the landline."

It didn't occur to her to shout for help, even though there were people going about their business on the High Road.

They ran on, widening the gap between them and The Man, but he followed them doggedly. Finally, they were at the end of their road and running down it to the house. Chloe saw a man cycling up the road towards them. He was surrounded by darkness and had a sombrero on his head.

"It's another one of them!" she shouted, pointing him out to Vicky.

"Shit!" Vicky swore, "Run like hell!" and they both put on a burst of speed. Judging distances, it was a toss-up who would get to their house first. She reached into her handbag and got her keys ready to open the front door. By some miracle, they got there before the madman on the bike, who was shouting incomprehensible things at them in Scottish. As Vicky concentrated on getting the key in the lock smoothly, Chloe looked on in horror as the man on the bike pulled up, jumped off it and made for them, but then she was dragged inside and the door slammed into his face.

"Open the fucking door, you bitch!" Mexican Dave screamed as he battered it with his fists.

Vicky's pupils were huge as she reached down and double-locked the door before opening the door of their flat, getting them inside and double-locking it, too.

"Kitchen!" she said, and they ran down the short corridor. Vicky went to the knife block, took out the biggest one for herself, than gave a smaller one to Chloe.

"If anyone gets in, just keep stabbing them," then she snatched up the phone and dialled 999.

"Emergency, which service do you require? Fire, Police or Ambulance?"

"Police!" Vicky said louder than she intended.

"Police," the operator repeated and then there was a click and a pause,

"Hello? Police?" Vicky said.

"Fucking nutter!" It was the voice of an Indian man.

"Are you the Police?" Vicky demanded.

"Nutter! Fucking nutter!"

"Vicky!" Chloe screamed and Vicky turned to see The Man standing in the garden, balling his fists and seething.

The sound of the front door shattering was followed by the thundering of fists on the door of their flat

"I'm gonna cut you up, bitch!"

"Nutter! Fucking nutter!" the phone chimed in loudly, even though Vicky was holding it down at her side.

Then The Man stepped up to the patio door, pulled back his fist and slammed it into the glass. It shattered and he stepped inside, just as Mexican Dave crashed through the front door.

"Fucking nutter!" screamed the voice from the phone.

Chapter Thirty

The Truth Will Out

Chloe's scream had Ray up and out of the bed in half a second. He hit the light switch and immediately realised she'd had another bad dream. This time, Chloe was awake and crying, and Vicky was already cradling her,

"It's all right... It's all right," she repeated.

Ray rubbed his face and looked down at them. What was happening? Why was it happening? He looked at the clock – five past four. Christ! Another broken night's sleep! Just what he didn't need.

"Are you okay?" he asked, coming back to the bed.

Chloe cried uncontrollably for a couple of minutes and then finally was able to tell them about the dream.

As she spoke, Ray ground his teeth – The Man again! He realised that he hadn't had time to put his description through the system to see who the bloke was. That would be high on his list for the day!

When Chloe had finished, he asked,

"Do you need anything? Glass of water? The loo?"

"Loo," she said, and he helped her out of the bed and took her down the corridor.

Chloe was shaky and felt dreadful, but she told herself that at least it was just a dream. Ray stood outside the bathroom and waited. God, what a mess! They'd had none of this nonsense before Chloe had seen the child psychologist. It MUST have something to do with that. This was the problem with messing about with people's minds – especially when they were kids. He decided he'd take some time off and go to see this woman when Chloe went to her next appointment.

"All done," said Chloe when she came out. Ray put his arm around her and they walked back to the bed. Vicky was standing by the bed and when they entered, she forced a smile,

"Let me tuck you in," she said, as Chloe jumped in and got under the covers.

Once she'd tucked her in, Vicky gave her a kiss,

"I just want to have a quick word with Ray and then we'll be right back, okay?"

Chloe nodded and Vicky kissed her again, then turned to Ray and indicated they should head down the corridor. They padded to the kitchen, Ray switched the light on and turned to Vicky,

"What's up?" and then he noticed that she looked deathly pale, as if something was very, very wrong,

"You alright?" he asked, putting a gentle hand to her shoulder.

"It's Chloe's dream," she said, looking drawn and sick,

"I was having it, too."

***

It was seven when Ray left the house for work. He had a ton to do and he wanted to fit in a visit to Andy, but all the way in, the only thing he could think about was the previous night. He had been so sure that the nightmares must have been triggered by the trip to the psychologist, but when Vicky had said that she had been having the same dream... it didn't make sense. How could it be? Could she have been mistaken and muddled Chloe's dream with her own broken sleep? No. He could tell that she was speaking the truth. And anyway, to get that confused she'd have to have some serious mental problem, which Vicky clearly didn't have. But what the fuck was going on? Two people couldn't have the same dream at the same time... could they? Ray seemed to be at the heart of a whirlwind, watching every different part of his life being uprooted and spun into the air around him. As he stood, crammed into the tube train, he rubbed his eyes. God! The lack of sleep was really getting to him. When the alarm had gone off and he'd got up, he'd had that horrible feeling of being wrenched away from sleep. That feeling of coldness and fragility, and the sense that he could somehow feel exactly where his kidneys were. He stared about the train only half-seeing the other passengers. He'd have to pull himself together, because there was a high likelihood they'd caught Andy's attack on camera and that he'd be having to brief people about a manhunt. He groaned internally. Why did Chloe have to have that dream last night?

When Ray walked through the door, Emma thought he looked like crap. What had happened at home now? His wife and daughter had no idea how lucky they were, and yet they kept making his life difficult. If she had her way...

"Morning, Em'," Ray said with something resembling a smile, "Got any good news for me?"

"Um..." she looked flustered.

"What is it?" Ray said warily.

"It's better to see it for yourself than have me try to explain it," Emma said, indicating her computer screen.

"Watch," she said and clicked her mouse.

Security footage from a camera on Westminster Bridge played on the screen. Nothing much was happening, but then the footage changed to snowy interference for about thirty seconds before the picture came back.

"So?" Ray asked. His brain felt foggy and sluggish.

"So, that bit of static matches the moment when the person who attacked Andy would have been crossing in front of this camera."

"What?"

"There's more," Emma said reluctantly. She could see Ray wasn't ready for this, but she had to tell him,

"Every camera between New Scotland Yard and the scene of the attack has the same problem. Even our own security cameras in front of New Scotland Yard."

"What?" Ray's tired brain seemed to have a one-word vocabulary.

"What I'm saying is that we have a burst of static on the cameras outside New Scotland Yard at 12.03, about a minute and a half after we see Andy leave the building. We see Andy walk along the Embankment, then turn left onto Westminster Bridge. All the cameras catch that. But from 12.03 each camera in sequence has a burst of static as if someone has gone in and wiped each recording so we can't see who was following Andy. Every camera that would have caught the attack shows nothing but static for the duration of the assault. One minute Andy's walking along, then there's static, then he's down. And it's the same with the cameras on the other side of the bridge. All of them have periods of static after the attack. The only thing we can point to is that the person escaped faster than most people can run, but probably not fast enough to be in a car or on a motorbike. So, they were probably on a bicycle."

"Fuck me!" Ray groaned. The one thing that could've given them a lead was a pile of shit!

"And you've double checked..." he began.

"Everything. All the camera footage is the same."

Ray sat down and put his head in his hands. What was happening? It was unprecedented! How could anyone tamper with... but no, that was the wrong question... *who* could tamper with security cameras in one of the most sensitive parts of London? Only someone with top security clearance and access to everything... one person came to mind and she was in her late twenties, five foot ten, athletically built, with white hair and a penchant for power suits and stealing his cases.

"Fucking bitch!" he hissed through gritted teeth.

Emma looked shocked and he had to quickly backtrack,

"No, not you. You're great – better than great, you're a marvel. I was thinking of someone else," he flapped,

"Um... I'm going to have to go..." he continued, getting up, "I need you to pull any security footage you can from a wider area around New Scotland Yard in the twenty minutes before the attack. Whoever they're trying to hide might show up on their way to the attack. Okay, got that?"

"Yes, boss, but where are you...?" Emnma said, but he cut her off,

"Make this priority one. I want that footage!"

And then he was walking briskly towards the door and calling Oliver Fernsby's phone.

Ray was prowling around the foyer of the Treasury like an angry tiger when Oliver Fernsby arrived to show him upstairs.

"Good morning, Detective Inspector Ennis..." he began, but Ray interrupted,

"Cut the crap and take me to the Snow Queen."

"Of course, follow me."

Oliver walked at a good pace to help dissipate some of Ray's anger and, when they were halfway down the long corridor towards the stairs up to the office, he said,

"You're not alone, you know."

"What?"

"You're not the only person to call her the Snow Queen. I think it's the white hair..."

"And the way she annoys the hell out of people!" Ray added.

Oliver smiled,

"Well, I really couldn't comment on that."

Ray's face relaxed a bit and Oliver gave himself a small pat on the back. Maybe the long spiral stairs would also help to tire their visitor out a bit? Oliver was right. By the time they reached the top, Ray was puffing. It was the lack of sleep – nothing seemed to be working properly.

This time, Elizabeth Russell was waiting for Ray in Oliver's office, standing looking at a file. Her purple trouser suit and mauve shirt were an arresting combination.

"Hello, what can I do for you?" she asked with cheery bonhomie, fixing him with those disarming violet eyes. Ray railed against her internally. No! He was angry and here to have things out and he'd bloody do it this time!

"I think you know exactly why I'm here!" he accused.

"Well in that case, I think you'd better come in," and, since she could see he that he looked like an exhausted wreck, she added, "Coffee, Oliver! Strong and plenty of it, please!" then she led him into her office.

"Shall we sit?" she asked, indicating the chairs near the window.

"No, I'd rather stand," he said, barely holding back the anger he wanted to unleash.

"Okay, what's the problem?" again, her calm voice, beautiful features and beguiling eyes threatened to extinguish the flame of his anger – it was now or never.

"I know you think you're above the law, but tampering with CCTV footage on police premises is a criminal offence. I'm investigating the attempted murder of a serving police officer and I will see you prosecuted for obstructing justice."

"I'm sorry, but you've lost me," she said, quite genuinely.

"Come on, don't play the innocent!" Ray retorted, his voice rising, "How the fuck did you tamper with the footage from every camera between New Scotland Yard and the far side of Westminster Bridge?"

"Oh!" Elizabeth Russell exclaimed. This was an interesting and unexpected twist!

"God, you're pathetic! Can't even come clean when you're caught red handed. You people in Whitehall are all the same – just out to protect yourselves and fuck the rest of us!"

Elizabeth Russell was standing in the most neutral pose she could as she replied,

"May I say something?"

Ray nodded, fighting the urge to pace.

"I honestly don't know what you're talking about..."

Ray made a noise that made it clear he thought that was horseshit,

"No, I'm serious. Whatever's happened to that footage has nothing to do with me. I can see why you might think I'd have done it, because it is sneaky, high-handed, requires the highest security clearance and interferes with yet another of your cases..."

"Yes, it fucking does – and it's a very personal case," Ray interrupted, fighting his emotion over seeing Andy in that bed and being unable to do anything about it.

"But this wasn't me..." how could she make him believe her? It was time for the truth.

"I'm going to do something I haven't done since we met," she said,

"What, not fuck me over?" Ray replied bitterly.

"No, I'm going to be totally honest with you," and this time, when she fixed Ray with her violet eyes, they weren't sparkling, but hard as flint. His anger died instantly.

"Let's sit down."

This time, Ray took the offered chair and sat down. As she sat opposite him, her face brightened,

"Oliver, perfect timing. No, don't worry about pouring the coffee, just leave us to it," and the ever-efficient Oliver shimmered out of the room.

Elizabeth Russell poured coffee into the two cups and said,

"Help yourself to milk and sugar – and biscuits. So, this case is not what you think it is," and she stirred two lumps of brown sugar into her black coffee.

"Then what exactly is it?"

"It's nothing to do with people traffickers or Russian arms dealers. I mean, they are at the peripheries, but they're not what this is all about. This is about a creature that's been in London killing people for thousands of years," and she went on to explain everything about Krowos and his network of evil.

"Bullshit!" Ray spat when she'd finished.

"There are some days I wish it was, but it's true. And the reason I know some of this is thanks to Andy."

"Andy?"

"Yes, he's a very instinctive sleuth – I'm surprised he hasn't got further in the police force – but he uncovered the evidence that linked this Krowos to three other attacks identical to that of Florence Gichuru. The earliest one was in 124 A.D. in Roman London near the grove sacred to the god Krowos."

"Andy discovered that?" Ray was more than surprised.

"All in the Crime Museum archive. And that's why they tried to kill him. They specifically didn't want you to find that out."

"Why not?" Ray asked, drawn in. Then he immediately shook his head and said,

"No, don't answer that. It's nuts. I mean, you expect me to believe this bollocks, but... how does it all work?"

Elizabeth Russell poured herself another cup of coffee and stirred in the sugar. How could she put this in simple terms?

"Okay, there is more than just the physical reality we see around us..."

"Don't tell me – like 'auras'," Ray said, putting on a mock spooky voice.

"Yes."

"That's the sort of nonsense my seven-year-old believes in," Ray threw the words away, but for Elizabeth Russell, a major piece of the puzzle fell into place.

"Your daughter sees auras?" she asked, sitting slightly forward in her chair.

"So she claims. She's got visual stress and dyslexia. It's most likely part of that," Ray countered.

This is why Krowos is so interested in Ray and his family, Elizabeth Russell thought. Ray would be a great addition to the team, and his daughter was a ball of psychic energy. Nice combo.

"Beyond this physical reality," she continued, "There are other planes of existence and other dimensions, which are populated by lots of things. Some are like us and others really aren't. Occasionally, beings from these other places cross over into our world and when they do, they broadly fall into three categories: Watchers – they can't interact with this world at all and simply observe what's happening. They're the ones that give people the creepy feeling they're being watched..."

"This is such nonsense," Ray muttered, drinking some coffee. He'd give them this much – they made damned good coffee, even if they were batshit crazy.

"The second group are benevolent – they are able to interact in our world and they try to help people. Then there's the third group – they are... malevolent. They are able to interact with this world and they want to harm people. Krowos is one of those. Most of these intruders are linked to a particular place where the barrier between this world and their home plane or dimension is at its thinnest. In the case of Krowos, he is directly linked to an old spring that starts right under the offices of Global Actuaries Limited. Which is why I needed you to back off for your own safety."

"Does taxpayers' money fund this rubbish?"

"It did once, but these days it's covered by three hundred years' worth of good investments. Now, when we first met, I asked you whether anything odd had happened to you in the previous couple of days and you lied to me when you said no."

Ray shifted uneasily in his seat.

"And you've lied to me every time I've asked that question since – I'm not offended, in fact I'm impressed with how well you lie. It's a very useful and under-appreciated skill. But those lies aren't helping you. I'm guessing that things have been happening to you and your family that you can't explain logically. From the look of you, you've been losing sleep."

"My daughter's been having bad dreams..."

"Don't tell me," she interrupted, "They're about an angry old man in an overtight raincoat."

"Yeah," Ray said without any feeling. He was struggling to take it all in.

"And you've seen him, too, haven't you?"

"Yeah."

Elizabeth Russell leaned across and refilled Ray's coffee cup.

"Right now, he's probably the most dangerous man in London," she said, "He is the leader of Krowos' acolytes – oh, and by the way, Titheridge had everything right. Every one of the sixty-eight people he killed were evil and were vicious killers. So far, you've been lucky..."

Ray didn't feel very lucky.

"That man in the raincoat could have killed you and your family at any time, but he's seen something in you - and especially in your daughter – that Krowos wants."

"Okay, if I play along with this delusion for a minute – what could this thing see in me that would make it want me?"

"You're successful, well-connected, a good leader – who knows how far you can get in the Met over the next ten years? A senior copper would be very useful to a creature that requires a steady stream of human sacrifices. But most attractive of all, it can see the darkness in you."

"Bollocks!"

"I see it, too. The reason you're so good at catching criminals is because you really understand how they think. You're right up at the top of the circle where policing and criminality meet. Yes, you're on the side of justice, but what separates you from criminality is wafer thin. That's why I originally thought you might work well in our department. You need a certain moral flexibility to do what I do," she said, thinking about the deal she'd just struck with the Druids.

"And do you still think I could work here?" he asked.

"No. Your world view is too inflexible, which is why we're still having this conversation."

Ray gave her a sour look.

"What would I have to do to make you believe me?" she asked, "Because right now, I need you on my side and not getting in my way."

For the first time, Ray was seeing a different side to Elizabeth Russell. Gone was the friendly, polite civil servant. Now there was a tinge of anger and the temperature in the room seemed to be dropping.

"I have a big fucking monster sitting in Candlewick, gorging itself on human blood, and I'm going toe to toe with it in the next couple of days," she said and, as her passion rose, so the temperature and the light level in the room dropped further,

"It is more dangerous than you can comprehend and I need all my concentration and energy to kill it. I frankly don't have the time or bandwidth to waste holding the hand of a stubborn, closed-minded fuckwit who can't see that he's hopelessly out of his depth and that his pig-headed world view is putting his family in mortal danger. So, how can I convince you that I'm telling the truth right here, right now?"

The room had become cold and very dark, with the only light seeming to emanate from Elizabeth Russell, who shone like an amethyst. Ray felt the crawling sensation of fear in his stomach, but he mustn't show it. He had to be strong.

"It'll take more than some trick of the light to convince me," he said.

She stared him down and her voice spoke inside his head,

"You know, I can make you do what I want."

Ray shook his head and put a hand to his ear.

"I'm in your head right now. If I wanted to, I could make you open that window and jump out. Shall I do that? Will that make you believe?"

"This is rubbish!" Ray said, but then he made a surprised "Whoa!" as he lurched up out of the chair,

"Hey!" he cried as his legs started moving him jerkily towards the window.

"Admit that you're wrong and that I'm right, or I will drop you out of the window," her voice said in his head.

"No, this must be a dream. This can't be happening," but he was still moving towards the window. Then his thoughts turned to the time when he'd chased The Man.

"Oho!" Elizabeth Russell's voice in his head was crowing, "So, you tried to chase the man in the raincoat and it was just like this – weird, incomprehensible and frightening. And I like the way you've named him 'The Man'. I think I'll use that."

"No! How could you know that?"

"Because I'm in your head you idiot. Fuck! Don't you get it? You're just a tiny speck in a vast ocean and you need to let go of the idea you have any control. You're nothing. You can't even stop your hands from opening the window."

Ray watched in horror as his hands deftly opened the latch on the large, round window. He was desperately trying to pull his hands away, but his body was no longer his own, and now he'd opened the great window and was moving right to the lip of it. He looked down and the tips of his shoes were hanging over the edge of the long drop down to the pavement.

"It would be so easy..." her voice purred inside his head and he could feel himself leaning forward.

"No!" he shouted in rising alarm. He was leaning out into space and soon he would be past the tipping point.

"I think we've heard enough from you," she said within him and suddenly, he felt his lips meld together.

"Mmmm! Mmmm!" he tried to scream for help, but nothing came out beyond a virtually inaudible murmur.

And now he knew he was past the point of no return, but instead of falling to the flagstones below, he slowly kept leaning forwards. Eventually, he was staring straight down at the ground and his body was sticking out of the side of the building at ninety degrees. He was still trying to cry out, more in anger than fear, but nothing came.

There was a pause and Elizabeth Russell came to stand by the window looking out,

"How's the view?" she laughed and then, with a twizzle of her finger, she made Ray turn over so that he was looking up at her. She was standing with her legs firmly planted at shoulder width and her fists on her hips looking down at him imperiously, her white hair swept by the breeze and her violet eyes flashing with triumph. What was she?

"Duh! I'm a witch," her voice sounded in his head and echoed like the toll of a bell.

She let that sink in, then beckoned to him with her finger. He rose from horizontal to vertical until they were face to face.

"Don't look now," she smiled, "But you're standing in mid-air."

Ray couldn't move his head, but he could just strain his eyes enough to see she was telling the truth.

"Now do you believe?"

Yes. The thought happened before he could control it.

"Good. Now, if you and your family want to survive to see next week, you will go home, pack your bags and drive straight to that static caravan near Cromer."

But how did she know...?

"Because I'm in your brain! Christ! I thought you were clever. How many times do I have to explain? I'm in your brain right now and I can see everything in here. And let me tell you, you've got a lot of repressed shit."

Now she moved in close so that they were eye to eye and this time the words came from her exquisitely drawn lips,

"Leave this to me. Take your family. And fuck-right-off," and she punctuated the order by flicking her index finger right between his eyes.

Chapter Thirty-One

The Choices We Make

Ray started with a jerk and looked around him in confusion. He was sitting on the tube, rattling towards... he didn't even know where he was going, or which line he was on. He looked at his watch – nearly one in the afternoon. What the fuck? What just happened? Had it just happened? One second Elizabeth Russell had been there in front of him, and the next...

The train slowed and pulled into Waterloo. Ray thought about Elizabeth Russell. Was any of that real? Something deep within him said 'yes'. The doors opened and Ray made a split-second decision. He scrambled out of the train on rather wobbly legs and made for the exit. While he tried to work out what the hell was going on, he'd do something useful and see Andy. The hospital was only a few hundred yards from the station and what he needed was quiet time to think. Being with Andy would be perfect. He came out of the station and swayed down the polluted canyon of York Road towards St Thomas' Hospital. He knew that he ought to be going home, that his wife and daughter were in danger and that he'd agreed with the Russell woman to leave town, but something made him want to delay all that. Maybe it was pride, or his 'pig-headed' nature, but he had to do something to show that he was still in control. His mind was his own, not Elizabeth Russell's – even if she was a witch who could suspend him sixty feet above the ground. Did she really do that? Was she really a witch? Fuck! He didn't even know which way was up anymore. All he knew was that there was no way he was telling anyone about it. He'd be certified in an instant. Could the stress of the last week have cracked his mind?

When he entered the hospital, Ray pulled himself together and decided to be in the here and now. He made his way to the ICU and when he presented himself at the nursing station, he showed them his police ID.

"One of your colleagues is in there with him. She's only just arrived."

"Oh, thanks... but can I still...?" Ray asked.

"Yes, but no more than two of you, please," the large, happy-looking Filipino nurse replied, handing him a gown, gloves and a mask.

"Thanks," Ray said and walked down the corridor.

"Emma."

Ray's appearance made her start. She was on the far side of the bed and her head had been bowed, looking down at the cannula in Andy's arm.

"Boss!" she cried out in surprise.

"Sorry, didn't mean to startle you," Ray said quietly, slipping around the end of the bed to join her.

"You nearly gave me a heart attack!" and her eyes, which were the only feature of her face not covered by her mask, showed she'd been spooked.

"How is he?"

"Bit better than yesterday, but they've still got him in a coma..." and at this point, her voice wavered.

"Hey, I know... it's okay," Ray said, putting an arm around her shoulders and giving her a squeeze. She felt warm through the thin cotton of the gown and her shirt.

"It just seems so wrong. Who would do this to Andy?"

"What, apart from his ex-girlfriends? I don't know," and Ray was pleased to hear a small laugh from her.

"It just shows, though... one day you're here, and the next..." she trailed off.

"Yeah... I guess the moral of the story is, life's for living," Ray said, then he realised his arm was still around her and he withdrew it gently.

"What's happening with the CCTV footage?" he asked.

"They said they wouldn't be able to get some of it over until after two, so I thought I'd come and see him. Didn't want to just hang around."

It seemed like a fair reason. Andy meant a lot to all of them.

"Are you all right?" she asked. Although his face was covered, she could see he was even more exhausted than he had looked earlier.

"Yeah, fine. Just had a stressful meeting," then he decided to be a bit more honest with her,

"I'm going to bring forward my holiday and head off tomorrow."

"What?" Emma sounded shocked and very concerned, "With Andy here in the hospital like this?"

"Well..."

"We need you to manage the case," she said with urgency, "Andy needs you... I..." then she trailed off and her pent-up emotion burst and she started crying.

"Hey, hey, it's all right," and Ray was holding her shaking body close to his. He enfolded her in his arms and, with her face buried into his shoulder, he could feel the intensity of her feeling. He rested his chin on the top of her head and his senses were filled with the scent of spring breezes from her shower gel. Her slim, taut body was calming now as her sobs subsided, until she finally stopped and he let her relax, slipping his hands across her back to gently grip her shoulders. She looked up at him and, wiping tears from her eyes, she said,

"Sorry,"

"Nothing to be sorry about," he said looking down at her. The tears had taken away some of the toughness she always projected, and then he looked into her eyes and felt something unexpected. She saw his reaction and reached a hand up to his mask, took it off as her other hand took off her own, drew his face to hers and kissed him. He resisted slightly at first, but then, as her lips explored his, he kissed her back and now they were exploring each other. They parted for a moment, their eyes communicating more than words ever could, and then they were locked together again. His left arm slipped around her waist, pulling her close. She was so slim that she seemed to meld into him, so that it was difficult to tell where he ended and she began. One of Emma's arms squeezed him to her, while the other hand ran across his strong buttocks and gripped them. She could feel his manhood growing firm against her stomach. She wanted it. Now.

"Take me home," she said when they came up for air.

Ray hesitated. What was he doing? What had he done! He shouldn't go with her... but the electric feeling of attraction was impossible to resist.

"Come on," he said and they walked out of the room together, leaving Andy alone.

As they went down to the basement exit, Emma knew that she had to keep stoking the fires, because once he was outside in the cold light of day, he might ignore his desire and go back to his family. Fortunately, there was a cab right by the door and she was able to get him into it before he could think through what they were doing.

"Vauxhall Grove, please," she said, closing the door and turning Ray's face to hers. They kissed again, and again there was that electro-chemical connection that left them both slightly breathless. She thanked God that it was only about five minutes back to her place. She wanted him so much it hurt and she couldn't let him slip through her fingers. For his part, Ray was too tired and confused to think. He could only feel, and this felt good. Unlike the complicated, difficult world outside the cab, this seemed simple. Everything else seemed so intertwined and impossible to navigate, but here it was just two people making a powerful connection. The simplicity of it lifted the weight of work, the responsibilities of parenthood and the complications of marriage from him.

Ray didn't really notice his surroundings when they arrived at her place. He saw a white-fronted Victorian terraced house, and then they were through the front door and straight into her ground floor apartment. It was dingy and the entrance hall was cluttered, but Ray wasn't focussed on that. Emma was now the centre of his world and she was kissing him and drawing him into her bedroom. Pausing only to throw some clothes off the unmade bed, Emma was all over him. It was an incredible rush to feel her desire for him as her fingers worked efficiently to unbutton his shirt while she kissed him deeply. He slipped out of his shoes while she took off his shirt and ran her hands over his lightly muscled body, then kissed his chest. He began to search for the buttons of her shirt, but she simply said,

"No," and pushed him backwards onto the bed. He was hardly down when she'd taken off her shirt and bra. Her athletic kick-boxer's physique was toned and tanned and exciting. As he watched, she stripped off her trousers to reveal slim, muscular legs. Then Emma stepped out of her white sports thong and stalked towards Ray, keeping her predatory eyes locked on his. She got onto the bed and crawled up him with a knee either side of his legs until she was straddling his midriff, then she was kissing him with ever greater urgency.

His hands delighted in the softness of her skin, the feel of the curves of her body and her small, tight ass. Somewhere deep inside, part of him was thinking how different it was from being with Vicky. Emma's scent and physicality were new and thrilling, and that need she had for him was like a drug. Was there anything more arousing than being desired? Vicky loved him, but the desire had gone from their lovemaking years ago. This was... incredible. Emma could feel his desire beneath her and she slid down him to quickly undo his belt, button and zip. She pulled at his trousers and boxer shorts together, swung a leg around so that she could pull them off and, once they were out of the way, her leg swung back and she was straddling him again. She was past all thoughts of foreplay. She had only one desperate need – to envelop him and hold him deep inside her. She was more than ready for him and she reached down to guide herself onto him with an expression of perfect rapture. And when she had every inch of him inside her, she leant forward, gripping his wrists and pinning them to the mattress. Then she looked deep into his eyes and rode him hard.

Maybe it was the pressure of the last week, but the intensity of their fire was barely quenched over the next three hours. Whenever it seemed that the flames had died down, one of them would re-ignite them. Finally, Emma wrapped herself around her man and, with a smile of a mission accomplished, she fell into perfect, untroubled sleep. Ray felt gloriously knackered, but as he drifted into sleep, he knew that he would have to pay a price and that the currency would be guilt. When they awoke over an hour later, their kisses still fizzed with energy, but they both knew he would have to go.

"Can I have a quick shower?" he asked.

"If I can come in with you," she smiled and then, in her bath/shower, she knelt as the water cascaded over them and drained him to the last drop. She was determined to make sure there was nothing left for his wife when he got home. Afterwards, she got up and they washed each other, still feeling that thrill of the touch of someone new.

"What will we do tomorrow?" Emma asked, with her head resting on his chest as the water ran over them.

"We'll just try to be ourselves and work hard to find out who attacked Andy."

"What about your wife?" and Emma's lip curled in distaste as she thought of that other woman, who was now yesterday's news.

"You let me deal with that," he said calmly, working hard not to betray the bewildering confusion he was feeling. What he needed now was a good night's sleep. Was it too much to ask?

When Ray arrived home, he was only slightly later than usual and was greeted by Chloe jumping into his arms for a big hug. He carried her back into the kitchen and put her down before giving Vicky a warm kiss and squeeze.

"You smell very fresh and breezy," she said.

"I had to have a shower at work," the lie came so easily and smoothly that it sounded like the most natural thing in the world.

"How's Andy?" Vicky asked with concern, instantly forgetting anything about showering at work.

"They've still got him under, but they think he's getting stronger," Ray replied, "Wat'cha cooking?"

"Chilli con carne with rice and nachos and... I've made guacamole from scratch," Vicky said proudly, pointing to a bowl of green goop on the kitchen top.

"Nice!"

"You bet – it's got extra coriander in it!"

"Good day?" he asked.

"Quiet one. You know, after last night..." and Vicky shot a glance at Chloe, who had gone out into the garden and back to the drawing she'd been doing when Ray had arrived.

"I'll try to get her out to the new playground at Streatham Common tomorrow..."

And that was how the evening went. Easy chit-chat and the comforts of a happy, stable home. As the evening progressed, Ray sometimes felt as if he were watching someone else's life rather than living his own. It was all so divorced from what had happened in the afternoon, that it was a bit surreal. How could he have done what he'd done and slip back into this so easily? It didn't seem possible, and yet there he was, playing Uno with his family, laughing and joking, and sharing warmth and camaraderie with his wife. It didn't quite compute. He wondered briefly, as he oversaw Chloe brushing her teeth, whether this was how Vicky had felt when she'd been banging Ed. Maybe that was why he wasn't feeling horribly guilty, because he knew that this was simply making things even? Although he'd never wanted to get back at Vicky for what she'd done, the fact that she had done it certainly made it easier to justify his afternoon with Emma. And what was going to happen between them now? It had been incredible, but could it really compete with a comfortable family evening?

"And the insides of your teeth," he said when Chloe looked like she was about to stop brushing.

"Orry," she replied with a mouthful of toothbrush and toothpaste.

Ray knew that whatever was happening with Emma couldn't be permanent, because at the end of the day, his family were most important. Even with all the complications and responsibilities, this was real and what he'd done with Emma was more like a dream, or a film he'd seen.

"Right, where are you sleeping tonight?" Ray said with a yawn – even with the nap he'd had in Emma's arms, he was knackered.

"How about sleeping in your bed tonight?" Vicky suggested, giving Ray a look that told him she wanted more than just sleep. Ray groaned inwardly.

"Um..." Chloe was thinking. She'd had a nice day, but what if The Man came back in her dreams?

"It's okay if you want to come in with us," Ray said, trying to sound helpful, but not so enthusiastic for her to join them that it would arouse Vicky's suspicions.

"But it might be good to have all that space to yourself," Vicky said with an encouraging smile.

"Okay, I'll sleep in my own bed, but can we leave the hall light on, just in case?"

"Of course," Vicky smiled and she led Chloe to her own bed. Ray followed and they took it in turns again to read chapters of Matilda.

Once they'd read about a quarter of the book to her and finally tucked her in, they went to the kitchen to clear up. As Ray picked up the tea towel to start drying things from the dishrack, Vicky stood in his way with a look in her eye that he knew very well.

"So..." she said, running her forefinger down the centre of his chest and looking into his face with a certain intent.

"So?" Ray said innocently.

"So, shall we get an early night?" and as she spoke, she put her arms around his waist.

"Yeah, that would be nice," he replied, looking down at her. He really did love her and, whatever she thought about her own body, he loved that, too. But as they held each other, there was none of the electricity of the afternoon. Ray was finding the juxtaposition of his time with Emma and that moment with Vicky weird to say the least. Vicky went on tiptoe to kiss him and he met her halfway. Although Vicky kissed him with passion, Ray still couldn't feel that thrill Emma had given him. Maybe it was because he was so tired, but Ray knew it was simple familiarity. Two people who'd been together ten years just couldn't feel the same heat as they had when they'd first started going out. Otherwise, they'd wear each other out or explode.

Soon they were in bed and Ray worried he had nothing left. This was confirmed when Vicky came onto him. In spite of her best efforts with her hands and then her mouth, the most he could manage was a semi. Vicky looked gloomily at his failing member, lolling over on his upper thigh. She worried if it was her. She'd put on a few pounds recently. Maybe he didn't find her attractive anymore? She couldn't remember a time when he hadn't got an erection. Maybe...

"Sorry, beautiful, it's no good," Ray said gently, "I'm so tired and stressed, it's... if I could string together a few nights' sleep it'll be fine. In the meantime, why don't I do something just for you? Come on, take off your nightdress," and he started to pull the light cotton up her thighs. Although she always felt a little self-conscious naked, she liked the way he looked at her. She could tell he still liked what he saw and when he started to kiss her all over, she closed her eyes and relaxed into it.

Ray knew her body well, knew what she liked and didn't like, and what would take her to the heights of pleasure. After taking his time to worship her round and exquisitely soft behind, he turned her over and kissed up the insides of her wonderfully fleshy thighs and then set to work with his tongue. They say that familiarity breeds contempt, but Ray didn't find that the case in the bedroom. He took comfort in knowing exactly what Vicky needed to climax and was relaxed about the fact that his dick had never had anything to do with it. He watched and listened and felt her slightest reactions to what he was doing and matched his movements to her. He loved this. Was it because it gave him a feeling of power to be able to create such a strong response in her? Perhaps. Or perhaps it was simply the fact that even though they'd had their rocky moments, he loved her, loved the feel and smell and taste of her, and enjoyed giving her pleasure? Whatever his reasons, after she had reached repeated climaxes, he took comfort in the way she held onto him in their dreamy post-coital cuddle.

When the lights went off, Vicky fell asleep quickly, leaving Ray thinking about what had to be the strangest day of his life. In the morning, he'd tell Vicky to pack so that they could leave for Norfolk in the afternoon. He would have to go into work to clear up a few things and make sure Andy's assault was being fully investigated, but then he'd be off. And what would he do about Emma? Christ! He'd got himself up a creek there. He didn't like to think about how messy things could get at work and at home if she decided to make life difficult. He sighed. Emma would have to wait until he got back from holiday. And what about the elephant in the room – Elizabeth Russell? Did he believe any of what she'd said? Surely it was all garbage! And yet, there she was running her own department in the Treasury. Should that alone make him believe her? Or should he believe her because she'd apparently taken over his mind and levitated him out of a window? What the fuck? Did that even happen? As he drifted off, he began to wonder if the whole day had been a weird dream. He should be so lucky!

Chapter Thirty-Two

Dead And Gone

After Ray left, Emma had a dull, sinking feeling at the thought of him going home to his wife and daughter. She could give him everything he needed and with none of the problems. Then she thought about Ray, about what they had done and that buoyed her mood. Yes! She'd finally got what she wanted. Now he'd come to see how much better things could be with her, and then... her eyes sparkled as she imagined their future life together. It was a life that didn't include Vicky or Chloe. She went through the living room to the kitchen to get some juice from the fridge. The kitchen, like the rest of the flat, was gloomy and messy. A discarded pizza box sat on the work surface and the sink was full of three-day-old washing up. Emma didn't notice it. Her mind was fixed on Ray – the feel of his skin and muscles, the way he smelled and the taste of him. She felt an ache in her loins and wished he was with her again. But there was a lot of work to do and she needed to have her mind clear. She'd go back to the office and put some time in. She wanted to have something to show Ray when he got in the next morning. Could his useless wife do that? No! It would confirm how much better Emma was than that dozy cow. Yes, that was the thing to do, but first, she needed to see Andy again.

When she arrived back at the ICU, the Filipino nurse was still on duty.

"Is it okay if I see Andy Harper again?" Emma asked.

"Wow, he's popular today," she smiled, then she looked at her clipboard and said,

"There's someone in there with him, but you can join them. So long as we don't have more than two at a time, it's fine."

"Thanks," said Emma, then she put on her PPE and walked to Andy's room, puzzling over who could be in there. When she opened the door, she saw the white hair of on old woman bent as if in prayer on the far side of the bed. Was it his nan?

"Hello?" Emma said quietly, not wanting to startle whoever the old woman was, but it was she who got the shock when the woman looked up. She was clearly in her twenties, very good looking and not wearing any PPE.

"Oh..." Emma stammered, "I'm sorry, I thought... er... I'm Emma, I work with Andy – who are you?"

Elizabeth Russell smiled back at Emma, immediately quelling her disquiet and replied,

"Natalie Krasnakova, pleased to meet you," and she held out her hand, which Emma briefly shook.

"And how do you know Andy?" Emma asked.

"Oh, sorry, yes – I'm Andy's ex... well, one of his many exes – you know what Andy's like."

"Yes, I do," Emma replied. She wasn't sure she liked this woman. Maybe it was the perfectly tailored purple trouser suit, or the lack of mask or gloves, but there was something not quite right about her and Emma was determined to find out what,

"It's funny, I don't remember Andy mentioning a 'Natalie',"

"Well, we broke up about two years ago. How long have you been working with him?"

"Getting on for a year," said Emma.

"That's probably why, then," Elizabeth Russell smiled, but as she looked at Emma White, she knew that something was off and that she was hiding something. Her aura was a dirty brown, although that only pointed to vague possibilities as to what could be wrong. No, there was some specific problem here, but this Emma White seemed to be a shifting sand... Elizabeth Russell needed to pinpoint what this woman was hiding behind that surgical mask...

"So, how did you meet?" Emma asked, just stopping herself from adding 'because you're not his type at all'.

"In the Hoop and Grapes."

Emma looked blank.

"It's a pub - the oldest licensed house in the City of London. That was just one fact I discovered on a guided pub crawl around some of London's oldest pubs. A friend of mine got it for me as a joke birthday present. Started at The George in Borough and ended up at the Lamb and Flag in Covent Garden. Bloody long walk, but I started chatting to Andy in The George and it gave us the chance to get to know each other as we got steadily more pissed. By the end of the day, I'd learned a lot about the boozing history of London and had got myself a new boyfriend."

Emma nodded along – yeah, that sounded like exactly the sort of thing Andy would do on a day off. History, beer, chatting up women – that was Andy.

"So, what do you do?"

"Lawyer... no don't worry," she said quickly, seeing the way Emma's eyes instantly narrowed, "Purely corporate stuff. I work in banks."

"Oh... so, if you don't mind my asking, why didn't it work out?"

Elizabeth Russell laughed loudly,

"You know Andy. Mister Footloose and Fancy Free didn't want to get tied down – at least, not outside the bedroom," she winked at Emma and was glad to see it made her uncomfortable,

"But seriously, I had the chance to work in Shanghai, I wanted to take it... Andy wanted to stay here and try to make Inspector... so we shook hands and went our separate ways. And I mean that literally. It was all very... Andy."

Yeah, Emma could imagine that, too.

"But now you're back," Emma said, "How did you find out he was here?"

That was the question.

"You know Charlie Denham?"

"Chief Inspector Denham?"

"Yes, that's him. He's a friend of a friend, so when I tried to get in touch with Andy and was getting no result, I gave Charlie a call and he told me all about what happened. So, I came here as soon as I could to give this old malingerer a kick up the arse."

Yes, that all made sense, too. As Emma looked at her, she could imagine she was the type who was a 'friend of a friend' of lots of people, even though she looked young.

"How about you?" Elizabeth Russell asked, "What's it like working with this daft bugger?"

"Kind of fun," Emma admitted and then she talked about Andy, his quirks and foibles at work, and his various extra-curricular shenanigans.

As Emma spoke, Elizabeth Russell concentrated hard to get a bead on her. On the one hand, she wasn't lying, but she was hiding something. What could it be?

"And I suppose he's a pain in his boss's arse – what's his name?" she asked and even behind the mask, it was clear that Emma immediately coloured as she said,

"Ennis. Detective Inspector Ray Ennis."

Bingo! This girl was having an affair with the good Inspector. But earlier on at her office, when she'd been poking around inside Ray's mind, there'd been nothing like that in there...

Elizabeth Russell's features betrayed nothing but polite interest in what Emma was saying, but internally, she was laughing! So, Ray Ennis, having witnessed her power and having been told specifically to get out of town for the sake of himself and his family, must have gone straight from her office and fucked the arse off his Detective Constable. What a twat! What was he thinking? Maybe it was some bizarre reaction to being told the truth? Maybe she'd gone too far by levitating him out of the window? Could his wounded pride and belittled manhood have sought out the easiest way to reassert themselves by shagging a junior colleague? Whatever his reasons, he was an idiot. His career would probably be totally scuppered if any of it got out. One word kept coming to Elizabeth Russell's mind and that word was 'twat'. Anyway, that had been his choice and so long as he stayed out of her way for the next couple of days, who cared? He was a funny one...

"But the main reason I'm here is Andy," Emma said, "I know they've got him in a coma, but apparently you hear everything around you, so I thought I'd come and talk to him."

"Oh, he isn't in a coma anymore,"

"What?" that was news to Emma.

"No, he was awake when I got here."

Then Emma noticed for the first time that the mechanical breathing aid had gone. She'd been concentrating so hard on this other woman, that she hadn't properly looked at Andy. This was incredible,

"What was he talking about? Did he say anything about his assailant?"

"I don't know," Elizabeth Russell said, "Just kept saying the word 'sombrero' over and over again. It was quite disturbing, actually. I was pleased when he fell back to sleep."

Emma looked surprised by this revelation.

"I wonder what he meant?" she said more to herself than to the ex-girlfriend. She decided that she'd get back to the office and see if there was any hint of a sombrero in the footage. If it did have any bearing on the case and she was able get somewhere with it, Ray would be very happy.

"Okay, well, thanks," she said to Natalie Thingummy – she'd forgotten the woman's name already,

"I've got to get back to work... um... nice to have met you," and by the time she was finished, she was halfway out of the door.

"Likewise!" said Elizabeth Russell, watching as the heavy door closed behind the retreating policewoman. And then she swung into action. She needed to organise his immediate removal from that all-too-public facility. While he was there, he was in danger from Krowos' acolytes and she shuddered to think what might happen if The Man paid him a visit. Yes, The Man was powerful and dangerous, and wouldn't think twice about killing a police officer lying in a hospital bed. There was only one way to ensure Andy's safety. Andy had to die.

She closed her eyes and her mind reached out to Oliver, to speak directly into his mind,

"Okay, Oliver, I'm getting him out of here now."

"Got it. I'll call the extraction team," Oliver's voice said in her head, "They'll be at the back door in five."

Oliver, who was sitting behind his desk, reached for the elegant candlestick phone.

"Good lad! Catch up with you later. Dill pickle," and he knew from the sound of Elizabeth Russell's voice inside his head that she was smirking.

"That's not funny!" he thought, but she had broken the connection. This was part of her quirky sense of humour. As part of his training, he had to be able to block psychic suggestion. Sometimes, to spot-test him, she would say something incongruous during a mind link. At the time it would seem throwaway and inconsequential, but over the next couple of hours, the need for whatever she said would grow until he finally had to get the thing. As he dialled the number, Oliver knew that he would have to fight the urge to eat a dill pickle. Could he resist her suggestion this time? He'd give it a damned good try, but he thought it was unfair doing it in the middle of an operation. Of course, that was why she'd done it. He could remember her saying,

"Do you think the creatures and entities you meet in the field are going to be playing fair? You've got to be able to do this under extreme pressure,"

As Oliver waited for the leader of the extraction team to pick up his phone, the first yen for a dill pickle hit him. Dammit!

Back in the hospital room, Elizabeth Russell stood up and leaned over to whisper into Andy's ear,

"Don't worry, handsome, this won't hurt a bit," then she slipped her hand down the front of his hospital gown, across his strong, hairy chest (she liked that in a man) and rested the palm of her hand over his steadily beating heart. She focussed her power and spoke words in a language that had been dead so long, there were only a handful of people in the world who would have recognised it. Andy's heart slowed, slowed, slowed... and then stopped. As it stopped, she pressed her lips to his and quickly drew the last of his breath into her. As the machines monitoring him went crazy, she withdrew her hand, then took her seat. Within thirty seconds, a couple of nurses rushed in.

"He stopped breathing and then the machines started making noises," Elizabeth Russell said calmly as the nurses quickly assessed the situation. One of them checked his notes,

"He's got a DNR order."

On hearing this, the other nurse switched off the machines and then turned to Elizabeth Russell,

"I'm sorry, but he's gone. He's got a..."

"I know – Do Not Resuscitate," she interrupted. Then, in a voice that the nurses felt more than heard, she said,

"I will stay with him. Please unplug all the machines and leave us alone."

Without another word, the nurses did as they were told and left.

Fifteen minutes later, Elizabeth Russell watched as the extraction team placed Andy's dead body on a gurney and covered it with a sheet,

"Right, give me five minutes and then take him down to the transport. Someone is bound to be watching to make sure that he's dead, so take your time and give them a good show. I will stay in the shadows and target anyone suspicious. Then I'll meet you at the facility. Yes?"

"Yes," said the four soberly dressed but very fit looking men who made up the extraction team.

A few minutes later, she made her way out of the hospital and walked briskly towards Westminster Bridge. It was a magnificent summer's evening in London with a pastel sky of blue, smeared with gold and red where the sun was dipping in the west. Naturally, the tourists were out in force to get their holiday snaps with the Houses of Parliament in the background. Anyone watching Elizabeth Russell leave the building wouldn't have suspected anything when she blended completely into the crowd on the bridge and disappeared. After all, it was busy and she was walking fast. They wouldn't suspect that she had cast a spell on herself and that now she was nothing but a shadow moving swiftly back towards the hospital.

She quickly got around to the exit where the bodies of the deceased were removed by funeral directors. She moved into a corner, where she could blend into the deep shadow, and watched her team come out of the door and load Andy into a hearse. The beauty of this, was that if anyone with advanced psychic abilities were watching, they would see that Andy was dead and that this wasn't a subterfuge. Now to see if anyone was on the lookout... she scanned the road around – a few more tourists (what the hell were they doing back there?), various hospital staff coming and going, a few passers-by and... hello! Well, that was brazen! In the bike lane on the other side of the road, a mad looking bloke in a sombrero was standing with his feet astride his bike, leaning on the handlebars and apparently taking a breather. His aura of total darkness made him stand out sharply against the world around him. No wonder Titheridge had been able to catch so many of them. Elizabeth Russell kind of appreciated this man's 'fuck you' attitude, but it was based on ill-founded arrogance. Krowos' followers thought it was a powerful god. If any of them realised how comparatively weak it was, they would be more on their guard.

Elizabeth Russell fought the urge to sweep across the road, stare into his eyes and rip his heart from his chest. If there was one thing that annoyed her more than entities from other dimensions pissing on her turf, it was the idiot humans who enabled them. However, she needed Krowos to think it was in complete control of the situation, because she was going to use its arrogance against it.

"You're going to be followed by a man on a bicycle. Continue as planned and let him observe," she said directly into the minds of her operatives.

A minute later, the hearse pulled out and turned right to go to Lambeth Bridge roundabout. Mexican Dave could see that there was no life in the person they'd brought out, but decided to follow anyway, just so there were no loose ends. Once the hearse was off, he pedalled after it with his sombrero solidly stuck on top of his head. Elizabeth Russell followed, a shadow on the wind. She was surprised that Krowos would send the man who'd committed the attack to keep an eye on the hospital. It was another example of its arrogance. The more she got to know Krowos and its ways, the more she disliked it.

Half an hour later, the hearse arrived at a funeral directors on Balham High Street and pulled in through the entrance between the terraced buildings that had originally been designed for a coach and horses. It stopped on the far side of the cobbled courtyard within and the four men got out. Mexican Dave hovered at the entrance, watched as the body was taken out of the hearse and into the building, and then turned to go back to town. His work here was done. The pig was dead and hadn't regained consciousness. Job done! Better cycle back for further orders. For her part, Elizabeth Russell momentarily considered following him, but then dismissed it. What would she find out from following him that she didn't already know? Besides, she couldn't keep Andy in stasis forever and, if she was being honest with herself, she wanted to be with him for a while. She had a busy night ahead, so a short oasis of calm appealed to her.

As a shadow, she swept into the courtyard, but halfway across it, she reformed her physical body out of the air and, without breaking stride, marched into the service entrance of Ebenezer Meers Funeral Directors. The door opened directly into the coffin making workshop, which was a large, square room with everything you'd expect to find in a woodworking space. The smell of fresh pine, wood glue, linseed oil and wood stain hung in the air alongside the faint smell of embalming fluids. Two doors led out of it. The first, to her immediate right as she entered, led into the coffin showroom at the back of the shop itself. The other door opened into a short corridor which ended in a large set of lift doors not unlike those at the hospital. Halfway down on the right was the door to the cold storage and body preparation area. Here the smell of embalming fluid was stronger. The scent of it reminded her that she ought to repaint her nails before the final showdown. She always liked to look good and, if things went wrong, she didn't want to die looking shabby.

She pressed the button, the doors opened and she stepped inside the generous lift, which had been designed for bulky loads. The lift began its descent and Elizabeth Russell smiled to herself. She was carrying Andy's life-force inside her and she could feel its warmth in her chest. He felt good. Maybe once this was over, they could... no, she mustn't get ahead of herself. One thing at a time. The lift doors opened into a cavernous area, which was split into a series of rooms and corridors by reinforced glass walls. The people that worked there called it the fishbowl. She walked straight down the corridor and finally opened a door on the left, which led into the only room with opaque walls. Inside, the extraction team were just putting Andy into a hospital bed when she walked in,

"Good work, everyone. There's a tab in my name at the Bedford if anyone fancies a drink. I'll be over there in half an hour, but don't let that put you off."

The men smiled and made various responses of gratitude, then left Elizabeth Russell alone with a nurse who had followed her into the room.

"Hi Lucy, how're you?"

"Great! Enjoying the sunshine while it lasts," the sun-bronzed woman replied in an accent that indicated South American origins.

"Okay, I'll just restart him and then I'll leave him in your capable hands," Elizabeth Russell said, then she went over to Andy. She looked down at his face which she felt just erred on the handsome side of East End bruiser. She stroked his stubbly cheek with her hand, then gently squeezed his mouth to open it as her other hand went to his chest and lay over his heart. She opened her mouth slightly and locked her lips to his as she breathed into him and simultaneously pressed down against his heart. She unlocked her lips and spoke some words from the long-dead language again. She concentrated her thought on his heart, pulled her hand back and gave his chest a hard thump.

Andy gasped back to life and his eyes opened.

"What the fuck?" he gasped – he didn't know where he was, but he was freezing cold!

"Hey, handsome," Elizabeth Russell smiled and the sight of her beautiful face looking down at him warmed him.

"I was just dreaming about you," he said.

"Sweet dreams, I hope."

"Weird dreams, like I was disembodied."

Yup! That would be about right.

"Don't worry, they're just dreams," she said, placing her hand against his cheek and stroking it gently with her thumb,

"We've moved you from St Thomas' to a private facility. Lucy here is your nurse,"

"Hello," Lucy smiled.

"And she's going to be helping you get better."

"Did I get impaled on something?" Andy asked uncomfortably as the pain in his chest stabbed with every word.

"Yes, you did!" she replied merrily, "You got an iron railing right through your chest. It was quite spectacular."

"Fuck me!"

Eventually... she thought, but replied,

"Yes, you were very nearly completely fucked, but thankfully they were dumb enough to try to kill you about two hundred yards away from a hospital. So, here you are on the road to recovery."

She didn't tell him that she was responsible for speeding him along that road or that a very powerful healing spell was the only reason he was off the ventilator. Over the next ten minutes they chatted easily, while Lucy sorted out his drugs and new IV drips.

"Ever been to the Hoop and Grapes?" Elizabeth Russell asked at last.

"Yeah, they do a good pint of Doom Bar. Although, if I'm honest, I'd rather drink..."

"No, don't tell me," she said quickly, "Let me guess..."

"All right."

She regarded him appraisingly, but decided she wouldn't cheat by looking into his mind,

"Let's see..." she said, "You're a native Londoner, but you're too old to have grown up with all the small independent breweries, so your main pub options in those formative years between sixteen and eighteen..."

"Legal drinking age in pubs is eighteen," Andy reminded her.

"Yeah, but look at you. I bet you were nearly six foot by the age of sixteen and you've got a lived in face, so you'd've got into pubs no trouble..."

Andy gave her a look that admitted she was right,

"So, in the late nineties your main choices would've been Sam Smith's, Courage, Young's and Fuller's. Now, Sam Smith's is piss. I think you're better than that, so that's off,"

"True. Can't stand them, and I don't know why they have so many pubs in central London. They're a Yorkshire brewer."

"I know, it's mad," she chimed in, then looked him over again, "Courage has a great heritage, and Courage Best and Courage Directors are great beers, but I don't think you grew up on them, either. So that leaves us with Young's and Fuller's. They both make good beer, there's no denying that..."

Andy nodded. He wasn't going to argue the point.

"Young's have London Original and London Special, but then Fuller's have London Pride and ESB..." and there it was – Andy's tell. As soon as she said ESB, she noticed the tip of his tongue appear at the left side of his mouth. Yes, he was imagining a well-drawn pint of ESB right now, seeing the dew on the sides of the glass, feeling the coolness in his hand as he drew the lightly foamed head towards his lips, and finally glugging down a good throatful, revelling in the smooth, rounded taste with its biscuity, toffee scrumptiousness.

"Fuller's," she said suddenly, "You're a Fuller's man."

"Sure?"

"I'd bet my house on it. Well?"

"Put it this way... I could murder a pint of ESB right now."

"Ha!" Elizabeth Russell was exultant, "I knew it! But I bet these days you go a bundle on craft lagers, don't you?"

"'Course. There are lots of great lagers out there."

"I'll tell you what, when you're up and about, why don't we go for a nice walk as part of your rehab and if it happens to start at The George in Borough and end up at the Lamb and Flag in Covent Garden, with various refreshments along the way, so be it," she said.

"It's a date!" Andy said before she could change her mind. Elizabeth Russell laughed,

"You've got to get better first, so that should give you something to aim for... now, I've got to go – I can't spend all night with a malingerer like you. Do everything nurse Lucy tells you to, and eat as much ice cream as you like. See you round," she said and gave his cheek a couple of playful pats, then left the room.

***

Later that night, deep in the heart of France, Gaston Verne stepped out of the shadows of the forest and into the sacred clearing. There, at its centre, the ancient 'Stone of Eternity' had been standing watching the comings and goings of men, animals and trees for over two hundred thousand years. Gaston's druidic robes seemed to glow in the light of the waning gibbous moon as he walked across the clearing. He breathed slowly and deeply, revelling in the scents drifting in the July air. Four more druids followed him out of the forest so that together they formed an arrowhead with Gaston as the tip. In his right hand, he held the oak shaft of the axe that had been forged to kill a god. The head of the axe was nothing like the sort used for chopping wood. It was a heavy executioner's axe with a squared off cutting blade one and a half feet in length, more like a giant meat cleaver than an axe. The light of the moon picked out silver writing that had been inlaid on both cheeks of the axe head. These were the words of power.

When the druid reached the Stone of Eternity, he gently laid the axe on top of it as the other druids fanned out around the rock to encircle it. Gaston Verne looked around at the great oaks that surrounded them and as their branches softly moved in the breeze, the druids began to sway with the natural pulse of the forest. All five druids raised their arms towards the fat, summer moon and together, they invoked Cernunnos, the horned god of wild things with the power to balance man and nature. Then, while the four druids chanted the words of power, Gaston called out,

"Oh Cernunnos the eternal, Lord of Animals, Ruler of the Wild, hear your servants, who bow before you. Bless this blade that was forged and tempered in holy flame and quenched in sacrificial blood that it might return Krowos the Deceiver to timeless space," and then he repeated the speech twice more as the other druids chanted the words of power again and again. As they performed the ritual, they could see the silver words inlaid on the axe head scintillate with sacred fire. In that moment, they knew that if wielded correctly, the axe would serve its purpose and send the false god back into the void. Then, under the fat moon, with the great oaks of the forest as their witnesses, they made a promise to Cernunnos that the first sacrifice when they returned to Anglesey would be in his name.

Chapter Thirty-Three

Favourite Things

Ten past five in the morning found Elizabeth Russell pacing her office. She was still wearing the purple trouser suit from the previous day because, as yet, she still hadn't finished work. After leaving Andy and having a swift half with the lads from the extraction team, she'd come straight back to her office to sort out the strategy for drawing Krowos out of his lair so that she could cut his umbilical cord. On paper, it was all fairly straightforward. At midnight five of her strongest psychics would launch an attack on Krowos from Finsbury Circus Gardens. Judging from its pride and arrogance, Krowos would go out to destroy them and, once it was out of its lair, she would cut its cord and that would be that. Of course, it wasn't without extreme danger – she needed Krowos to be a good distance away from her when she started cutting, because she knew it would turn and come for her the instant the first cut was made. She wondered how many swings of the axe it would take to cut all the way through that thick umbilical cord. Three? Five? Hard to tell. If it got to her before she cut through the cord, she'd simply have to face off against it. She didn't fancy that, but as it stood, the plan was undoubtedly the safest strategy. She really didn't like the thought of going into the building to confront it in its lair where it was at its strongest. No, the plan to draw it out could work – especially because Krowos and its acolytes had no idea that anyone other than the police were interested in them.

Then the moment she'd been waiting for came.

"I've got the axe!" the excited voice of Oliver Fernsby sounded in her mind.

"Well done, Oliver! Are you coming back in the car or the chopper?"

"Chopper," he replied, "Weather's clear, light breeze. Should be at the heliport in Battersea by seven fifteen and with you before seven forty-five."

"Excellent! I'm going to get some kip, so only contact me if it's life or death. Happy landings!"

"Sleep well," Oliver said and then he was gone.

"Fuck yeah!" she said out loud, then crossed the room to the big day bed in the corner. She kicked her shoes off as she went, took off her jacket and trousers, and laid them over the back of a chair. Then she slipped between two of the bearskins on the bed and happily allowed herself to sink into a deep, untroubled sleep.

When Oliver Fernsby walked through the door of her office at ten to eight, Elizabeth Russell was looking calm and relaxed in a generous silk dressing gown of red, gold and black. She was sitting behind her desk and her eyes glittered at the sight of Oliver carrying a long brown paper package in his hands.

"Where do you want it?" he asked.

"Right here on my desk."

He laid it down gently in front of her and stood back.

"No wonder Fraulein Maria loved brown paper packages tied up with string," she said, as her hungry eyes passed over the package, then her hands started pulling at the strings. Within seconds, the parcel was open and the axe lay glinting up at her.

"Oh," she said and her voice couldn't help but betray a bit of disappointment.

"Something wrong?" Oliver asked with concern. He hadn't checked the item himself, because he thought it would be rude after the chief druid had handed it to him with some ceremony.

"No, nothing wrong with it. I can feel it'll do the job admirably, it's just... I was expecting a bit more Gallic flair in the design."

Oliver inspected it – yes, it was rather functional.

"I was hoping for a lovely sweeping crescent of a blade, or a really traditional big-headed English axe – you know, something I could wield with dash, but this... it'll make me look like a butcher about to cut up ribs of beef," Elizabeth Russell sounded quite disconsolate.

"Surely it's *how* you brandish it that's important," Oliver said encouragingly.

"Yeah, I s'pose," she mused, "If anyone's going to make this look cool, it's me. Right, I'd better get a feel for it. While I do that, could you be an angel and get the coffee on?"

Oliver started for the door,

"Oh, and a spot of breakfast would be nice..."

"A pain-au-chocolat, cheese and bacon croissant, devilled kidneys and a side of kedgeree," Oliver said without emotion.

"I'm going to really miss you when you start field work," she said. Oliver smiled and left her to it.

She got up and walked into the middle of the room, holding the axe aloft at arm's length to check there was enough clearance and that she wasn't going to hack into the ceiling. Yes, plenty of room. She weighed the axe in her hand – it was, rightly, very top heavy. It would be perfect for chopping through the cord. She mimicked the motion of chopping straight down. Yes. That would be excellent. But could she fight with it? She swung it around her head as if to bury it in the chest of an attacker, then undertook a series of moves as if she was fending off multiple attackers. She used the shaft to block, the end of the handle to stab, and swung the head through different planes. It was good overhead and sideways, but slow in an uppercut. Obviously, you wouldn't want to be on the wrong end of such a blow, but she decided she'd only use that move in extremis.

By the time Oliver returned half an hour later, she was breathless and a little sweaty.

"How's it feel?"

"Pretty good – still wish it looked cooler. I mean," she said holding the axe before her, "If someone said to you, 'I'm going to get French Druids to make you an axe to send a foul creature back to its own dimension', you'd think 'Wow! That's gonna look amazing', and yet..." she trailed off and let the dull, oversized meat cleaver speak for itself.

"Still, I s'pose it'll do the job," she sighed as she slumped into her chair to take her breakfast at her desk.

"What're you having?" she asked.

"Just sourdough toast – some with Marmite, some with Dundee Orange marmalade."

"Sounds eminently dull. Right, I'm going to demolish this lot, then I'm going to do something very important."

"What?"

"I'm going to paint my nails scarlet to match my suit."

"Of course," said Oliver – that made perfect sense!

Chapter Thirty-Four

Chasing Shadows

Ray swam slowly back to consciousness after a delicious night of unbroken sleep. He hadn't set an alarm, because there was nothing pressing at work. It was a case of tidying things up and setting people tasks to do while he was away. He rolled towards Vicky, wrapped an arm over her and spooned against her. She stirred, but not enough to wake up. He lay there enjoying the cosy nest, but slowly the warm feeling of contentment was replaced by cool disquiet as he thought about what he'd done the previous day. Looking back on it now, it was madness. He could only imagine that between the stress of Andy being in the hospital and the insanity of his meeting with Elizabeth Russell, his mind had somehow snapped... but no. That wasn't why he felt that unpleasant sensation deep inside. The true reason he had slept with Emma was because he'd wanted to. He'd noticed that she was attractive the moment she'd arrived in the unit, but he'd never had the guts to admit it to himself. The moment she'd kissed him yesterday, he could have backed off and defused the situation, but he didn't. He had allowed himself to be seduced. That was on him and at some point, he was going to have to come clean with Vicky, but not today.

When they finally got up it was already nine and, as they set about fixing breakfast, Ray betrayed nothing of his feelings. He was bright and breezy,

"So, who fancies leaving for Norfolk today?" he asked, after they'd been chatting about their upcoming holiday.

"Yay!" Chloe cried. She loved their holidays in Norfolk.

"Today?" Vicky exclaimed, "We can't leave today!"

"Why not?"

"The booking..."

"Imagine the booking isn't an issue. Why can't we leave today?" Ray said.

"Well, because..." Vicky reached for good reasons, but found none, "Because we haven't done any shopping for it... I haven't checked that Chloe's clothes still fit... um..."

"All she needs is a swimsuit and her ordinary summer clothes. We'll hire wetsuits there and I'm sure you can easily pop down to Tesco's for picnic food for tonight. Anyway, have you got anything planned in the next two weeks?" Ray asked and both he and Chloe fixed Vicky with expectant looks.

"The follow-up with the psychologist," Vicky said and both their faces dropped.

"We can rearrange that. And anyway, I thought they were going to email us the results."

"They are, but..."

"And that'll give us more time to mull over what she thinks before going back to see her."

"Yeah, but what about the booking?" Vicky insisted.

"I've already brought it forward," Ray lied. It was on his list of things to do that morning.

"But why the sudden rush?" Vicky looked keenly at Ray.

"Blame the chief – it's his idea. Since we wrapped up our case and because Andy's out of action, he decided it would be best to get leave out of the way now."

"But he can't just say 'go on holiday' and expect you to go the next day!"

Ray looked her in the eye and tried to make it clear that something else was in play – something he didn't want Chloe to know about. Vicky picked up the cue and said,

"Chloe, do you want to watch TV while you have breakfast?"

"Yeah!" she said eagerly – what a stupid question!

“Okay, go on,” then, as Chloe parked herself in front of the telly, Ray and Vicky went down to their room and closed the door.

“Okay, what’s really going on?” Vicky asked quietly.

“After what happened to Andy, the chief thinks it’s safest if we get out of the way for a couple of weeks.”

“Why didn’t you just tell me that earlier?”

“I didn’t want to worry you,” he said, “And anyway, after the week I’ve had at work and what with Chloe waking us up every night, I’m probably not making the best decisions. Sorry.”

Vicky unbent and said,

“Yeah, it has been crazy... but next time, lead with the ‘we’re in danger and have to go’ thing, and I’ll hop to it, no questions asked.”

“Sorry,” Ray said again.

“Dozy muppet!” Vicky smiled and gave him a kiss, “Now come on, let’s get breakfast over with – I’ve got packing to do and you’re not allowed to blame me if I don’t pack everything you want.”

It was nearly half-past ten when Ray sauntered into the office. He was feeling pleased with himself, because he’d managed to sort out the booking for the static caravan on the way in. There had been a late cancellation and he was in the right place at the right time, so that side of things was sorted! However, his good mood disintegrated the moment he saw Emma. It wasn’t because of what had happened the previous day, but because her eyes were red from crying. He crossed the office to see her,

“Are you all right?”

“No,” she said and, as she looked at him, the tears were coming again,

“Haven’t you heard?”

“Heard what?”

“Andy died last night,” Emma said, and it was taking all her emotional strength to stop herself from clinging onto him for comfort.

Ray was stunned. Everything seemed to become muffled for a few moments and the room swayed,

“But... but...” he had seen the doctor. The doctor had said it would all be okay, that the wound wasn’t as bad as it could’ve been,

"But...?" he couldn't even form the question.

"Internal bleeding. His liver. They think they missed something and by the time they realised, it was too late," this time Emma couldn't hold back the tears and Ray instinctively put his arms around a colleague in distress.

Emma held him close to her for over a minute until she got control of herself, then reluctantly let go of him,

"I don't think we'd even know if I hadn't decided to drop in and check on the way to work this morning. They didn't inform anyone."

Ray wanted to be shocked, but given the way the NHS was being allowed to wither, it didn't surprise him at all that the overworked staff had no time to tell anyone.

"Fuck!" he sighed. Well, that was that. He was in a daze, as if he'd been struck over the head.

"But I think I might have a lead on who did it," Emma said and Ray focussed on her,

"I did what you said and checked the CCTV from further afield and there seems to be a pattern – look," and she led Ray to her desk, where she had a Google Earth satellite map of London on her screen with a route marked.

"The route I've picked out here corresponds to the incidents of cameras losing pictures."

Ray looked at the screen and could see the route go from the Embankment, up Whitehall to Trafalgar Square and then up towards Tottenham Court Road.

"I started finding the pattern last night after you left," and here she gave him a meaningful look, which he held. He wanted to look away, but he didn't want to show her that he wasn't feeling the same way about last night as she was.

"And when I got as far as the requested CCTV showed, I went from there and requested more. Long and the short of it is, I've tracked this person all the way up to Camden, where they seem to have spent the best part of three hours in the late afternoon on Albert Street."

"How...?" Ray began,

"Because a security camera on the south end of Albert Street has forty-three seconds of interference at about seven thirty, but the security camera halfway up Albert Street, where it crosses Delancey Street, had thirty seconds of interference at three fifty-five. And from that point, the periods of interference continue back to one-o-clock on a route that tracks across half of northeast London. I gave up when they got over to Haggerston."

"So, our attacker stayed in Albert Street for three hours," Ray mused, "That is brilliant police work, Emma," he said warmly.

"Thanks Ray... boss," Emma stumbled as she tried to stay professional with the man whose body she had owned the previous afternoon.

"We need to get up there," said Ray, "Knock on some doors, find out if anyone saw anything. But it's going to be difficult with nothing to go on."

"Oh, but we do have something," said Emma excitedly, "Last night when I went to see Andy, there was a woman with him..."

"What did she look like?"

"She looked young, but she had white hair..."

"Yeah, I know her," Ray said.

"From when she was going out with Andy?"

"Yeah," Ray said without a moment's hesitation. If that was the story Elizabeth Russell was peddling, then he'd corroborate it,

"Bit of a bitch, to be honest," he added – just because he was corroborating her story didn't mean he couldn't riff on it,

"Andy was lucky when they broke up."

"Yeah, who wants to date a corporate lawyer?" Emma said with distaste,

"But the point is, she said Andy had been awake and had kept repeating one word – sombrero."

"Sombrero?" what the fuck? Ray shook his head. Could Andy have got a look at his attacker and seen a sombrero?

"You think Andy saw someone in a sombrero?" he asked.

"Maybe. It's worth asking."

"Okay, I've got to see the chief first, then you and I are going to Camden."

Within half an hour, Ray and Emma were in a car and heading up to Camden. As Emma drove expertly through the traffic, Ray thought about Elizabeth Russell. If she was involved, then maybe the Andy situation wasn't all that it seemed. She certainly had the power and levers to move Andy to an unknown location, presumably for his own safety. She clearly liked him, so maybe she'd decided to protect him? Or she just happened to be there when Emma visited and then Andy had died later. But it seemed weird that he'd recover consciousness, come off the ventilator and *then* die of a complication. Whatever the truth, he took the decision not to share this information with Emma. The less she knew, the safer she was.

"Are you still leaving today?" she asked, keeping her eyes on the road.

"That's the plan. I was going to go home at three, but I'll push it back if we get a lead here."

Emma reached her hand across and ran it down the inside of his thigh, where she rested it on his crotch,

"I'm going to miss you," she said, "Feels like you're going to miss me, too."

Ray was feeling that electricity again and, in spite of himself, part of him was keen to take up where they'd left off the previous day.

"Yeah," he said through gritted teeth.

Emma took her hand away to change gear and laughed at the look of pained self-restraint on Ray's face. She had nothing to worry about. He could be away for six weeks and within five minutes of seeing her again, he would be under her power. Her slightest touch would be enough to lock him back into her. She loved the thought that she had that control over another woman's man. Ray was hers now. Vicky had lost him and anything he did with her was just going through the motions. They came to a red light and, when they'd stopped, she looked across at Ray. There it was! When their eyes met, there was that palpable connection. She could see that he wanted her, that he was hers, body and soul. For her part, she wanted to pull the car over and fuck him right there on the kerb. The atmosphere in the car was crackling with energy. Emma smiled archly – soon he would be hers forever and there was nothing that his wife could do to stop it. Emma almost felt sorry for her… almost.

When they finally arrived at Albert Street, they were both glad to be able to get out of the car. The tension of painful desire was much harder to deal with than the oppressive heat of a baking London day.

"Odd or even?" Ray asked.

"Even," Emma replied.

"Okay, we work our way up the street and if either of us gets any joy, we call the other over, yes?"

"Got it, boss," she said happily. Yes, this was just how she'd imagined it could be – lovers at night and tracking down criminals by day.

Ray crossed the street to the odd side and knocked on the first door.

It took over an hour before they got any joy, but finally, Emma heard Ray whistle at her to get her attention. She looked away from the hassled woman she'd been talking to, who had to keep stopping her rambunctious cockapoo from escaping the house and running around the street. Ray was gesticulating for her to join him, so she said,

"Thank you for your time, sorry to have bothered you," and jogged across the street to join Ray and a dishevelled looking middle-aged man on the doorstep of his house.

"Sorry, sir, could you please repeat what you just told me?" Ray asked.

"Sure, yah! So, I was at home… um… I'm working on a screenplay…" the man said in a very upper crust, public school accent,

"And my study overlooks the street. Well, I saw a man in a sombrero sawing away at one of the railings outside that house," and he indicated the one house in the street that had been allowed to fall to rack and ruin,

"He was there for hours. Looked a bit crazy to me, so I didn't want to confront him – especially as he had a saw."

"Did you get a good look at him?" Ray asked.

"Bloody impossible not to. He was literally there for hours. So, he was average height, fairly average build, black hair with dark eyes and the most enormous lower jaw – never seen anything like it. Very shabby clothes…"

Ray looked the man up and down – he couldn't talk. He was wearing grubby pyjama bottoms, no shoes or socks and a threadbare T-shirt. And his hair was an overgrown tangle, but he was posh, so it counted as eccentric rather than mad.

"It was a dark blue shell suit and what was particularly incongruous was that he was wearing black brogues with no socks. I thought to myself – what a funny combo. I wondered whether he might be homeless or something, you know? Anyway, he really wanted that piece of railing and when he finally got it, he took a file out and sharpened the end of it for about half an hour. Then he left with it tucked under his arm like a lance."

"Are there any other details you can give us?" Ray asked.

"Yah, actually there is. He kept shouting things in the most ridiculous sort of Scottish accent. It was hot, so I had my window open and I had to listen to him chuntering on."

"A Scottish accent..." Ray was noting it down when the man stopped him,

"No, it wasn't a Scottish accent. It was a bad attempt at a Scottish accent. God knows where he was from, but it wasn't Scotland."

"Thank you, sir... would you be able to come down to headquarters and work with our team to build up a visual image of this man."

"Well, I don't know... I'm trying to finish this screenplay, y'see..."

"Do you have a very tight deadline, sir?" Ray asked.

"Um... No, not as such. It's more of a spec piece of work, but I still want to get it done..."

Ray gave the man such a withering look that he immediately back-tracked,

"Having said that, of course, I can surely spare some time to help the boys in blue," then he realised that might sound sexist, so he quickly fumbled to add, "Or girls in blue – or transgender folk in blue for that matter. Um..."

"Thank you, sir. If you could please give your details to Detective Constable White, we will contact you in the next six hours to set up a convenient time for you to come in," Ray said and then he turned to Emma,

"You get his details. I'm going to look at the railing."

When he got over to the set of railings in front of the big Victorian terraced house with boarded up windows, he could immediately see which bit had been removed. There were metal shavings all over the ground, but beyond that, there wasn't much to see. The house itself looked like it had been secured by a professional company, with a robust front door and an alarm flashing away to show it was 'on'. Okay, so there was nothing to go on there, but... as Ray stared at the scene, he was picturing the Google Earth route that Emma had mapped out. Whoever Mister Sombrero was, he'd have to sleep sometime. Maybe they could track camera interference back to a particular place? He took out his phone and called headquarters to arrange CCTV footage from the Haggerston area and told them that it was likely they'd need to keep asking for footage from different cameras around the city. He was just finishing the call when Emma came to join him.

"He's a right one," she said, "Is there anything sadder than an ageing trustafarian with delusions of adequacy?"

Ray smiled and replied, "There's nothing else here, so let's get back. Anyway, I've had an idea."

They were back in their office by two and, while Emma put the description of Mister Sombrero out to officers on the beat, Ray started looking through CCTV footage. He was caught up in the prospect of tracking down the bastard who'd attacked Andy and totally forgot that he was supposed to be getting in the car and leaving for Norfolk around four. When Emma joined him, they were able to speed things up and had soon tracked the patches of interference back to nine in the morning at...

"Centre Point," said Ray, unsurprised, "Our well-spoken layabout did say he thought Mister Sombrero was homeless."

Sure enough, there were no incidents of camera interference in the area until just after two am the previous night.

“So, he spent the night either in one of the homeless hostels or sleeping rough somewhere near Centre Point,” Ray said, and Emma could hear the excitement in his voice,

“All we’ve got to do is go over there now and ask around at the hostels. Someone’s bound to recognise him – it’s not like he’s ordinary looking. Come on,” Ray said and he started for the door.

Emma glanced at her watch as she followed him,

“Shit, it’s past four – weren’t you supposed to be home already?”

“Damn!” Ray hissed as they got into the lift, “It’s okay. Vicky won’t mind. It’ll give her more time to get ready. I’ll text her when we’re on the road and tell her I’ll be back by seven. They can have an early dinner or something. Would you mind dropping me home, though?” he felt a bit guilty as he glanced across at Emma. It was weird asking her to drop him back. What if Vicky saw her? What if they ended up chatting? Christ! That would be awkward.

“No probs,” Emma smiled. She didn’t mind at all. Taking the man she owned right back to the door of his loser wife flicked a switch of desire inside her. And if she could see the loser, all the better. Yes, then she could look into the eyes of the woman she’d robbed of her man. She could have a bit of fun with this...

“Mexican Dave?” said the friendly-looking woman with greying dreadlocks at the reception desk of the third homeless hostel they tried, “What’s he been up to now?” and she had the look of mild amusement that an aunt might have on discovering her cheeky nephew had been caught doing something slightly naughty again.

“You call him Mexican Dave?” Ray asked.

“Yeah, everyone does – because of the sombrero. I’ve never seen him without it in three years,” said the woman who’d introduced herself as Shiloh.

“Does he stay here often?”

“Most nights.”

“Was he here last night?”

Shiloh swept back a couple of dreadlocks and consulted the night logbook.

"No. But it was a hot night, so maybe he decided to camp out. Some of our customers like to do that in summer."

"We need to talk to this man urgently. There is a possibility that he's been involved in a serious assault..." Ray said, but Shiloh cut him off,

"No! Not Dave! He's eccentric, but he's harmless. He's never given us a moment of trouble in all the time he's been coming here."

"I'm sure that's true, but today we need to speak to him. We need you to call us the moment you see him," and Ray's stern gaze made Shiloh faulter.

"Yes, yes of course. There was never any question that we wouldn't..."

"And will you ensure that all your staff are alerted?" Ray interrupted.

"Yes," she said quietly, looking away.

"When was the last time you saw him?" Emma asked.

"Me personally?" Shiloh puffed out her cheeks as she thought, "Sometime yesterday morning. He was off out on his bike."

"Do you have a file on him?" Ray asked.

"Of sorts... just bear with me..." she said and went through a door into the office behind the reception desk.

"If we're lucky, they've got a photo of him," said Emma.

"Yeah..." Ray was thinking about what he would like to do to Mexican Dave if he caught up with him.

"Here we are," said Shiloh brightly as she returned with a thin file, which she handed to Ray.

He opened it and skimmed the details. There was nothing of much use, only that he'd turned up out of nowhere five years before and was a bit weird, but not a drug user or a troublemaker. Ray's fingers felt the distinctive texture of a photograph amongst the pages and pulled it out, hopeful to see exactly who they were dealing with.

"What the hell happened to this?" Ray asked, laying the photograph on the desk.

The photo was a group shot with various staff members and hostel users enjoying a Christmas party. In the middle, was a man in a dark blue shell suit and wearing a sombrero, but his face was unrecognisable, as if the photographic paper had melted during developing.

"That's the best picture we've got of him. For some reason they never come out."

When Ray and Emma left the hostel ten minutes later, Ray was feeling distinctly unsettled. He wanted to get home and get home now! There was something about that photograph that had set off a sense of deep disquiet inside him. They'd spent all day following the trail of a man who could only be tracked by the interference he seemed to cause on CCTV. Ray had assumed that this was all some trick by Elizabeth Russell to cover her movements, but now he was sure that wasn't the case. Mexican Dave must be one of *them*, one of the people that Ms Russell claimed were the acolytes of this strange blood demon. This was a man who could not be filmed and whose image could not even be captured on a photograph. That was weird. It was weird, and Ray could see it with his own eyes. Suddenly, he had the horrible suspicion that Elizabeth Russell was right and that something supernatural was going on here. And if that was the case, then he should've already got out of town. She'd told him to leave with his family yesterday afternoon, but instead of doing that, he'd made choices based on pride and ego. Now his family were on their own and unprotected. Not only that, but he'd left them all day so he could go chasing around town. Why? To avenge Andy? Maybe. Or maybe it was all to feed his ego by pursuing Andy's attacker and catching the bastard? Had he only been doing it all for himself? Whatever the case, he wanted to get home.

"Okay, so I need you to liaise with Kevin Braugham on this," Ray said as Emma took the car through the heavy central London traffic. Emma knew Detective Inspector Braugham, but didn't really like him. He was fat and when he looked at her it made her feel like she was some dessert he was eyeing up.

"Yes, Ray," she said. In the privacy of the car, she reckoned she could call him that and, when he didn't protest, she felt a little glow in her stomach.

"He'll take the credit, but I don't mind. So long at this psycho's off the streets, that's all that matters."

They stopped at a red light and Emma's hand went to Ray's thigh again and stroked up to his groin. Ray didn't stop her, but there was something different this time. Emma wasn't getting that electric sensation.

"You all right?" she asked.

"Yes, I just want to get home," he replied, distracted. He checked his phone and was somewhat comforted by the 'thumbs up' reply to the text he'd sent about an hour and a half earlier. Should he give Vicky a call? No, that would create a weird situation for the rest of the drive.

Seeing Vicky's emoji reply made Ray much more relaxed. As Emma drove them over the river and off towards south London, Ray thought about the day. Maybe he'd overreacted? Maybe everything Elizabeth Russell had said was bollocks? He'd probably get home to find Vicky and Chloe had had a lovely day and were stuffed to the gills on the picnic they'd bought. Yeah, that was it. Everything was fine and he'd done the right thing chasing down the case. Even Emma seemed to have calmed down. They were coming into Brixton and she hadn't tried to feel him up since central London. Yes, he was literally on the home straight now and, as they went up Brixton Hill for the last mile or so, Ray allowed himself a smile. When Emma finally pulled over opposite his house, their goodbye was a little awkward, but cordial.

"Have fun," she said, trying to smile.

"I'll give it a go," Ray replied – did she realise that when he returned, he would have to break it off between them? It was hard to tell.

"And good luck capturing Mexican Dave," he said.

"Thanks."

"Okay... see you," said Ray and he closed the car door, crossed the street and disappeared into his house.

Emma watched him go with trepidation. This was a big moment for her. Would he make the right choice and ditch his loser wife and her troublesome brat? Emma knew that his only path to true happiness was as her lover. She could give him so much if only he had the sense to choose her.

Chapter Thirty-Five

Get Up And Go

After Ray left for work with promises that he didn't have much to do and that he'd be back by four, Vicky got straight down to the packing with Chloe's 'help'. Out came two suitcases, which were left open on the big bed, one for her and Ray and the other for Chloe. This quickly started filling up, but not with clothes,

"Do you really need fifteen soft toys?" Vicky asked as Chloe trooped into her room with two dogs, a mammoth, a monkey and a cat in her arms.

"Yes," Chloe replied seriously, "I don't want any of them thinking they're less loved than the others if I leave them behind."

"But you can't bring all of them – we don't have a suitcase big enough," Vicky protested. It was the same conversation they had every time they went away,

"Why don't you have a meeting with all of them in your room and get them to vote on which three you're going to bring with you?" she suggested.

Chloe put on her thinking face and, after a few moments' careful thought, said,

"Yes, that's a very good idea. If they vote, then it'll be their decision and no one can say I'm picking favourites. Well done."

Vicky probably could have done without the patronising praise at the end, but she was glad to see the pile of toys go back to Chloe's room,

"And while you're doing that, I'll pack your clothes," she said, but Chloe wasn't listening any more – she had an important meeting to chair.

By the time Vicky had finished the packing, Chloe appeared with Mister Snuffles the cat, Spotty Dotty the Dalmatian and Pig. Pig didn't have a name, because she was a no-nonsense animal, who didn't believe that names were necessary.

"Pig will ride in the back of the car with me," Chloe announced.

"Fair enough," Vicky smiled, "Put her in your backpack along with everything else you need. It's a long journey, so I've already packed the Ipad..." and before Chloe could interrupt, she added,

"And yes, I've loaded everything onto it."

Chloe wouldn't let her forget the time last year when they took a long journey and Chloe hadn't been able to watch Bob The Builder because Vicky had neglected to download the episodes to the device.

"Thanks Vicky," Chloe said, thinking that it was nice that Vicky was finally getting the hang of things.

By one-o-clock, they were all packed and all the bags were neatly lined up by the front door. Since Ray had conveniently missed the packing stage, Vicky thought the least he could do was lug the bags out to the car and load them all in. She regarded the bags and tried to imagine how it could all fit into their Skoda Octavia... well, that was Ray's problem now.

"Okay, Chloe, let's get down to Tesco," she called down the corridor. No response,

"Chloe," she called again. Silence.

"Chloe, come on, don't muck about..." Vicky said, walking down to Chloe's room, but what she saw when she opened the door was quite disturbing.

Chloe was sitting on the edge of the bed, staring towards the door with her eyes very wide open and a look of terror on her face. She wasn't seeing Vicky, but something else. Something horrific.

"Chloe!" Vicky cried, running to her daughter and giving her shoulders a shake.

This did nothing. It was as if Chloe was in a deep trance or having some sort of fit. Vicky shouted her name and shook her again. Still nothing.

"Fuck!" she swore. What should she do? She didn't want to slap her – that had been traumatic enough with Ray next to her giving her moral support. Should she throw water onto her...

Suddenly, Chloe gasped loudly, making Vicky jump,

"Are you all right?" Vicky asked as Chloe stared about her with terror in her eyes,

"We have to run!" Chloe said, leaping off the bed and trying to drag Vicky to the door.

"Wait, what? What is it? Are you all right?"

"No, we have to leave now!" Chloe insisted as she put her full weight into dragging Vicky out of the room.

"Why? What is it? Talk to me, Chloe!"

"*He's* here!"

"What? Just stop and breathe... Who's here?"

"THE MAN!" Chloe shouted, "I saw him and he's come for me."

Vicky looked out of Chloe's window onto the tiny light well between their house and the one next door. It was empty and Chloe's door had been closed, so there was no way she had seen anyone.

"I think you've had some sort of..." Vicky began, but trailed off. What could Chloe have had? It wasn't a dream...

"...some sort of fit. You need to sit down and let everything get back to normal."

"No, we need to go!" Chloe insisted, "We need to get in the car and drive away. I saw him, he's next door and he's killed Mr and Mrs Clarke."

Vicky felt an unpleasant sensation shiver through her, but wasn't about to throw sense and reason out the window. Chloe had had a weird fit and that was the end of it. But she was still desperately trying to drag Vicky out of the room and they were at the door.

"Chloe, stop it!" Vicky said firmly, "You've had a weird waking dream. Nothing has happened. There is no man here and I'm sure Mr and Mrs Clarke are fine."

"No, but I saw them! I saw them dead!" Chloe insisted. She'd seen them right there in front of her!

That was the clincher for Vicky.

"Darling! Darling! How could you see them if you're in here and they're on the other side of that wall?"

"Er… I don't know, but I saw them!" Chloe was cross that it all seemed so muddled, while Vicky could feel her words had taken some of the insistence out of Chloe's tugging at her arm,

"It's a dream. It wasn't real. In fact, I'll prove it to you," Vicky said with confidence. She stopped struggling against Chloe and instead walked past her out of the front door of their flat and then out of the front door of the house. Chloe followed, although with some trepidation – what if The Man was out there?

As Chloe carefully put her head out of the front door, Vicky had already gone around the front of their house to Mr and Mrs Clarke's next door and she was ringing their bell.

"They'll be fine, just you see," Vicky said with a sympathetic look at Chloe.

There was a long pause. Vicky rang again.

"They might be out…"

Or dead.

Chloe looked on anxiously, ready to run.

Vicky tried one more time. Suddenly she wasn't quite as sure of herself, but whether they were in or not, there was still no way Chloe had *seen* them.

Chloe watched in rising panic. They *were* dead, she *had* seen them and now she and Vicky were in terrible danger!

"I told you!" said Chloe when another ten seconds had passed, "Let's go!"

"Wait!" Vicky ordered, "I hear movement inside."

"It's The Man!" and Chloe was so choked with fear that she could hardly get the words out.

"It's fine," Vicky insisted, focussing her gaze on Chloe, even as the door opened,

"Oh!" Vicky said in a mixture of surprise and shock as she turned to the figure that had answered the door,

"Sorry to bother you, Chris... um... what are you up to?"

The ageing man who had come to the door was covered in soot and dirt.

"Sorry, were we making too much noise?" he asked, "We've had part of the spare room ceiling come down, so we were just pulling down the rest before it falls down."

"Oh, that's terrible!" Vicky sympathised, then she thought quickly,

"Well, we did hear a bit of a thump, so I thought I'd just come and check you were both okay."

"Oh, sorry about that..." he began,

"No, no, no don't worry. You weren't disturbing us or anything. Besides, I needed to let you know we're going away today for a couple of weeks, so..."

"Don't worry, if anything goes wrong, I've still got your key. Do you need us to go in regularly to water plants or anything?" he asked.

"No, we should be fine... but Chloe should see you, you look so funny all dusty."

"Of course," and then he leaned back inside his house and looked at himself in the mirror by the door, "Oh dear, what a mess!"

Vicky beckoned to Chloe to come out and see, and she did so reluctantly. Although she didn't want to, she couldn't help but smile, because Mr Clarke was standing there all dirty, with his hair in a horrible tangle and black marks all over his usually pale features."

"There, you see? Nothing to worry about," Vicky said to Chloe, before turning back to Mr Clarke, "She does worry a lot."

Mr Clarke smiled and waved at Chloe, thinking to himself that she also screamed quite a lot. And usually in the middle of the night.

"Anyway, sorry to bother you, Chris. I'll let you get back to it and we'll see you in a couple of weeks."

"Have fun!" he smiled and waved to them both as he closed the door. Two weeks without being woken up by the kid next door yelling and screaming – it would be like a holiday at home!

"See? Everything's fine," said Vicky, putting her arm around Chloe as they walked back into their flat.

"But it all looked so real," Chloe replied in a small voice.

"Hey, look, it's okay. Forget about it. C'mon, let's go to Tesco, get the picnic stuff and maybe a treat – they've got that Krispy Kreme doughnut display..."

Vicky was pleased to see Chloe's face brighten,

"Tell you what, why don't we walk down there and come back on the bus? It's a lovely day and we're not getting much stuff. We can enjoy the sun and stretch our legs on the way. Especially as we've got a long drive ahead of us later."

Chloe wasn't so sure about the walking, but she nodded. She felt a bit silly about what had just happened and didn't feel she could say no.

The walk along the High Road and then down the hill towards Streatham Common was bright, with the sun in their eyes most of the way. It was also quite hot and there was a lot of traffic belching out fumes, so Vicky had to admit to herself that it wasn't quite the refreshing walk she'd been hoping for. In fact, both of them sighed as they entered the big supermarket with its wonderfully cool air conditioning. They looked at each other,

"Okay, so maybe the walk wasn't such a great idea," Vicky admitted and they both smiled,

"But at least the bus almost goes to the end of our road," she added as she got a trolley.

Of course, a child's pester power can be expensive at the best of times, but when they've just had a strange shock, it's hard for a parent to deny them anything. Consequently, they ended up with a bit more to carry than Vicky had intended when they got through the checkouts forty-five minutes later. As they left the store, Vicky had two bags in each hand and Chloe had one lighter one.

"Not far to the bus stop," Vicky said, as much to make herself feel better as to reassure Chloe. They walked along in the shade of the imposing glass and steel storefront of the large supermarket, until they reached the far end, which was right next to the bus depot.

"Crap! That's our bus!" said Vicky and she started jogging as best she could with all the bags, while Chloe trailed just behind her. The double-decker looked like it was about to leave, so they put on an extra spurt of speed to make it before the doors closed, more falling into the bus than getting onto it. Vicky, who was now a bit sweaty, overladen with bags and lacking some dignity, tried to sound casual as she thanked the driver for waiting for them and tapped her travel card onto the reader. It bleeped loudly.

"Upstairs or down?" she asked as they shuffled into the sparsely populated bus.

"Up," replied Chloe.

Vicky immediately regretted offering Chloe the choice as, the moment she started up the narrow stairs, the bus lurched forward.

"Bugger!" Vicky swore as she desperately clung onto one of the rails with a spare finger that wasn't required for carrying the bags. With her body turned slightly side on to the stairs so that she and the four bags could fit, Vicky toiled up the narrow stairs and, as the bus bounced and turned when it joined the traffic, Vicky damn near lost her balance. She would have tumbled back down the stairs had Chloe not been right behind her to give her a shove at an opportune moment.

"Thanks," she said, emerging from the top of the stairs and looking back down at Chloe as she did. Chloe, however, had just got to the point where she could see all the way to the end of the top deck, and was suddenly rooted to the spot, staring with her eyes popping.

"What is it...?" Vicky began, then her throat suddenly constricted as she looked to the back of the bus.

There was The Man. Vicky recognised him instantly from Chloe's description and from the dream they had both had about him, but to see him actually standing there in front of her was stupefying. He was staring at them with furious eyes, his fists balling and his breath hissing through his teeth, as darkness seemed to gather around him like a cloak. After a moment of utter mental chaos, Vicky blurted,

"Run!" and all but pushed Chloe back down the stairs. They stumbled down to the lower deck and Vicky ran to the front,

"Stop the bus!" she shouted at the driver.

He looked straight ahead and pointed to the sign 'Do Not Distract The Driver' next to his cab.

"There's a fucking psycho up there and he's after us!" Vicky yelled.

The driver looked ahead as he manoeuvred the bus through the traffic.

"Let us off the fucking bus!" she screamed, "He's trying to kill us!"

While Vicky swore at the bus driver, Chloe was looking up at the ceiling above them with wide-eyed horror as she listened to the steady footsteps walking along the aisle of the upper deck.

"We've stopped – open the fucking doors! Please!" Vicky begged as the bus halted for a zebra crossing.

"Next stop is fifty yards away. Please sit down and stop verbally abusing me," the bus driver said evenly without looking across at her.

And now the footsteps had got to the top of the stairs. Chloe automatically retreated to be closer to Vicky as the thump of the first boot came down onto the top step.

Vicky tried to calm herself and sound more rational,

"I'm sorry I shouted, but there is a man up there who has been stalking me and my family. Please let us off the bus."

Thump. The Man was on the second step.

"I can't do that," replied the bus driver without emotion, "Anyway, there's nobody up there."

The Man stepped heavily onto the next stair.

"No, because he's coming down the stairs to get us!" Vicky shouted with rising fury – why wouldn't this idiot understand what was happening?

Another thump. Two more steps and they'd be able to see his feet.

"You two were the only passengers to go up there," the bus driver said.

The sound of the heavy boot on the next step was like an explosion to Chloe.

"He'll be down the steps in a few seconds and bloody attacking us, you fucking arsehole!" Vicky screamed.

The heavy boot came down hard on the next step.

"Please!" Vicky begged and then suddenly the bus stopped and the doors opened, "Thank you!" she shouted and dragged Chloe out with her just as The Man's boot could be seen landing on the next step down.

"We're at the bus stop anyway, you mad bitch," the bus driver said to himself as he watched the crazy woman and her unhappy kid run off up the road with all their bags bouncing around them.

This was bad. Vicky and Chloe were over half a mile from their house and some of it was uphill. After running the best part of fifty yards, Vicky looked back at the bus stop but couldn't see The Man anywhere. They were on a busy part of the High Road, where the traffic was only single lane each way and there were a lot of people around, so maybe he'd lost himself in the crowd.

"Come on!" said Vicky, encouraging Chloe to jog with her.

They jogged on up towards a major junction and as they went, the bus came up and overtook them.

Vicky had never experienced her blood run cold until the moment the bus roared past them in the direction of their house. She looked across to see The Man standing at the middle set of doors and staring at her with a dreadful leer on his face. He was trying to get ahead of them!

"No, no, no!" she cried, but then she saw they had a chance. The traffic light was red and the bus was stopping.

"Dump the bags and sprint!" she shouted, letting go of the four bags that had been holding her back. Chloe dropped hers, too, and together they ran up the hill and past the bus. Vicky's skin crawled as they passed within a few feet of The Man as he stood impotently balling his fists behind the glass doors that wouldn't open.

Now they were running across the junction and the next bus stop was in sight. If they could beat The Man to it, they might have a chance of getting home first.

"Phone Ray!" Chloe shouted, and, still running, Vicky reached for her...

"Dammit! The bloody thing's out of battery..." she swore as the phone stared blankly back at her.

Then came the sound she didn't want to hear – the unmistakeable roar of a double-decker bus accelerating. The lights must have changed. Fuck! This was going to be tight. They were now only about twenty yards from the stop. If they could just get past it before the bus... Vicky and Chloe ran headlong, but the bus swept past them with The Man now grinning as he waved to them. But then came salvation! The car immediately ahead of the bus needed to turn across the oncoming traffic. Meanwhile, the traffic coming the other way was heavy. Vicky, still running, watched the bus slow, then stop. It couldn't have been more than ten yards from the actual bus stop, but there was no way the driver was going to let anyone off in the middle of the road. She and Chloe ran past the bus again, but this time The Man's face was nothing but gnashing hatred.

And then they were past the bus stop. He couldn't cut them off and, even better, the traffic ahead was at a standstill. But the two of them couldn't slow down, even though their lungs were burning and Chloe had a stitch. There were still a couple of bus stops ahead where he could cut them off. They ran on, dodging through the shoppers who were oblivious to everything except their own narrow lives. They passed the first bus stop, but as they got to the next crossroads, they could hear the familiar roar of the bus coming up behind. This time, they were saved by the traffic lights, which turned red just as they could feel the bus at their heels, and then they were dashing across the road, looking ahead to the final bus stop before their house.

"Keep going!" Vicky gasped, digging deep into her energy reserves. They mustn't falter now! She glanced back at Chloe and felt a burst of pride that in spite of the pain of sprinting so far, Chloe still looked determined and hadn't complained once. But there was the bus, pulling away from the lights. Vicky turned back and tried to put on an extra burst of speed, but there was nothing left in the tank. She was at full tilt. Either they would make it, or they wouldn't.

They could feel the bus looming behind them as they were engulfed in its shadow, like that of a great shark in the ocean. The bus just beat them to the stop, but Vicky knew that bus drivers rarely hurried when it came to opening and closing doors, so they kept running. They pelted along the side of the bus and they were just past the central set of doors when they opened with a pneumatic hiss. The Man stretched out a hand and snatched at Chloe as she passed, but caught only air, and now it was a foot race. Vicky and Chloe against The Man. Mother and daughter ran on with everything they had, while The Man walked after them at no more than a brisk pace. With every step, the gap between them increased.

"It's okay, it's okay," Vicky was gasping as she dragged Chloe along, while she kept looking back at The Man and his hate-filled eyes,

"We'll get home, lock the door and I'll call the police from the landline."

It didn't occur to her to shout for help, even though there were people all around them on the High Road.

They ran on, widening the gap between them and The Man, but he followed them doggedly. Finally, they were at the end of their road and running down it to the house. Chloe saw a man cycling up the road towards them. He was surrounded by darkness and had a sombrero on his head.

"It's another one of them!" she shouted, pointing him out to Vicky.

"Shit!" Vicky swore, "Run like hell!" and they both put on a burst of speed which neither of them thought they had. Judging distances, it was a toss-up who would get to their house first. Vicky reached into her handbag and got her keys ready to open the front door. By some miracle, they got there before the madman on the bike, who was shouting incomprehensible things at them in Scottish. As Vicky concentrated on getting the key in the lock smoothly, Chloe looked on in horror as the man on the bike pulled up, jumped off it and made for them, but then she was dragged inside and the door slammed into his face.

"Open the fucking door, you bitch!" Mexican Dave screamed as he battered it with his fists.

Vicky's pupils were huge as she reached down and double-locked the door before opening the door of their flat, getting them inside and double-locking it, too.

"Kitchen!" she said, and they ran down the short corridor. Vicky went to the knife block, took out the biggest one for herself, then gave a smaller one to Chloe.

"If anyone gets in, just keep stabbing them," then she snatched up the phone and dialled 999.

"Emergency, which service do you require? Fire, Police or Ambulance?"

"Police!" Vicky said louder than she intended.

"Police," the operator repeated and then there was a click and a pause,

"Hello? Police?" Vicky said.

"Fucking nutter!" It was the voice of an Indian man.

"Are you the Police?" Vicky demanded.

"Nutter! Fucking nutter!"

"Vicky!" Chloe screamed and Vicky turned to see The Man standing in the garden, balling his fists and seething.

The sound of the front door shattering was followed by the thundering of fists on the door of their flat

"I'm gonna cut you up, bitch!"

"Nutter! Fucking nutter!" the phone chimed in loudly as Vicky held it down at her side.

Suddenly, as she looked at The Man outside the patio doors and was deafened by the bloke hammering on the door, Vicky realised this was just like the dream!

"It's the dream!" she said to Chloe excitedly, "This is just the dream we had. All we have to do is wake up..."

Hope flickered across Chloe's face – they were asleep and all they had to do was wake up... she concentrated and tried to wake up, but it was no good.

"I can't wake up!" she shouted.

"Me neither!" said Vicky, with rising terror. Why couldn't they wake up?

"Look, it doesn't matter," Vicky said, holding Chloe's gaze with hers, "We know it's a dream and that nothing bad is really happening."

Then The Man stepped up to the patio door, pulled back his fist and slammed it into the glass. It shattered, and so did Vicky's hope that they were merely in a dream and that everything would be all right. As The Man stepped through the shattered patio door, Mexican Dave crashed through the front door. Behind him was an Indian man with a grin full of crooked teeth holding a mobile phone.

"Fucking nutter!"

"Get behind me!" Vicky ordered. Whatever this nightmare was, protecting her daughter was her first instinct. But if this was a dream, and they both knew it, why hadn't they woken up? As Chloe ducked behind her, The Man lumbered towards them with his arms outstretched like a Mummy from a black and white movie.

"Wake up! Wake up!" Vicky shouted at herself. Why the fuck wasn't she waking up? As The Man lunged at her, Vicky couldn't get out of his way, but deflected his hands upwards with her left arm as she stabbed into his unprotected left flank with the knife. By some miracle, it went between his ribs and sank into the side of his chest up to the hilt. The Man made a quiet 'Oof' sound and pulled away from her. Vicky lost her grip on the knife just as Mexican Dave leapt at Chloe, slapping the knife from her hand and crushing her beneath his weight, knocking her out cold on the hard floor as they skidded three feet beyond Vicky.

"No!" She screamed, but before she could react, The Man's powerful right hand caught her by the throat. She scrabbled at it with her own hands, tearing at his skin with her nails, but the pain was unbearable as he crushed her windpipe. He lifted her off the ground and her legs were kicking as the room started to go blurry around her. Fuck! This wasn't a dream! The pain and the panic were all too real. She felt her flailing foot hit something, but she was falling into darkness and all she could think of was how she had failed Chloe. As The Man held Vicky in the air, Roaming Rohit hobbled around him and looked at the wound in his side. A great bloom of blood stained the honey-coloured coat around where the knife was sticking out of him.

"Fucking nutter!" he said, then took the handle of the knife and pulled it out. He turned towards Vicky, who was still kicking and struggling. Rohit didn't like the kicking and struggling. He wanted it to stop, so he pushed the blade into her midriff.

"Fucking nutter!"

A sound choked out of Vicky as he withdrew the blade and she thrashed harder, so he pushed it in again,

"Fucking nutter!"

And again.

"Fucking nutter!"

And again.

"Fucking nutter!"

Then the kicking stopped.

The Man dropped Vicky and she slapped onto the blood-soaked floor. He indicated to Mexican Dave to get Chloe out. Mexican Dave bundled her unconscious body into the sack he'd brought with him and carried her out to Tommy, who was waiting in his cab outside. Jane Hardiman was sitting in the back of the cab and helped Mexican Dave get the child in.

"All right, Dave?" Tommy asked.

"Aye! Bit fuckin' messy and she stabbed your man, but nothin' we can't handle. Adios!" Mexican Dave cried, slapping the side of the cab as Tommy drove away. Mexican Dave went back inside to see how things were going. As he walked back into the kitchen he was amazed by two things – how quickly The Man and Roaming Rohit had eviscerated the woman and how elegant Rohit's handwriting was.

Chapter Thirty-Six

Consequences

Emma was about to drive away when Ray let out a cry like nothing she'd ever heard. She was immediately out of the car and running towards his house. As she got to the front gate, she noticed that the door of the next house was half open. What the hell was going on? She ran into Ray's house, down the corridor and skidded to a halt when she got to the kitchen. She was so shocked, she was unable to make any sound whatsoever. Ray was kneeling in the middle of a floor awash with blood. Above him, a naked woman was hanging by her intestines tied to the flex of the ceiling light. Emma felt her gorge rise, looked away, put her hands on her knees and bent over, trying not to throw up. Ray was sobbing loudly and repeating that it was all his fault over and over again. After about a minute, Emma had control of herself and turned around to look at the room again. Across the wall on her right, a message had been written in the blood of the hanging woman, it read:

"We have Chloe. If you don't want to see her end up like your wife, you will come to us at ten pm tonight. You know where we are. Do not tell anyone about this or Chloe dies."

"Fuck..." Emma whispered. She looked at her watch – seven fifteen. Less than three hours to go.

"Ray..." she said quietly, then she walked across the tacky, congealing floor and put her hand gently on his shoulder. He turned towards her with a pitiful look on his face,

"What have I done?" he sobbed.

"What have *you* done?" Emma was confused. Why did he think he was responsible for this nightmarish atrocity?

"She told me to go. She said I was out of my depth and she told me to go, but I didn't believe her. And now Vicky's..." he couldn't bring himself to say the truth out loud, "Why was I so stupid?"

So, it had been his wife who had warned him to get out of town. Now the sudden holiday made sense!

"I'm here for you, Ray," Emma said and as he knelt before her, she brought his face to her midriff and held him to her as he cried for his dead wife. Yes, he was crying for his dead wife, but it was Emma that he was clinging onto. She would be his rock and when all this was over, he would be totally hers. She stroked the smooth skin of his head and thought through the situation. Saving his daughter would be his top priority and she would help him do it.

"I'm so, so sorry," she said, gently trying to soothe him and soon his sobbing was calming down.

"Listen... now, listen to me Ray," she said, in a calm but firm voice, "What's happened here is... beyond horrific, but we only have about two-and-a-half hours to find Chloe. Can you think where they might have taken her?"

"Global... Actuaries," Ray choked out.

"Okay, so, if you want to save Chloe, we've got to get over there before ten, but we've got to get our shit together and think up a plan. Can you get up?"

Ray nodded and tried to get up, but slipped in the blood. Jesus! He was kneeling in Vicky's blood! She was all over him! He stifled a scream of horror by shoving a bloody fist into his mouth, and then his mouth was filled by the metallic taste of her. Christ – the horror was unending! Part of him wanted to die right there. Vicky was gone and he wanted to be gone, too, but there was another part of him that was screaming for him to get up and save Chloe. Save Chloe and wreak vengeance upon the animals that did this to his innocent wife. The voice was screaming for him to cut them up and stamp through their blood. That voice was louder than the one that wanted to die, so when Emma held out a hand, he gripped it firmly and lifted himself onto his feet.

"Right... right..." he said as his brain tried to catch up with the situation. But it was all too much! Vicky had been... Ray started to look back at the torn, eviscerated body of the woman who had been the love of his life, but Emma took control. She took his face in her hands and turned it to her,

"Focus, Ray! There will be time for mourning later, but right now we've got a job to do. Come on!" and she led him out of the room by his hand.

She closed the door to the room of horror and led him into the bathroom.

"Take your phone and keys out of your pocket," she said and he followed her instruction like an automaton.

She leant over the bath, pulled the shower curtain across it, then ran the shower, fiddling with the temperature until it was right.

"Shoes off and get in," she said.

"What about my..."

"Your clothes are fucked anyway. Get in there."

Again, he did as he was told. He was in such a daze that getting into the shower fully clothed didn't seem strange at all. The water on his bald head felt good. The white noise of the shower head and the chaotic, yet constant feel of the water raining down on him were soothing. He didn't know how long he stood there before Emma said,

"Strip."

He took off his sodden clothes with some difficulty and handed each item to her, which she put into the sink. Soon he was naked.

"Here," Emma said, handing him a bar of soap. He started to wash himself under Emma's wanton gaze. She wished she could step in there and wash him herself, run soapy hands across his firm chest and lightly muscled flanks until finally giving him an intimate soaping... but that was for another day. Now that the wife was dead, there would be plenty of time for enjoying every inch of Ray's body. Right now, they were on a clock which was inexorably ticking down.

"Keep washing, I'll get you some clothes," she said and left him to it.

The simple process of showering and washing brought Ray back from the precipice of despair and, when he stepped out of the shower and turned it off, he was able to think. He grabbed a towel and dried himself, then put it round his waist and went to the sink. He found his trousers and unclipped his push dagger sheath from the back of the belt, then walked into the hall. He hesitated, looking at the closed door that led onto the unthinkable. What he'd seen in there... had any of it been true? Part of him wanted to check, but most of him wanted to leave it. Then he saw the bloody footprints on the hall carpet... oh God! It was true! He took a step towards the room of death, but stopped himself. If he was going to rescue Chloe, he'd need to be totally in the present. He had to channel his unquenchable grief to give him the power to smash the bastards who'd done this. It was with swelling anger that Ray entered the bedroom. Emma noticed the change,

"How are you feeling?" she asked and immediately knew how lame it sounded. What do you say to someone who's just experienced that?

"Vengeful," he replied in a tone she didn't recognise. It was harsh and flinty.

"I hope these are okay," she pointed to the clothes on the bed.

"They're great. Thanks, Emma," he said, looking into her eyes. She felt the dark energy from him. Yes! That was what they needed. He started to dress and she said,

"I've got a feeling something bad has happened next door. I'm just going to check it out before we go, okay?"

"Sure thing," he replied, and she went back out to the car to get her taser. She wasn't about to go into a possible charnel house unarmed.

As she left the house, Emma was struck by how wonderful and summery it was outside. The sun was still hot, even though it was well past seven and the street seemed relaxed and... normal. She crossed to the car, got the taser and looked back at the two houses. Their ordinary faces, bathed in the golden light of a July evening, gave no hint of the potential horrors within.

Emma found that strange and jarring. She hoped that she'd find nothing untoward in the other house, but there was something about the way the front door was hanging that gave her an unpleasant sensation in her gut. She walked back across the road trying to look relaxed and keeping her taser out of sight. The last thing they needed at this point was any fuss. If anyone called uniformed officers out, there was no way they were going to be able to rescue Chloe in time. When Emma got to the door, it had clearly been forced. Now she held the taser at the ready as she moved into the house. Unlike Ray's, it hadn't been split into two apartments, so the downstairs rooms were general living spaces.

"Hello?" she called, "This is the police. Is there anyone in the house?"

Silence.

God, the house was still...

She looked in through the open door of the front room, which was furnished with antiques in keeping with the period of the house. It was clear. She looked up the staircase that ran straight up from the front door to the first-floor landing. No signs of a struggle and, aside from a few black footprints on the sandy-coloured carpet, everything looked fine. She decided to clear the downstairs first, then go up, and moved carefully down the corridor to the side of the stairs, holding the taser at the ready in front of her.

The door halfway down the short corridor was pushed to, but not fully closed. Emma prepared herself and then gently pushed it open with her foot – just the downstairs toilet. She turned and headed along the corridor to the room at the end. Again, the door wasn't fully closed and she was just about to push it open, when she noticed a familiar smell. Someone was dead beyond that door. She took a breath, held the taser ready and pushed open the door. Unlike Ray's house, the killers hadn't taken time here. If anything, it looked like someone had rushed through the house towards the back door and killed the people inside along the way. The man and the woman were slumped in different parts of the room. The woman was next to the sink in a slowly drying pool of her own urine. Her head was at a very wrong angle to the rest of her body and Emma imagined a strong man entering and breaking her neck before she even knew what was happening. Emma moved towards the man, who was at the far end of the kitchen/diner, lying face down on the floor with his hand outstretched towards the handle of the back door. The hilt of a kitchen knife was sticking out of his back. So, whoever had done this had marched in, killed the woman, taken the knife (possibly from the drying rack) and gone after the man, who had tried to escape out the back, but hadn't made it.

Ray had just clipped his push daggers to the back of his belt when Emma came back.

"Well?"

"Two dead. A man and a woman..."

"Chris and Ginny," Ray said hollowly.

"I've closed the front door so that it won't arouse suspicion. Once we've done what we need to, we can call it in," Emma said and Ray nodded in agreement.

"I know where we can get handguns," she added.

Ray looked at her and, for a moment, she didn't know if he approved or not,

"Good. We're going to need them," he replied and she felt very relieved,

"We can think through what we're going to do on the way," he said and walked into the hall. Again, he looked down the corridor to the closed door at the end. Images of what lay beyond flashed through his head. Every image was beyond belief. It was a film. That was it... It was just a film he'd seen. He had to keep telling himself that, because the truth would crush him. He shook his head to clear it and headed out to the car, closely followed by Emma, who locked up behind them.

"I've got a selection of police issue handguns at my place," Emma admitted as she drove down the hill towards Brixton.

Ray gave her a look of surprise, but said nothing.

"I know. It's bad. And you don't want to know how I got them, but they're what we need right now, so..."

"Okay... what's our plan? We can't just go in with all guns blazing," Ray said thoughtfully, "We need to strike for the head,"

"Simon Montague?"

"Exactly! He's the one in charge. If we can get him, take him prisoner then we've got a chance to swap him for Chloe..." then Ray thought about the building,

"Me and Andy had a look round the back of the building and found something odd."

Emma looked at him with curiosity as he continued,

"There seems to be a security black spot right where the back door is. In fact, the way we reckoned, it might be possible to approach and enter the back of the building from the alleyway to the south without being caught on camera at all. And that includes the cameras from the buildings around. We thought it was a sure sign they didn't want anyone to see who was going in and out of that entrance. Now we can use it to our advantage."

"Okay, so that's our in – what then?" Emma asked.

"I think we'll just have to improvise. They won't be expecting two of us and they certainly won't expect us to be carrying firearms. That might be all the edge we need..." then Ray's face clouded.

"What?" Emma asked.

"I can't believe I'm risking Chloe's life with such a thin plan. What if there's shooting? Can I really put her in that danger?"

"I hate to say it," said Emma, "But she's already in serious danger and if you don't go, or you tell anyone else..." and she left the sentence unfinished. From the look on Ray's face, he was clearly remembering the message written on the wall.

"I know, but I still feel like it's a flimsy plan."

"We can make it work. We *must* make it work," Emma said and she reached over to take Ray's right hand and give it an encouraging squeeze. He liked the feel of it and returned the squeeze. That small moment gave Emma much more pleasure than it should have. This was a very odd situation. There she was, helping the man she loved avenge the death of his wife and rescue his daughter. Was it any wonder that her emotions were all over the place?

When they got to her flat, she told Ray to wait in the car. She ran in and went to the locked cabinet in the bedroom. Inside were half a dozen handguns of various makes and models, with boxes of bullets. She grabbed what she thought they'd need and ran back out to the car.

"Here you go," she said, handing Ray a Glock 17M, "Clip's ready to go and here's a spare."

She gave him the spare mag and he looked at it, with its dull, brassy live round sitting in the top. Seventeen rounds per magazine... Ray did the maths – sixty-eight rounds between the two of them would be more than enough firepower. He looked over at Emma and, not for the first time, was impressed by her capabilities.

"I guess we'd better go," he said, but before he could do anything, Emma leaned across and kissed him fiercely.

"Sorry," she said as she sat back, "I know everything must be raw, but I had to do that. You know, just in case we..."

"It's okay," Ray replied hoarsely.

Emma could see he was contending with too many conflicting emotions, but eventually most of them would pass. All they had to do was get through the night and things would become simpler. She put the car into gear and they drove into the gathering twilight.

Chapter Thirty-Seven

The Best Laid Plans

Once her nails were painted and fully dried, Elizabeth Russell set to work on the important matter of getting her mind, body and spirit ready for the difficult night ahead. Everything was in place – the psychics were ready; she had a watch on Global Actuaries Limited; and she had the tool for the job. Now it was all about her. Still wearing her dressing gown, she went to the large map of Britain on the wall behind her desk, stretched out a hand and pushed firmly where Sheffield was marked. There was a click and a secret door opened in the wall. She stepped through, felt for the light switch and closed the door behind her. It was a large room with sage coloured walls and a thick, patterned maroon carpet. Yes, it was a bit OTT, but the original cream carpet had been hopeless – the slightest blood spillage and it was wrecked. The wall to the left of the entrance had two large built-in wardrobes, while the back wall was dominated by a long, oak apothecary cabinet that stood three feet high. An array of drawers, each with a card slipped into a slot in the front and marked with the name of whatever was inside, tantalised the curious. The wall above the cabinet was hung with a selection of weapons and magical equipment from swords and maces to wands and sickles. The wall to the right had a full-length mirror in the middle of it, with a Louis the Sixteenth dressing table and chair on one side and a gentleman's clothes horse on the other. Further along, near the front wall, a door opened into a grand bathroom with a cream tiled floor and walls with large tiles from floor to ceiling made of what looked like lapis lazuli.

Elizabeth Russell walked across to the apothecary cabinet and rootled around in various drawers, taking out a selection of herbs and powders. She laid them out on top of the cabinet – she would need them for her cleansing bath. She went over to the built-in wardrobe, slid a door open, took off her dressing gown and slipped it onto a hanger. Beneath it she was wearing nothing but her underwear, which she took off. She took a moment to aim at the open-topped laundry basket in the corner nearest the secret door and said in her best darts commentator's voice,

"Here she is... two darts left for the world championship... she needs double top and a bullseye..."

Then she threw her pants, which flew in a delicate arc to land right in the middle of the basket. She gave a fist pump and said,

"That's the double top! Now all she needs is the bullseye..." and she folded the bra so that the cups rested one within the other and took aim again. She released and, for a moment, thought it might not make it. And she was right. The bra ended up stuck half in and half out of the basket, lolling miserably over the side,

"Oh, what a disaster for the young lass from Sheffield. That surely is the end of a promising career. Now she'll have to go back to fettling geese in her dad's goose quarry," she said, then turned away from the treacherous bra and headed towards the bathroom.

The very white skin of her face and neck and the vee of white skin that spread from her neck to the valley between her breasts were all most people ever saw. In a low-cut summer shirt, she looked provocative, but normal. However, beyond the small area of virgin white skin, the rest of her body was adorned with hundreds of tattoos. Each one was a religious symbol and they covered every possible civilization from Sumerian (she had the winged goddess, Lamma, inked on her left forearm), to the Peruvian Norte Chico people, whose leering Staff God was tattooed just above her appendix scar. Her shoulders and arms down to her wrists were an intricate tangle of sacred imagery. Dragons, bears and eagles vied for space across her chest, stomach and back, alongside Quetzalcoatl, the Aztec feathered serpent, as well as Maori, Viking and tribal symbols from across Africa. The tattoos continued down across her buttocks and groin, down the front and back of her slender, but strong legs and all the way to the tips of her toes.

Every point of her body that could be used to strike – her knuckles, shoulders, elbows, knees and feet (including her heels and soles) – were inked with symbols to fight evil. The Christian cross; the Celtic triquetra; the symbol of Damballah from Voodoo; symbols for Gye Nyame and Aban from West Africa; a left pointing arrow from a First Nation American religion; the symbol for the central Asian sky God Tengri; the symbol of Allah; the Viking helm of awe and terror, Aegishjalmr; the star of David; and the Taoist Yin-Yang were among the symbols that gave spiritual power to every attacking move she made. However, there was even more to Elizabeth Russell than met the eye. A thin scar ran along the hairline across her forehead and down towards her temples. It was the only visible sign that the flesh of her forehead had been surgically pulled down so that the symbols that were tattooed across her knuckles could be laser etched onto the front of her skull. The same had been done under her hair across the back, each side and across the top of her head so that any strike from her head could cause serious damage to almost any supernatural foe. The laser etching didn't stop there – it had been done across the bones of her knuckles, elbows, shoulders, knees and feet.

She also had defensive symbols tattooed at every entry point to her body from her private parts to the inside of her nostrils, the inside of her upper and lower lips, around the entrances to her ear canals and the most visible ones, which were on her eyelids. The result was that spiritually, she was a living weapon. She walked into the large bathroom and flicked on the lights, which were star ceiling lights in the pattern of the northern night sky. They gave a relaxing, twinkling light which glinted off the large, copper bateau-style bath in the middle of the room. The far end of the room was a huge walk-in shower, next to which three freshly laundered white bath robes were hung. On the wall between the door and the shower, there was a vast marble basin, with an array of toiletries around it, above which a large, antique mirror hung, reflecting the light from the starry bulbs in the ceiling. A lavatory and a bidet in simple white porcelain on the far side of the room completed the bathroom furniture. Fitted to the wall next to them was a broad, chromed towel rail with a selection of fresh white towels.

Elizabeth Russell went straight to the sink, washed her hands and then picked up a bullet-shaped laxative suppository of her own making. She wetted it under the tap, then inserted it and thoroughly washed her hands again. If she ever knew that she was going into battle, she always made sure that she was purged beforehand. There had been a time, early in her career, when she'd been halfway through wrestling a demon out of a child when her bowels had opened. It had been embarrassing, messy and the townsfolk had laughed her out of the neighbourhood. After that, she'd sworn it would never happen again. The 'recipe' of the suppository was from a wise man in the Caucasus Mountains and it worked quickly and efficiently.

Within five minutes, it was done and she was able to get into the shower and fully cleanse her physical body.

When she was out and dressed in a white bathrobe, she turned the taps on for the bath, before going through to the dressing room and collecting the ingredients she needed. She placed them by the sink and lit the two candles in silver holders on either side of the mirror, repeating an incantation to draw the power of light to her. She took off all her silver rings, the face of each of which was etched with the same sacred symbol as the tattoo on the knuckle beneath them. As she mindfully took each one off, she acknowledged the truth that she didn't *need* to wear them anymore, because the tattoos and etchings in her knuckles did the job, but they reminded her of her past. Long before the tattoos and surgery, those rings had often been her only weapons in fights with evil beings. Each had its own story to tell and they were part of her. Also, she'd got used to their comforting weight and they enabled her to pack a punch if she was ever in a fight with regular human beings.

Soon the bath was full and she slowly added each of the ingredients, concentrating on the role she wanted it to play in her purification and saying it out loud. She began by sprinkling the water with pink Himalayan mountain salt, then added rue, laurel, mugwort, rosemary and St John's Wort. Once all the ingredients were added, she hung the bathrobe on one of the spare hooks, took one of the dry ones to place it on the towel rail and was finally ready to get into the bath. Ensuring that she was facing towards the door and, holding a clear quartz crystal to amplify her strength and intention, she stepped into the deliciously hot water, lay down and relaxed. With slow and even breaths, she opened her spirit to the universe, feeling the flow of energy as positive strength flowed in and tension flowed out. She floated in blissful harmony and let her mind freewheel, letting go of plans, schemes and concerns. She lay in the bath simply being.

Two hours later, Elizabeth Russell emerged from the secret door behind her desk fizzing with energy, and her freshly pressed black shirt and scarlet trouser suit announced that she was ready to take care of business and look good doing it. Her apparently light, sporty pair of black trainers masked their true function – the non-slip rubber soles were anti-static, fuel resistant and heat resistant to a hundred and thirty degrees. Their steel toecaps would be undetectable to anyone right up to the point when she kicked them. The final touch was a short necklace with stones of black tourmaline, red jasper, aquamarine, black onyx, carnelian, hematite, bloodstone, black obsidian, tiger's eye and green aventurine, strung on the entwined hair of a powerful eighteenth-century Inuit shaman.

So, she was cleansed – now all she had to do was meditate and then she'd be ready for whatever Krowos might throw at her. She walked over to the day bed, scooched into the middle and sat with her legs crossed. She cleared her mind and began to meditate. Although her body didn't move, her mind slipped through time and space to the Simtokha Dzong, the oldest castle monastery in Bhutan. She stood before its white walls in the brilliant sunshine and looked around at the surrounding bowl of hills blanketed in trees, that made it appear as if the monastery was a rock in the midst of a swelling sea of green. In the distance, to the north, she could see the white peaks of mountains over four thousand metres high looking down with benevolence on the sacred place. She loved it there, especially in the summer when the flowers of the surrounding garden added their dashes of red and pink to the vista. Maybe it was because the air was thinner at over two thousand metres above sea level, but the colours always seemed so vivid there, and the deep blue of the sky, with the green of the hills made her feel at peace with creation.

She walked up the stairs ahead of her and into a cool passageway with a high ceiling and walls painted in ochre, across the courtyard beyond and up more stairs into the brightly decorated rooms of the central building. She directed her steps to the main chapel, sat before the statue of Buddha and made herself one with existence in the Palace of the Profound Meaning of Secret Mantras. Although she had travelled to sacred sites on every continent, this was where she was able to fully lose herself in the flow of the universe. This was where she could shed her physical form and unburden herself of ego and the layers of life experience that had shaped her psyche. This was where she could be her true self, a being of light that was so much more than Elizabeth Russell, the simple girl from Sheffield, who once, a long time ago, had walked the ten miles to Bamford Edge to sell her soul to the Devil.

While her body spent an hour sitting on the day bed in her office, her soul spent an aeon gathering strength and power for the night ahead and, when she finally opened her violet eyes, they shone with an arcane power. She slipped off the bed and walked over to the desk. As she moved, she was light and lithe, full of a coiled energy that made her feel incredible. She took the heavy axe from her desk as if it had no weight, walked to the centre of the room and gave it a few good swings. Yes, that felt good! Now all she had to do was watch and wait for the night to come and the battle to commence.

***

It was just after four pm when Elizabeth Russell got the sinking feeling that her plan might be unravelling. A voice spoke directly into her head. It was Jo, one of the psychic operatives who were watching the Global Actuaries building,

"A cab's just arrived and the female passenger has just taken a sack into the building."

"And?" Elizabeth Russell replied directly into Jo's mind.

"Looks like the sack contained a child. Whatever was in it was human and alive."

"Show me what the woman looked like, please."

Jo did so.

"Thanks. And did she go into the building?"

"Yes, she went in and the fat cabbie went off again. He's missing the end of his left arm."

"Okay, that's good to know. Keep me posted."

Elizabeth Russell sat in silence.

"Bollocks!"

It looked like they were going to sacrifice a child that night. Having an innocent child caught up in the middle of it certainly complicated things. Maybe she should postpone the plan? And then what? Allow them to feed a child to that abomination in the cellar? She ran her hands through her hair, then entwined her fingers behind her head and leaned back in her chair. What to do?

Over the next two hours, she worried at the problem, but decided to stick to the plan. There was no way they would attempt a human sacrifice during daylight hours. In The City during summer, people worked later, so she reckoned that they would wait until most people in the area had left work. If she was lucky, they wouldn't do anything before ten. If they were doing anything involving the moon, then that might push things back later. Moonrise wouldn't be until after half-ten and it wouldn't pass the meridian until after half-three. That was their most likely time for a blood sacrifice if they used the influence of the moon... IF they used the influence of the moon. The fact was, she had no idea how they summoned Krowos. There was a real chance that the child in the sack had already been sacrificed.

At around six, things started to gather momentum, as Jo began talking into her mind again,

"One armed cabbie's back. Just dropped off a rather dashing man with a military bearing."

"All right, Jo, try to keep your desires on a leash," Elizabeth Russell smiled.

"I'd like to keep him on a leash," Jo replied archly, "I'll let you know anything more as and when. Peace!"

Okay, the new person might complicate matters even further, but that didn't mean...

"Sorry, me again. A madman on a bike wearing a sombrero just arrived and went in. He's got a terrible black aura."

"Aha! That's Krowos' herald and occasional assassin. He's very dangerous. Are you fully concealed physically and psychically?"

"Yes," said Jo, "Catch you later."

Elizabeth Russell was now worrying about Jo. She was a warm-hearted person and a brilliant psychic, but wasn't quite cut out for this sort of potentially dangerous field work. She favoured chunky jumpers and flowing hippy skirts and always had a pair of spectacles on a cord around her neck – hardly SWAT material. Another person arrived in the now familiar cab ten minutes later,

"Middle-aged bloke; average height and build; looks thoroughly uninteresting – aside from his black aura," Jo said, "But he's going in through the back like the others, so he must be important."

"Right, thanks Jo. And you're sure you're safely stowed somewhere they can't see you?"

"Too right, mate!" Jo exclaimed – she didn't intend getting maimed by some creature from another dimension. No, she was strictly observing and making sure she wasn't observed back.

"Oliver!" Elizabeth Russell shouted from her desk.

"What?" he shouted back from his desk on the other side of her closed office door,

"Is the car ready?" she shouted.

"Yes, it's right outside and ready to go," he shouted back, then his voice came politely into her mind,

"Why are we shouting?"

"Because all this silence is driving me mental!" she bellowed through the door, then she got up from her desk, strode across the room and dramatically opened the door to see Oliver at his desk,

"It looks like tonight's turning into a shindig for evil fuckwits," she said in a measured voice, "It might be wise to have an ambulance on hand, just in case everything goes south."

"Righto!" Oliver replied, "Anything else?"

She searched the ceiling for inspiration, found none, gave a cursory,

"Nope!", turned on her heel to go back into her lair, remembered something halfway through and spun back around to face Oliver as if she'd meant it,

"One thing – once I'm on site, I think we'll need a road diversion in place to close off Cannon Street. We don't want the risk of collateral damage."

"Of course," he replied, and she spun on her heel and marched back to her desk.

Oliver smiled. She often had such outbursts when things were getting particularly tense. He certainly didn't envy the fact that the whole operation was her responsibility. Of course, every operation of the Regulator's department was her responsibility, but this one seemed to be getting somewhat complicated. And it was all on her shoulders.

"More people have arrived," Jo's voice interrupted Elizabeth Russell's thoughts, just as she'd cleared them nicely.

"Tell me,"

"Got an elegant Chinese woman and two rather sub-par men. One of them is Indian with a very pronounced limp and the other is a very angry-looking old man..."

"Let me see through your eyes!"

Jo immediately complied, allowing her to effectively take over her body.

Elizabeth Russell sat forward at her desk in Whitehall and her violet eyes rolled back in their sockets until only the whites were visible. At that instant, her vision transferred to Jo's from her vantage point overlooking the back of Global Actuaries Limited. Yes, that was The Man all right... and it looked like he'd been in the wars. He looked even more like death than usual, was holding himself very stiffly and the left side of his coat was bloody from his armpit to the hem around his knees. Elizabeth Russell took in the rest of the scene as the three people went inside and the cab drove away. Back in her office, her eyes rolled forward and the link was broken.

"You've got to keep yourself hidden from that old man, Jo," she said with urgency, "He is very powerful and very, very dangerous, even if he's carrying an injury. At the first sign of a possibility he might be onto you, you've got to get out, right?"

"You got it," Jo replied, but without her usual bubbly delivery. If The Regulator said someone was dangerous, then they were bloody dangerous!

Jo went back to her surveillance and Elizabeth Russell rested her chin on the palm of her left hand as she leant on her desk. This was all looking sticky! Even though she was primed and ready for action, she knew she wasn't invincible and she really didn't fancy tackling Krowos and his acolytes single-handed. But the fact was, that with two of her senior officers out of the country and the third in hospital, she was the only person in Britain with the skills to do the job. She toyed briefly with the idea of getting Titheridge involved, but then discarded it. It was too late in the day to bring him up to speed and he was bound to be a loose cannon. No, this one would be down to her... but how could she thread the needle of this problem in such a way that she wasn't taking on all of their enemies at once?

"We've got a celebrity arriving," Jo's excited voice suddenly said into her mind,

"Who is it?"

"Ever heard of a singer called Shiny Starrr?"

"No," Elizabeth Russell replied.

"Oh come on, she's had loads of hits. You know... Shiny Starrr - spells her name with three R's."

"Fuck me – what an idiot! And she's there, is she?"

"Yes, went in just now, but this time the cabbie's parked up and gone in, too. He is a huge man!"

"Hmmm... so if the cabbie isn't going out again, then maybe they're all assembled?" Elizabeth Russell pondered,

"You know what? I'm going to come over now," she said suddenly, "I have the feeling that I need to be there not here. So, sit tight and I'll see you in about half an hour."

"Got it," Jo said and the connection was broken again.

Elizabeth Russell was up from her desk within a heartbeat and heading for the door with a stony look on her face,

"Right, come on, Oliver, we're off!" she announced as she crossed his office towards the outer door.

Oliver scrambled to follow his boss, who was looking powerful, focussed and crackling with energy as she flung open the outer office door.

"Hang on," Oliver said, but she wasn't stopping as she marched out onto the iron gantry to the top of the spiral stairs,

"I'm not waiting around for you to get your shit together," she called over her shoulder, "You've got to be ready to move at the drop of a hat!"

"No, you've forgotten the axe," he replied calmly.

The footsteps on the iron gantry stopped, paused, then started coming slowly back to the office,

"Well, I cocked up that exit, didn't I?" she said as she crossed Oliver's office again and went into her own. While he went to stand ready by the outer door, he could hear her chuntering to herself in the other room,

"What a total tosspot! You'd forget your head if it wasn't screwed on. Fuck's sake! It's only the most important thing here... what a wanker!" and then she emerged from her office and trudged across to the main door with the axe in her hand,

"Right, let's go," she said bitterly and led the way to the stairs. As he followed, Oliver couldn't help but smile.

One of the perks of running an invisible department in the Treasury was the car that came with the job. Generally, Elizabeth Russell couldn't give a monkey's toss about cars, but there was something about the black, vintage Jaguar 420G as it basked on the kerb side that made her smile. At over sixteen feet in length, it was more like a killer whale than a car. It had an air of power and a certain amount of menace about it as they burbled across London in the failing light of the summer's day. In the comfort of the blue-grey leather seats, she looked out as the city slipped past. They drove through the inevitable mess of Parliament Square and passed Big Ben. On the bridge ahead, Andy had been impaled by the man in the sombrero. Elizabeth Russell's eyes narrowed – she hoped to meet that man later on and give him Andy's kind regards. However, their business was north of the river, so they took a left onto the Embankment and drove along it all the way to London Bridge. The view of old and new buildings made her think of the churn of the old city and how it was constantly reinventing itself. She wondered briefly what Krowos thought of it all. It was certainly different from pre-Roman times. Was it just luck that the creature had found a place in one of the oldest parts of the city to push through into their world? Could it have known that the rock and spring it had anchored itself to would one day be at the centre of one of the world's great capitals? Part of her was keen to find out, but her experience of such creatures was that they weren't particularly chatty when faced with possible disconnection from our world. Usually, they fought tooth and nail, and afterwards there was neither time nor opportunity to find out anything interesting or useful.

Soon, their driver turned off Lower Thames Street and into Fish Hill Street, where he parked up.

"On foot from here," Elizabeth Russell said, and she and Oliver got out of the car.

"You head over to the north side observation point and relieve Quentin. Tell him he's done for the night and there's a tab at the Red Lion until six am. I'll take over from Jo at the south side observation point. Keep in touch and watch out. This lot are dangerous."

"Good luck," Oliver said, then walked briskly up the hill.

Elizabeth Russell went down the hill and along Lower Thames Street before wiggling her way back up to a delightful Victorian building in light-coloured red brick on Laurence Pountney Hill.

"I'm here, Jo," she thought and a moment later, Jo came back with,

"On my way!"

Elizabeth Russell stood in the street and waited, looking through an iron railing at the small garden next to the building. Incongruously, in the maze of stone, concrete, glass and steel, two large plane trees loomed at either end of the garden. Their crowns rode higher than the four storey Victorian building she was about to enter, and the fact made her smile. The trees stood as a reminder that if ever humanity fell apart, plants would take back the city within a hundred years. After about a minute, Jo came to the door and opened it,

"Sorry," she said, "I do find all these stairs a little hard,"

"Not a problem," Elizabeth Russell smiled and then gave the small, puddingy woman a warm hug. Jo might not be fit, but there was a strength and solidity about her that was comforting.

"Come on in," she puffed and led the way through the building which, unlike its elegant frontage, had been horribly modernised so that inside it had the anonymity of the sets used for The Office. Once they had negotiated three flights of stairs and various corridors, they got to the observation room, which looked out on Laurence Pountney Lane and the back of Global Actuaries Limited.

"It's been all quiet since we spoke. I do hope that poor child is going to be all right," Jo said in between heavy breaths.

"I think they'll be fine until after midnight. Listen, why don't you head off?"

"Wouldn't dream of it. I want to stay here and be your back-up."

"You know that isn't necessary. Anyway, who's going to stop Quentin getting pissed at the Red Lion if you don't get over there?"

"Fair point. All right, I'll stay for a bit and then head off. How's that?"

Over the next half hour, the two of them made the best out of a lull in the activity across the street. Jo was good company and her incessant chatter stopped Elizabeth Russell from getting too introspective. But, as the time wore on, she felt that things were getting more likely to kick off and she finally said,

"Jo, I think you'd better head home..."

"Look!" Jo said, pointing to the back door. The Indian man with the limp had come out, closely followed by the madman in the sombrero. As they appeared, Oliver spoke into their minds,

"Heads up, you two, The Man's just come out the front door."

"And we've got two out the back," Elizabeth Russell replied.

"Holy shit! He's phasing!" Oliver cried, "One moment he was by the front door of the building and the next, he was on my side of the road."

"Okay, stay calm, Oliver. From the way the two back here are acting, it looks like they're doing a perimeter check. Yeah, they seem relaxed. Mister Limp is heading down Martin Lane and the Mexican's coming towards us."

"The Indian chap's gone out of sight down the lane," said Jo.

"Yeah, and the Mexican has disappeared behind our building. Right, I'd better go down and intercept him," Elizabeth Russell said, but before she could move,

"I've lost sight of The Man!" Oliver said urgently, "Repeat, I do not have eyes on The Man."

That wasn't good, but what she saw a few moments later pleased her even less.

"What the fuck is he doing here?" she said out loud as she watched Ray Ennis and his female DC make a dash to the back of the building. They must have waited until the Mexican was past them and then bolted. She watched as they fiddled with the lock and in a couple of seconds, they were in.

"Christ on a fucking bicycle! Those two are going to ruin everything!" Elizabeth Russell exclaimed.

"Which two?" Oliver asked.

"Detective Ennis and one of his colleagues have just gone in through the back door," she replied, her mind whirling through possible scenarios. Bollocks! Every one of them was messy!

"All right, people, we are now improvising. I will take care of the three musketeers, you two keep your eyes open and let me know if you see anything."

Jo and Oliver both answered in the affirmative and Elizabeth Russell got up,

"And Jo, I need you to guard this with your life," she said, resting the axe against the wall before running from the room.

Chapter Thirty-Eight

Three On One

As Elizabeth Russell ran down the stairs, she thought about The Man and the fact that he was phasing through space and time. He was able to materialise anywhere he could clearly visualise. It was a neat trick but, like all powerful spells, it drained the caster's energy. She was tempted to do it herself but held back. How much psychic energy would she need to deal with Krowos? She couldn't risk it. For now, she was just going to have to shift her arse the old fashioned way, and she took the last few flights of stairs two at a time, almost crashing through the front door at the bottom of the final flight. As she stumbled out into the street, she wondered where the bloke in the sombrero had got to. The area was a maze of narrow alleys. Laurence Pountney Hill headed up towards Cannon Street and halfway up it, Suffolk Lane led off to the left. The alley straight ahead of her between the high buildings ended in a T-junction, the righthand half of which looped around to become Suffolk Lane. Elizabeth Russell took a gamble, ran up the hill and then cut left into the top of Suffolk Lane. The cobbled road was barely wider than a car and the five storey buildings on either side of it made it seem even narrower in their darkening shadows. She ran forward to where the lane doglegged to the left and opened out in front of an elegant Georgian building in cream stucco, with a sweeping staircase up to the black painted front door. And there, walking up the cobbled hill, was Mexican Dave. He tilted the front of his sombrero to look at her,

"Where the fuck d'you come from missy?" he asked in his ridiculous accent.

"From the hospital where the man you ran through is recovering nicely," Elizabeth Russell replied.

"Bollocks!" he spat, "We know he's dead."

"Like you 'know' that Krowos is a god and not just some chancer from another dimension conning idiots like you?" Elizabeth Russell gave a derisory laugh as she saw the flicker of doubt in his eyes.

Mexican Dave roared with anger, then charged at her. It was a clumsy attack, which caused his sombrero to slip off the back of his head, and she neatly stepped aside and allowed him to lumber past her,

"Not so easy when your victim can see you coming," she said, thinking about how this fucker had skewered Andy through his back.

Mexican Dave stopped and turned to face her, but before he could move, Elizabeth Russell sprang forward and delivered a left to his gut. He doubled over with an 'Oof!', but managed to avoid her follow-up right knee to the face, spinning away so that her momentum took her through empty space and left her flank open to attack. A flick knife flashed out in his right hand, but she parried the blow with such force that his right arm broke in two places just above the wrist, leaving him hopping about and yelping in pain.

"You fucking bitch!" he wailed, cradling his broken arm and stumbling backwards.

"Detective Sergeant Harper says hi," she smiled, her violet eyes sparkling with relish at the feel of the bones breaking against her right hand - not simply because of the pain it inflicted, but also because she now knew which symbols he was most vulnerable to. On her right knuckles were the star and crescent, a Tengric symbol, a Celtic triquetra and a cross. One or more of them had done the trick. With that knowledge, it was time to push home the attack.

She flashed forward, faster than he could see, and the first thing he knew of the attack was the starburst of agony as her right uppercut connected with the enormous target of his oversized chin. The effect was spectacular. Her fist shattered his jaw, tearing the skin and flesh so that the lower half of his mouth flapped down to his neck. Mexican Dave was done. He slumped to his knees, making a horrible gargling noise as he tried to breathe, despite the blood spurting down his throat from his severed maxillary artery. Elizabeth Russell stood over him while he clutched at the air, as if he might somehow be able to catch hold of life itself and cling onto it. With every passing second, his stressed heart pumped his lifeblood out of the gaping mess of his mouth. Part of her wanted to grab him by the hair, lift him up, look deep into those dying eyes and tell him what an evil, useless waste of humanity he was... but she'd learned long ago that it rarely helped. They usually didn't hear much amid the tumult of impending death, and if they did hear, they almost never cared. So, she stood back and let him bleed out. The humane thing would have been to give him a coup de grace, but she stood watching Mexican Dave choking and gurgling and vainly scrabbling for life. That was more than he deserved.

When he finally slumped backwards, she had the urge to give Mexican Dave's body a further kicking before setting it alight, but she had two more of Krowos' servants to hunt down. She ran down the hill to Upper Thames Street, then along to Arthur Street. It was a wide road crowded in by faceless corporate offices of concrete, steel and glass, and cluttered by a mess of construction work. No sign of Mister Limp, so she jogged up past the diggers and other equipment that had been abandoned for the night, until she reached the junction of Martin Lane - another narrow, cobbled canyon. Roaming Rohit limped his way agonisingly around the corner of an alley about twenty yards up the lane and when he saw her, he stopped. Their eyes met and then his face broke into his white, toothy grin as he said,

"Fucking nutter!"

Elizabeth Russell instantly dropped to one knee and clutched the sides of her head as if it was being pulled apart. Roaming Rohit limped his way slowly towards her, his weaselly eyes boring into her as she desperately fought against the pain.

"Nutter!" he said once he was standing over her, using all the power Krowos had bestowed on him to tear her head in two,

"Fucking nu..." but as he opened his mouth, Elizabeth Russell's hand struck upwards with the speed of a snake. Suddenly, her thumb was in his mouth, wedged to the roof of it as her first and second fingers stabbed into his eyes. Before he could even scream, she pushed him back, gripping his mouth and eyes like a bowling ball until she slammed him against the smooth, stone side of the nearest building. With her fingers clenched onto the bones of his eye sockets, she smashed his head backwards against the wall, pulled him away and smashed him back, over and over again with such speed and fury that in five seconds his shattered skull had destroyed his cerebellum.

She let go of his face, and her forefinger slipped out of his right eyeball with an unpleasant sound as his thin body crumpled to the ground. She looked down at him as his limbs, no longer controlled by his brain, randomly twitched and writhed. His now sightless eyes were a mangled mess with blood and vitreous humor running down the sides of his face. Annoyingly, he was still alive. She bent down, took his head in her hands and broke his neck without a second thought. His attack had been strong and would have been enough to overcome most psychics, but she was another matter. She'd faked the reaction to his attack well enough for him to think it had been working. More fool him. Now he was dead. So much for the promises of power Krowos had probably made to him. She shook her head. Why, when faced with a clearly evil supernatural power, did anyone ever side with it? Surely it was obvious that if the powers of darkness exist, then so must the powers of light? So why choose the darkness? She couldn't understand it.

She looked around – unlike Mexican Dave, Rohit was visible from a main road, so she grabbed his hands, dragged him into the alley and propped him up against the side of a dumpster that couldn't be seen from the street. It really wasn't a heroic end for the self-proclaimed Nawab of Newington. Now all she needed to do was find The Man.

"Anyone got eyes on The Man?" and her thought transference made her voice sound in Oliver and Jo's heads.

"Nothing here," Jo replied.

"I lost track of him a few minutes ago," Oliver responded, but then he cried out and was silent.

"Shit!" Elizabeth Russell swore and had to make a split-second decision. Time to phase, whatever the consequences! She visualised herself in the north side observation point where Oliver was and spoke the words of the spell. The next instant, she was there in the echoey, half-finished office space of a building under construction.

The Man was holding Oliver's face and staring into his eyes. As she watched, her assistant's hair turned grey and then white.

"Put him down!" she ordered in a voice of commanding wrath.

The Man turned his head, his watery blue eyes full of hate, and made a low, guttural growl. He threw Oliver aside like a rag doll, hitting his head on the wall and knocking him out cold. Then The Man turned and faced Elizabeth Russell full-on. His arms were ramrod straight at his sides and his fists were balled as he stood there seething through gritted teeth. She could feel that he was drawing in strength for an attack. Common sense would dictate that she should attack before he was ready, but she didn't. She knew nothing about him other than that he was far more powerful than the two men she'd just dispatched. She wanted to size him up before fully engaging, so she circled around him, putting herself between him and Oliver. She watched as a black void opened around The Man. The void was fascinating. It was pure darkness, a hole through time and space to some unimaginable place of evil in the great Beyond. Against that background, Elizabeth Russell didn't even see the black cords shoot out of the darkness to wrap around her wrists, ankles and throat.

Suddenly, her world was pain as the cords tried to pull her arms, legs and head off. She strained against them, burning cold against her flesh, but they were too strong for her. As the cord around her neck cut off her airway and simultaneously started stretching the tissues connecting her vertebrae, she had a flashback to the day she'd been hanged. That day, she'd entered a calm place as her brain was starved of oxygen, but then desperate panic had followed on its heels. This time would be different. Even as her hip and shoulder ligaments strained to breaking point, she concentrated her power and blades of light burst from her, severing the black cords, which slithered back, screaming into the void surrounding The Man. She staggered and heaved in a great gulp of air as she held up her right hand. The blades of light flew to her hand and formed into a spear which she threw into the void. The spear flashed through the darkness, flying deep into the core of that nowhere space. There was roar of pain from the darkness and the walls of the building shook as the void collapsed in on itself.

As The Man stepped back to steady himself, Elizabeth Russell rubbed her throat with her left hand. It was painful. If she survived, she'd have one hell of a bruise,

"It's just you and me now, old man," she said hoarsely, and her eyes glittered as they held his in their gaze.

"Mors tua, vita mea," The Man replied through yellowed teeth.

As they stood, staring each other down, their wills locked. Wow! He was a strong one! And old. In fact, ancient. As their spirits struggled for supremacy, she could sense his experiences. Yes, she could feel the weight of around two thousand years behind him. After all, who resorts to speaking Latin in a fight? A Roman. So, The Man had been with Krowos since the early days – no wonder he could phase through time and space, conjure the darkness or recover so quickly from a stab wound. Age had not weakened him. He was stronger for it and supremely confident. As confident as the day he had taken part in the final rout of the Druids in Anglesey. Even then, he had been Krowos' man.

The Man and Elizabeth Russell stood ten feet apart, locked together with their eyes. Physically, they were still as statues, but the stillness belied the psychic strength they were expending. They were like Greco-Roman wrestlers standing in an apparently motionless clinch. To watchers it might seem as if nothing was going on, when the reality was that every muscle was straining to overcome the foe. As The Man put all his spiritual energy into taking down the little bitch in front of him, he left no energy for protection. So, even while Elizabeth Russell started to bend under the sheer weight of his onslaught, she was able to read his memories, thoughts and fears. He was a Gaul, born in the city of Agedincum and at sixteen he had joined the Roman army and come to Britain, where he quickly came under the sway of Krowos. The creature had immediately spotted the boy's psychic strength and offered enhanced power for his loyalty. And his first major task for the god was to ensure the destruction of the Druids...

Sweat was now pouring down Elizabeth Russell's face as she struggled to fend off the stronger man. Yes, she was sure of that now. Psychically, he was older and stronger than she. This was a fight that she couldn't win! His power was oppressive and she was buckling under him, but would his past be the key to her future? Why had Krowos been so keen to see the Druids destroyed? They had left him to his own devices and hadn't even begrudged his human sacrifices. The fact was, Krowos feared the Druids, because they knew how to kill him. Their magic could undo his power – which meant that the symbol on her right knuckle that had caused so much damage to Mexican Dave was the Celtic triquetra. But although these thoughts took only seconds to go through her mind, it was too late for her to win the psychic battle. The Man almost had her pinned and now he was trying to absorb her soul as his voice sounded within her,

"Mors vincit omnia!"

Death conquers all.

"Yes!" she said out loud and then she did something The Man had never seen before. She closed the psychic connection between them. Suddenly, he was fighting nothing! How could she do that? It was impossible! Once two wills were engaged, it was a battle until the total victory of one and the annihilation of the other.

Elizabeth Russell laughed. It was a full belly laugh that echoed around the big, empty room.

"Two thousand years old and you've never learned how to break a spirit link?" she asked, wiping the sweat off her forehead with her sleeve,

"Maybe you should've got out more? Learned from someone other than Krowos. It's got rather limited knowledge."

The Man hated her mocking tone and gathered his anger to kill her. This time, Elizabeth Russell didn't wait around, but was across the space between them before he could even blink and delivering a vicious right hook into his injured flank. The power of the blow winded him and left him doubled over, but she pressed home her attack and he cried out as the steel toecap of her right shoe smashed into his left kneecap. He started to drop, but an uppercut into the wound in his side stopped him falling, with the impact snapping a couple of his ribs. With a groan, he phased across the room to get away from this strong magic that was hurting him to the core. Elizabeth Russell phased across the space and as she materialised, the right hook into his flank landed with a hideous crack.

Now the wound where Vicky had stabbed The Man had fully opened up again and was bleeding freely. He limped backwards away from the bitch – he had to get away from her, had to get back to Krowos, had to heal... The Man disappeared and was almost instantaneously on the first-floor landing of the concrete stairwell. It was dimly lit by a single security light and, had Elizabeth Russell seen the sly look on his heavily lined face, she wouldn't have been so quick to phase after him. As she appeared in the stairwell, she was enwrapped by his strong arms, which simultaneously lifted her off the ground and squeezed the breath out of her. She was caught with her arms pinned to her sides and unable, because of his big belly, to kick or knee him anywhere. Now he was looking into her face with a disturbing leer and, as she dragged in a strained breath, the stench of sulphurous eggs from his mouth almost made her gag.

"Sic desinit," and his grin widened as he watched her leaning back and the muscles of her neck straining in agony.

"Yes, so it ends," Elizabeth Russell gasped, and her eyes fixed him with a stare as cold as death.

All her strength went into the headbutt and The Man's nose exploded under the blow, spraying blood in a wide arc across the unpainted walls of the stairwell. He loosed his grip as he stumbled back, blinded by pain and the blood in his eyes. He couldn't see Elizabeth Russell leap high into the air to bring her forehead down on his face again with even more force. The second hit shattered the bones across the front of his face, caving it in as the power of the Celtic triquetra etched into the bone of Elizabeth Russell's forehead exponentially increased the deadly force of the blow. And now he was falling backwards to strike the concrete floor with a muffled slap. Everything was blurred and he couldn't think. There was too much pain. And it wasn't simply physical, she had struck to the essence of his being. The bitch had Druidic magic. Where did she...? He grunted with pain as she jumped down onto him, lying on the bare concrete, and punched him on the stab wound again. The agony! And now she was in a frenzy, ripping apart his coat and shirt, then hitting him again and again on the unprotected stab wound, and he couldn't defend himself as the welter of blows struck home. Her fist slammed into him again but this time, she didn't withdraw it and his chest was overwhelmed with agony as she pushed deeper and deeper into him. And then there was such a sharp pain that it made his eyes flash open very wide, and she was pulling and tearing inside him. His last view was of the sweating face of the young woman with white hair, her violet eyes sparkling in triumph... and of the heart, torn from his chest held before his eyes.

Elizabeth Russell was sure The Man was still conscious as she jammed his heart into his mouth. Kneeling over him, she watched carefully as life left his body. Her chest was heaving and she was soaked with sweat from the exertion. She leant back, looking to the ceiling with a prayer of thanks to the powers of light on her lips. As she slowly got off The Man's corpse, a thought struck her,

"Oliver!" she gasped and immediately ran back to the big room where her protégé lay on the floor.

She bent down and laid her hand on his head, speaking words of healing. As Oliver started to come round, she contacted Jo,

"Jo, it's me. I've eliminated the three men. Oliver's been through the ringer and has had a knock on the head. Could you come over and look after him?"

"Of course," Jo replied, "And the axe?"

"Bring it, please."

"Will do."

Oliver moaned and put his hands to his head as he struggled to a sitting position. He looked at Elizabeth Russell,

"Sorry. He jumped me."

"I'm just glad you're alive," she said, examining his features. His hair was now as white as hers.

"He opened doors in my mind that I never even knew were there," Oliver said weakly, "Then he showed me... he showed me..." and he faltered, sobbing at the insanity of what he'd seen.

"I know," she replied, "The ultimate truth at the heart of the universe... the terrifying reality of pure good and pure evil... the screaming chaos of existence... yada, yada, yada..."

Oliver looked up at her,

"You... you've seen it?"

"Of course I've seen it – how do you think I got this?" and she pointed at her hair.

"But... but... how do you cope with the knowledge?"

"It is what it is," she shrugged.

"But what's the point if none of this makes any difference?" Oliver said, his hollow eyes staring into the chaotic abyss once more.

"The point is... you have choices. You can choose the life you want to lead – in the light or in the dark. Ultimately, life only has the meaning you give it and the most important standards you can meet are your own."

Oliver still looked a bit shellshocked.

"Listen, this was going to happen to you anyway,"

"It was?" he asked.

"Yeah, as part of your training, I would have shown you The Truth in controlled conditions. And maybe you'd have walked away from it with that lovely dark hair you used to have."

"Wow. I did not know that."

"None of our trainees do..." she said and then waved away whatever Oliver was about to say, so she could continue,

"But the great thing for you is that you've experienced this in the field. A truly evil man has tried to turn you insane during a life-or-death struggle and you've come through it – unless you've gone insane... have you gone insane? Who's the Prime Minister?"

"Who cares?" Oliver said irritably.

"See? You're fine," she said and patted his cheek, "And this will make you so much stronger. To get through a moment like that in the field is very impressive. Now, come on, it's best to walk it off," and she heaved Oliver up,

"And here's Jo, bang on time."

Jo puffed into the room, holding the axe with both hands,

"All these bloody stairs! Oh shit – Oliver's seen The Truth."

"Yes, and I need you to talk him down and keep him moving, while I go and destroy the fucker in the building across the road..." then a thought struck her,

"And while I'm doing that, I've got to somehow keep those idiot cops and the sacrificial child safe. Bloody hell – what a clusterfuck!" Elizabeth Russell complained, taking the axe from Jo's hand before marching purposefully across the empty office.

Chapter Thirty-Nine

The Temple Of Krowos

It was the smell that brought Chloe back to consciousness. The stench was unlike anything she'd ever experienced and, as her eyes opened, she fought the urge to vomit. What was this? There seemed to be a big rubber ball in her mouth, held in place by straps that ran around to the back of her head. It was forcing her to breathe through her nose and that was hard enough even without the appalling smell. She was lying on a white tiled floor with her hands tied behind her back in a large, circular room lit by flaming torches. Where was she? Vicky! Where was Vicky? The last thing she remembered seeing was The Man attacking her. Chloe had a terrible feeling in the pit of her stomach. Vicky was gone and now she was in the place where the thing from the darkness lived...

Krowos.

The word formed in her mind and she realised with terror that she was not alone in the room. Her bulging eyes were drawn to the circular hole in the middle of the floor. The pit that seemed to absorb light.

I am here, child.

Again, the words formed in her mind. Chloe concentrated to throw whatever was forming the words out of her head, but was met with a deep chuckle,

You cannot stop me. Even now, when I'm at rest, your powers are no match for me.

Chloe struggled into a standing position and tried to move, but was chained to the block of stone behind her.

Welcome to your new home. Soon we will be properly introduced. And then...

Chloe's eyes widened, filled with terror as the voice described the intimate details of what it would do to her and how it would keep her there forever, feeding off her and torturing her. She tried to close off her mind, but it was impossible. She wanted to die. Why couldn't she just die?

Because I won't let you. Not for a very, very long time.

***

Once Ray and Emma saw Mexican Dave and the Fucking Nutter leave the back of the Global Actuaries Limited building, they got ready to run over to the back door. They had arrived about ten minutes earlier and hidden themselves behind two huge pots containing tree ferns on either side of the entrance to a nearby building. Once they saw that both men were out of sight, they made their break for it, running fast and low across the delivery area. When they got to the door, Ray used his lock picking tools to open it and they were in. Both of them had their Glocks drawn and Emma closed the door gently behind them.

"Where now?" she whispered, looking around the loading area with the large lift, a set of doors with stairs beyond them going up and a set of doors with glass panels through which they could see the stairs heading down. They hardly noticed the open service window set into the wall on their left with the unlit room behind it. Ray said nothing, but indicated that they should go up. That was where Simon Montague was most likely to be. When Ray got one on one with him, he'd make that stuck up bastard wish he'd never been born for kidnapping Chloe. As Ray began quietly opening the doors to the upper stairs, there was the unmistakable, loud crack of a taser being fired, instantly followed by the sharp pain of the probes embedding themselves in his leg, and then the fizzle of the electricity as it took his body in its fist.

Ray fell forwards and his gun clattered to the floor. As he looked back, he could see Emma standing looking surprised. A big man in a blue football shirt was leaning through the service window behind him holding the taser. Why didn't she...

"Put the taser down now!" Emma said quietly as she moved forward to point her gun at the chest of the big man.

He dropped the taser and put his arms above his head.

"You all right?" she said to Ray.

"No. Fuck, that's painful!" and Ray knew there was more pain to come. While Emma indicated for the big man to leave the booth, Ray pulled the probes out of his leg. Each sharp flash of pain made him wince, and he swore quietly as he picked up his Glock. He got up on slightly shaky legs and wiped his head with a handkerchief, then turned to face the man.

"What happened to your arm?" the question was out of his mouth before he had a chance to stop himself.

"Accident," Tommy replied.

"Is that cab outside yours?" Ray asked, mastering himself.

"Yeah."

"Give me the keys,"

"Why?"

Ray pushed the tip of his gun into Tommy's fat cheek,

"Because if you don't, I'll blow your fucking head off."

"In my right front pocket," Tommy said, apparently unperturbed by the gun pressed into his flesh.

Emma reached in and got the keys, then handed them to Ray.

"What do we do now?" she asked, "We can't cuff him."

Ray looked at the stump of the man's left arm. That was tricky. Maybe he could be of some use to them?

"What's your name?"

"Fuck off," the man replied.

The instant smack of the butt of Ray's gun into his mouth caused him to cry out and stumble back. Ray's outstretched foot sent the big man crashing to the floor. Before he could even put his hand to his bleeding mouth, Ray was on top of him and forcing the barrel of the pistol between the bloody, broken teeth,

"Listen you fat fuck, tell me what I want to know, or I will kill you right now. What is your name?" and he took the gun out of his mouth and rested the barrel just under the man's left eye.

"Tommy,"

"Do you know who Simon Montague is?"

Tommy nodded.

"Where is he?"

"Down... downstairs."

"In the basement?"

"In the temple."

"I knew it," Ray said, looking up at Emma, "I knew that 'archaeological site' stuff was bollocks. They've been using the old temple for satanic rituals."

"No..."

Ray flashed Tommy a vicious look.

"No, it's not that temple. There's another one... deeper underground."

"You know where it is?"

Tommy nodded.

"Take us there but remember one thing – if you try anything... anything at all, I'll kill you. My daughter's down there and I will kill anyone who gets between me and her. Got it?"

Tommy nodded again.

"Right, let's go."

Tommy led them down to sub-basement C.

"How do we get in?" Ray asked.

"The fob's on the keyring," Tommy replied. His mouth was throbbing and every word was painful.

Ray pulled out the car keys, selected a black fob and placed it on the pad. The door clicked and Ray opened it, indicating for Tommy to go first.

As he walked into the oppressively hot, spa-like corridor, Tommy tried to think about what he could do to warn the others.

Ray and Emma were using their tactical training to silently communicate and, as Ray pushed Tommy's face to the wall, Emma sidled up to the entrance of the changing area.

"Move and you're dead," Ray whispered into Tommy's ear, then crept over to join Emma. Ray used his fingers to count down: three, two... one!

They darted into the room, guns pointing forward, but the large, empty space stared blankly back at them. Ray indicated the showers and Emma gave them a quick check. She gave him a thumbs up and they left the room.

Ray put his gun into the back of Tommy, who was still facing the wall,

"Lead the way."

The three of them went down the corridor with its deep terracotta walls until they reached the door at the end.

Ray tried the fob on the scanner by the door, but nothing happened. He looked sternly at Tommy,

"Sorry, it needs my fingerprint," he said quietly and placed his hand on the scanner. The door opened and Ray prodded Tommy to go inside. Now they were in the red room and, as Ray looked around at the depictions of depravity on the walls, he felt a deep pang of guilt. How could he have allowed his daughter to end up in a place like this? Why didn't he get his family out when he had the chance? He knew that, whatever the outcome of the next few minutes, he would be tormented by those questions for the rest of his life. He tried to clear his thoughts and focus on what was ahead. He glanced across to Emma for reassurance and, though she looked very tense, the nod she gave him buoyed his courage. He pushed Tommy towards the nail-studded wooden door. Destiny lay beyond it.

"Open it and go through," he whispered to Tommy, whose hand went to the iron loop and twisted it to open the door. All three of them were sickened by the stench of rotting flesh that burst out of the door, but the time for stealth was over, now came action.

As soon as the door was opened, Ray kicked Tommy forward and because his big belly caused him to lose balance, he sprawled onto the white tiled floor. Ray was in the room half a second later, pointing his gun at the still figures dressed in white robes who were standing around the edge of the huge room. The low-level, flickering light from the torches hung around the walls, made it harder to see, but the white robes on the dark background made them easy targets.

"Armed Police! I need all of you to get down on the ground now!"

The sound of someone trying to call to him through a gag drew his attention and his breath caught as he saw Chloe standing on the far side of the room, chained to some sort of monolith.

"Chloe!" Ray cried with a terrible, hollow feeling in the pit of his stomach.

She could only reply with a grunt, muffled by the ball gag strapped in her mouth as she struggled against the chain with her hands behind her back.

"She is unharmed... for now..."

Ray turned and pointed his gun at Simon Montague, who was carefully walking towards him across the room.

"Stop!" Ray commanded.

"Whether she remains that way really is up to you," Montague continued and Ray felt rage and hatred boiling up inside him at the sound of that entitled, smug voice.

"I am an armed police officer. Stop or I shoot!" Ray shouted, taking aim at the chest of the approaching man.

"I don't think you will," Montague smiled, "I don't think Chloe would want to see..."

The five gunshots in the enclosed space were deafening and Ray's ears were ringing as he realised that Simon Montague was still walking towards him unscathed. Ray panicked and raised his gun again,

"Please don't..." Montague began, putting up a hand for calm, but again the room was filled with the sound of another five shots. Montague stopped and put a finger to his ear and opened his mouth wide as if he were trying to equalize air pressure in his ear.

"Please stop making that awful racket, can't you see your gun's no good?" Montague said.

Ray raised his gun again, but stopped. The cold muzzle of a gun at the base of his skull told him to stop.

"Drop it!"

"Emma?"

"Drop-it!" Emma repeated and Ray complied. He was shoved in the back towards the monolith opposite the one where Chloe was struggling.

"What are you doing?" Ray couldn't understand.

"I'm doing what needs to be done," she replied, "Stop! Turn towards me with your hands behind your back."

Ray did so and Tommy and two of the figures in white came forward and used cable tie handcuffs to tie him to the chain fixed into the top of the stone monolith. Tommy retreated, giving Ray a foul look.

"Emma...?" Ray was bewildered.

"Sorry about the blanks in your gun, but I know what your temper's like... I had to do this, Ray. It's the only way we're going to be together. You know, I've always loved you..." she said, coming close to him,

"Then why are you doing this?" Ray said aggressively as he struggled against the cable ties.

"I loved you from the moment I saw you just over a year ago, but I knew you couldn't love me because..." and she looked towards where Chloe was standing,

"But then The Man saw you... you know which man I mean,"

Ray visualised him in his dirty raincoat,

"He saw you and he also wanted you – for very different reasons to me, thank God. He could tell how I felt about you – he's gifted like that – and he came to me about six months ago with an offer. I could have you if I gave myself to Krowos and convinced you to give yourself to him as well. I said yes without hesitation."

Krowos! So, Elizabeth Russell had been telling Ray the truth. This was a cult and Emma was one of them. Looking at her now, she seemed a bit unhinged. She was full of restless energy and couldn't stop pacing up and down. As she spoke, Ray became calmer and focussed. He still had a chance to get out of this if only he could get her gun. Unseen by anyone else, his hand reached for one of the push daggers clipped to the back of his belt.

"And now we're so close, Ray," Emma said, looking at him with longing,

"You have a very simple choice. Give yourself to Krowos and Chloe will be safe. Give yourself to Krowos and we can be together forever. He has the power to make that happen. And all we have to do is be loyal to him."

"And sacrifice innocent people," Ray said bitterly.

"No one is innocent," Emma replied, "And anyway, when you've been touched by Krowos, you will see that those we sacrifice are nothing. Just wasted DNA."

Yes, when he was touched by Krowos, Ray wouldn't even care when the god consumed his daughter. And he would consume her. That had always been part of the bargain Emma had made. She wanted no traces of Ray's old life to spoil her bliss, and Krowos needed the child's precious psychic energy. It was a win-win.

"And what if I say no?" Ray asked, hoping to buy time as he started cutting through the cable tie with the blade of the push dagger.

"Then Chloe will die. You don't want to die, do you, Chloe?"

Emma rushed over to the girl, who was moaning in discomfort and fear.

"Look - she's terrified!" Emma pointed at her and then walked back to Ray, "I hate to see her like this as much as you do. You can stop all this with just one word."

"But Vicky..." Ray began.

"Don't pretend you cared about her!" Emma screamed, and then she looked across at Chloe,

"You know where your father was yesterday afternoon?"

"Please, no..." Ray said, looking in shame at the ground.

"He was with me and I was fucking him. All afternoon."

Ray glanced at Chloe and in that moment, he knew he had lost everything. The 'say it ain't so' look, which he couldn't allay, broke his heart. Ray bowed his head and cursed his stupidity and weakness.

Emma walked towards Chloe,

"Where was his love for your mother when he was so greedily gobbling my pussy?" Emma was revelling in the destruction of the relationship between father and daughter,

"Where was his love for your mother when he was emptying his balls into my mouth?" yes, that hurt! The child looked disgusted and bewildered.

Emma turned away from the doomed child and walked back towards the man she loved. Yes, he looked broken and humiliated now, but once he'd been touched by Krowos, he would forget all this. This moment when the great Ray Ennis stood humiliated before her would be a memory she would always carry. And any time she might have doubts about his love for her, or worry that he really had loved his wife, she could picture this moment as a reminder of her power over him. Emma approached him, ran her fingers gently down his cheek, then kissed him viciously. She looked back at the broken child,

"See? He loves me."

The slight turn of her head gave Ray the perfect target as he punched forward with the push dagger between the knuckles of his free right hand. The blade sank into Emma's carotid triangle, just under the line of her jaw and he twisted the blade. She made an "Uuh!" sound as he pulled out the blade and blood fountained from her severed carotid artery. Her left hand went up to put pressure on the wound, but it was no good. People were screaming and she could see the blood spraying onto the white floor, then she began to totter as the room spun around her. She wanted to raise the gun and shoot the brat, but strong hands wrenched it from her and she fell backwards to the hard floor.

Ray snatched Emma's Glock from her hand, praying that she had real bullets in it. Montague ran towards him to get the gun and Ray shot him in the face at three feet. The force threw him backwards and Ray was on to his next target. Tommy's broad back was an easy mark as he hefted his way towards the door. The first shot tore into his left lung, the second went through his back and lodged in his liver and the third shattered two vertebrae in his mid-spine. He collapsed ten feet from the door and lay there bleeding out. Ray turned and saw an older woman was going for Chloe with a knife. His shot hit her in the hip and she went down screaming in pain. He turned back towards the door, where a girl who looked like the singer Shiny Starrr was opening it. The shot caught the tip of her shoulder and she cried out, but slipped through the door. Ray looked this way and that for his next target – there! The middle-aged man running from one monolith to another took two shots to bring down. Behind one of the monoliths, The Captain had been counting the shots. Ennis was only eight down, which meant he had another nine in his clip. This was not a good position. Two more shots and a woman's scream told him that Tiger Lil was down. Silence descended and The Captain tried to make his breathing as quiet as possible as he listened hard to what was going on.

Someone was moving across the room,

"Chloe, are you all right?" it was the cop.

The child began sobbing.

"Let me get you out of this..."

A pause.

"There! You okay?"

"Vicky's dead," the girl was stating a fact.

"I'm so sorry..." he said, then there was the sound of something being cut.

"Run to the door and wait for me," he said, followed by the sound of a child's running feet. What was going on? The Captain didn't dare look. A woman groaned. Plane Jane – she'd only been winged in the hip. The Captain listened as careful footsteps crossed the room to where the woman was groaning. When it came, the gunshot seemed inevitable. Now there was silence. The Captain wished he had any kind of weapon, but there was nothing.

Ray watched Chloe run over to the door and wait there, then he looked around at the destruction he had wrought. And there lay Emma in a widening pool of blood that was running towards the hole in the middle of the room. Her breath was fluttering and she must be near to death. Ray was overcome with a cold rage and walked over to her and knelt with a knee on either side of her chest, so that he could watch the last of her life drain out of her. She turned her head to look towards the hole in the floor, but he turned her head back and forced her to look at him. She was the biggest mistake he'd ever made. Maybe seeing her die would lessen the anguish he felt that Vicky had paid for that mistake. His eyes locked on hers. Yes, everything must be going dim now...

The Captain risked a look from his hiding place. Ennis was kneeling over the woman cop and was totally focussed on her. If The Captain was quick and quiet, he could just get to him before Ennis could react. He darted forward with a sniper's speed and stealth, but before he was halfway, he was facing the soulless muzzle of the Glock pointing straight at him. The first shot hit him full in the chest, the second in the belly and the third in the shoulder. The Captain's momentum skidded him off to the right and he lay still. Now Ray turned back to Emma,

"I hope that hurts, you bitch."

But as she started to sink into oblivion, Emma's face twisted into a smile of triumph,

"Krowos, take this blood and come to us!" she choked, then her eyes glazed and she was dead.

Chapter Forty

God Of This Earth

Ray knelt above Emma for a few seconds more, looking down at the woman who had played so brilliantly on his weaknesses. She had destroyed his life... but as he looked at her with contempt, he kept some for himself, because deep down he knew that most of the responsibility lay with him. He couldn't take the thought, which was accompanied by the image of Vicky strung up from the light flex.

"Come on," Chloe shouted from the door. She knew that Krowos would come when Emma's blood ran into the pit. She knew, because Krowos had told her while she'd been chained to the post. He had told her how they would summon him and all the things he wanted to do to her. She didn't want any of that to happen.

Why wasn't Ray moving? Chloe screamed,

"Ray!" and when he turned to look at her, she ran out of the room, hoping that the sight of her leaving would make him follow. She was across the red room in a heartbeat and wrenching open the door to the corridor beyond. She sprinted down it to the door at the end and was opening it when Ray came haring out of the red room.

Then the entire building shook.

"Run!" Chloe shouted, her eyes wide with fear as she ran up the concrete stairs. Ray soon caught her up and, as they ran, a mind-splitting howl came from somewhere below. They put on more speed, finally bursting through the double doors into the service area by the back door. Ray had the key to the taxi in his hand, unlocking it as they crashed out through the back door of the building into the bruised, shadowy gloom of late dusk.

Chloe dived into the back and Ray got into the driver's seat, quickly scanning the controls,

"Where the fuck's the starter?"

Why did every electric vehicle have to have its own special way of doing things?

"There! Look!" Chloe squealed, pointing at a knob on the central console next to the gear stick.

"Got it!"

Ray looked at it, hoped it was like the other electric car he'd driven and pressed the brake pedal, then turned the knob.

"Thank fuck!" Ray cried, as the cab switched on and he put it into 'drive' to sweep around the side of the building and up towards the glittering lights of Cannon Street.

"Seatbelt on!" he shouted as they went. He slowed at the end of the narrow side street and was about to turn right when he saw Elizabeth Russell running towards them through the gloom with an axe in her hand,

"Left! Fucking go left!" she screamed, pointing west down Cannon Street. Ray turned the cab left and put the pedal to the floor. He wasn't about to argue with a woman who was covered in blood and wielding an axe. The cab lurched forward and accelerated with a 'zwing' noise as Ray drove straight towards the distant dome of St Paul's Cathedral and the bright lights of Westminster.

Elizabeth Russell ran to the corner of Global Actuaries and flattened herself against the wall, speaking low and fast in an ancient language. She could feel Krowos coming and she didn't want him to be able to see her, so her spell would shield her from his vision. And then she heard it. The manic, thumping of multiple tendrils as the creature galloped up from its pit. A wave of hot, foetid air crashed into the street like the shockwave of an avalanche breaking down a mountain, and then Krowos was there. It emerged from the side street, barely a yard away from her and she couldn't help but feel a shiver of fear flash through her. Krowos loomed ten feet above her, raising itself on its rear tendrils and turning its bulbous, baby-like face first to the right and then to the left, sniffing at the air. Elizabeth Russell stood motionless as it started to move to follow Ray, but stopped. It turned its eyeless face directly at her, sniffing. She didn't dare breathe. Her hands gripped the shaft of the axe firmly, ready to defend herself. It sniffed... sniffed again, then turned away and careered down Cannon Street after the black cab. Once its twenty-foot maggoty body was past her, the umbilical cord started spooling out down the street as the thing gained pace in its pursuit of the cab.

Suddenly, she realized she had a major problem. In her original plan, Krowos was due to be stuck in Finsbury Circus Gardens, held there by her psychics. She had envisioned herself hacking away at the stationary three-foot-thick cord until she was through it. But right now, with it moving past her at speed, there was no way she'd be able to strike two blows in the same place. The only way her plan could work was if the thing was standing still, and right now it was running towards the city of Westminster at about thirty miles an hour!

"Shit!"

Maybe if she struck one heavy blow, it would stop and then come back at her and she could keep hacking at the same spot?

It was worth a try...

In the cab, Chloe started screaming when she saw Krowos emerge onto Cannon Street. This wasn't a dream. It was real! It was *real*! IT WAS REAL AND IT WAS COMING FOR HER!

Chloe's screams made Ray look in the rear-view but all he could see was the empty street behind them.

"It's all right," he said, slowing the cab as he half-turned back to Chloe, saying,

"There's nothing there. We're all right. We're safe now."

Chloe looked in terror at the obscenity flailing after them,

"Don't slow down!" she screamed – Krowos was gaining fast.

"But there's nothing there," Ray said in a calming tone.

Chloe could see Krowos catching up with them. What could she do? What could she...

Chloe's face distorted with anger and her eyes flashed lightning blue as she screamed in a voice that pierced Ray's marrow,

"See it!"

And, in that moment, Ray's world collapsed. He saw Krowos under the streetlamps... saw the great, eyeless baby head with its wide mouth full of teeth, saw the maggot's body, propelled forward by fat tendrils, and saw the grotesque umbilical cord trailing behind. It couldn't be! It was all wrong! It was a nightmare made flesh! This wasn't like discovering that aliens existed. That was possible. But this... this was impossible. Involuntarily, Ray's foot hit the accelerator. This was a thing of evil, a creature from some place beyond the universe. It didn't fit into the laws of nature. In fact, it shattered them. What could he trust? Nothing! Nothing was as it seemed. Ray's eyes bulged as he stared into the rear-view at the thing chasing them down. And the darkness surrounding it... it wasn't the natural darkness of the night. From this darkness, he could hear screaming from the abyss. Why could he hear the screaming? WHAT WAS THAT THING?

"Look out!" Chloe yelled and Ray looked away from the rear-view too late to avoid clipping the lamppost. They veered across the road, he tried to correct, overcooked it and the cab flipped. There was a split second when the only things keeping them in their seats were their seatbelts, then there was a crunch, another moment of weightlessness, then the crumple and screech of metal as the car skidded along on its side until it came to a halt. "Oh shit!" Ray gasped. He felt like his lungs had been displaced to the left.

"Chloe?"

A low moan told him that at least she was alive, then he suddenly became horribly aware of a heavy, erratic thumping sound. A look in the cracked rear-view showed Krowos galloping towards them. The abomination was coming for them and they were trapped sideways in the fucking cab! Ray swore as he undid his seatbelt and fell downwards towards the passenger door, which was crushed against the asphalt.

And then, horribly, the erratic thumping stopped.

"Krowos is here!" Chloe whimpered.

Tendrils smashed through the window of the driver's door, showering Ray with broken glass and there was the painful sound of tearing metal as the tendrils tore the door off. Then the great, baby face came down to the door. Without eyes it couldn't see them, but it could smell and feel and taste them. Their terror was delicious! Tendrils slipped into the cab and grasped Ray around the waist. He screamed, trying to cling on to anything as he was dragged from the cab, but even as he held onto the lip of the doorframe, he knew it was over. He was ripped away from the cab and held up in front of that face which had haunted the nightmares of Londoners for two thousand years. Tendrils held his arms out to the sides and wrapped around his torso, but his legs were free to kick. The thing opened its mouth and released a multi note cry that was simultaneously a high-pitched squeal, a mid-range bellow and a low-range tone that seemed to vibrate the organs in Ray's body. He added to the tumult with a scream of his own as the pain of that awful sound threatened to tear his soul apart. And then the wide mouth opened and Ray realised he was being lowered towards it. He was kicking his feet and trying to pull away from the stinking jaws of the creature, but it was no use. He screamed as he was lowered down... down... down... snap!

Elizabeth Russell watched impotently as Krowos chased after the cab. As it went, its slimy umbilical cord slithered out after it. She'd have to just start hacking and hope for the best. She raised the axe, but stopped. The distant crash of the cab flipping over drew her attention.

"Fuck me!" she gasped. How the fuck had he managed to crash the car on an empty street? She'd specifically had all traffic diverted around the area to avoid just that sort of problem, and yet he'd managed it. But this might work in their favour. Once Krowos got to them, the cord would stop moving and then she could start chopping. She centred herself and prepared to say the words of power. Still the cord slipped past her until finally Krowos got to the wrecked car and the cord stopped moving. Right! It was now or never! Elizabeth Russell spoke the words of the spell that would finally send Krowos back to its own dimension and then, with all the force of her being, she brought the axe down on the cord.

As she'd spoken the words of power, the silver writing etched on the cheeks of the axe had lit up with the flames of the sacred fire and, as the blade met Krowos' slimy flesh, it sliced deep, hissing like a hot iron in cold water. The putrid, grey ooze that filled the umbilical cord sprayed out, covering Elizabeth Russell from head to foot. She spat and gagged, wiped the stuff from her eyes and swung again. Three hundred yards away down Cannon Street, Krowos roared in agony, but in that moment, what chilled Elizabeth Russell was the simultaneous screech that came from deep below Global Actuaries. Down the street, Krowos threw Ray aside as it turned to face the new danger. Ray, who had lost consciousness when both his legs were bitten off above the knees, rolled across the road. The paramedics from the ambulance that had parked in the pedestrianised area at the end of Queen Street never saw Krowos. All they saw was a man raised up into the air, then thrown across the road. They ran straight to him and began emergency care.

Krowos reared up and began running back towards Elizabeth Russell. This had always been the bit she'd dreaded, because now it was a simple race between her and the creature. As she swept the blade down again and again onto the first cut, she was glad to see that the axe was cutting through the stinking flesh fairly easily. Now she was in a frenzy, hacking and swearing, not daring to waste time looking up at the monster running towards her. The sight would not have helped her. Darkness was spreading from Krowos as it bounded towards her with its slimy, flailing limbs. Its wide mouth was snarling and its fat, maggot's body undulated sickeningly. As she put all of her physical and psychic strength into every blow, Elizabeth Russell hoped that Krowos wouldn't have the sense to stop and yank the injured length of umbilical cord away from her. Fortunately, wounded animals don't tend to be very rational, and in the mayhem of the moment, Krowos wasn't thinking about anything other than killing whatever was attacking it. But it couldn't perceive anything there! How could this be happening? And then, suddenly, it could smell and sense the woman chopping away at its cord with an axe. Her spell had dissipated as she used all her psychic energy on cutting the cord. Now Krowos had a target, it could attack! Krowos let out a shriek that was so unearthly, it caused Jo and Oliver, watching from the building across the street, to be instantly sick.

Krowos launched itself at the woman, its tendrils outstretched to tear her apart, when the axe struck through the umbilical cord and hit the pavement beneath with a metallic crack and a shower of sparks. Elizabeth Russell turned, axe in hand, ready to defend herself from the huge creature, but as soon as the cord was cut, its power was gone. As Krowos flew through the air it became smaller and smaller. When it hit the pavement with a splatter, it was barely a foot long. Elizabeth Russell shouldered the axe and walked over to the still shrivelling 'god' that had caused nothing but chaos in the world where it didn't belong. Now it was only about six inches long - an insignificant, stinking, ugly little creature writhing on the ground. It turned its sightless face up to her and made a high-pitched wailing sound.

"No!" Elizabeth Russell said firmly,

"You're not immortal and you're not a god. You're just a malevolent little scumbag intruding in the wrong fucking dimension. You know what death looks like? The sole of my shoe," and she very deliberately placed her left foot on top of its head and crushed it with her full weight. As it let out a nauseating squeal she could feel the head giving, giving, the tiny baby face distending, the squeal rising in pitch, then pop! A burst of yellow pus exploded across the pavement.

Chapter Forty-One

The Unfamiliar Shore

Elizabeth Russell sighed. That was that, or was it?

"Ray..." she said, dropping the axe so that she could phase to where the upended cab lay.

She appeared at the scene and saw the two paramedics desperately trying to save Ray's life, but he was teetering on the brink after a catastrophic loss of blood. Elizabeth Russell looked at the broken man. Should she save him, or was it a greater act of mercy to let him go? Then she thought of the child and her decision was made.

"Go to the child in the taxi!" she commanded in a voice that could not be resisted and the two paramedics picked up their equipment and ran to the cab.

"I need your strength. Channel through me!" she said, connecting to Jo and Oliver and a moment later, she felt her body charge with energy as if she'd downed a pint of espresso.

Elizabeth Russell stood above Ray and she spoke the words of three different spells to save his life. Ray's eyes briefly fluttered open and he saw an angel hovering above him, its violet eyes radiating power and a silver halo crackling with spiritual energy around its white-haired head. Then, thankfully, healing oblivion took him.

Ten minutes later, Elizabeth Russell watched as Ray and Chloe were loaded into the back of the ambulance. He was unconscious on a stretcher and she was looking tiny and cold, wrapped in a silver shock blanket. But even in a traumatised state after enduring the unthinkable, Chloe radiated a golden light. No wonder Krowos had wanted her. She was special. To a creature that fed on psychic energy, she'd have been like an all you could eat buffet. It would have kept going back for more again and again until it had finally drained her of everything. If it had shown self restraint, it could have made her last for years. Elizabeth Russell literally shuddered at the thought of how close that poor girl had come to plunging into a living hell. Thankfully, they'd averted that, but what now? Of course, the Department of The Regulator would see that they had the best possible physical, emotional and spiritual care, but Elizabeth Russell was worried for their future. Ray was of particular concern. She could tell that he had seen Krowos and, given his fixed views on the world, she knew there was a chance he might have permanently lost his mind. And Chloe? Kids were resilient, but sometimes shocks like she'd experienced could send them down unpleasant paths. Elizabeth Russell would have to keep a very close eye on her. She wondered where the mother was, little realising that she'd find out later that night. Part of her wanted to blame Ray. Had he followed her advice, his daughter wouldn't have gone through hell and he'd have his legs and his sanity. Stubborn pride could be a very dangerous thing... but she couldn't totally blame him. If there was blame to be laid at anyone's door it was hers. She could have forced him to leave London. She could have been quicker to unravel the truth about Krowos. Hell, she could have noticed that the fucker had been commanding a cult in London any time over the last three hundred years... yes, the buck definitely stopped with her. She looked at the father and daughter tucked into the back of the ambulance. They were flotsam washing up on an unfamiliar shore after a violent storm and there was no guarantee that they wouldn't be dragged back into the sea with the next wave and lost forever in the ocean's vastness.

The doors closed and the ambulance pulled away. Elizabeth Russell stood with her hands on her hips in the empty street under the eerie streetlights, watching the ambulance depart. Her scarlet suit was torn and covered with stains of blood and the putrid grey gunk that had sprayed out of Krowos' umbilical cord. Her face was a mess of gore, and thick gobbets of grey ooze clung in her hair.

"All right, Bess?" Jo puffed, as she and Oliver arrived. They had hurried the three hundred yards to catch up with her and Jo was already sweating.

"Fine," she said, smiling, "Although I think I need to shower and change before they'll let me in the pub. Come on, drinks are on me..."

***

By the time Andy Harper and Elizabeth Russell were ensconced at The Counting House on Cornhill, the golden September afternoon was giving way to evening. When they finished their pints of ESB, shadows would be darkening and seeping out into spaces from which the daylight had banished them.

"Halfway!" Andy said, raising his glass to toast the mid-point of their pub crawl. Elizabeth Russell clinked his glass and took a long draw on her pint. Oh yeah, that hit the spot.

"Nice to finally get a pint of ESB," she said, "I mean, The George and the Hoop and Grapes are great pubs, but..."

"ESB," Andy smiled. He looked at her beautiful face and into those dreamy, violet eyes and wondered for the nth time why he was so lucky to be with her. She smiled back at him and he felt a warmth in his chest. It was the smile she reserved for the man who had won her heart. They held each other's hands, relaxed, happy and sipping at a liquid wonder of the world.

She had been at Andy's side throughout his two-month convalescence and had helped his mental recovery even more than his physical one. When he'd found out what had happened to Vicky, Ray and Chloe, he'd been shattered, but Bess had been there for him. Having her made all the difference. Everything was so easy with her. She was his instant best mate. She was funny, clever, independent and really seemed to care about him. Why a girl like her would want a battered ageing git like him was unfathomable, but he was rolling with it. It was like the best dream he'd ever had, but it was real. No point in wrecking it by over-thinking it. Even his recovery had been straightforward, and now he was pretty much back to full strength. That certainly made Bess happy. She was a powerful personality, but she clearly liked a man who could make her feel protected. Maybe that was why she was attracted to a lummox like him? And yet... there was much more to her than met the eye. He'd always felt that was the case, but when he first saw all her tattoos... that was when he'd known that her life was a vast, undiscovered country and that it would take time, effort and patience to explore it. He took a long sip at his pint and looked over at her – seeing the little lines around her mouth that creased when she smiled gave him a warm feeling that was unlike anything else in the world. He really was the luckiest man alive.

When they came out of the pub and directed their steps towards the Old Bell Tavern on Fleet Street, a cool wind was blowing. Elizabeth Russell – Bess - buttoned up her long, midnight blue cashmere coat and put her arm through his. After Krowos, it had been a long clean-up and she was glad to be out on the town knowing it was pretty much all tied up. The only loose ends were Chloe and Ray. It appeared that the next wave had indeed swept them back out into the ocean... Ray's physical wounds had healed, but he was locked inside his own mind with the knowledge of Krowos. He was now, and would probably always be, residing at a very comfortable, but very secure psychiatric facility just outside London – and Chloe was at his side. Once Ray had regained consciousness after the attack, he had begun screaming and nothing could stop it. Only Chloe had been able to bring him peace, and now she was using all her psychic strength to keep him calm and even happy in his own limited way. Although Bess was sad this was all that Chloe was doing with her abilities, she understood. Chloe had admitted that she had made her father see Krowos in order to save their lives. She had said it was her fault that her father was broken and that she must be the one to mend him. How could anyone argue with that? So, Bess would keep a close watch on the girl, and colleagues would help Chloe hone her powers. But one day her father would pass on, and who could tell how Chloe might react to that? That was for the future.

Bess and Andy walked on through the gathering dusk and when they turned out of Queen Victoria Street onto Cannon Street, St Paul's Cathedral rose up ahead of them in the distance. As they sauntered towards it, she deliberately didn't look back down Cannon Street to where Ray had been mutilated barely a hundred yards behind them. She didn't look, but her mind picked over the aftermath. Clearing up the nightmare of Ray's house and covering up what had happened to the neighbours had been difficult; questioning all the staff at Global Actuaries Limited had been laborious; relocating the company had been annoying; and clearing out Krowos' lair had been utterly unpleasant. But, once they'd got the excavators in and dug down the sixty feet to the site where the umbilical cord had been attached, she'd finally been able to make sense of it all. The large rock the cord had been attached to had been turned into a link to another space. That rock had since been crushed, dissolved and its liquid remains evaporated in a laboratory, so that the link to the other space was gone. She had been wrong about Krowos. It wasn't a creature that had deliberately pushed itself into this world from some other dimension – its mother had pushed it into this world. Somewhere, out in the darkness and chaos, there was a malevolent creature puncturing different realities to spread its offspring throughout existence. Krowos hadn't been fully formed, but was a slow-growing foetus, still linked to its mother when the cord had been cut. The scream from the pit in Krowos' final moments had come from her in that other space. Bess dreaded to think what Krowos might have become had it grown up – and the thought that its mother was out there birthing these abominations truly made her blood run cold.

"You cold, Bess?" Andy asked. He had felt her shiver.

"No, I'm good," she said, then she stopped,

"Come here, handsome," and she drew him towards her by the lapels of his jacket and kissed him as if he was her entire world.

***

Brian Titheridge was whistling 'Somewhere Over The Rainbow' as he walked across the large, clean operating room. For the last few months, he had been tasked with tracking down and interrogating the servants of Krowos – now the creature was gone, he felt safe enough to think of its name, though he still couldn't bring himself to say it out loud. Things were going well. He'd hunted down an even dozen of them so far and had more lined up for the coming weeks. He was back in the house near Peckham Rye - the garden had a lovely Autumnal feel to it - he had a nice clean place to work, didn't have to sneak about in the shadows and was really enjoying life. He especially liked his new boss. Elizabeth Russell really got it. She fully understood that the servants of Krowos had to be eradicated to the last man or woman, and that extreme violence was the only way to get the truth out of them. Each of the twelve he'd 'talked to' so far had eventually been forthcoming with their contacts. *Yes, they all talked in the end,* he thought as he picked up his home-made jumbo apple corer device. He walked back across to the operating table, where Shiny Starrr was lying naked and fully restrained. He had already been 'talking to' her for about seven hours, but so far, she'd said nothing useful.

"You're not going to enjoy this," Titheridge said, holding up the instrument in front of her face,

"But I am," he smiled and, for the first time, he saw real fear in her eyes.

Yes, they all talked in...

The End.

Afterword

Please review this book!

Reviews make a huge difference to the success of a book, so if you enjoyed Malevolent, please consider leaving a review on Amazon or your favourite book review site. I'd very much appreciate it.

If you want to see what I'm up to, then you can find me on Facebook

I try to keep news about what I'm having for lunch (with pictures) to an absolute minimum, but if I'm having something incredible, I do reserve the right to post it.

Or, if Facebook isn't your scene, you could throw yourself into the abyss of chaos that is my website VJNash.com

There, if you are brave enough, you can sign up for my newsletter. It's free, I don't harvest or share your data and it's crammed with exclusive info on what's coming up and access to the occasional short story.

Printed in Great Britain
by Amazon

56886431R00243